# FINDING HARMONY

# What Reviewers Say About CF Frizzell's Work

**As Seen on TV!**

"I loved this so much! It was absolutely fantastic and one of those stories that I started reading and found impossible to put down. It drew me in straight away. The tension between Peyton and Ronnie was sizzling straight away with a good amount of humour built in to lighten some of the intense mood around their first show. How C.F. Frizzell did this, I'll never know, but the chapters about the paranormal activity had such amazing build ups and cliff-hangers that they were just amazing! An experience you really do have to have for yourself."—*LESBIreviewed*

**Exchange**

"CF Frizzell really knows how to write tension! A great read, a real roller coaster of emotions with a sensational love story."—*Kitty Kat's Book Review Blog*

**Night Voice**

"CF Frizzell has written a beautiful love story, a romantic tale that will have you cheering on Murphy and the lady who has stolen her heart. …There was just enough angst and plenty of hot sex in this excellent book to keep anyone hooked. Emotions ran high and how all of those involved communicated their feelings made for a very interesting read. I loved it."—*Kitty Kat's Book Review Blog*

"I very much enjoyed it. The main characters felt real and likeable. The connection between them was palpable and the slow build-up was a pleasure to read. The supporting characters were also well developed. …I liked the author's writing style and will keep an eye out for her future works."—Melina Bickard, Librarian, Waterloo Library (UK)

**Stick McLaughlin: The Prohibition Years**

"[E]xciting reading and a story well told!"—*Golden Threads*

Visit us at www.boldstrokesbooks.com

# By the Author

# FINDING HARMONY

*by*
## CF Frizzell

2025

# FINDING HARMONY

ISBN 13: 978-1-63679-741-0

THIS TRADE PAPERBACK ORIGINAL IS PUBLISHED BY
BOLD STROKES BOOKS, INC.
P.O. BOX 249
VALLEY FALLS, NY 12185

FIRST EDITION: JANUARY 2025

CREDITS
EDITOR: CINDY CRESAP
PRODUCTION DESIGN: SUSAN RAMUNDO
COVER DESIGN BY JEANINE HENNING

# Acknowledgments

Synchronizing several different worlds in *Finding Harmony* proved maddeningly tricky to write, and just as intricate as the story's characters found to produce. But friends and family certainly made all the difference in the world.

For helping preserve my sanity through the creative process, I must acknowledge the invaluable and candid input, unrelenting support, and immeasurable patience of very special people.

A huge thank-you goes out to remarkable BSB authors Jesse J. Thoma and Holly Stratimore, an accomplished musician in her own right; to Rachel Hampton and Julie Logwood of our cozy writers' group; and to my astute, sharp-eyed Goddaughter, Casey Brown. Thanks for lending your love, time, and creative minds—and for showing me no mercy. *Seriously.*

And, as always, I bow to my wife, Kathy, for her generous heart and endless stamina in reading and critiquing this manuscript so many times. You even battled through illness (yours and mine) to help me make *Finding Harmony* what I trust is a fulfilling, heart-warming tale.

Finding harmony really is what it's all about.

# Dedication

Kathy

Because of you there is perfect harmony in every note.

# CHAPTER ONE

The stage floor vibrated beneath Harper's feet, and the bass notes pulsed upward, into her thighs. Drumbeats pounded like heartbeats, throbbing, demanding from deep within her. The rhythmically erotic full-body massage pushed reality beyond everything except the lyrics at her lips. Arching back, Harper's body quivered as she thrust words into the mic with all the strength left in her lungs. She prayed her voice would hold out as she rode the lead guitar's screaming harmony line through the impossibly long final note.

Spent and drenched in sweat, Harper dropped to her knees at the song's crashing climax, the end of this second encore, the grand finale of her band's Head Wind national tour. Sound switched off, stage lights went black, and the mammoth crowd erupted.

Harper raised her head and pushed her hair off her wet face as the house lights came up. Still kneeling, she smiled back at the thousands of wild, appreciative fans.

Decker leapt from his drums to join her at center stage, and she was grateful for his assist to her feet. Guitarist Rhea threw an arm around her waist and Harper looked from one to the other with equal wonder.

"The end," she managed, her voice worn to a croak.

"Fuck, yeah!" Decker shook her by the shoulder.

Rhea snugged Harper to her hip. "You. Are. Amazing."

"No. *We* are." The whole band gathered across the front of the stage and each of them waved to the crowd. "Look out there. We killed it."

As Storm took one last bow, Harper imprinted the scene, the feeling into a lasting memory. Each tour always closed like this, resonating like a glorious lifetime achievement. The six-month Head Wind tour, which promoted their album of the same name, pumped up the fame and fortune with sold-out concerts and a slew of original hit songs.

She knew they'd all earned the right to feel like teenagers on the last day of school. Exhausted, but no less ecstatic, they left instruments and gear to the care of their roadie crew and hurried after their manager Harry to the rented limo in the back alley.

Harper wiped off her theatrical eye makeup as they paraded through the doors, glad to be rid of her signature provocative look for at least the foreseeable future. Her body demanded a long, hot shower at their hotel, and she couldn't wait to ditch the skin-tight leather bra and pants. They were scorching hot, literally, and she figured she'd dropped ten pounds in sweat tonight. *Hell of a way to stay in shape.*

Eager for the cool spring air, she stepped out behind Zee, her bass player, and plunged into a sea of fans. The crush of bodies made it hard to walk, and being patted, grabbed, and bumped made the car seem miles away, but she managed to autograph whatever was shoved at her until she reached the sanctuary of the vehicle.

Sitting up front, Harry turned around to address them as their driver began inching through the crowd. Harry's meticulous grooming had taken a beating getting aboard and he amused everyone when he gave up fussing with his hair and yanked his tie loose.

"Champagne's in your rooms and plenty of food. As usual, make sure you all eat, don't just drink."

"Fuck that, Harry. I'm guzzling. Don't think I have the strength to chew, anyway.'"

They laughed at Smitty, their keyboard player. No one doubted him.

Decker and rhythm guitarist Primma slapped at the windows to fans still desperate for a parting connection. "I'm with Smitty," Decker told Harper over his shoulder. "The bubbly better be cold."

"Oh, I'm guzzling, too," Primma said, "but starting with this." She opened a Gatorade from the case at her feet and passed one to Harper.

"Listen up," Harry went on. "I was approached by two different record labels tonight. Didn't expect that. A bidding war for Storm could force our company's hand, which would be *very* nice. I'm going to look at the numbers myself, once this dust settles."

Lead guitarist Rhea nodded appreciatively. "Nice position to be in. We'll take it."

"Damn straight, we will." Smitty slouched in his seat and elbowed Harper. "Wait till the live album comes out."

Harper poured more Gatorade down her throat and looked to Harry. "When's that? Six months?"

"Late fall, although they're already going over the material. We shouldn't hear from them until August sometime."

Taken from their wild show in Philadelphia in March, the recording package was projected to net them millions, far more than their previous two albums. Harry considered his successful pitch to their label to be his personal triumph.

"It'll be great not to have dates and times hanging over us for a while," Zee said.

Head Wind had been Storm's fifth tour in its six years of existence, and their biggest production to date, so the idea of having the summer off seemed unimaginable. Harper let it wash over her like that shower she wanted. Maybe she'd have a chance to reassess her tiny condo in San Mateo and find something in LA, closer to the music industry. Regardless, right now she looked forward to quiet time and reviving the songwriting muse that had abandoned her during the recent nonstop months. Storm's upcoming Hawaiian getaway couldn't come soon enough.

The after-party at the hotel was already in full swing when they arrived and, as usual, showed every indication of growing out of control. Harper caught Harry's eye across the room and just shook her head at the loud, crazy scene. Considering she was running on just adrenaline, she wondered how long she'd last, where her endurance—and willingness—to celebrate all night had gone.

Partiers spilled out of various rooms and into the hall and Rhea nudged her as they wound through the crowd. "Time for our second wind. Maybe our third." Someone stuck a joint into her hand, and she hit off of it before passing it to Harper. "We were fucking hot tonight, weren't we?"

Her lungs still primed, Harper inhaled with gusto as Smitty waltzed by and gave each of them a bottle of champagne.

"Phenomenal," Harper said. She took a long drink, relished the cooling of her scratchy throat before she exhaled. "God. When it clicks like tonight?" She tapped Rhea's chest. "But I want us to rethink some of our arrangements. You should sing more. Your voice is too good to just play lead."

Rhea shrugged modestly. "I'm down with that, but you're Storm's voice, even when it struggles."

"It's been doing that a lot lately, hasn't it?"

"Well, yeah. Shit. I thought you were gonna blow it out tonight." She pointed her bottle at Harper for emphasis. "We need this break coming up."

A suggestive arm sneaked around Harper's waist from behind and she noted Rhea's amused recognition. A body pressed against her back and a familiar voice registered in her ear.

"I finally caught you!"

Harper whirled into the arms of her best friend, Denise. "You made it! Damn, it's good to see you!"

"I met…Well, I got a little distracted. Anyway, I finally caught you." She squeezed Harper tightly and stepped back to give her a once-over. "You *know* you scream 'Fuck me' in this outfit." She pinched Harper's bare midriff and made her flinch, then she plucked at the center of Harper's flimsy bra. "And when did your girls get this yummy?"

Harper slapped her hand away. "You're out of control already."

"These leathers—or what there is of them—worked perfectly for that last song, by the way, all skin, glistening under those lights."

"I was sweating my ass off."

Denise accepted the joint from Rhea. "Did you guys plan that second encore?"

"Yeah, but by then, we had nothing left, and my voice was crap."

"Oh, but the audience was *so* into it. LA crowds will go all night."

Harper still reveled in that sound, thousands of voices singing her lyrics, propelling Storm to its thunderous finish. They really had blown the roof off the place. Unfortunately, though, some of her body parts had started complaining already. Her shoulders and arms ached, her throat blazed, and she may have tweaked her shoulder, running that gauntlet through the crowd.

She winced and threw back more champagne. "I think I need something more *medicinal* than this."

Denise sighed. "Being thirty-six means we're not invincible anymore."

"Not even close." Harper sent Rhea a sideways look as they maneuvered toward the liquor table. "You, however, are the disgusting picture of youthful vigor. It must be where you get your energy." Rhea's rail-thin frame made it hard to imagine she drove their music so hard. She could handle any guitar lead, any riff or instrumental break with a wizardry that brought audiences to their feet.

"Hey, thirty-one means my kid days are gone, honey. I work for love of the sport."

They clinked bottles.

Denise cleared her throat pointedly. "Speaking of 'love of sport,' I'm going to venture into this wild animal kingdom and find that someone I met earlier."

Rhea grinned and ran a hand over her buzz cut. "You mean your 'distraction'?"

"Ah yes," Harper added, "your 'distraction.' Any chance you got her name?"

Denise ignored their teasing. "Hey, I know she's a fellow Chicagoan, and we're a long way from home."

"Oh, well, hell. In that case, by all means."

"Stop smirking, both of you. She's very sweet…and looks great in leather." Denise eyed Harper from head to toe again. "She doesn't *slay* it like you, but then, no one here could." She kissed Harper's cheek. "Wish me luck."

"I do. Call me in the morning."

"*Later* in the morning." Denise poked Rhea in the arm affectionately and slipped into the crowd.

Harper poured some Maker's Mark from the dozens of bottles on the table and lingered over the bourbon's soothing feel as much as its taste, all while surveying the happy faces, her chosen family. Strangers were mixed in, attached to a bandmate or crew member, but that was nothing new. They were all here because of something she had created six years ago. Thank God, we've made it. Moments like this made it seem like a lifetime had passed along the way.

"Am I losing touch, or does everyone have twice my energy right now? It's almost four o'clock."

Rhea laughed. "I was toast an hour ago, but my room is just as full as this one. Yours probably is, too. We'll have to kick them out."

"Lovely." *I think I'm more like burnt toast.*

"You know, I'm glad Head Wind is done, but what a run it was."

"God, yes. Let's not even *think* about topping it," Harper said as they squeezed through the clog of people at the door. "Maybe not for a long while." Bringing the curtain down tonight on their lengthy tour had her walking on air, but, damn, she was dragging. The whole scene, the grueling schedule, the workload, the public presence, all of it sometimes bordered on too much. "I might be getting too old for this, Rhea."

"We're *all* feeling old right now. Why do you think we blur the lines like this?" She toasted her with the bottle.

Harper laughed, but she wasn't about to fortify herself with gallons of alcohol. That reckless period was behind her. "I know we joke, but it comes to mind a lot these days. Slowing down looks better and better."

Rhea slung an arm around Harper's neck. "Sad words, my friend, but I hear you. How about we let Hawaii do its magic on us, okay?"

Harper clinked her bottle to Rhea's. "To Hawaii."

"No shit. Wheels up in a week."

"Can we go now?" she asked, more than half serious. "I have things to square away at home, so I could be a little behind you guys, but I'll be there."

"Good. We're counting on it." Rhea gave her a squeeze before releasing her. "Okay, this is where I split. Hey, if I don't catch you in the morning, I'll see you in Maui and we'll, you know, go get lei'd."

Laughing, Harper pulled her into a hug. "I love you. You're the best."

"And I love you back. *We're* the best, baby."

Harper was sad to see her slip away. Their sisterhood came through a special bond, a musical connection impossible to describe. They'd met years ago, back when they'd each been into the impromptu jam scene at clubs in New Jersey, and been through the trenches together ever since, so parting at this moment left her a little empty.

Harper wandered dutifully through the insanity, expressing thanks and handling the laughter, compliments, and one-liners with mechanical ease. Another bourbon helped. Occasional flirtations amounted to harmless fun, and she found her crew foreman's sister surprisingly tempting until she promised to alter Harper's reality a little too much.

Too worn to fight off the Maker's Mark, Harper wobbled back to her suite and evicted the stragglers sprawled across her furniture. Bed called. Loudly. And, like most nights *or days*, she didn't mind falling into it alone.

Not that she'd taken to the practice easily. Breaking up with Chelsea after three years had been a painful lesson in dividing love between woman and career. And filling the ensuing void by making and taking seductive invitations had grown old fast. She'd more or less quit playing that pickup game last summer, and tonight, she just wanted her brain to go silent.

When her phone chimed throughout her empty room at eight o'clock that morning, Harper wasn't particularly gracious. Unable to open her eyes, she grabbed it off the nightstand, hit the silencer, and tossed it. *Gimme a break.*

Less than a minute later, even with the pillow over her head, she heard the damn thing vibrating on the bathroom tile. Muscles awakened sore and resentful as she stepped wearily over party debris and her discarded clothing on the carpet. When she bent to retrieve the phone, her brain sloshed mercilessly, and she squeezed her eyes shut. She forced them open, and then to focus.

"Seriously?" The gravel in her voice felt as menacing as it sounded. She took the phone back to bed and answered the call via speaker. "Mom." She cautiously set her head on the pillow. "It's early here in LA." She dropped the phone to her chest and laid a forearm across her eyes.

"Oh, I know, Harper, but this is important, and I did wait until your concerts were over. You *have* stopped traipsing all over the country, haven't you? And you're free now? Wasn't last night the end of it?" Harper didn't know where to begin. Her mother took advantage. "Anyway, I had to make sure I reached you. That always takes a miracle, and you know it."

"Please tell me what's so important." They hadn't spoken in weeks, but there was always a crisis in Mom's Florida world.

"What's the matter with your voice? You sound awful."

"I was asleep. What's up?"

"When's the last time you visited your grandmother?"

Harper opened her eyes to her guilt. She adored Gram, but sucked at showing it. She'd written her last letter…five months ago, shortly after Christmas? *If only Gram wasn't afraid of email and the computerized world. Didn't we all meet in Tampa? When was that?*

"Well, we always get together at your place for Christmas, so—"

"You didn't make it this year *or* last year. So, when's the last time?"

"You mean actually visited her?" *When did we play in Boston?* She shook off that thought, knowing she hadn't ventured to rural southeastern Massachusetts in ages.

Her mother exhaled hard. "God, you're making this so difficult. Yes. When's the last time?"

"Um…Hell, I don't know, Mom. A long time ago. Maybe eight or nine years?"

"Dear Lord, Harper. You've only seen her at our house, haven't you? Once, maybe twice a year? And haven't visited her since your twenties? Tell me that's not true."

Harper frowned at the phone. *I need to figure that out.* "Is she okay?"

"Now you ask. Hmph. She is at the moment. Listen. Your father and I have been up here with her for a couple of days, but we're heading back to Tampa now. He has to prepare for his annual meeting, so I'll call you from home tonight and we'll talk."

"Wait! No." Harper sat up too fast and her head and stomach lurched. She snatched up the phone. "Tell me now. What's wrong with Gramma?"

"Her difficulties are mounting." Harper felt her rising pulse subside. The world was not ending. "She didn't want to talk about it, but I dragged it out of her."

"How is she managing? I know she's slowing down, but…Is she still running the store?"

"What do you think? Of course, she is. She's in denial, minimizing her troubles, if she mentions them at all, but we could see right through her. I can't fathom why she still insists on living by herself, running that damn old place."

"Yeah, I remember." Harper lay back down and rubbed her forehead. Fond, youthful memories tried to blossom through the sludge in her head. *Popsicles, bike rides, barbecues, star gazing, fireflies…*

"You *do* know she's eighty-three. Her situation isn't going to improve. It's time she faced facts."

"So, you're saying…What *are* you saying?" She pinched the bridge of her nose. "She should give it all up?"

"Before something tragic happens, yes, that's what I'm saying. Really, Harper. She can't continue pretending it's 1960 or whatever, playing shopkeeper—for which, I might add, she already relies on help."

"But Gramma has more fight in her than the both of us combined."

"Please. The evidence is clear as day. She's dropping things, has trouble picking up her pills. You can hardly read her signature anymore. She can't lift things like she used to. Her arthritis is advancing, and the decline is obvious. Now, she says she won't be staying with us through the holidays this year, so what does that tell you? There's a lot more to that than she's letting on."

"Well, she—"

"Gramma needs to give up that place once and for all. We can't have her this far away, so your father and I have decided that moving her to the assisted living facility near us in Tampa is the ideal thing to do."

Harper sat up again. "Are you kidding?" *Ideal for whom?*

Now, she was awake. She scavenged Tylenol from her toiletry bag and trudged to last night's ice bucket, scrounging for something non-alcoholic in the water.

"The time has come," her mother declared. Harper popped the pills, cracked open a bottle of spring water, and poured it down her sore throat. Her mother continued. "I know she won't like it, but—"

"Won't like it?" Harper laughed. "Did you discuss this with her? I bet she shooed you right back to your condo meetings and pickleball leagues."

"Don't be rude."

"There's no way Gramma would agree to some *facility*, no matter how close it was to you. No way. Not even if it was right next door to her own place. The store is everything to her, Mom. She's been there all her life. She'll never change her mind."

"Listen to me. That capable grandmother you remember isn't who she is today. What she's been able to manage in the past will be impossible for her very soon. I don't expect transitioning to something better will be easy for her, but it is necessary. You *do* need to see the issue here."

*For your sake or Gram's?*

Harper wandered to the window, bravely parted the drapes, and surrendered to the late May sunshine and the real world. Squinting down twenty-two floors to the bustling city, she tried *not* to see her mother's point. But too easily, she imagined Gram hobbling around the crowded old store, sagging against the counter trying to make change, following a regimen of prescriptions to remain healthy and pain-free. It hurt to think Gram's life may have come to that.

"I see the issue." *Most likely, it all* is *catching up with her.*

"It's a downward trend, and Lord knows what it means. Her life should not become some brutal daily struggle, so it behooves us to see the big picture, to think long-term. I daresay we should have started sooner. We need to assure Gram's quality of life for the time she has left."

"I don't disagree," Harper said, sinking onto the edge of the bed. "She deserves that, except I'm sure she believes that living as she does *is* quality living."

"Well, it's not. She needs help with all sorts of routine things and she's going to need more. We're all thankful a neighbor is there for her every day, but that's not quality of life. And what's ahead will make that point in capital letters."

"So, what about the store? It gets sold?" She wanted to hide from the answer. The old place was a part of her childhood, where she'd summered for years.

"Oh, selling it is long overdue. It needs a ton of work anyway."

"God. How did she react to that?"

She needn't have asked. World War III probably had broken out. Moving, losing the store would break Gram's heart, and Harper wished she had been there to form her own opinion of the situation, at least to referee. But if Mom's assessment was accurate—and not her usual histrionics— Gram *should* make the change to something easier while she was still able to enjoy it. *If Mom's right.*

"She didn't react well. Once she stopped crying, she became furious. We tried to be reasonable, implored her to be reasonable, but she wouldn't listen to us. This is imperative, Harper. The time really is now." She huffed into the phone as Harper waited apprehensively for whatever came next. "You've always been her shining star, Harper, so for Gramma's sake, you have to go and take care of this."

## Chapter Two

F rankie didn't care how many rabbits or muskrat or even deer might be watching. She peeled off her filthy clothes on her cabin's back deck and went inside to shower.

In less than a minute, hot water began pulsing the dirt, dust, and flecks of leaves and weeds off her skin. Keeping nature from overtaking her cranberry bogs was a necessity and a monthly, back-breaking battle.

She scrubbed at the bloody scratches and residual dirt, knowing she'd do it faster if only she had the energy. This was the fifth and, thankfully, the last day of such work, extending the long, top-heavy line trimmer down over rounded embankments, shearing off invasive vegetation that rimmed her crop's eight acres. But the job satisfaction was worth the full-bodied weariness.

A wave of pride rushed through her as she washed. Running her own little homestead and achieving enough success to live comfortably were a work in progress, like that of any farmer, and it kept her on her toes, mentally sharp, and physically fit. She'd been at this for almost three years now, having broken free of a long, crippling relationship, and rebuilt the identity and self-worth she'd sacrificed during that time.

At the moment, however, Frankie simply looked forward to succumbing to a cold beer on the deck. Maybe for an hour.

She had promised Stella she'd cover the evening hours for her tonight at Crossroads General Store. Plus, she knew Stella was bursting to chat about her granddaughter's impending arrival, and although that probably meant Frankie would hear every last detail of their family life, including things she'd already heard, she was happy for her aging friend.

Stella and her throw-back store had grown on Frankie from the minute she'd met them three years ago. They were each other's only neighbor for miles, and from day one, Stella had welcomed Frankie's visits and the help she volunteered. She'd given her a key after only two weeks.

Frankie had long since given up trying to understand how this woman had stolen a piece of her heart. She still figured it had something to do with the innate draw of family. Her own had been close and supportive, but today, without them or siblings or grandparents, she'd apparently made the most of this connection.

She kept a watchful eye on Stella's advancing arthritis and the decline in her physical abilities, even though the woman's will and spirit were as spry as ever. As half of the "dynamic duo," as Stella called them, Frankie lent all the help she could spare, and it had become increasingly necessary. She hoped this granddaughter was truly aware of the situation.

In clean jeans and T-shirt, she headed for the store, hopefully refreshed enough to last her through the evening. Admittedly, it would be another long day, although Crossroads was no bustling marketplace and offered more quiet time than stress. She slowed her truck at the intersection and eyed the deserted gravel lot, wondering if Stella's granddaughter would wax nostalgic over the weathered 1920s building.

Frankie dearly hoped she saw beyond its isolated stance in the meadow. Would she appreciate the deep, shaded porch, or the gingham curtains fluttering in the windows, or the hanging geraniums Stella no doubt had watered this morning? Would she remember lazy summer evenings in those rocking chairs or customers lingering in conversation?

Frankie could feel all of that in her bones and her ties only reached back a few years. Nights she spent playing guitar on that porch would stick with her forever, and she'd always hear Stella singing along and the bullfrogs chiming in at sunset.

Generations had passed through the place, and even though the exterior called for fresh touches, there was a special comfort here, a dignity that deserved to be respected and appreciated. Roots, something Frankie took to heart.

She'd heard Stella's many stories of this landmark store, the family homestead, and how she'd come to live in the first-floor addition in the back. She had grown up living above the store, eventually moved back into it when she married, and Stella still glowed whenever she recounted those many summers here with her granddaughter.

But Stella hadn't seen her for a couple of years and only received a letter now and then. God only knew how long it had been since she'd visited. So, what did that say? The beloved granddaughter was "just so busy" with her rock band, bouncing all around the country. So much for appreciating family. Yes, making assumptions was wrong, but how did you dismiss an absence like that?

She parked in the back lot and headed for the steps, grinning at Stella's favorite music playing inside. Countless customers had learned to appreciate the likes of Perry Como, Brenda Lee, and Ray Charles just by coming here.

The old screen door slapped shut behind her and she called out as she passed Stella's apartment, then the stairway to the vacant one upstairs, and then the storage room. "Hey! Avon calling! Is the boss here?" In the kitchenette, she lowered the volume on the stereo under the counter and heard Stella chuckle.

"Oh, Frankie! No one but me knows what 'Avon calling' means anymore, silly."

"Exactly. It's our secret code."

Walking a bit slower than usual, Stella primped her gray hair into place. The bright expression on her cherubic face said she was delighted by Frankie's arrival, but those silvery eyes looked worn. She would never admit it, however.

"What were you up to that I interrupted?"

"Nothing, dear. I was just going to rest a moment on the sofa. Let's sit outside."

Frankie followed her onto the front porch and drew a Coke from the refurbished Coca-Cola cooler chest, wondering, as she frequently did, just how many generations had performed this ritual. She swiped icy water off of the glass bottle and pried off the cap at the chest's built-in opener.

"You come, sit." Stella tapped the rocker next to hers. "Who knows what you've been working on all day." She rested her hand on Frankie's arm. "You're an angel, Frances Cosgrove. I'm so lucky."

"Shh." Frankie patted her hand. "How else would I hear the latest news?"

"Uh-huh. Thank you for covering for me tonight. I'm just feeling a little worn out."

"My pleasure, you know that." Frankie enjoyed evenings here. "Babysitting" Crossroads at night was even easier than during the day. And Stella already needed a break. "Were you cleaning all day?"

"Oh, my place just needed a little housekeeping. I want it presentable when Harper gets here."

"You didn't clean your whole apartment, I hope." Frankie frowned at her. "We were going to do that togeth—"

"It didn't take too much. The bigger job is upstairs, even though you did it a few weeks ago, when my daughter and son-in-law were here."

"Well, do *not* tell me you went up there and tackled that apartment, too. You promised to tell me when you needed it prepped. I'm taking care of that, so don't even think about it."

Neither Stella's daughter Meredith nor her husband had been thrilled about staying at her childhood home, even though Frankie had done a bang-up job reviving the long-vacant apartment. In fact, Meredith hadn't seemed thrilled about anything—including Frankie—but Frankie had made the effort for Stella and was ready to do it again.

"When is your granddaughter due?"

Stella scrunched her shoulders in youthful delight. "Harper will be here tomorrow afternoon."

"Tomorrow?" Frankie wanted to run upstairs and get to work. "Well, that's great. I'm looking forward to meeting her. How long has it been since she's visited?"

"Oh my." Stella gazed out at the intersection. "Can't say as I remember the last time."

"That long, huh?" Frankie's opinion of this granddaughter slid a bit more to the negative side but she didn't want her pause to lead Stella there, too. "I'll remember to wear something other than work clothes."

"Nonsense. You're always presentable and I don't believe hard work ever looks bad on a person. You don't have to be clean and shiny, like now," she tipped toward Frankie, "but you really smell good." She giggled. "Harper will like you right away, just like I did."

"Well, thanks. That would be good." *Because we better get along.*

"Honestly, Frankie. I can't wait for you two to meet." She clapped her hands together in her lap, obviously excited. "She's single, you know."

Frankie laughed and shook her head. "I see. Behave yourself."

"I'm just saying." She patted Frankie's arm again. "But, honestly, there's so much for you two to talk about. You play the guitar and so does she. She can talk about her band, and you can tell her all about your little farm and your berries."

"I doubt she'd be interested in my world, Stella. I'm sure it's a far cry from what she's used to. Has she played music a long time?" Frankie saw herself as an above-average guitar player, but spending time with a pro could be fun, even educational.

"Ever since high school and I believe she's been with this band for quite a few years now."

"Would I know the band? What's their name?"

"Hm. Meredith must have told me at some point." She frowned toward the floor, thinking hard. "It's a one-word name." Her head jerked up. "Storm. Yes, Storm is the name."

Frankie reared back in her chair. "You're kidding. Storm is your granddaughter's band?" Watching Stella nod, she still couldn't believe it. Storm was one of the hottest new bands in the country, appropriately named for the fury they generated on stage. *She's coming here?* "Stella. Storm's a big deal."

"Meredith said she thought they'd become successful. I'm so happy for Harper. Isn't this exciting?"

Frankie was floored. "Harper plays guitar for Storm."

"Yes. She created the band. She's the lead singer."

"She...Holy..."

"Oh, but, knowing Harper, I'm sure she'll fit right in here and relax like old times. I bet she'll help in the store, too, and will pick up so much from you."

"From me?"

"Of course. You explain things so much better than I do. She never learned about running Crossroads, you see. When her grandfather and I shared all her summer vacations, she was just a child. Now, I should tell you that she's the ambitious type and can be a little headstrong, but not to worry. *You* know how things are done here." The twinkle was back in her eyes.

Frankie had a hard enough time getting past Harper's notoriety, let alone the idea of showing her the ropes here. Wouldn't Crossroads just bore her to tears, be too slow a lifestyle for her? *And who the hell am I to re-introduce her to this place? I didn't grow up here.*

"Geez, Stella. I mean, well, I'll do what I can, of course, but you and I have become a pretty good team here, and if she doesn't know any—"

"Eh!" Stella raised a frail hand.

Frankie tried not to see the crooked fingers, the tell-tale results of her arthritis. "I'm serious, Stella. As your granddaughter, Harper has the right—"

Stella shook a finger at her. "And you're practically my granddaughter, too, you know."

Frankie's alarm tripped over that thought. She'd often wondered if Stella saw her that way—and actually didn't mind. Hell, the attachment was mutual, Frankie couldn't deny it, but her "adopted" status didn't measure up to Harper's.

"No one should ever stop appreciating the past or learning new things," Stella continued. "Yes, you may have to teach her, explain deliveries and what goes where and when, that sort of thing, but she's always been a quick learner, very sharp."

"Teach her?" Frankie's reservations churned in earnest. "But, really, who am I to—"

Stella seized Frankie's chin in her cool fingers. "Hush now. I know how sweet you are with people and how much you love Crossroads. That's why I know everything will work out just fine."

"Uh-huh."

"I can't wait to have my two favorite girls here together."

Frankie took a long swig of her Coke and got to her feet, touched by Stella's affection but all too aware of her own limited authority. She had housekeeping chores to prioritize in a hurry, but her brain was stuck on *who* was coming and how to deal with her. One thing was certain: She was about to learn a lot about Harper, the star, the delinquent granddaughter, the woman. *Time to buckle up.*

She needed to vent what now had morphed into frantic energy. She had plenty of to-dos on her list but was short on time, so she was grateful when Stella abruptly decided to do a little sweeping. Frankie leaped at the chance to tackle the upstairs apartment before Stella attempted it, and armed with fresh linens and cleaning supplies, she bolted to the second floor.

Her mind raced as she hustled through the cleaning process, dusting and vacuuming, paying special attention to aging knickknacks and family photos. Would these things register with Harper? She had no idea if Harper still harbored a shred of devotion to Crossroads or if she had become some high-flying diva who couldn't be bothered. And, on top of all that, Harper could pull rank, being Stella's blood relative. Getting along could require some tact.

Pretending to need a break an hour later, she checked on Stella and found her sitting on a dining chair in front of the produce bins. "Iced tea, Stella?"

"That sounds lovely." Stella stood with effort and moved to a stool at the counter. "How are you doing upstairs? It must be warm up there."

"A bit, yeah, but the bathroom's clean, and the kitchen floor is drying now. Almost done." She gestured toward the fresh produce. "That's a good idea, going through the veggies. Are you finished?"

"I am." She paused to sip her tea. "You know, I lost quite a few tomatoes. I told Terri that she picked that bushel too late. I shouldn't have accepted them."

"How many?"

"A good ten pounds, I'd say." She nodded at Frankie's groan. "I know. She prides herself on those greenhouse tomatoes, but I'll have to mention it."

Frankie smiled inwardly at Stella's reluctance to hurt anyone's feelings. She looked around at work awaiting her in the store, knowing Stella already was too tired to get to any of it. Leaning on the counter, she hoped her own energy would last through tonight.

"Listen, since you've finished the veggies, why don't you take that break now on your couch? I'll finish upstairs soon and take over down here."

"Don't *you* ever run out of steam? You must be sampling that nutritional stuff you put on your berries."

Frankie laughed. "I could, you know. It's organic. But no. I just pace myself. Unlike someone else in this room."

Stella waved off Frankie's tease. "Fine. I'll go take a break." She inched off the stool, rounded the counter, and put her glass in the sink. "But first, I'll make us a little supper."

"Thanks, Stella, but I'm good so you rest. I might grab something later. You be sure to eat."

"No wonder you're so slim." She shuffled toward her apartment down the hall. "Nothing but muscle on your bones, Miss Cosgrove. I'm making us BLT sandwiches before I settle in for the evening. Don't argue with me."

Frankie watched after her. "Thanks, Stella." She couldn't refuse. Nor would she. Sandwiches for both of them meant Stella couldn't skip a meal without Frankie knowing.

Having finished prepping the upstairs apartment, Frankie began chores in the store and made short work of sorting magazines and sundries, dusting and restocking the shelves, and double-checking the produce bins. All while imagining a flaming rock star parading around Crossroads.

She reorganized the little display of her own cranberry creations, proud of her jarred sauces and relishes. *Yes, Harper, it's called "canning."* Stella had insisted Frankie display them on the shelves up front as "the least I can do" for the help Frankie lent her. But Frankie couldn't stop wondering if Harper would appreciate any of it.

# CHAPTER THREE

Frankie smiled ruefully into Joe Lamont's aging frown. She enjoyed his company and endless sentimental reflections but hoped he would be her last customer tonight. Her mind was as weary as the rest of her.

"So, you don't figure Crossroads will ever sell beer, huh?"

"Come on, Joe." She bagged his cigarettes, corn chips, and Cheerios, the latter being what his daughter probably had sent him to get in the first place. "How long have you known Stella? You know how she feels about that."

"I'll tell you what I remember. I remember us as kids, always hanging 'round this store." He shook his head, pulling money from a tattered wallet. "But I'm seeing her here a lot less these days. No offense, Frankie, but the place feels different when she's not behind the counter."

"Don't worry." She wasn't about to let his hang-dog expression linger. "She just ran out of oomph this afternoon, preparing for Harper tomorrow."

"Now, that little girl was a hellion, you know. She always kept Stella on her toes. My money says it'll do both of them good to have her back again."

"And my money's with you, although I think Harper's vacation is only for a few months. God knows, Stella worked enough today to keep her permanently. That's why she needed to crash early, otherwise...well, you know. Every second she's able, she's right here."

"Stella's got spunk, all right." His enthusiastic nod shook strands of hair out of place and exposed his balding head. "But, I'm telling you, nights like this would pass quicker if she sold beer. Business would pick up. For years, I've been telling her."

"I know, but that's Stella."

"Well, wouldn't you enjoy a cold one, sitting on that porch, playing your gee-tar?"

Frankie shut the drawer to the hulking cash register and handed him his change.

"If you join me some night with that banjo of yours, maybe I'll have a cold one for each of us."

"Bah. I've heard you play. You're too good for me. I only tinker with the Gibson."

"Not true. I've heard *you* play that antique beauty of yours. And you know that a banjo picker needs a guitar player, Joe." She held her hands out wide, presenting herself.

He paused at the door, bag in hand. "Maybe I'll take you up on that." The goofy grin took twenty years off his face.

"I dare ya!" she called as he ambled out to his station wagon.

Frankie shut off some of the lights and retrieved the lone bottle of Coors she'd stashed in the back of the kitchenette fridge. Stella wasn't an alcohol fan, not after a drunk driver killed her husband, so Crossroads didn't offer spirits. Occasionally, folks just dropped by to say hello and brought their own to hang out, but they always made sure Stella spotted the responsible ones among them drive away.

She returned to her guitar and the old stool on the porch, eager for more chill time. She inhaled the sweet night air and acknowledged her remarkably good fortune of having two serenely special places to be. She couldn't help but wonder if Harper ever enjoyed anything similar, living what had to be a hectic life. Did she even "do serene" at all?

Frankie wouldn't trade her own situation for anything. Five minutes down the road, home offered a little porch, comfy lounge chairs, a sizeable firepit, and bullfrogs. Here, Stella had her share of frogs, as well as every cricket on the planet, acres of moon-washed meadow, and those happy echoes of times gone by. Simply irreplaceable.

Tranquility on the porch, especially lit by a pair of antique lanterns, provided the perfect organic fit for an acoustic guitar, so Frankie unwound for the last hour of the business day by strumming through her eclectic repertoire. She touched base with her favorite artists, roaming comfortably from blues and bluegrass to folk and pop.

Then she polished her latest challenge, a markedly altered and subdued version of Storm's driving "Send Me Down." Having heard the trending tune so often in her truck, she'd worked out its chords, transposed them to her vocal range, and learned most of the lyrics. Slowing its pace to a ballad allowed the melody to shine, and the more she played it, the more she liked it.

"Damn good for an amateur." She shook her head at the coincidence of all coincidences. "Of all songs." She set the guitar aside and took her Coors to the rocker, then punched in "Send Me Down" on her phone. "Stella's granddaughter." So hard to believe.

Ready to watch Harper in action, she had just leaned back when a car cruised into the parking lot and swung parallel to the porch steps. A middle-aged woman with wild blond curls stuck her head out.

"Quiet night, huh, Frankie?" A junior high school teacher, Vicky was one of Stella's favorite customers.

"Hey, Vic." Frankie stepped down to the car window. "Yeah, quiet but nice. Warm for the beginning of June, isn't it?"

"Oh, I'll take it. Did Stella call it quits early? I was just wondering if her granddaughter had arrived yet."

"Tomorrow. Stella wore herself out today, getting ready for her."

Vicky shook her head. "I swear. There's no stopping her sometimes, is there? She must be so excited."

"Beyond excited."

"I'm happy for her. It's been a long time, hasn't it?" Frankie nodded. "I'll swing by another day and say hi."

"Do that. I'm sure Stella would love to introduce you."

Frankie extinguished the porch lanterns, and with guitar in hand, latched the screen door, and then locked the big wooden door inside. She straightened the two sets of tables and chairs at the front windows and glanced around before turning off the last light.

The hominess Stella had maintained here through the years was tangible. It simply felt right. She offered so much in such a small space and loved welcoming everyone to her nostalgic little world. Now, here in the dim light, Crossroads' companionship struck Frankie again, as it always did, even though she thrived in a singular lifestyle on wide-open spaces.

The little dining area and the three stools at the counter were more than sufficient, and the old potbelly stove provided all the cozy warmth anyone could need. The other half of the room offered a double refrigerator/freezer case, walls of shelving, and aisles of rolling racks, all filled with everything from fresh produce, canned goods, and dog food, to duct tape, Wiffle balls, and cough syrup.

On her way out, she made sure she had ingredients to make her popular cranberry muffins here in the morning, then switched off the kitchenette light, double-checked the doors in the hallway, and finally locked the back door behind her.

*This will be your life for a while, rock star Harper. You up for it?*

With two large suitcases, carry-on, and guitar case tucked into her rented Audi, Harper cruised off the highway and onto back roads she hadn't traveled in ages. She blinked behind her large sunglasses as the wind shifted in the convertible and threatened to send them and her ballcap off into the woods. The fresh air was welcome, though, because jet lag was bound to overtake her in a few hours, and she couldn't let it start now.

"At least there aren't any traffic lights," she mumbled. Waiting wasn't her strong suit, not even for red lights, and she didn't appreciate idle time bringing certain things to mind, like the band and crew she'd left behind.

Leaving that closely knit circle felt like cold turkey withdrawal. They had charged full-tilt through those last shows, *pedal to the metal, as they say*, and stopping on a dime had come with all the grace of a head-on collision. Motor home living, strangers' advances, sandwiches on the run, the "life" was behind her for the summer, but that perpetual drive forward was ingrained and slow to relent. And when you worked nights, days could be difficult.

Storm's ascendancy had ramped up the crazy life to a serious degree, but she'd asked for it, and despite the grind, she counted her blessings every day. Storm deserved to ride the Head Wind high for a while. She just wished she could have spent more time enjoying the ride with everyone.

Bandmates had sympathized with her about needing this trip, however, and she shook her head as she drove, remembering the raucous, all-night send-off they'd thrown for her. She imagined each of them now, lolling on some Hawaiian beach, but, as much as she longed to join them, she had to take advantage of this opening in her schedule to fly East.

At least crossing the country this morning had allowed some semblance of calm to set in. All she really had to worry about was a nostalgic New England summer and some "normal world" responsibility. Persuading Gram to "think long-term" would be a challenge, but she had a summer to achieve it. Plus, her stamina and her weary vocal cords would enjoy the quality recovery time.

Privately, she worried more about her voice with every performance, and knew she was lucky that the daily rigor had ended when it did. These days, a Janis Joplin raspiness filtered into the Miley Cyrus power that had won her the hearts of millions. Although many said the new growl was sexy and she liked what it lent to their hard-driving sound, it definitely would shorten her career if she didn't pay attention.

So, the more she thought about this trip, the more beneficial it felt. Casting off the grueling demands of touring gave her a thrill, but, most of all, recharging to come to Gram's aid, to deliver a happy, care-free future for her meant the world.

An incoming call broke through the music in the car, and Harper smiled at the sight of Denise's name on the dashboard screen. She hiked the volume to hear over the whooshing wind.

"Hello, Chicago."

"Hey, travelin' girl. How's the Massachusetts weather?"

"Amazingly beautiful right now and probably better than yours."

"Listen. I'm reporting in about my date last night. You know, the one you could have doubled with me if you had stopped here on your way."

"Right. And I'd still be there now, wouldn't I? Besides, you're forbidden from staging set-ups for me, if you remember."

"Wuss. So, you want the juicy details?"

"Like I have a choice."

"She was...God. I might have to marry her."

"I pity the woman."

"She's a mason. The work she did around her pool is breathtaking."

"She has a pool, huh?"

"Honey, she's got a lot more than a pool."

"Ahh. And masons have amazing hands, right?"

"You're so right," Denise said with a laugh. "Whew! Okay. I can't think about her right now. So, are your people in Hawaii yet?"

"Yeah. The whole band left a couple of days ago. Some of the crew, too, I think. Rhea texted me last night. She said Smitty still hasn't sobered up and apparently doesn't intend to."

"Sounds par for the course. He needs to keep his hands on a keyboard at all times."

"True. Oh, and Harry said the studio's nuts about the live album."

"How come I don't hear a happy smile?"

Harper shrugged as she drove. "It just means we'll be back on the road, pushing the album. And we'll need some new material."

"So...?"

"I'm just a little too tired to think about all of that yet."

"Fine. Now, tell me about this Frankie person. He's your grandmother's helper?"

"Apparently, yeah."

"Well, is he young? Old? What?"

"I really don't know. She didn't say much, just that her 'right-hand is a farmer.' Knowing her, he looks like Tom Selleck, because she loves him."

"Well, the woman has good taste, although you might prefer JLo or Kristen Stewart."

"P!nk."

Denise hooted. "Oh my God. That works! P!nk would absolutely *kill* a shopkeeper's apron."

"And just the apron."

"Ah-ha! Our renegade's not dead after all."

"Hey."

"So, you really don't know anything about this guy?"

"Doesn't matter. Gram trusts him."

"But what if he's a dick?"

"Such a supportive friend you are. He won't be."

"Are you almost there?"

"Five minutes. You should see this area. Things have grown so much since I was here last, but there's still nothing. Woods, fields. There are a few side streets now, and some houses here and there, but this two-lane just has a highway connection and not much else. It's a miracle that Gram's kept Crossroads solvent out here all these years."

"Well, keep your phone charged. You're on your own out there in Nowheresville, going to a dinky old store in the middle of some cornfield with a strange guy—"

"You're doing it again, being *supportive.*"

"Hey. I'm your best-est friend in the real, ugly world. Call me. Don't forget."

"Cross your fingers and wish me luck, girlfriend."

"Good luck, shopkeeper, but you won't need it. You'll be fine. Love you."

"Thanks. Love you, too. Bye."

"Bye. Call me!"

Harper wiggled her toes in her Nikes, enjoying the comfort and freedom that, hopefully, also applied to the rest of this day and many more to come. Thankfully, the stars had aligned this way, and freed her time for Gram, to do what mattered most and then some.

It would be good to see Crossroads again, to help Gram while passing time on Memory Lane. Convincing her to make the Great Move would be rough, but she felt up to it. And dealing with a whimpering little shop wouldn't run her into the ground the way touring did. It wouldn't bring artistic satisfaction—and she'd miss that, probably even need it—but flashing back to those innocent summers here long ago would be sweet. Besides, she was only staying for the summer. Maybe she'd even find some inspiration and return to Storm with new songs.

The two-lane curved just enough for Harper to see the intersection ahead and the expanse of open fields—with the familiar two-story farmhouse plunked in the middle. Memories made her heart skip.

When was the last time someone painted that sign, she wondered. Paint peeled from the large "Crossroads General Store" declaration beneath the two upstairs windows. The "Dan & Stella Anderson, Proprietors" that she remembered from so long ago had worn off and brought a twinge of loss.

The entire house needed a fresh coat of paint, that much she could tell from across the deserted intersection. The baby blue plank siding had faded to a forlorn gray, and the white accents cried for a boost. Trimming those yew trees at the corners of the porch would help, too. At least all the red flowers hanging along the front were as pretty as ever, and that American flag fluttering off the corner post looked new and proud.

"My God, it's been a long time." Idling at the crossroads, she tried to take it all in. "Still looks the same, though, Gram, but it does need work."

*There's bound to be a buyer somewhere, right? Hopefully, a buyer with heart because this can't go to just anybody.*

The only sign of life at the store was the dusty pickup at the porch steps, although she thought she spotted movement inside.

"Well, here we go." She took a breath, crossed to the gravel lot, and parked beside the truck.

A large, busty woman wearing a cowboy hat, filthy jeans, and T-shirt strolled out onto the porch and trotted down the steps to her truck. She passed in front of the Audi, and surprised Harper when she paused and patted its hood.

"Nice ride." She winked and continued to her vehicle.

Harper found herself smiling. "Thanks," she called out as the woman drove away. "*Very* interesting clientele, you have, Gramma."

Leaving her cap and glasses on the seat, she got out and retucked her shirt into her jeans. *Life is like being on tour, one unique performance after another.*

# Chapter Four

Harper stopped at the bottom step and gazed up at the porch, the rockers, the wood-framed screen door. She had to smile at her own child-like wonder. She'd figured it out on the plane, just how long it had been: a weekend blur of a visit nine years ago. Before that, only a couple of visits since her teens. The routine of summering here had ended at fourteen, when she'd become addicted to that annual music camp in Tampa.

Now, as she enjoyed a voice out of the 1950s crooning from inside, a torrent of memories came rushing back. Thankfully, Gram still loved music, especially the old songs, and, apparently, her helper Frankie respected that. *So glad he's a decent guy.*

She assessed each of the four porch steps and was impressed to see that they, as well as the porch flooring, looked relatively new. Smiling at the sight of the old Coca-Cola cooler chest, she lifted the lid and suddenly saw her ten-year-old self. Bottles still stood in frigid water. *No way.*

Just as she remembered, the screen door squeaked when she opened it, and the old plank floor inside creaked beneath her first steps. She stopped and looked down, found herself scanning for scuffs and scrapes she'd made a lifetime ago.

Catching herself adrift, Harper slowly turned and took it all in. *How I spent my summers then...and now. Some people vacation in Hawaii.*

The world of her past embraced her. A sweet feeling of home permeated these walls, so remarkably familiar. And then a flicker of the present crept in, a stark reminder that her ultimate objective was to guide Gram away from this forever.

Harper took a deep breath. *Because you're a loving, realistic granddaughter.*

Antiques still blended with present-day necessities everywhere she looked, covering every wall, filling practically every surface. The big pickle jar on the side table, the alluring penny candy case, the coffee grinder… The delicious aroma of something freshly baked sucked her deeper inside.

*Someone has to be here.*

She called out. "Hello?"

*Must have caught Gram indisposed.*

The floor creaked as she crossed to the counter, and she ran her palms over the Formica, anchoring herself as if touching her past would link her to her present. The scent of strong coffee settled her whirling thoughts. So did the scratchy, definitely substandard sound coming from the old stereo. The muffins looked delicious beneath that glass dome.

The little kitchenette appeared surprisingly none the worse for wear, and, behind the counter now, she was taken by the relatively new stove and griddle. Spotless, like everything else. Gram needed an updated fridge, though, and she almost laughed at herself for the assertion.

The rear screen door snapped open down the hall, startling her out of the past, and heavy footsteps clomped closer. It was the purposeful sound of someone on a mission, and she geared herself to meet the special man who had become Gram's friend.

Unexpectedly, a smooth alto began accompanying the oldies tune on the stereo. *Okay, this is too much. He sings on key? Enough already.*

"You're sure to fall—Whoa! Uh…Hi."

The tall, rangy woman stopped before her shaggy hair did, and it flopped into her eyes. She managed to swipe it back while juggling a crate of vegetables, and the corded muscles in her arms flexed.

*Well. Hello.*

The woman blinked and took an extra beat before speaking. "Sorry. I was out back and didn't hear you come in."

Surprised innocence on such bold, striking features was adorable and caught Harper off-guard.

"Hi. No, ah, it's…it's no problem. I…um…" *Smooth.* Watching the woman stride past, Harper tried to sound coherent. "Ah…Maybe little bells on the door would help."

"I was thinking about that just yesterday," the woman said from the far side of the store. She grunted as she deposited the crate near the bins of fresh produce. "Just sorting out a delivery," she explained unnecessarily and returned to the kitchenette.

Harper realized she was standing in the middle of it, and backed up, out of the woman's path.

"Fresh from the farm?" she asked. *No, the liquor store, stupid.*

"Yeah, Terri's zucchini and bell peppers. Good thing, too. We were out." She leaned over the sink and began scrubbing her hands. "Can I help you find something?"

*Maybe a little composure?*

Obviously, this woman had been hard at work. Damp spots discolored the red T-shirt that clung to her back and disappeared behind a slim cowhide belt. The hips and rear pockets of her bleached jeans were streaked with dirty handprints. *And I'm here staring at her ass. What did she ask?*

"Our coffee's still decent, if you're interested." She nodded toward the coffeemaker and Harper caught herself looking for an espresso machine. *As if.*

The woman ripped off paper towels to dry her hands. "Is it still morning?" she asked generally and tipped back to read the Felix the Cat clock above the counter. "Yup. Got another thirty minutes."

Harper looked up as well and was amused by the familiar cartoon collectible.

The woman tossed her paper towels into the trash bin nearby, then hustled to the stereo and switched it off. She bent forward and wiped her face with the hem of her shirt, as if it was an afterthought.

"Sorry, but if you're looking for Stella, she just went to do a little shopping in town with a friend," she said, her voice muffled against the fabric. "She might be gone a couple of hours." She tucked in her shirt before turning.

Her collar-length auburn hair somehow matched the color of her eyes—which locked onto Harper's and sizzled.

"So." She planted both hands onto nonexistent hips and offered a cheeky, roguish grin.

Harper couldn't help it. She grinned back. *Are you who I think you are?*

The woman's chiseled jawline hitched, and Harper enjoyed seeing a little nervousness poke through that rugged facade. But then a dimple flashed near her chin, and Harper bit her lip. *Oh, now that's just not fair.*

"Harper Cushing?"

The smokey voice was a lot more captivating than the question. But in Harper's moment of hesitation, and perhaps impatient because of it, the woman cocked an eyebrow.

"I'm Frankie Cosgrove." She took a few steps closer, her large hand extended, and Harper sensed a little trepidation in both of them.

Frankie only knew that her feet had moved reflexively. Inbred manners must have offered her hand to this dark-eyed beauty who definitely had escaped every freaking one of her YouTube videos. No bewitching makeup or mouth-watering outfit now, just form-fitted azure shirt and snug white jeans, and a penetrating look that rode a dazzling smile. Her magnetism was powerful, inescapable.

"And you're the famous Frankie."

"I'm really pleased to meet you."

Harper's hand filled hers with a comfortable warmth, a softness her own calloused palm couldn't offer, and a very pleasant—distracting—tingle rippled up her arm. The long, smooth fingers formed a solid grip, however, and conveyed all the fire and confidence of her grandmother.

Oddly, Harper's killer smile made standing still difficult and Frankie forced herself not to shuffle self-consciously. She liked the voice, though, reassured and steady, in a comfortable register. Was there a hint of grit in her sound? *Nice.*

"Me, famous?" Frankie asked. "Look who's talking."

"Please." Harper laughed lightly as she shook her head. "That's the last thing I want to think about. Can we bury all that for a few months?"

"Fair enough." *We can try.*

Frankie gave her credit for the humble approach and thought it might not be such a big deal after all, considering few people around here were tuned into Harper's scene or Storm's music. But she was aware enough to know that dismissing Harper's notoriety would be hard. Just looking at her, Frankie saw "star."

"So…you're early," she said, already trying not to flounder. "Stella was expecting you later this afternoon."

Harper clasped her hands in front of her and leaned back against the counter. "I lucked out and scored an early flight. I hope being early hasn't created a problem." Sharp-eyed, she tipped her head slightly, inquisitively. She practically glowed with self-assurance.

*Sizing me up?* Frankie acknowledged a whisper of caution in the back of her mind.

"Oh, no. Not a problem at all."

"I really am happy we've finally met, you know. Aside from 'Frankie's my right hand,' Gram told me nothing about you." The corner of her mouth curled upward suggestively. "I confess. You're certainly not the Frankie I was expecting."

Her midnight eyes searched Frankie's face and appeared quite eager for Frankie's return volley.

"Stella led you on?"

"More like *didn't* lead rather than *mis*led. Shame on me for assuming you were Francis with an 'I' instead of an 'E.' My bad."

"Well, correcting things to an 'E' had become my life's work so I gave it up a while ago. I don't care anymore." She shrugged. "Frankie swings both ways now—the *name*, that is. *I* don't."

"Duly noted."

Frankie caught the quick smile. "Just so you know, she wasn't very forthcoming with me, either. I mean, I don't know if I expected anything in particular, and honestly, there was no sense dwelling on it anyway, but…"

*But what? Am I rambling?* "You've got her look in your eyes."

Harper batted her lashes. "Well, thank you. That's a good thing."

"That's a *fierce* thing. I'm shaking."

Harper laughed, a throaty sound, easy on the ear.

"I'm trying to picture you and Gram arguing," she said.

"Thankfully, that hasn't happened often."

"But I bet you never win, do you?"

"Never." *And God help me if you have her stubbornness, too.*

"That's Gram, all right. No surprise, there."

"Well, then, so…welcome back to Crossroads. How does it feel? How long has it been?"

Harper held up a palm. "I shouldn't admit it, but quite a few years, and before that, way too many. It's more than a little humiliating." She gazed around almost longingly. "Amazing, that being here now feels as good as it always did. The memories are coming fast and furious, trust me."

Trust could come too easily. Already, her body was willing to offer this stunning woman a lot more than that.

"You must have a million memories." Frankie watched her wander to the front room and evaluate the place. *Are you ready to "fit in," as Stella expects?* "Is it very different from back in the day?"

"Hasn't changed a bit, really, and that should be impossible, right?" Harper drifted to the fresh produce area and pressed down on the hanging scale. "God. This is still here. I broke it when I was about seven. Did you know it can't take a child's weight?"

Frankie grinned. "You don't say."

"Boy, I found out fast." She inspected how it was hung from above. "Wow. This chain…Right here is where Grampa fixed it." She withdrew her hand, as if the memory was too much.

"Remember this?" Frankie held up a long pole with grippers on one end and laughed at Harper's wide-eyed reaction.

"Oh, look at that!" Harper took it reverently. "You have no idea how much damage I did with this thing."

"And how about this?" Frankie slid open the candy case, tossed her a Tootsie Roll, and noted the deft, one-handed catch. "Kids take all day deciding what they want."

"I did, too, every day," Harper said, unwrapping the candy, "until Gram put me on restriction. Two pieces a day because I already had too much energy." She eyed the case affectionately. "Heaven is being eight years old with free access to penny candy."

A thumb hooked on her back pocket, Harper munched on the Tootsie Roll as she wandered, pausing to touch and gaze at things. Frankie tried to focus on items that attracted Harper's attention, not on Harper herself, but that was impossible.

High-end clothes wrapped every curve of her slender figure flawlessly, and the black braid extending between her shoulders somehow added to her modest height, boosted a bit by those brand-new Nikes. Contrasting with her public image, she glowed with youthful innocence as she stood in profile, lost in the framed black-and-white photograph of her grandparents.

Frankie went back around the counter and leaned on it. *Physical support.*

"You know," Harper said softly, "even the sound of footsteps on this floor takes me back in time."

"I get that." *I'm glad you get it, too.*

"Man, so much stuff." Harper scanned the shelves and bins, goods stacked on the floor, the rolling racks that divided the merchandise area into three skinny aisles. She carefully pushed a rack aside, then rolled it back into place. "Ingenious."

"Better to have things roll away than crash to the floor."

"Oh, believe me, I remember what that was like." Harper strolled to the potbelly stove and fingered the wildflowers in the vase on top. "I wasn't here much in the colder months, but I do know this stove kept it cozy. I bet it still works, doesn't it?"

"Like a champ."

"Somehow, that figures." She took another wonderous look around, sighing as she crossed her arms. "Boy, what some touching up, some upgrades would do for this place."

*Excuse me? Where did that come from? How much "touching up"? And exactly what needs "upgrading"? You haven't been here fifteen minutes.*

Harper turned and eyed Frankie keenly, her distant look of remembrance replaced by dutiful scrutiny. "How do you think Gram would react to changes?"

"Changes? Depends, don't you think?" Straightening off the counter, Frankie stopped her hands from clenching by sliding them into her back pockets. "Off the top of my head? Not well."

"Hm. But how is business, Frankie? It always was just okay. Is it any better these days?"

Frankie could feel her guard rising. If there was more behind Harper's question, then this was a topic for the boss. All she felt authorized to reveal was that Stella's bookkeeping was hard to read, but accurate to the penny. *Maybe she'll give you free rein with the books like she's given me.*

"Crossroads gets by comfortably, but your grandmother knows best. I-I'm not here all the time."

"Yeah, damn. I guess I put you in an awkward position, didn't I? I apologize for that. I'd just like to see the complete picture, you know? To understand where she's coming from, how hard she's trying. I need to know if it's taking a toll on her, and I'm sure she won't level with me."

"She doesn't level with me much, either, but you'll see for yourself soon enough. How long are you staying?"

"The summer, although that's not cast in stone. I need to reconnect with Gram. Way too much time has been lost between us and that's my fault, so... Ironically, this hiatus from Storm came at the perfect time, and I can recharge while catching up with her. Everything just fell into place."

"I'm glad—for you and Stella. She couldn't be more excited. She's been telling everyone you were coming."

Harper smiled toward her shoes. "I owe her lots of long dinners and hours of rocking on that porch."

At least Harper realized her importance in Stella's life and was eager to show her. Stella adored Harper and evidently the feeling was mutual, although Frankie sensed it actually took coming here to remind Harper of that fact.

"Stepping back in time is wild," Harper admitted, "but stepping into your own past is mind-blowing."

Harper was lucky her step back was mind-blowing in a heartwarming way. Frankie would never take a step back. Her own mind-blowing step had been heart*breaking* but into a future she loved. Wondering about Harper's intentions here now had Frankie a little uneasy.

She exhaled hard to shake the feeling and forced a lighthearted smile. After all, Stella's favorite person in the world had arrived. And she was disarmingly captivating.

"Well, let's get this show on the road." Frankie rounded the counter. "So you can hang with Stella when she gets back. I'll give you a hand with your luggage, help get you settled upstairs." She winked as she headed to the front door. "That'll blow your mind some more."

# CHAPTER FIVE

The stairway to Gram's old apartment—and Harper's childhood summer home—sent yet another wave of déjà vu through her as she bumped her way up with her guitar case and carry-on. Thankfully, Frankie already had helped her haul those ridiculously heavy suitcases.

From the top of the flight, Frankie grinned down at the guitar. "A woman after my own heart." She relieved her of it as they entered the quaint living room. "Maybe we'll pick some, when we have time."

Harper registered that concept instantly. Frankie played guitar, apparently, and Harper wondered how well. And didn't all amateur guitarists presume they should play together? If Frankie hadn't sounded so genuine, Harper would have been annoyed.

Besides, Frankie's "pick some" reference was a countrified version of the jamming Harper did with Storm, and if that meant cannibalizing her hard-earned style into some hay seed sound, she had no desire to even open the case.

Actually, she had more important objectives, the first of which was reacclimating herself to this place—with its loud, flowery wallpaper, tired couch and recliner, and threadbare braided rugs. They reached into her memory and stirred her senses. So familiar, like the hints of talcum powder and sunbaked dust that drifted on the room's freshly cleaned scent.

"Yeah," she answered vacantly. "We'll see."

She headed for her bedroom to drop off her bag but surreptitiously watched Frankie set the guitar case between the couch and coffee table. *Thank you for choosing such a protected spot.* Harper returned and caught her leaning in the doorway to Gram's old bedroom.

"Forgive the cliché, but do you come here often? Up here, I mean."

"Rarely," Frankie said softly. "At certain times of the year, when the store's busy, we use this for storage. I do make a point to check on things now and then, run the water, the stove, but I generally try to stay out of Stella's way. Her generation prides itself on independence and privacy and I respect that."

"But sometimes they pride themselves on it to a fault."

"Oh, for sure, and that's when our generation, the *smart kids* step in."

Harper grinned but wished she had been a "smart kid" for Gram during all their lost years. She certainly intended to be one now. Frankie's care for Gram appeared incredibly sincere and Harper couldn't help but be touched. The tenderness in her eyes was telling.

"When she had COVID," Frankie continued, "I checked on her constantly and it drove her a little crazy, losing some of her independence. She was hard on herself, too, for 'inconveniencing' me." Her face brightened suddenly. "But we'd been vaccinated, so she never developed a bad case and we beat it."

*No one ever told me Gram had been sick. Did I ask?*

"Well, I'm very grateful you were here. I bet she was a handful to care for."

"Yeah, well, I can be stubborn, too."

Harper didn't doubt that. Frankie's stubbornness probably came with that abundance of athleticism and sinewy muscle, too, and she didn't need *those* thoughts creeping into her current concerns.

Feeling Frankie's eyes on her, Harper made the rounds in the room, raising the blinds a bit higher and opening windows a few extra inches. The steady breeze off the meadow was refreshing and helped set aside thoughts of those discerning eyes.

"Maybe I'll throw all these curtains in the wash for her," Harper said, "now that I know my way around. Thank you for the grand tour, by the way. I'll probably toss all the linens in, too."

"Everything's clean. Vacuumed, dusted, linens and towels—"

"Seriously? She needn't have gone—oh. Did you…?"

Frankie strode into the kitchen, disregarding the question.

"Of course, you can use the kitchenette downstairs if you want," Frankie said, "but I thought you might prefer having this full kitchen to yourself. Anyway, so…" she opened the fridge, "I brought up milk, yogurt, eggs, butter, and bacon. That's a fresh pitcher of Stella's favorite iced tea, which you might like. Actually, it's really good. And the loaf of bread's there because this place gets warm on summer days." She shut the door. "There's more stuff in the cupboards. That fan in the corner works great. I got one on wheels, so you can move it into your bedroom if you want. Sorry, but your grandmother hates AC."

Harper just looked at her, beyond impressed. "Is there anything you *don't* do around here?"

Frankie shrugged. "Things have become a little harder for Stella, lately, maybe since the holidays, so I kind of slipped into a bigger role—carefully, so she wouldn't notice. After a while, she must have realized she couldn't fight it."

"Well, what you do for her, *have done* for her is amazing. I assume you met my folks a few weeks back."

"I did."

"I don't imagine my mother expressed her appreciation, but I certainly want to. I can't thank you enough for everything. And I seem to remember Gram saying something about you running a farm, too? How do you ever manage?" To Harper's limited frame of reference, Frankie surely looked the part, capable, wiry strong, and down-to-earth. *Handsome* came as a distracting bonus.

"A farm, yeah, I do, so I have to juggle a few things, but she's become pretty special to me, Harper, I won't deny it. All this is who she is, so…" she grinned haplessly, "so here I am."

"Yes, here you certainly are." *And my brain had better stay on track.* "Come on. I want to learn more." Harper switched on the fan and waved her to follow. "It needs to cool off up here so let's continue this downstairs."

"The porch is definitely the place to be," Frankie said as they descended.

"And I really want to hang some kind of bell on that front door."

"So, strangers don't appear out of the blue in the kitchen?"

Harper stopped at the bottom of the stairs and looked back, up into Frankie's dimpled smirk.

"Smart-ass."

Frankie's devilish grin lingered as she squeezed past Harper.

Crouched at a cabinet, she pulled out a strip of leather with bells attached, and then a sizeable cowbell. "See? Had them right here. I did have good intentions."

"Never doubted it." Harper took the strip of bells and jingled it. "Too soft." The cowbell's clang made her blink. "Shit. That will wake the dead."

"Then we have a winner, at least until it annoys the hell out of everyone." Frankie put the strip of bells away. "I'll hang the cowbell today. How's that?"

Hands on her hips, Harper grinned. "Why do I get the feeling you're going to wear me out?" The double meaning struck her instantly and, feeling herself blush, she turned to the fridge before Frankie could respond. "I know it's midday, but I could use a beer."

"Ah. Good luck dealing with Stella about that." Frankie nodded toward the front door and Harper gladly followed her onto the porch. "Crossroads offers this elegant selection of thirst-quenching ice-cold beverages—as you might recall." Frankie gestured regally toward the cooler chest, then extracted two nearly frozen bottles of water.

"Oh, God yes. Thank you. Perfect."

"By the way, you should know that we divided this chest in half. Regular size on the left, kid-size on the right." She pulled out a miniature Coke. "The tonic's in glass, too, and no twist-offs, just like old times. They are mixed with the waters on each side."

"'Tonic,' is it?" Amused by the term, Harper dropped into the comfortably cushioned rocker. "I haven't heard it called that since I was little." She watched for Frankie's reaction, observed everything about her, and tried not to get caught.

"Blame your grandmother," Frankie said, resting her lanky frame against the railing and crossing her ankles. She wiped her wet hand across her thigh. "If you call it 'soda' or 'pop,' you'll get the lecture about disrespecting Massachusetts tradition or something. She won't hear of it, like it's unpatriotic. It doesn't matter that 'hair tonic' was a thing, once upon a time."

"Man, some things never change." Harper sipped her water and pressed the bottle to her forehead. "You don't, by any chance, have a pool at your place, do you?"

"No pool. A pond about three times the size of this house. Do you fish? I stocked it with catfish. Oh, and there's Momoa, a great-granddaddy snapper."

"Momoa? Clever name, but snapping turtles eat fingers and toes, so no thank you. Tell me that you and your boundless energy didn't dig the pond yourself."

"Hell no." Frankie moved to the rocker beside Harper's and groaned as she sat. Harper wondered if she'd stay put for more than a minute. "It's a spring-fed pond, off the swamp. I draw from it for irrigation."

"What do you irrigate?"

"Cranberry bogs."

"Really? I saw a display of cranberry things inside. Are those yours?"

"They're my creations, not my berries. Not yet, anyway."

"Funny, but I don't remember cranberries growing around here in my younger days. Guess I never paid much attention."

"The place had been abandoned for years when I bought it."

"How big is your farm?"

"I have fourteen acres in all. Eight are bogs, and four of them I planted a few years ago."

"By yourself?" When Frankie nodded, Harper just shook her head. "You don't have…Oh, what do you call them…farm hands?"

"I work alone, but this October will be my first real harvest, so I'll need to recruit some gluttons for punishment to help me."

"Christ, you're ambitious." Somebody could make a fortune bottling whatever it was that empowered this woman. Turning all that energy and physicality loose on the land was undeniably intriguing. *Frankie* was intriguing. "Can't say as I have a damn clue about cranberries, except for those little clips you see at Thanksgiving, those commercials where people are wading around in berries."

"Those are 'wet-picked' berries and the most common. They all go to sauce and juice. But mine will be 'dry-picked,' no water involved. They're the unsung heroes of Thanksgiving."

"Really. Please say you don't pick them by hand."

Frankie laughed. "No. The vines don't grow much higher than your shin, so you harvest them like you'd mow your lawn, with walk-behind machines. Mine are the berries you buy in bags. They're considered fresh fruit, so they bring a better return."

"Sounds like harder work so they should be worth more."

A little smile appeared on Frankie's slim lips and Harper couldn't tell if her brief assessment had been accurate or appreciated. She really hoped for both. She didn't want to insult her. She enjoyed Frankie's direct, efficient approach, and her honesty was a welcome change from her own world.

"You're exactly right," Frankie said. "I'll show you around my place sometime, if you'd like."

"Well, now you've made me curious. So, yeah, I think I would." Surprised to actually mean it, Harper raised her water bottle. "Here's to spare time."

Frankie joined her toast, then turned those charismatic eyes on her. "So, what's the 'Harper Cushing Story'?"

Automatically, Harper heard standard publicity lines in her head, and she almost cringed. This wasn't some media event. Hell, it felt like Storm lost a touch of its luster with each passing minute here, but, curiously, she didn't feel exposed by what was left to tell. And that was a little eye-opening. So was a compulsion to share.

"My world is a completely different trip, Frankie, so different from this, from yours." She shook her head. "I did the quit-school-to-play-music thing, deep in college debt and not caring one crap about how to get out of it. I spent quite a few years with different bands until I found a comfortable fit and we started making money."

"Well, good for you. I'm all for doing what you enjoy."

"Storm's so busy, and God knows I'm grateful, but I've let far too many years pass, being out of touch with Gram. She'd always been closer to me than my mother or father." Harper shrugged a shoulder. "Sometimes parents just prefer to do their own things. Mine live the 'sunshine life,' as you know." She hoped that conveyed enough about them.

"I know Stella goes there every winter. That's when a couple of us fill in for her here, but it sounds like you guys don't see much of each other."

"Not really, no. I try to catch up with them in Tampa for the holidays, but it's tricky with Storm's schedule. I didn't make it, these past two years."

"Family hasn't visited Stella in the three years I've been around, not until very recently."

"I have to hang my head about all of that. I have contractual excuses, I suppose, but my folks don't." She took a drink and snickered. "But that's probably just as well."

"Ah-huh. I've met them, remember."

"Impressive, aren't they?"

Frankie just grinned. "And I'm guessing they're not thrilled about you and Storm."

"Let's just say that very few of my life choices have thrilled them and Storm definitely is not one. We rarely speak, and when we do, they don't ask, I don't tell."

Frankie nodded pensively and Harper wondered what she thought— and how much more, if anything, she should offer. *Yes, the life is a traveling circus of parties and sex and money...and music, too. Don't ask if I've ever had reservations.*

Frankie turned in her seat to face her. "Have you always been into the kick-ass stuff Storm does?"

"Since my late teens, I guess. Those rebellious years, you know? No stage feels big enough when your message *has* to defy gravity." The precocious years, she mused, and recollections made her smile.

"So, the fire burns deep."

"Well, once I realized people liked the stuff I wrote and how it was delivered, I was hooked."

"I have to confess, I would've picked country to be your style, not an alternative type of rock."

"Country? Not even close. Why?"

Frankie shrugged. "Just a feeling. Growing up, you spent a lot of time here and I just thought it might have left a mark."

"Interesting. And you might be right, to a degree. Those lazy summers here may have kick-started the creative juices, but I was a suburban Florida kid at heart, eager to bust out."

"Are you still?"

"Oh, hell, yeah." Harper was glad when Frankie shared her laugh. "Making a massive crowd bounce to your rhythms, hearing thousands sing your lyrics? It's a major high and we're seriously addicted."

"Sounds like you can't wait to get back to it."

"Oh, of course, but this break comes at an ideal moment to spend with Gram and to give my voice some much needed time off. It was trash when our tour ended a couple of weeks ago and had already made us reschedule a few dates back in March. The ol' vocal cords might be aging faster than my spirit."

"So, being here will also be good for you professionally."

Faint high-pitched chatter brought Harper up straight in her seat and she gestured to the intersection. "First customers of the afternoon?"

Frankie grinned across the parking lot. "Once they're home from baseball, they're off on their bikes. Wouldn't be Saturday afternoon without them."

Three boys, probably eleven or twelve years old, peddled at full speed toward the porch steps and skidded dramatically to a dusty stop.

"Hi, Frankie," the tallest said. "Water time."

The three scrambled onto the porch and crowded against the ice chest, jostling each other as they grabbed small bottles from the water. The littlest boy was left to flip the heavy lid closed.

"Hey, guys. This is Ms. Cushing," Frankie said, a hand extended to Harper. "She's Mrs. Anderson's granddaughter."

Each boy offered a "hi."

"Hi back," Harper said. "I used to ride my bike everywhere around here, too. I spent almost every summer with my grandmother back then."

"Bet that was a long time ago, right?" the tallest boy asked, and Harper heard Frankie laugh.

"Well, yeah. Thanks for reminding me."

He pulled a wrinkled dollar bill from his pocket and handed it to Frankie. The others did the same.

"Thanks, Frankie. Gotta go."

"Yeah, thanks, Frankie!"

"Bye, Ms. Cushing!"

They peddled off as fast as they'd come, and Harper took note of their familiarity with Frankie and the store.

"Best deal around," Frankie said, flattening the bills against her leg.

"Just a dollar for the water?"

"Well, they're little bottles."

"How much for the regular ones?"

"Dollar fifty."

"Really? Aren't they two dollars in the real world?"

"This is a better world."

# Chapter Six

T rapped at the knees, Frankie lost her balance, slid across the front of her tractor, and hit the ground like a felled tree. Thankfully, she was out in the middle of nowhere on her bogs, because toppling dirty, sweaty, and legless onto the gravel road was embarrassing and sure as hell pissed her off.

With the rubbery chest waders still bunched around her knees, she sat up and wrestled to extract each leg, each foot from its attached boot. Getting out of these things was just one more reason she hated them. She knew better than to lean against something—and not sit—to take them off.

After considerable yanking and shaking, she freed each foot, then heaved the waders onto the pile of mucky sticks and leaves in the tractor's dump cart. She wasn't thrilled to have spent the entire morning sloshing around, clearing an irrigation ditch of the massive debris clog generated by last night's wind. At least water now circulated freely around the bogs.

She wondered if Stella was sparing Harper any of Crossroads' tedious work. *It's been a few days, and they must have settled in together. I should have checked on them by now.* Not knowing just how well Harper was handling things ate at Frankie's sense of responsibility.

Most likely, Harper was still adjusting, and Stella was still reveling in her company, but Harper had better be stepping up, even when Stella declined the help, which she did too often.

Frankie almost laughed at the idea of the California rocker dragging herself out of bed at dawn to help with the rush of coffee-deprived commuters. Did she remember all that Frankie had told her? Figured out the old cash register? How long did it take her to find something for a customer? Did she enjoy hauling in cartons of stock or lugging bundles of newspapers to the recycling bin out back?

"How's life treating you now, Harper?" Frankie was willing to bet Stella already had cooked her a roast, baked her bread, and made her one of those rich German chocolate cakes. "You'll probably end up getting spoiled rotten."

Frankie shifted her tractor into gear to dump the load, but the machine wouldn't budge. Distracting thoughts vanished when she saw that both left tires had gone flat. She must have run over something serious on her way here from the barn.

*Of course, this has to be the farthest point away.*

She ran both hands through her hair and growled at the sky. Of all her work equipment, the tractor was the most vital. She had one spare tire but would have to hit the hardware store to buy another—if it was in stock.

She started the long walk back to the barn with little to do but think.

Sometimes, problems tested her patience, her physical stamina, but she was proud of how far she had come. She'd been totally overwhelmed that first day, coming face-to-face with her new life. Three years ago, when that winding dirt road through the woods opened up and revealed fourteen acres of weeds, an abandoned cabin, and a ramshackle little barn, the misgivings and doubt had crushed her heart in a vise.

Bordered by swamp and woods, and cross-hatched by ditches into a multitude of sections, her rectangular-shaped acreage originally had been half its current width. She had doubled it in her first year, which made that new far corner truly far now. She looked back at it and the hobbled tractor. Her fledgling sections had become ridiculously demanding, but she wasn't about to slack off now.

She flexed her shoulders against the memory of all those obstacles that had made her want to turn and run. How she prevailed through that early period, she still wasn't sure. Amazing that she had had the time and energy to lend Stella back then.

But the farm remained her heart's ambition and God bless Stella for being the get-up-and-go cheerleader she'd needed. Damn, it had been *so* worth it. This fall, her little farm would produce a payoff her bank account desperately needed. *Come hell or high water.*

Ironically, she empathized with Harper, so out of her element. Stepping off a raucous concert stage and into her past, she was bound to be slammed by life's adjustments here, and it sounded as if she had paid some dues along the way. Frankie could relate. Living the life you wanted, pursuing your goals took guts and landing on your feet was seldom easy.

But she chafed at the idea that Harper could—consciously or not—bulldoze her way through Stella's Crossroads life. Good intentions sometimes got bulldozed in the process, too.

❖

Laughter from out front in the store broke Harper's concentration. The bookkeeping records she had spread all over Gram's kitchen table weren't as happy and gay. Enlightening, for sure, but not upbeat by any means. Elbow on the table, chin in her palm, she puzzled over how Crossroads survived from month to month. Red ink here and there said "barely," so the lighthearted goings on in the store right now struck a sad note for her.

However, an incoming call from Frankie gave her spirit a welcomed boost.

"Hey, Harper. Just me."

"Hi, me."

"Calling to see if you'd torn your hair out yet. How are you doing?"

Harper smiled at the phone. "Good, so far. No crisis to report. I'm fumbling around a little less each day. The boss says she'll keep me, so there's that. Thanks for checking in."

"So, you're finding your way around alright?"

"Mostly. Crossroads may be compact, and I'm grateful, but it's still left me confounded at times. I've rearranged some things to more logical places, and that's helped."

"Rearranged things?"

"Yeah, and that may have thrown Gram a few curves, but she'll catch on."

"But she has things set up in ways to help her remember. You know, 'everything in its place.' For years."

"Oh, she'll adjust. In fact, she'll find stuff easier to reach now."

Frankie responded curtly. "Did she do the rearranging with you?"

"Yes." The sudden challenge in Frankie's tone struck her. "She did. Well, for a while. You know how stubborn she can be. She lasted about ten minutes, then a customer came in and Gram left me to my own devices— which was just as well, I guess."

Frankie went silent for a long moment. Apparently, moving things around in the store bugged her as much as it had Gram. But, like Gram, Frankie would adapt. Rearranging merchandise wouldn't be the only change she'd probably have to make, but it didn't mean she'd completely restructure the store, either. To really gauge Frankie's temperature on the matter, Harper offered another thought.

"And I wanted to ask your opinion of Crossroads' hours. Would opening at eight o'clock be *that* big of a deal?"

"You mean not open at six?"

Frankie's incredulity gave her away.

"Yeah," Harper pressed on, "and don't you think staying open till ten is excessive?"

"What does Stella say?"

"I haven't mentioned store hours to her yet. I'm a little hesitant."

"And you should be because Stella will flip. I can't say the night hours are all that productive, but the six o'clock opening is legendary, Harper. Stella looked forward to a happy, nostalgic summer with you, not one of disarray and frustration. Changing Crossroads can't be helping her sleep well at night."

"Hell, I'm not *trying* to upset her, Frankie. Gram's well aware that the family is concerned about her going forward and that some things *have* to change."

The tone of this conversation had changed, too. She didn't want to end up at odds with Frankie. The summer would be long and grueling if they spent it butting heads, especially when Frankie could be a vital ally in her cause. Besides, she liked Frankie and enjoyed her company.

"I understand. Just thinking about Stella, that's all."

The sharp edge in Frankie's voice had softened and Harper was relieved.

"I appreciate that. I do. I want her to be happy, too, and to see that change has an up side. I'm trying to be as mindful, as considerate as possible, but I know it's difficult—for all of us."

"Yeah, well, as long as she's handling things alright, I guess that's the most important thing."

The call left Harper pondering the many avenues to her quest, and the level of tact required. Frankie's loyalty to Gram and the store were touching but couldn't factor into this. Gram's well-being definitely did, and Harper vowed to tread as lightly as she could.

And at the moment, Gram was decidedly content. Harper could hear her chatting brightly about someone's newborn. Then the cash register rang, and coins bounced on the floor.

She went out to pick them up. Gram's arthritic fingers failed her at least three times a day, it seemed. Harper didn't want to embarrass her, but knew she needed help, and having Gram realize it was important.

She arrived at Gram's side and offered a smile to the customer. "Hi. Donna, right?"

The young woman smiled. "Yes. Hi, Harper. Have you learned everyone's name already?"

"I'm getting there. I've seen you here before, haven't I?"

"Donna's a regular," Gram said. "Well, when she's not studying. She works part-time for a housekeeping company but she's getting a business degree."

Donna rolled her eyes. "I hope," she told Harper. "Online classes will be the death of me."

"Well, don't give up. Everyone should pursue her dream."

She bent to collect the loose change, but Gram stopped her with a tap to the shoulder.

"I got this," she declared proudly, and used a tall-handled dustpan and broom to sweep up the change. "No problem." She picked out the coins.

Harper sighed at Donna. "As you can see, keeping up with this one is a challenge."

Gram smiled as she smoothed some of Harper's loose hair back into place. "And I've told *this one* to slow down, that she doesn't need to rush all the time."

"I just want to get caught up on things, Gram," Harper said, bagging Donna's purchases, "so you and I can get lazy on the porch." She winked at Donna.

"A method to the madness," Donna said. "I'm happy for you both." She collected her grocery bag and Gram edged along the counter and walked her to the door.

Harper went to the storage room and gathered items to replace what Donna had bought. Arms loaded with flour and canned goods, she paused at the counter to take in the view through the front window. Gram dead-headed a hanging geranium with a little less of her trademark precision and sacrificed several healthy blossoms in the process. Then, she leaned against the railing and sighed heavily toward the quiet intersection.

The ponderous sight brought a lump to Harper's throat. She left her items on the counter and navigated carefully through the screen door without alerting the cowbell. She stepped up behind Gram and gently placed her palms on the thin shoulders.

"Penny for the lady's thoughts."

Gram reached to her opposite shoulder and covered one of Harper's hands with hers. "Honey, this old lady's thoughts aren't worth a dang, let alone a penny, but thank you for asking."

"Well, that's not true at all." She hugged Gram back against her. "Your thoughts always have been and always will be worth a fortune to me." She kissed her cheek. "Now, spill, girlfriend." She nestled her cheek against Gram's ear.

"Your mother hasn't the faintest idea about this place, Harper. She wants me to let it all go."

"Did she call you again?" Harper fought the urge to call and scream at her mother.

"We chatted a little last night, yes."

Harper groaned. "Mom's looking out for you, that's all. She doesn't have a clue about a lot of things, you're right, but she means well."

"Oh, I know, but..." Gram offered a hand toward the parking lot. "If I'm not here, Crossroads probably will close." She patted Harper's arm. "I know what you're seeing in those books in the kitchen, honey. It's not great. And I know Meredith is hoping you'll persuade me to her line of thinking." She turned from Harper's hold and settled into a rocker. "I'd prefer to persuade you to mine."

Harper crouched before her, wishing desperately that this was easier.

"Just let me get my own sense of things, okay, Gram? Then you and I will talk, not Mom. And meanwhile, we'll enjoy our summer."

Gram looked toward the parking lot again before turning uncertain eyes to Harper.

"What do *you* think I should do?"

Harper's heart beat harder in her chest. "I want you to take stock, Gram. Take stock of your abilities, of what's required of you here every day, and apply the wisdom you've always applied to your decisions."

Gram looked away again. Life-changing decisions didn't come easily, but they should be one's own and Harper *so* wanted Gram to feel reassured in making them. She didn't like sounding like a politician, but thought being tactful mattered more. Gram probably heard something else entirely.

"Freddie said he might be back tomorrow."

"Freddie, the bakery delivery man?"

Gram nodded. "He said his manager may not accept the check I wrote this morning. He couldn't read my writing." She looked down at her hands. "It's a little hard to grip the pen these days."

Harper's first reaction was to get Gram into electronic banking but wondered if that might simply prolong the inevitable. *One more thing working against her.*

"I'll help you with that when he comes tomorrow."

"He comes early, Harper."

Harper grinned. "I promise to be up. You're spoiling me, letting me sleep while you're down here, working. My body clock needs to get used to the time change, so I'll start setting my alarm to get up early."

"Frankie will be here tomorrow morning." A smile created more tiny wrinkles at the corners of Gram's eyes. "It's a muffin morning. They're out of this world, fresh from the oven, you know, and you'll get first dibs."

## CHAPTER SEVEN

In the far corner of the store, Harper carefully cut open a five-pound bag of coffee beans and only spilled a handful when Gram called from the counter. Harper yelled "Nice to meet you" to yet another customer Gram was introducing and concentrated on filling the glass cannister.

She was straightening the shelves when, for the second time today, she discovered herself humming to a favorite old song on the stereo. Gram certainly wouldn't take to the raw, tenacious music Harper made these days, but she did have great taste in the oldies, and the familiar music provided a comforting backdrop to Harper's new daily routine.

Passing through the kitchenette to the storage room, she gave the Felix clock a glance and wondered where the day had gone. Sleeping through her alarm and starting at ten o'clock could be a clue. Maybe she was still stuck on West Coast time or "tour" time because adjusting to this daytime activity was tough.

When Gram opened Crossroads at the ungodly hour of six, it evidently was normal to find two or three commuters waiting on the porch for coffee and muffins—*which had already been made because Frankie had come and gone.*

In the storage room, Harper assessed the "system" of boxes stacked beyond eye level and knew who had built it. Some cartons were deceivingly heavy, too heavy for Gram to manage. *Oh, Frankie.* Every other morning, she magically produced muffins and vanished back to her realm like some phantom, only to show up later to help wherever needed. It was impossible to find fault with her generous heart.

Harper finally found the box she needed, halfway up a stack, and began removing the higher ones to get at it. But her disruption collapsed a half-empty box in the middle and the entire stack tipped forward.

"Whoa! No!" She shoved both palms up against the shifting boxes and accidentally bumped the adjacent stack in her rush. It swayed toward her, and, as if in slow motion, both stacks toppled.

Harper grabbed a box as it hit her face, but others crashed against her, and she cursed colorfully as they knocked her to the floor.

"Hey! What's—" Of all people, Frankie appeared in the doorway, obviously amused to find Harper sitting amidst the mess. "Are you finished?"

Harper just glared.

"Well, are you okay?"

"Yes, I'm okay, dammit!"

Frankie hurried to help her to her feet as Harper shoved boxes aside. Her cheek hurt, her shin bled, and her toes throbbed. Her ego felt worse, but her temper flared. She snatched a box off the floor and started a new pile, not caring where.

"What the fuck, Frankie? Did you booby-trap this room?"

Frankie chuckled as she rounded up loose cans that had rolled away. "Really, are you alright? Some boxes are he—"

"Heavy. Yeah, no shit. What the hell were they doing, up so high?"

"That's my fault. I'm sorry. I should've warned you. We have to stay a step ahead of Stella." She located the box with a torn flap and began refilling it. "Sometimes Stella will rip open a box to get at stuff, like she did with this one, and that undermines all the others."

"What if this had happened to her?" Inspecting the scrape on her shin, Harper immediately decided to rearrange the room her way. "There'll be some changes made in here. And damn fast. Consider yourself put on notice." At least Frankie appeared appropriately chagrined.

"I messed up. I—"

"What's going on back here?" Gram looked between them and around the room. "I heard the crash."

"Just boxes stacked too high, Gram, that's all." Harper scolded Frankie with an evil eye, then chastised Gram with a finger. "And you cannot be pulling things out of the middle."

Guilty, Gram looked beyond Harper to Frankie and bit back a grin. "Um...I have to check my brownies." She hurried across the hall to her apartment.

Harper spun to Frankie, who immediately cast her grin to the floor.

"You're just as much to blame," Harper said, "and you know she'll keep right on doing it."

"Unfortunately, you're right. She will. I've warned her a few times already. So, one step ahead."

"Great." Harper puffed loose hair off her forehead. "God, with the two of you...I need to get more sleep."

"I'm sorry about all this. I should have noticed that she'd been nibbling away at the pile. I meant to put some of these boxes on the floor. I hope you're okay." She gently turned Harper's cheek aside and the delicate touch sent a surprising flutter through Harper's chest. "You'll get a bruise there," Frankie said, "below your eye."

Harper swallowed hard at the contact, watching Frankie examine her cheek. "I-I thought I caught the box in time." Those concerned eyes flickered up at her and Frankie withdrew her hand.

"I'll get you some ice."

"Thanks, but I think I'll live."

"Eh, you might not say that tomorrow morning. Be right back." She took off for Gram's apartment.

Harper exhaled hard at the mess around her feet. "God dammit." She had to pay better attention, stop daydreaming about songs on the stereo, that breeze on the front porch, and how out of sync she obviously was from the real world. And now Frankie.

"Here, try this." Frankie hurried in, somehow looking apologetic, hopeful, and gallant all at once. "Crushed ice." She set a bulging cloth into Harper's palm, and Harper had to force back a grin when Frankie guided her hand to the right spot. "This is my fault," Frankie continued. "I mean, damn. You're barely here a week and already I've given you a black eye?" She shook her head. "I should've waited at least a month."

Harper *did* grin now. "Your contrition is *so* touching."

Frankie busied herself creating two short stacks of boxes, then steered Harper by the shoulders to sit on one. "I'm sorry," she said again, sitting on the other stack. "How's your leg? Do you want a Ban—"

Harper quickly set her free hand on Frankie's shoulder. "No, thank you. It's just a nick. Besides, if Gram sees you getting me anything else, she'll probably call an ambulance."

Frankie laughed. "True, although she feels bad. She knows why the boxes fell."

"Well, if it means this won't happen to her, then I'm glad it happened."

"Oh, I didn't say that. She didn't repent, she just feels badly for you."

Harper laughed lightly but immediately winced. "Don't make me laugh."

"Hurts, huh? Is that cold enough?"

"Will you stop worrying?"

"Have you ever had a black eye before?"

"Once, when I was twenty-one. Our bass player was standing too close, and when he turned, I caught a machine head just below my eye."

"Ouch! That's a big tuner to take in the face."

"Yeah, and it was a big ouch. I saw stars. It took a lot of makeup to hide that shiner."

"I got mine at about twelve, a bunch of us playing football. A friend and I were the defensive line, and we closed the gap between us, head to head."

"And you had to go to school with your shiner?"

"Oh yeah. Teachers teased but kids didn't. City kids, you know. No big deal."

"Boston?"

"Roslindale. That's almost Boston."

"How does a city girl end up out here growing cranberries?"

Frankie shifted on her seat. "You never know where love will take you."

"Ah. But you tackled your farm all on your own, right? Oh…sorry. I didn't mean to pry."

"No big deal. She had a family operation going when we met, and I really got into it. Fifteen years of 'us' and no 'me' turned out to be too many. I had to move on to something that made me happy." She shrugged. "Funny, how clear hindsight can be."

Harper watched the dimness brighten in Frankie's eyes. *Fifteen years?* She was a "giver," that much was clear, and she was stronger for it.

"You're still giving, Frankie."

"I guess, but I'm *me*, too, so it's okay. I can't be one without the other."

"Good. You shouldn't be. Somehow, I don't think that's who you are."

Frankie held her gaze for a long moment. "Tell me who *you* are."

Suddenly very self-conscious, Harper took the ice off her cheek and inspected the little bundle. Frankie's patient silence was loud, and she sat waiting, watching, until Harper forced herself to look up.

"Who *I* am? No one's ever asked that before. I…I'd say I'm too independent for my own good, but I'm smart enough to know it—usually," she added with a little smile. "Thank God, I'm a lot smarter today, than when I thought I was the next Pat Benatar, shoving my band down everybody's throat. We're pretty aggressive on stage, but that's where it stops, for me, anyway. I've outgrown the wild and careless lifestyle."

"Why do you think that is?" Frankie urged Harper to put the ice back on her cheek. "Why you outgrew it. You still love what you do."

"Of course." The words had never sounded so automatic. "Music is my lifeblood, like exercise that keeps body and mind in tune. But I don't need it the way I used to." She flashed back to arguments with her mother and shook her head. "Back then, it was all about refusing to be ignored. I *had* to be heard."

Frankie sat back, nodding. "Were your folks into music when you were young?"

"No. My folks have always been into real estate and country club socials. So, I was all about being heard."

"And now you have thousands screaming for you whenever you step to the mic." Frankie grinned modestly. "As somebody who's hurled before playing for an audience, I can*not* imagine what that's like."

"Oh, I went through that, too, Frankie. Believe me. The first time I saw a couple hundred people waiting for us. And the first time there were two thousand. When it came to ten thousand, I hyperventilated and almost blacked out." Frankie laughed. "But, Jesus, there is nothing on earth like it. When they're all singing back *to you*?" Harper shot a prayerful glance at the ceiling. "Your feet aren't even on the floor, let me tell you."

"How the hell do you remember lyrics at moments like that? Chords? I'd be…I don't know. Frozen."

"No. It sweeps you up and you're off, into it, consciously or not."

"Man. It's a far cry from begging to be heard."

"Very far. I've been there for a couple years now, and it still feels that way."

"And today, is there a touch of redemption in that?"

The heavy question surprised her, but Harper appreciated Frankie taking the issue to a deeper level.

"I'll confess to that, sure. But time's too precious to waste on redemption. And I'm no kid anymore. I just want to make music that I like and that, hopefully, pleases listeners. It's okay if everyone's not into it, and the genre doesn't necessarily matter either, but it has to feel right to *me*."

"Exactly. I get that."

"So, like I said, I guess I'm independent by nature."

"You're a lot more than that."

Frankie ran both palms down her thighs as if she was nervous. When she stood and looked around the room, Harper didn't doubt it. They *had* shared a lot, and Harper realized her heart rate had kicked up a notch.

"We should straighten out this mess," Frankie said.

"Let me." Harper set her ice bundle aside and got to her feet. She did want to organize things *her* way, not as high as Frankie's reach.

"I'll help y—"

"Don't worry about it. But thank you."

"Well, aside from this, you're doing okay here?"

Harper nodded. "Overall. I'm gaining more insight by the hour, I think. About Gram and Crossroads. She burns so much energy through the mornings and really slows down in the afternoons. And *you*…" She shook her head. "How *do* you do it?"

"I just need to keep busy, a habit from the past."

"So, what *did* bring you here today? You just happened to pop in and catch me in my most embarrassing time of need?"

"I was just dropping off that crate of cukes and peas for Terri. Her gardens are taking over the world right now. Catching you in action was just good timing."

"Uh-huh. Well, thanks a lot." Harper didn't know what else to say. She was seriously distracted by that smile, that damn dimple, and seeing Frankie run a hand through her hair, Harper could almost feel that cool silk between her own fingers.

"Look, really, Harper. If you need anything, remember I'm not far."

"Good to know. Thanks."

Frankie stepped to the door. "I have to go, but—"

"Will you be back later?" The expectant look on Frankie's face made Harper wonder how she'd sounded. *Okay, so I'm hoping for it.* She hurried to elaborate. "Gram will be bummed that you've left."

"Please tell her I've got a project going right now. She'll understand."

"I'll do that." Harper joined her in the doorway. "I should check on her."

"I'm surprised she hasn't come to check on *you.*" Frankie studied Harper's bruise pointedly. "Come here, under the light." A hand on Harper's shoulder, she urged her back beneath the ceiling light.

Harper caught herself before she placed a hand on Frankie's chest. Such contact just seemed acceptable, considering she felt oddly closer to Frankie somehow. But she'd come all this way to "feel closer" to Gram, not Frankie, and standing here, inches from that dynamic physical presence wasn't helping.

"It might turn a little blue but not bad," Frankie said. "I think the ice helped."

Harper looked away from Frankie's mouth, across her cheek, and their eyes met. Frankie's softened dangerously, and Harper felt her composure slipping. Whatever this was, it needed to be put in its place. And fast.

"I'm glad you stopped by."

# Chapter Eight

Wrestling with her better judgment these past few days made daily work difficult, but Frankie couldn't get past that exchange in the storage room. She'd texted Harper the next day, just to check on the black eye situation, of course, and had been tempted to text more, but didn't. The heat in Harper's eyes, the luxurious feel of her cheek, that seductive voice, they had ganged up on her when she'd driven away, and still wouldn't let go. She liked it more than she should, far more than she'd ever expected. And that shook the walls she'd built around her spirit and scared the hell out of her.

*She's only here a little while, so smarten up. And stop touching her.*

But when she pulled into the parking lot, the sight of grandmother and granddaughter working side-by-side made her smile. They were tackling the little garden beds at the corners of the porch, although Harper was on her phone while Stella raked.

"Harper's trimming these yews." Stella grinned from beneath her flowery sun hat. "It's about time she did some real work around here."

"Hey!" Harper interrupted her conversation to yell from the side yard. "What was that?"

Frankie laughed. "Yeah, I can see she's working hard." She did think the yews looked good, considering Harper probably had never played gardener in her life.

"She's really done a good job, don't you think?" Stella asked. "We accomplished a lot this morning. Well, until she got that call from someone in her band." She leaned closer and whispered. "I wish they'd let her enjoy her vacation. She gets business calls almost every day."

Frankie watched Harper pace as she spoke into the phone, her free hand chopping air as if marking beats. "Music is her life, though, Stella. And she's kind of a big-shot in the business, you know."

Stella watched Harper as if from afar. As in *long ago.*

*She's all grown up, Stella, but she's here for you now.*

"Let's go sit a while," Frankie said, setting a hand on her back. "I could use a drink. Bet you could, too."

As they headed for the porch, Harper slid her phone into her hip pocket and followed them up the steps.

"Sorry about that. Our album's entering the editing phase now and we need to pay attention." She sighed hard. "We think engineering is overreaching, so we've scheduled a Zoom huddle to strategize. We can't allow them to minimize our input."

"Do you guys need to be there?" Frankie half expected Harper to start packing.

"Not yet. We'll see how the samples come back first, then decide if we need to swoop in. I'd thought what was sent the other day was okay, but the guys weren't as satisfied." She wiped her face with a paper towel from her pocket and, as if renewed and returned to the present, she flashed Frankie an optimistic smile. "Good morning."

The sincerity in that welcome stirred Frankie's self-control. "Hi. You guys are really going at it, today."

"You got that right." Harper pointed at Stella. "Who are you and what have you done with my sweet gramma? I'm going back to Cali where it's more fun."

Frankie really hoped she wouldn't anytime soon. "If it's any consolation, you're doing a terrific job." She opened the ice chest as she spoke to Stella. "Those yews will be easier to decorate at Christmas."

"Oh, that's right!" Stella lit up at the idea, obviously ready to start decorating now.

Frankie passed each of them bottles of water, then left payment on the lid. Harper glanced at the money and sent Frankie a sideways look that said she still disagreed with the meager price. But Frankie winked knowingly and steered her away from that topic. She didn't want to think about Harper's "changes" and "upgrades."

Standing so close now, she was taken by Harper's presence all over again. Just a trace of shadow showed beneath her eye, and Frankie took a touch of pride in her ice remedy.

"Your eye's clearing up fast."

"Yes, thank God. Thank *you*. My cheekbone's a little sore, but I'll take it."

Frankie forced her attention to her drink. Harper's tank top and shorts were hard to ignore. They showed off her luscious figure in a glistening, rosy-red tan. With a lifestyle built around nighttime gigs, she most likely didn't spend much time in the sun. Nor had she probably given much thought to caution.

"You're hot."

Harper hiked an eyebrow as she raised her bottle to her lips. "Excuse me?"

Frankie grinned at her reaction. "Be careful, working in the sun. Where's your hat?"

"Upstairs."

"Ah-huh. And sunscreen?"

"I put some on earlier, *Mom*."

The playful look in Harper's eyes almost made Frankie catch her breath. She could have lost herself in that look if Stella hadn't been watching.

"Just saying," she added with a shrug. "We forget, all wrapped up in what we're doing. The sun's caught me too often and those evenings were killers."

Harper extended her arms to inspect them. "I suppose I need more."

"And don't forget your legs." Frankie tried not to admire them for too long. Harper's glance caught her, and Frankie quickly turned to Stella. "They'll burn, too."

"Oh, absolutely," Stella said. "They're too lovely to ignore."

Frankie and Harper shared a glance as they drank simultaneously.

"Frankie, guess what we did once things quieted down yesterday morning," Stella said, settling onto a stool. "We rearranged the storage room. It's completely different now. Oh, and guess what else." She beamed up at Harper. "We're having our sign painted!"

"Yeah, I got a good price yesterday," Harper explained, "so I called this morning and set it up. They'll be here next week, and it might only take a day or two."

"Excellent. Same colors?"

"Yup," Stella said. "Red lettering on white with the blue border, like it's always been, and just in time for the Fourth. I can't wait."

Harper's willingness to spruce up the old sign came as a promising surprise. It took some of the sting out of her eagerness to "upgrade" Crossroads, and Frankie hoped any such future changes would be as thoughtful and would make Stella this happy.

"It *is* exciting, isn't it?" she said. "And when it's done, we'll hang the buntings off the porch." She turned to Harper. "I think I put them upstairs in your living room closet."

"I'll find them." Harper patted Stella's hand. "I'm happy you still decorate for the Fourth. I always felt it was 'our' holiday, yours and Grampa's and mine."

Frankie appreciated the sentiment in Harper's gentle tone, her doting expression, and how she made Stella smile. Maybe she shouldn't worry so much about Harper's intentions here, but she still couldn't help wondering. Was she paying for the sign work?

*That's none of my business.*

"Well, you two will have your holiday again this year, and that's great." Stella leaned forward and poked Frankie's hip. "Did you get your tire?"

"I did. Three, in fact. I'm just coming back now. It took a couple of days for the store to get them, but I should be good for a while. So, now I'm out of excuses and have to get back to work."

"A woman came in for coffee today, first thing, asking for you," Harper said, eyeing her curiously. "Allison? She asked if you were going to be here tomorrow evening. Apparently, she's eager to hang with you."

*Lose the smirk, Ms. Cushing. There's no deep, dark secret.*

"That's Allie Trumbol. She's a firefighter and a mean guitar player. Now and then, a bunch of us get together here and pick for a few hours."

"Here on the porch?"

"Yeah. One night, there were so many of us, we took everything out there, in the parking lot."

"Friday of Memorial Day weekend," Stella added. "Oh, what a night. People came and sat in their cars to listen. They parked all around. Even Brenda spent some time in her cruiser. It's such fun, Harper." Stella inched forward and whispered behind her hand. "Even I sing along."

"You have a sweet voice, Stella," Frankie said. "Some of the others, not so much, but that's not important. It's all about having a good time."

Stella nodded vigorously. "I bet you would enjoy it, Harper. You'd spare your voice, of course, but you'd have fun."

Frankie genuinely hoped she would accept. "We play all kinds of stuff, none of it polished, but everyone would welcome a pro sitting in."

"Well, thank you for the invite."

"Now, Frankie," Stella began, "don't go wearing yourself out. Save some energy for tomorrow night."

"I'm watching the weather, Stella. That thunderstorm they've been predicting could arrive overnight, so I have to make sure the levees are secure." She dropped her empty water bottle into the recycling basket nearby. "I was lucky to get the tractor tires when I did. It's time I made use of them."

"If anyone else inquires, I'm telling them you'll be here. Oh, wait!" She hurried inside, still talking. "I have brownies for you. Don't leave yet!"

"Thank you! Don't rush!" Frankie stopped moving toward the steps and, without thinking, set a hand on Harper's arm. "Sunscreen," she said, leaning to her ear, "*all* over."

Harper turned her head just enough and returned the whisper. "Are you offering?"

Frankie's heart skipped as they stood nearly cheek to cheek. Harper was quick, and her foxy look was impossible to resist. "I'm good with my hands."

"I'm sure you are. And I make music with mine."

"Mine can make a little music, too."

"And I asked if you're offering."

Frankie inched back and lifted her gaze from the curl of Harper's lips.

"Okay, here we go." Stella and the cowbell broke the spell with a flourish. "This is for you." Frankie had a container of brownies in her hands before she could blink. "Now, don't eat them all tonight."

"Wow. No promises, Stella." She pecked her cheek. "Thank you. Nobody bakes better brownies." She sent a quick smile to Harper. "Remember: sunscreen, working in the sun."

"Oh, I won't forget." Harper couldn't hide her grin.

She wouldn't forget. The sensation of Frankie's delicate touch lingered. The breathy tease continued to reverberate everywhere else. Thankfully, she'd managed to keep her wits about her and respond in kind.

She inhaled and exhaled as subtly as she could. Bold, unexpected flirting rarely left her jittery, but now her nerves were racing, and she was even a little short of breath. *What am I, fifteen?*

She focused on Gram's fond expression, following Frankie's truck as it disappeared down the road. *Frankie can do no wrong.*

"What do you really know about her, Gram?"

"Frankie? Oh, well, quite a bit, I'd say." She sat back, those eyes examining Harper's face for intent. "Interested?"

Harper tried to dismiss the question with a little chuckle. "She's an intriguing character, for sure."

"Uh-huh. 'Intriguing,' you say. Well, she's actually a private person. No close family, that I know of, and maybe that's why she's so attached to this place."

"And to you."

Gram smiled. "Her previous relationship went sour after a lot of years. From what she's said—and hasn't said—she had to break it off. I gather there was a lot of emotional stress."

"Abuse?"

"Not sure, but maybe. But Frankie's doing what she loves now. She's said it helped her find herself again. That smile is genuine."

"I don't hear many survivor stories like that in my world, just lots of stress and struggle. Not many happy endings."

"You've achieved, Harper. You can pick and choose the life you want, although it would be nice to see a glimmer of love in your eyes."

"Oh, please don't worry about that. I don't. Storm's life is constantly spinning. It's one of the reasons behind our name. We all just take things as they come."

"I see. Well, I'm certainly not going to nag, but you should relax tomorrow night, join in with some new friends—and Frankie, of course."

The temptation of spending more time with Frankie felt a little dangerous. And a down-home picking session just didn't hold much appeal at all. At least Harper had appointments lined up for tomorrow and didn't have to make up an excuse or disappoint Gram with a lie.

"I have some errands to do later tomorrow and can't say how soon I'll be back."

"But they're lovely people. And you need to hear Frankie. Everyone wants to play and sing with her. She's a crooner, you know."

*Yes, I remember our first meeting. Vividly.*

"I do like the timbre of her voice."

"Is that right? My, if you could manage even a quiet little song, I would just love to hear you two together."

"Singing would be risky, Gram, and, besides, I doubt we even know the same material."

"Well, I understand about your voice, honey, but you could still play, right? You're a professional and Frankie handles everything that friends throw at her. Do you know that she can't read music? Not a note."

"She plays by ear?"

"That's what she says."

"That's what I always did, until I had to learn sheet music with the band."

"So, see? You can do both. Please give tomorrow night some thought, won't you?"

"I'll think about it, yes."

"Oh, good. Frankie likes you a lot, Harper. I can tell. And I think you like her, too, don't you?"

"Yes, of course. She's very nice and thoughtful, especially to you."

"And to you, from what I've seen. She's such a hard worker and somehow always finds time to help out here. She's so attentive. I can't imagine how someone could have taken advantage of that. She has a wonderful heart."

*Gram.*

"I've seen nothing less, it's true. You're so lucky that she's nearby and has such a flexible job."

Gram smiled. "Has she invited you to her place yet?"

"She has. The day we met."

"Are you going?"

"Sure, sometime, I suppose."

"Oh, do go. It's impressive, what she's accomplished there—and all by herself. She's such a genial person for someone so solitary. It's almost not fair."

"Who's to say why we take the roads we do, Gram."

"True. When she's here, she brightens up the place. And when you're *both* here, it just makes my heart happy."

The day's labor bore down and, once Harper had seen Gram off to bed, she meandered onto the porch and half-sat on the railing, afraid to settle into a rocker for fear of falling asleep. Mornings at Crossroads came horribly early.

*Would it really cause a revolt if Crossroads opened at eight? And if it closed at eight, we'd be spared these last two hours of nothing. It's time we got down to it and talked about hours, price increases, things that could improve Crossroads' salability.*

The weight of it all turned the tranquility enveloping her now into numbing isolation. At least the breeze was soothing. The honeyed scent of warm hay hung in the twilight, and she inhaled greedily. A simple pleasure, but another one of those things she'd taken for granted as a kid. Even the crickets were in fine voice, and she welcomed the rhythmic accompaniment.

A thunderstorm tonight seemed highly unlikely, considering the beautiful evening. Maybe Frankie just overstated her concern to escape back to her bogs. Harper hadn't considered that solitary nature at all until Gram brought it up, and now it colored all Harper's thoughts about her.

*Do you enjoy being a loner now? Your past obviously toughened you, but how can you still be so kind, so...enticing? Amazing, you're still single.*

Harper laughed lightly at her wandering thoughts. She'd lost count long ago of how many women had come and gone from her life because... because none of it had felt real? Only once had a woman stolen her heart— and life on the road had broken it. Those had been impossible circumstances, but nevertheless, *she* had broken Chelsea's heart. The "life" was as costly as it was large.

Suddenly, the sound of barking dogs startled her onto both feet, and she grabbed her phone from her hip pocket. There were times this ringtone irritated the hell out of her, but not now. Seeing Denise's name delivered a wave of comfort. She settled into a rocker and answered the call.

"I may not have uplifting conversation," she began, foregoing a hello. "I'm beat."

"Hey, nice to hear you, too. Why are you beat? You out pickin' corn today?"

"I told you. There are no corn fields around me. Just crickets."

"How're things with your cranberry farmer?"

"Fine. We haven't knocked heads yet, if that's what you're expecting."

"'Knocking heads' wasn't what I was shooting for."

"She comes here for Gram."

"So you say. No innuendoes or, you know, subtleties? No way she's ever had someone like you in her cranberry life. Tell me she's not freaking dead."

"I've caught a look or two, but…" She warmed at the memories of their storage room encounter, the sunscreen flirtation.

"Uh-huh. And what are *you* looking at? C'mon, for God's sake. Give your bestie a break, huh?"

"She's terrific with Gram, got her wrapped."

"Okay. This is boring."

"Look. I already told you what she's like and that hasn't changed since our last conversation. She's got this…reserved strength that's hard to describe and she wears it well, doesn't have a clue how sexy it is."

"Well. Now we're getting somewhere."

"Satisfied?"

"For now. I'll expect more substance next time." Harper sighed. "So, moving on, have you heard from Sasha?"

"Not since last week, when she said my condo had been sold." Harper chortled. "She's probably bought her own in Hawaii by now. Why?"

"Her daughter put an odd little comment on Instagram the other day, something about the *Tonight Show*. It's probably nothing. The girl's only thirteen."

Harper sat up. Her agent would have reached out. "Sasha hasn't made contact since we wrapped in LA."

"How did you miss it? You gotta keep up, girl."

"Have I told you it's different here and I've been a little busy? Oh, and I'm trying to learn how to do something new. It's called sleeping at night. So, what did she post?"

"Just that she'd love to see the band on the show."

"What does that mean?"

"Well, honey, you better break radio silence and find out."

Harper squinted at nothing in the dim light, thinking hard against a rising headache. The only obligation Storm had in its immediate future was arranging the live album from their tour. However, if promoting it on the *Tonight Show* was in the works, that would be big.

"Okay, I'll get in touch. Another must-do."

"Do I have to come to Nowheresville to be your freaking secretary?"

"You do quite well just like this, thank you."

"God. So, aside from Farmer Frankie, what else is going on there?"

"Gram and I have worked out a system of covering nights so she can retire early. Of course, I'm also trying to get up early to spare her on that end, too. It's tricky. And Frankie helps, if we need her."

"Does Frankie miss being there? It *was* her gig before you showed up."

"I don't think so. She hasn't let on, if she does. I think she's backed off because she knows I want to reconnect with Gram. Plus, I've been taking care of things here—or trying to, anyway—but I do get the feeling Gram misses her. I may ask her to come around more often."

"Right."

"For Gram."

"For your grandmother. Sure. I *do* have to come to Nowheresville, don't I? Dammit, Harper, did you ever think she could be someone special?"

"What? God, come on, Denni. Fantasy is one thing, but you're really reaching." She massaged her right temple.

"Bummer. Nowheresville isn't doing a damn thing for your love life."

"I'm not here for my love life."

"Or your sex life."

"Not for that, either."

"You're allowed to have one, you know."

"Let my life return to normal first, will you?"

"Ha. As if 'normal' was keeping your bed warm. Shit, Harper. Face it: You need a spark, girl." She let out a resigned breath. "Too bad Nowheresville is just what it sounds like, fucking dull."

"You know, if I could ever get enough sleep, I might even get used to it."

"'Get used to it'? Shit. Hurry up and get the hell out of there, will you? Don't forget you've got a sweet spot waiting for you in WeHo."

Harper sighed, imagining life in the diverse, electric world of West Hollywood and the adorable little house she'd found online. "Yeah, I know." She just had too much on her mind to get psyched about it right now, that's all.

"So quit the 'getting used to it.' It's scary, especially with Frankie nibbling at your common sense."

"Yeah, well, that seductive charm of hers is a little hard to ignore. There's a…I don't know, an intimacy to it that gets under my skin. And when she hits you with those eyes? Christ."

"Ah. So, now she's seductive. And you've mentioned the eyes before, by the way."

Harper replayed her words in her head. *Just being honest.*

Denise cleared her throat. "Not that you've given her much thought or anything."

# CHAPTER NINE

Frankie swore at the water streaming through the levee. She'd been waging war all morning, shoveling and patching breaks in the banking. This trouble spot refused to be denied, and she refused to let swamp water carve a Grand Canyon sluiceway onto her fragile new sections of bog.

She lugged the last of a dozen sandbags into the break, then buried the pile with shovelfuls of gravel and clay. She slammed the loose earth into place with the back of the shovel repeatedly, packed it as hard as she could, then added more, then more. The patch held.

She sagged onto her tractor and poured water over her steaming head, cursing the early-morning deluge that had caused this problem.

"Enough of this shit for one day." She'd neglected regular maintenance in this area recently and had paid the price.

The late June heat made answering the demands of her inaugural crop so much harder. Acres of tiny pale green buds had begun to blossom, and their miniature white flowers now dotted the bogs. Soon, eight acres would be covered with them, as fragile and beautiful as light snow, and then berries would form. Her livelihood begged for attention, no less than a child in the family. She *had* to be more diligent and a lot less distracted.

Stealing time away for Crossroads had always been tricky, and these days, with Harper handling things over there, she worried about it more than ever, but this year her time here truly mattered. She'd spent nearly all her savings, worked herself to the bone for this, and the time to reap the fruits of her labor was approaching fast. An entire year's income depended on her attention to detail, and she couldn't afford to stray.

She motored around the bogs and back to the barn, only to find her friend Terri lounging on the cabin porch. That robust personality and Stetson hat always brought a smile. Along with her wife and teenage daughter, Terri boarded horses and grew far more vegetables than she needed on her acreage several miles away. Frankie and Crossroads regularly benefitted from Terri's gardening obsession.

The stool disappeared beneath Terri's beefy frame and the water bottle in her hand looked terribly insufficient. She had a heart as big as her body, which seriously outdistanced Frankie's five-foot-ten.

Frankie stepped onto the porch and pulled up a stool. "Hey, farmer."

"Hey, farmer, yourself." Terri handed her a bottle of water. "Just at Crossroads so I got you one, too. Harper said I'd find you here."

"I *had* to get caught up here. Dirty work."

"Yeah, it shows."

"Right, and look at you." Frankie gestured to their clothes, all splotched with dirt. Frankie's jeans were wet from the thighs down, and she kicked off her boots and peeled off her socks.

"How was Harper doing?"

"Okay, it seemed. She had a little trouble finding the Scotch tape for a kid and I had to show her, but I think she's managing."

"Where was Stella?"

"Taking a nap. Harper said she'd dozed off watching TV, so she let her sleep."

"Yeah, Stella sneaks in those late morning naps all the time. She claims she does it intentionally."

"Right."

"Probably just one of many things Harper's noticed by now."

"Nature's going to take its course, Frankie. Nothing you can do, really." Frankie tried not to think about it. "So, speaking of nature, how are your berries looking?"

"They're good. Everything's starting to bloom. With luck, it'll be a huge haul, come October."

"Good for you!"

"You realize I'm drafting you for harvest. I have three picking machines ready and a fourth I'm working on, so I'm going to need all the help I can get. But it's tricky, finding people."

"Well, count me in. And my Ginny, too, when she's not teaching."

"The problem is I need daytime availability, and everything rides on the weather and temperature. There can be twenty people here, ready to go on a perfectly sunny day, but if the berries are wet…" She shook her head. "If they're wet from the rain or the sprinklers overnight or heavy dew, then we're screwed. Everything gets postponed."

"Damn. Even if they're just damp?"

"Gotta be dry because these berries won't be fast-frozen. They're warehoused as-is for packaging, so if they sit around wet, they turn to stinky useless mush."

"Cripes, Frankie. Whatever made you choose this world, some midlife crisis? I thought you had a brain in your head."

Frankie laughed. "Let's just say I got hooked on it, once upon a time. Lots of frustration and back-breaking work, yes, but lots of bountiful harvests, too. *You* can appreciate working outside almost every day, not to mention during the fall in New England. Can't beat that and you know it."

"As if picking a fight with Mother Nature is fun."

"I don't really fight with her, and neither do you with your crops. It's a cooperative effort, and mine starts with finding enough people with flexible daytime schedules."

"How many will you need?"

"Eight or nine, I think."

Terri nodded. "We'll get them."

"Thanks. A few regulars at the store have volunteered, too, so I'm optimistic." She held up the bottle. "And thanks for this."

"Two bucks, now."

Frankie stopped unscrewing the cap. "That's what you paid?"

Terri sent her a look as she removed her hat and tucked back loose strands of hair. Wearing that Stetson had given her hat-head and, with that knob of a ponytail at the back of her neck, she didn't appear to have much hair at all. A severe look for a large woman with a puppy personality. Frankie waited anxiously as she drank half the bottle.

"Yup," Terri finally answered. "Didn't take Harper long to raise the price, did it?"

Frankie simmered and figured Stella must have lost that argument. Maybe if she said something, Harper would think twice about spoiling more of Crossroads' old-time feel. "Sorry about the price."

*Eliminating all disposable plastic will be next. Won't be able to argue that point either.*

"Nah. Forget it. Everybody's been expecting changes anyway, with an outsider in Stella's ear."

"Yeah, well, that's a damn shame."

"People have noticed Stella's not at the counter as much now."

"They have?"

"Well, they miss her. And there's the other stuff, the gossip." Terri hitched a shoulder. "Already, there's talk that Harper will modernize the place, change things, like prices." She held up her water bottle. "I even heard a rumor she's going to shut the doors for good."

"That's crap. She doesn't own Crossroads." The thought made Frankie's stomach turn. "Where do people get these ideas?"

"From some obscure thread of conversation that has nothing to do with reality."

"I need to remind Harper to watch out for that. And if she gets carried away, changing things, that'll ruin—"

"Careful, Frankie. You don't own the place either."

"I know, but don't I have *some* right to watch out for it, for Stella? Who's been looking out for them these past few years? Not Harper. Not in a lot of years."

"But she's within her rights to make changes. You're not. You can't resent her legit connection—or be jealous of it."

"Ugh. Yeah, I know." She rubbed her face with both hands. "I *am* trying to stay objective. You think I'm jealous? Hell, I *like* Harper, and maybe more than I should, considering what she could have up her sleeve. It's got my brain working overtime."

Terri sat back, assessing Frankie with a discerning eye.

"What?" Frankie snapped.

"I'm beginning to see the real issue here. Obviously, you aren't."

"Well—"

"Somebody's finally broken through that lone-wolf thing of yours, hasn't she?"

"What? A woman from Never Never Land? Not true."

"Bullshit. That's what has your head spinning. Give it up, Frankie. You survived having your spirit crushed for years and you came out the other side, ready to tackle the world. So, go for it."

"Please. Get real. The issue is whether Harper's going to run roughshod over Stella and the place she loves."

"You're sulking because Harper outranks you and you want to stand your ground, but you're too lost in Never Never Land to figure out how. The *real* issue is you're hot for her."

Typical Terri. Somebody always had a crush on somebody. No way she really could be on to something.

But Frankie knew her mind wandered too often these days. Maybe she really wasn't doing such a great job of keeping her head on straight. Why had it become so hard to stay away, to avoid texting, to simply go the hell home when they're together? Was it really all about Stella? How many times lately had she caught herself ogling like a teenager? Hell, how many times lately had Harper caught *her*?

*Shame on me, because at the very least, it's embarrassing.*

Unlikely that Harper ever missed a thing. Her fast-paced world was known for shrewd instincts and self-preservation tactics, and now she was applying them to Stella's cause. We're definitely in two different leagues, Frankie mused, even though she liked having Harper in hers, at least for a little while.

"Yeah, so there's a lot I like about her—but so what? Being here is just a touch-and-go thing for her, come in for a landing and then fly away. I can't lose sight of that." She snickered. "Besides, who am I to her? Compared to what she's got going on? If anything, just summer entertainment. The 'helpful neighbor down the road.'"

"That's fucking horseshit, Frankie, and you know it. If your brain was really telling you that, your gut wouldn't like her."

"Yeah, well, aside from her temporary stay here, it would be nice if I didn't have to worry about what she has in mind for Stella and Crossroads. All of this has to be about Stella, not me."

"So, talk to her, for Christ's sake. Find out. But use a little diplomacy. Don't let what you don't know screw up what could be a mind-blowing summer." She rapped Frankie's shoulder with a backhand. "Nothing wrong with *enjoying* each other while she's here. She'd probably appreciate a little fun, huh? And God knows, you're too freakin' rusty for your own good."

"Stop." Frankie shook her head. "I've been burned before. I'm not getting swept down some dead-end road." Keeping the sharp, vibrant Harper Cushing at arm's length seemed smart. Frankie just couldn't be sure it was possible.

"For fuck's sake, Frankie. You don't have to marry her just because you screw around for a couple of months."

"I know that."

"Sure, you do. You're afraid things might go too far. I get that. But, Frankie...Wow. *Harper Cushing*? I mean, come on." Terri swiped her hat off to lean toward her. "There's common ground between you two. Go exploring."

"Are you done now, Coach? Man, you're brutal." Frankie straightened and rolled her shoulders.

"She's really likable, Frankie, down-to-earth friendly and, on top of that, she's jaw-dropping beautiful. When Stella introduced us on her second day here, a little piece of me melted at her feet. Those eyes? That smile had me weak in the knees. And add *Storm* to that image? Shit. It was a total mic drop moment. She's so much sweeter than you'd expect from some rock star. I was speechless. Me."

"Yeah, I felt that way, too."

"Pretty sure she's available, too, you know."

"She is, according to Stella, although I can't imagine why."

"Doesn't matter. She knows you're single, right?"

"Oh, by now I'm sure Stella's told her. You know, when she first said her granddaughter was coming, I never thought she'd be particularly special. And who'd have thought she'd be *somebody*? I just figured, okay, fine. Good for Stella."

"Well, from everything I've read, she's been living the high life for a while. Storm's been up there, near the top of that scene for a few years, so maybe she used to be a player, but I haven't read any recent mention of it. She's probably guarded just like you."

"All I know is that it's just getting harder to concentrate around her and that's a pain in my ass. She's…" Frankie waved a hand in futility. "She's intoxicating and my brain shuts off and there's this pull I can't do anything about. I have to keep busy, or I forget what the hell I'm doing."

"Glad to hear you admit it." Terri took another drink and sighed dreamily. "What are the odds, you think, of innocent little ol' Stella bringing you two together?"

"That thought crossed my mind, too. She gets this devilish look in her eyes sometimes. But really. She has to know we're from different planets."

"But what if Harper lets some of our laid-back living sink in? It can happen. What do you know about her?"

"Just that she summered here as a kid, then quit school to play music and joined a band. Oh, and her folks are a waste of time, so it's not surprising she grew close to Stella."

"Have you two played any?"

"No. I asked but she didn't sound too enthused."

"Well, keep asking. Everyone's getting together tonight, right? Maybe we can coax her into it."

"I don't think acoustic stuff is her thing."

"Funny," Terri said with a smile, "I can see her as a country diva, glittering all over the stage, but…Storm? Man, she's totally badass."

"She said her voice has been giving her trouble."

Laughing, Terri stood up and clapped Frankie's shoulder. "Look out, my friend. You know she can wail."

# CHAPTER TEN

Terri handed Frankie a beer from the little cooler at her feet, and everyone cheered when Joe raised his and led a toast to Stella. Frankie could see her blush even in the yellow lantern light and she wished Harper had been here to witness it. Stella loved all this and it showed. Her biggest pitcher of iced tea and an overflowing platter of cookies and brownies were set up on the table inside, as always.

Earlier, the sweltering evening had been a sleepy one for Frankie. She'd served only a handful of customers since the supper hour and taken her time preparing the porch while Stella did her baking. Off on "errands" since late afternoon, Harper probably had gone all the way into Boston. Even Stella didn't know Harper's business but hoped she would return in time to join the gathering. Frankie had her doubts, figuring Harper would make the most of the time away to connect with old friends in the city.

But the great mystery of the "errands" ate at her. Worrying about the rumors Terri had heard pushed her curiosity about Harper's grand intentions toward suspicions, but she couldn't picture Harper doing something to crush Stella's spirit. Frankie considered risking overstepping and inquiring. Terri's suggestion that they talk about it had sounded good, but could she really make a difference?

The porch had filled up fast once Joe arrived with his banjo, and by nine o'clock, she'd turned her attention to the lively gathering. They played and sang along to a random mix of tunes that only a few of them knew at any one time, but nobody cared when someone forgot a verse or struck a wrong chord. Everyone thoroughly enjoyed these sessions, regardless of how amateur they often sounded.

Besides, Terri really was in good form on her mandolin tonight, those big paws somehow manipulating the little instrument with ease, and Joe had his dearest friend on Earth, his vintage Gibson, ringing strong. Allie Trumbol and Vicky's husband Tom joined Frankie on guitar, and everyone tried their best at harmonies, with plenty of support from spouses, friends, and Stella. Overall, the collective sound was fairly decent and undeniably uplifting.

Somehow, they all finished a bright popular song on the same beat, a rare event, and they applauded each other roundly.

Vicky suddenly pointed to the intersection. "Hey, looks like Harper's home." Everyone on the porch waved as Harper drove to the back of the building. "She'll join us out here, won't she?"

"I'm hoping so," Stella said.

"Hey," Allie leaned toward her, "I heard you two are repainting the sign. That's great." The others agreed. "It will be good to see it bright and peppy again."

"My favorite part," Joe said with a little pat to Stella's knee, "is that you're putting 'Stella Anderson, Proprietor' up there, too—as it should be."

Stella sent him a shy smile. "Thank you, Joey."

Their affection for Stella was touching. The refurbished sign would show everyone that Harper cared for her grandmother, but it carried a foreboding of changes that concerned Frankie and probably troubled Stella, too.

Virtually all prices had jumped noticeably to pay for the sign work; Harper hadn't risked investing out of the store account or her own pocket. Frankie noted that, to their credit, these friends had politely avoided mentioning the price hikes.

Maybe after an hour with this group, sharing this lighthearted air, Harper would hang out with her later and open up for a while. They really needed to talk, and Frankie crossed her fingers that some music might pave the way.

She set her guitar in the stand beside her stool. "I'll go invite her." A chorus of encouragements and the cowbell's clang followed her inside.

Arriving in the kitchenette, Harper tossed a folder of papers on the counter and shook her hair free of its scrunchie. She offered a grin, trying to disguise her appraisal of Frankie approaching from the opposite side. Barefoot and in black cargo shorts, Frankie wore a faded sleeveless denim shirt closed by several snaps at her midsection. A few descriptors came to mind, all of them way beyond "nice."

"Hi." Harper cleared her throat. *A little hoarse tonight.* "Quite the gathering out there." The deep, hard-earned tan on Frankie's arms continued across her chest, up her throat to her face. Her eyes glowed with a mesmerizing coppery heat that threatened to set Harper's insides aflame.

Thankfully, someone on the porch tinkered with a mellow version of an Aerosmith song and stole Harper's attention. The tune was being customized in a way she'd never considered, and she gave whomever it was a mental high-five for creativity. She pointed toward the porch.

Frankie nodded. "We've been on a roll." She radiated energy.

Playing music with a group pumped up your adrenaline, Harper knew that for a fact, so Frankie probably was running on that. Her enthusiasm seemed limitless, considering how long she'd been awake today, and that made Harper realize how long she'd been at it, too, and she stifled a yawn.

"Bet you're glad to be home," Frankie said.

Harper had to agree, but the concept of "home" struck her more than usual, in light of today's difficult appointments. They had provided valuable information, but discussing assisted living facilities, personal aides, and marketing the building had been hard. It had made for a trying day and evening.

Frankie gestured over her shoulder to the laughing group outside, where someone was impersonating Dolly Parton. "Won't you come on out with us? The music's not to your standard, I'm sure, but the company is good."

Right now, Harper didn't know how she'd smile among the Crossroads loyalists. Her long-range plan to sell the property, once Gram moved on, would generate plenty of fiery opposition, but there really was no other practical recourse. She needed a sit-down with Gram, and then, probably, Frankie, and soon. She'd be an emotional wreck in a week if she kept things to herself much longer. Already, she felt frayed around the edges.

"I hate to be a buzzkill, Frankie, but I'm beat. I really need to crash. Do you think they'll mind?"

"Well, I'm bummed and they will be, too, especially Stella."

Harper couldn't bring herself to sit among them right now, even though the home-grown porch music was intriguing, almost tempting, and music had always been her salvation. "I'm sorry, but tomorrow comes early, and this has been a really long day."

Frankie tilted her head and an inviting spark glimmered in her eyes. "Just poke your head out, at least? Flash that gorgeous smile?"

Walking to the door, Harper shook her head at Frankie's triumphant grin. *You have no idea how irresistible you can be, do you?*

"Flattery doesn't always work, you know."

Frankie gently took her arm and stopped them between the front windows and the door, shielded from the view from the porch. "Not flattery. Just the truth."

The direct message in Frankie's eyes said she hadn't been flirting. If she had, then this went beyond all the flirtations Harper had received in the past because she felt it to her core.

On impulse, she traced a finger along the opening of Frankie's shirt. "Truth can be a dangerous thing, Frankie Cosgrove."

"I'm not dangerous."

"Oh, yes you are."

The screen door squeaked a half-second before the cowbell clanged, and they stepped apart as Gram shuffled in. Stopping abruptly, she glanced between them and waved toward the door.

"There you are. We thought you got lost, Harper. Are you joining us?"

Harper urgently tried to stifle the swirling in her chest. Touching Frankie—a totally spontaneous gesture—had shot her heart rate through the roof and, God, if she hadn't enjoyed every breathless second.

"I'm afraid I'm going to pass on this one," she said, ushering Gram back outside to the rocker. Disappointed groans came from everyone who overheard. "Hi, you guys. Look, I'm sorry, but I need to chill tonight. Thanks for the invitation, though. I'm just getting used to these damn hours you all keep, remember, so, maybe next time. Okay?" She hugged Gram and kissed her cheek. "I promise," she whispered.

Upstairs, Harper dropped onto the couch and closed her eyes. Conflicting emotions of the day ripped through her like a hurricane, recklessly upending practicality, reason, and common sense.

She just had to focus harder to get through this…this what? This summer of helping and guiding Gram to a better life? Was that what she was doing, gathering advice on how to sell Gram's happiness out from under her? And was this hiatus from Storm supposed to be spent dodging live music? When did she become such a prima donna? What was with that?

And, of all things, could she really afford to let enchanting eyes take her breath away? Peer into her soul? What did they see?

The memory of teasing the opening of Frankie's shirt returned in vivid color, her own peach-tipped nail trailing along the coarse denim, contrasting against Frankie's bronze tan. Sensations remained so real, the heat off Frankie's skin, the weight of that second when their eyes met.

Harper brushed away the goose bumps along her arms. *Cut the flirting and stick to business. Temptations are always worse when you know better. When you* both *know better.*

Music from the porch below carried out into the night, up to her windows, and she quickly ceded her focus to her professional ear. There were sour notes, some missed timing, but, overall, the renditions of songs from various decades were surprisingly decent, even enjoyable. They said as much about the players' age differences as their genre preferences. They also said a lot about Gram's love for having friends playing music on her porch. Harper took that to heart, too, and filed it among the heavy business notes she'd collected today.

But each song choice seemed to capture her attention in a unique way. From a professional standpoint, and Harper hadn't reverted to that for some time now, the assorted arrangements were unexpectedly engaging. Back and forth they went for the next hour, bouncing through decades and genres.

The next song began with gentle notes, but the progression rang familiar and forced Harper to open her sleepy eyes. Then came Frankie's mellow voice and a softer, melodic rendition of Storm's "Send Me Down," a tune Harper knew better than anyone. She bolted upright.

*Did you learn it off of YouTube? Watch it being played? The live or studio version?*

Delivered at a slower pace, the lyrics in Frankie's smokey voice were gripping. They took on an easier feel, more pronounced, maybe even more meaningful than Storm's sharp, heavily punctuated commercial rock version. Harper drifted back against the cushion and absorbed their impact.

"Unplugged is such a different vibe. Really nice work, Frankie."

For the first time in weeks, she itched to play, to try the song *this* way, a far cry from what had landed Storm a spot on Billboard's Top One Hundred.

## CHAPTER ELEVEN

First light of morning flickered low through the trees as Harper sped down the road, eager to spot cranberry bogs or a small farm or anything that might be Frankie's place. A call or a text would have been too impersonal, and this was personal.

Her courageous attempt at baking Crossroads' famous muffins this morning had been a glorious success, especially for someone who hadn't baked anything since she was…maybe ten, and she was ridiculously proud of herself. It even made being functional before dawn a worthwhile scientific feat. More importantly, it provided the perfect trade-off for some of Frankie's time at Crossroads this evening.

After she had that difficult talk with Gram.

She switched off the news in favor of silence. She had to concentrate, meet with Frankie, and get back to open the store and let Gram sleep in for a change. She just had to do something about those unforgiving hours.

She slowed to read the Cosgrove name on the mailbox ahead and carefully turned onto the dirt road through the woods. "God, Frankie. How'd you ever find this place?"

The woodsy environs abruptly opened to a vast, flat expanse, covered by a fanciful array of huge fountains. Dozens and dozens of them. "Holy crap." Harper stomped on the brakes. "*This* is where you live?"

The sight was hypnotic. Everywhere she looked, high, arching sprays revolved gracefully, overlapped each other as they doused the flat, bushy ground. What kids wouldn't give to romp under all that spray.

Someone emerged from a shed many acres away and walked along the narrow sandy road that surrounded the property. Frankie, judging by her stride and lanky figure.

Harper drove a bit farther and parked at the little cabin ahead. Frankie's Toyota sat off to the side at the barn, which definitely lacked the cabin's workmanship and vitality. Brick-red shingles covered Frankie's cabin, a compact, sturdy-looking structure that couldn't contain more than a few rooms. She thought the porch looked more spacious than the house itself and its deep, overhanging roof was inviting. "Cozy little hideaway."

She grabbed the small container on the seat and welling anticipation surprised her as she headed off on foot.

She hadn't expected her senses to heighten at the simple prospect of seeing Frankie, but the walk was invigorating, her sandals loud on the gravel, and the scents of pine and earth refreshing. She found herself smiling in the warm, early-morning air, even when cool mist off the bogs landed on her face, arms, and legs.

Closer now, discerning the background hum of a motor, she listened to the fountains spew their towering arcs far and wide. Those positioned particularly close to the road fascinated her, stopping and reversing before they sprayed the road itself—and her.

"Morning!" Frankie yelled, closing from an acre away. "You found me!"

"So, I did!" Harper gestured to the aquatic choreography around her. "This is wild!"

Frankie scanned her domain as she approached, and Harper wondered how long she'd been at work this morning. In a sleeveless T-shirt and faded jeans, hair jumbled as always, she looked capable of tackling anything, including her, and Harper promptly shelved that thought.

"It is kind of wild, isn't it?" Frankie said, glancing modestly at her work boots. "Sometimes I can't believe it's mine."

"You set all this up yourself?"

"It took ten times longer and cost a lot more than it should have because I had no idea what the hell I was doing. This idiot learned the hard way to *read the damn directions*."

"I've never seen anything like it. You know, the Bellagio fountains in Vegas have nothing on you."

"Thank you for that."

"So, is this how you water your berries?"

"Sort of. This waters the vines, but really soaks the ground and roots, loads them with water to survive a day of scorching sun. I can't let all my babies out there die from thirst."

"That's what all the flowers are?"

"Yes, soon to be berries. They're very fragile right now."

"You must have to run these fountains a few times a day."

"They're called sprinklers, and no, this is the only time to run them. In the hot sun, water on the plants is like oil in a frying pan. Actually, the berries would boil, so once the sun comes up, you shut the pump down."

"And you do this all summer?" Harper couldn't take her eyes off the dancing water show or her mind off the dedication required for all this.

"Yeah, until the sun's not as hot, although you often have to guard against scorching September days, too."

"But once cooler temperatures come, you're all set?"

"Mostly. The berries are like apples. They ripen in the chilly nights. But not frigid nights. Frost is the enemy."

"Oooo." Harper grinned at her. "Nasty, huh?"

"Well, it's very serious. A frost can erase your entire year's income." The magnitude of that rattled into Harper's brain and she regretted making light of it. "Sun's climbing," Frankie stated. "Come with me to the pump house."

They retraced Frankie's steps to the shed while the army of sprinklers continued to catch snippets of sunshine and hurl sparkles into the air. She could watch them all day, but sensed Frankie watched them with an exacting, maternal eye.

"The war against frost is a little complicated to explain," Frankie said. "Bog temps are different from land temps, exaggerated. So, late nights in October, you can get a hard, bog frost that will freeze and destroy the berry's pulp. You run sprinklers to keep a protective coat of ice around the berries, and that way their insides can't drop below the thirty-two-degree freezing mark."

"That's pretty clever. So, you're out here doing this at night." *Hello? Duh.* Harper felt herself blush, but Frankie graciously didn't call her on it.

"If there's a frost danger, I'm out here, yeah. When that season rolls around, you live by an alarm that sounds when the bog temp drops into the danger zone. I can't afford the higher-tech automated equipment, so I have to start the pump myself. The bigger, rich growers never have to get out of bed."

It was a harsh image, Frankie tromping along this little road in the middle of a frigid night, but Harper could see it, and it almost made her shiver.

She followed her into the shed and watched her turn the key on the gritty old motor, like turning off a car ignition. As water in the pipes slowed to a gurgle, Harper hurried out in time to see all the sprinklers shrink into themselves and disappear. The entire landscape fell silent and still.

Frankie stepped up beside her, wiping her hands on a rag. "And then they're gone," she whispered through a grin.

Harper turned to her, momentarily lost in that dimple near Frankie's mouth. "I...Thank you for a fascinating show."

"Thanks for your interest." She tossed her rag inside and pointed to what Harper was carrying. "What's that you've got?"

"Hm? Oh, I forgot." She handed Frankie the container and clasped her hands behind her back. "My morning accomplishment."

"Muffins!"

"You don't have to look *that* surprised. I know puttering around a kitchen isn't my thing, but I pulled it off. They're excellent, by the way."

"I'm impressed. I'm sure they're great. Thank you. I can't wait to devour them."

"You're still welcome to come and bake them yourself, of course. I just…" She shrugged.

"You just woke up before dawn with the urge to bake muffins."

Harper smirked. "Right. A lifelong ambition, like cooking's my thing. No, it's a bribe, an invitation, actually."

"No bribe necessary, Harper. Do you need me to mind the store tonight?"

"No, just some 'us' time. Gram misses you, and I thought we could spend the evening together, the three of us."

Frankie was nodding, but Harper's anxiety didn't level off. Frankie probably was reading any number of things into that invitation.

"Sounds great," Frankie said. "Thank you. I'll be there."

"I hope it won't pull you away from stuff you need to do here."

"No worries. I'll be over around…six? What's for supper?"

"Gram says her fried chicken is a favorite of yours." Frankie nodded. "She's insisting on teaching me how to make it, so could I persuade you to come earlier?"

"Stella's fried chicken? And you, Susie Homemaker? I wouldn't miss it, but, really, I don't need chicken—or muffins—to be persuaded."

Harper sent her a sideways look. "You're a cheap date, Cosgrove. Come as early as you like."

Anticipation helped Harper cope with the anxiety about this evening's talk. She looked forward to Frankie's company already, even though she'd deliberately forced herself into a position of no retreat.

She was counting on an alliance with Frankie, couldn't continue to avoid discussing business, even if it meant spoiling a sweet, relaxing evening. It had to be just as clear to Frankie that Gram's limitations would take their toll sooner rather than later, so Frankie was bound to endorse the practical approach and, in Gram's eyes, that would carry weight.

Harper conceded that she also wouldn't mind tapping a little of Frankie's trademark confidence and strength for herself. And, maybe her big heart, too, and the rousing stimulation that came with it. It was a lot to acknowledge.

Frankie toyed awkwardly with the Tupperware in her hands, her long lashes fluttering, and suddenly she pulled her phone from her pocket and stepped closer.

Harper's pulse quickened when Frankie put her shoulder to hers.

"You know," she began in that heart-stopping alto, "I'm glad you're here. I really want to talk with you." She showed Harper the time on her phone. "How long can you—"

"Oh, shit!" Her morning schedule suddenly crumbling, Harper spun to face her. They were dangerously close, and she lurched back. "I-I lost all track—"

"It's okay. If Crossroads doesn't open exactly at six, the world's not—"

"No, I need to go." Nerves already on edge, Harper tried not to panic. She grabbed Frankie's arm. "I'll see you later this afternoon?"

"Yes."

"Good!" Harper hurried backwards several steps. "Sorry, Frankie." She turned and hustled to her car.

*God dammit. Fucking Cinderella, I am not.*

She cursed herself as she flew back to the store. She was doing a lousy job of remembering her purpose. She couldn't afford to get swept away by farms or fountains or frozen nights. Or Frankie.

The smell of fried chicken made Frankie's stomach growl and she itched to get back to where Harper was playing chef in Stella's apartment. She looked forward to lounging on the porch with Harper later, once Stella went to bed, and finally having that deep conversation.

But right now, she waited patiently at the counter as her customers, a young mother and her little boy, discussed candy in the display case. She checked their dozen eggs and wrapped a rubber band around the carton for safe transport.

"Okay," the mother said and sighed wearily at Frankie. "We've made some critical decisions."

Frankie went to the case and dropped the boy's selections into a little paper bag. "Good for now?"

"Yes, for *now*," the mother answered, more to the boy than Frankie. "For after dinner." They returned to the counter and Frankie rang up the candy, eggs, coffee, and package of English muffins.

"You're all set for breakfast, I see."

"I smell chicken," the boy said.

Frankie laughed. "Me, too. Mrs. Anderson's granddaughter is cooking, and I'm excited."

"We're having spaghetti."

"Are you going to eat all your supper?"

"He is if he wants any of that candy," his mother said, ruffling his blond curls before paying Frankie. "You know, my father still tells stories of coming here years ago, the same candy stories."

Finished bagging the purchases, Frankie leaned against the counter. "May those stories live on forever."

"For sure. That's why we still come here. It feels like family."

"We appreciate that very much. Thank you. Family is what it's all about." Frankie watched the boy run out to the car, like countless other kids through the years. The cowbell clanged in their wake.

She twitched when Harper's seductive, gravelly voice wafted down the back of her neck.

"If you prefer watching that attractive woman to eating my awesome fried chicken, I'll be deeply insulted."

Harper was so close behind her, Frankie couldn't wait to turn around. Harper didn't back up. The curl of her full lips made Frankie's mouth water.

"Take me to your awesome chicken."

"Right answer."

"Can't wait to dig in."

"I've been told that the best things to eat are—"

"The ones you get all over your face," Frankie finished. Watching Harper's dark eyes dance, she suddenly hoped she wouldn't blush.

*Great self-control.*

"Well. With *that* in mind." Harper smiled mischievously as she poked Frankie's chest. "Come with me to the kitchen."

Frankie held Harper's gaze for several beats. She wasn't sure what she saw but was willing to lose herself in those depths to find out. The heartbeat pounding in her ears made it hard to think.

She eased away and headed for the hallway, simmering with Harper's sleek presence prowling at her heels. There had been so many things she wanted to say and a few she'd considered doing, but her brain had abandoned her and shamelessly put other parts of her body in charge.

*Ten seconds, idiot, and Stella's going to see you sweat. Get your shit together.*

Blessedly, Harper stopped her with a hand on her shoulder just a step from the door.

"In case you wondered," she whispered, "I heard what that customer said back there."

Surprised to hear compassion instead of flirtation, Frankie turned to her. "That this place feels like family to her?"

Harper nodded. She wasn't playing now and it seemed important to her that Frankie understood.

"I'm glad you heard it." The direct testimonial said a lot about Crossroads.

"I did. I just wanted you to know that I get it." She nodded toward the door. "We better get back to Gram."

The three of them eating together added a special feel to the meal, the likes of which Frankie hadn't experienced in many years. Stella had been rather quiet through supper, but Frankie knew she cherished the family atmosphere. Harper probably did as well, although she wouldn't sit still, constantly fussing to make sure everything was perfect. *Flirting in the store couldn't have made her this nervous.*

Afterward, Frankie took charge of clearing the table but found it hard to convince Harper to stop working. She finally took her by the arm and guided her away from the dishwasher. Then, Harper surprised her by deciding they would sit inside, instead of on the front porch—and Stella agreed, which also struck Frankie as unusual. Something was brewing, and, as she finished cleaning up, Frankie pondered the darkening atmosphere.

"There's Gram's peach pie for dessert later," Harper said, when Frankie joined them in the living room.

"Sorry, but I hope it's much later. I can't eat again until winter."

Harper cleared her throat and leaned forward in her chair. "Frankie, I… This feels awkward but it's important. I wanted to talk to you about…"

"Are we getting divorced already?"

Harper frowned at her attempt at humor. Stella reached for the box of tissues.

*This can't be good.*

"It's a difficult subject, Frankie. Gram and I touched on it this afternoon, and…it's hard. It involves Gram's future."

Stella dabbed her nose. "Crossroads' future."

"That's true," Harper said, turning to her, "but yours, first and foremost."

"Crossroads is part of that, Harper. We're inseparable."

"And that's *not* really true, Gram. This is incredibly difficult, I know. I'm not oblivious to that fact, but we *all* have to see things for what they are. That includes seeing you here by yourself and seeing you running a store that only breaks even, year after year."

Frankie tried to sink deeper into the upholstered chair. She should have known Harper would get around to this. Hadn't she intimated as much that first day, wanting to know how the business was going, how Stella was faring? She didn't want to think Harper had been her mother's hired gun all along, assigned to blow all this away.

"If I may ask…"

"Of course, you may ask," Stella said firmly. "You're family."

Frankie set her hand on Stella's on the arm of the recliner. "Harper. What's the bottom line?"

Looking at Stella, Harper appeared to stiffen...or brace herself. "It's time we looked for a place for you that's not so isolated, that's safer, where you're not so alone, a place where you don't have the burdens you have now."

Frankie's heart flinched. This wasn't what she wanted to hear. Stella certainly didn't. And, although she didn't know if her brain or her heart was speaking, something told her Harper might not want to hear it either.

Stella gathered herself in her seat. "And I've told you that I'm fine right here. It's no more isolated and 'unsafe' here than it's always been."

"Your capabilities have changed, though, Gram. Living here is *not* the same as it's always been. Not anymore, and please forgive me for saying so, but it's going to get harder."

"Nonsense. I manage quite well. You've seen it yourself."

Harper glanced at Frankie and back to Stella. "I've seen what Frankie does here, and taking over for her, *I'm* aware of the work involved, what is done for you."

Frankie could feel her heart thrumming in her chest. She wasn't particularly happy, being in the middle of this family drama, but being such a part of Stella's daily life for so long made her a critical element in all this. That's why it hurt, seeing Stella heft such a mighty realization, and why she, as Stella's closest friend, needed to help—help both of them somehow. Realistically speaking, Harper wasn't wrong.

Stella withdrew her hand from beneath Frankie's and fumbled with her tissue.

"Have I become a burden to you, Frankie?"

"Stop right now," Frankie said, adamant that Stella believed her. "No, you have not. I enjoy helping out here, us working as a team." Stella flashed Harper a watery, defiant glare. "But," Frankie went on, "you know as well as I do that, if I wasn't here, you'd have to hire someone to do the *necessary* stuff—and you can't afford it. Where would that leave you?"

Harper let herself take a breath at Frankie's words. She was desperately grateful for this support, even though it must have nicked at Frankie's heart to speak it. Gram depended on Frankie for more than she realized, and bless Frankie for everything she did, but unfortunately the significance of it all was indisputable.

She moved to Gram's chair and knelt before her. "Frankie can't be here all the time, Gram, and I'm only here temporarily. I can't have you struggling to run a store on top of struggling with your personal, day-to-day functions. I-I can't...and I won't. That would take years off anyone's life, and I don't want it taking any off yours."

Gram wiped her eyes. "And you think some condo in Florida near your mother is the big solution."

Harper palmed each of Stella's knees and offered a faint smile. "Far be it for us to agree with anything Mom says, huh? But the premise is right: a little place, maybe a condo by the ocean, whatever locale interests you. *I* would encourage you toward assisted living, so you could have help at the press of a button."

"Oh, Harper." Gram looked away, obviously overwhelmed. "Those assisted living places…They call them 'facilities' for a reason, you know." She turned to Frankie. "You've made it possible for me to stay here. I know that and I appreciate it more than I can say."

"It's okay, Stella. Look, we all can be our own worst enemy sometimes, can't we, not seeing things that are right in front of us." She gave Gram's shoulder a little squeeze. "Nobody's kidding herself here, Stella. Yes, this is heavy stuff we're talking about, but there's no rush." She turned sharply to Harper. "Right?"

Harper almost recoiled at Frankie's abrupt question. The tone had been challenging, but she trusted that the earnest look sought confirmation for Gram, not an argument with her.

"Definitely no rush," she said, "and we'll work on it together." She paused, hoping to hear some agreement from Gram, but none came. "As difficult as it is, we have to be smart about it."

The momentary silence that followed made Harper nervous. She prayed Frankie would endorse her plan and thereby ease its impact.

"So, take your time and think it through, talk it out," Frankie advised Gram. "Remember, there are lots of benefits to those places, activities, transportation to go where you want, and you wouldn't have to depend on anyone. You'd have friends—and real neighbors, finally."

Relishing the support, Harper added, "We could decorate the place together, if you want, in any décor you choose. Upkeep would be a cinch for you." She softened her tone. "Right now, all I'm asking is that you think about it."

Gram sniffed and Harper noted Frankie's subtle exhale. This was just as exhausting as she'd feared, but Gram had to feel crushed beneath the weight of it all and Harper hated that.

Tissue at her nose, Gram spoke timidly. "And Crossroads?"

"Selling the store would cover all your expenses, Gram." Again, Frankie turned to her, but Harper didn't dare leave her statement unfinished. "Please remember," she wiped a tear from Gram's cheek, "all of this is down the road, not tomorrow."

That didn't help much. There was a "sooner than later" weight to this and she knew they all felt it. Her eyes blurring, Harper looked away. *It shouldn't hurt to be promising an easier life.*

"I never wanted to sell, you know," Gram said from behind the tissue. "I'd hoped to pass it on, keep it in the family." Harper blinked away tears. Gram's disappointment was clear, but the hint of resignation in her words came as a surprise. "You have your own life, Harper, I know, and you love it so. I can't saddle you with this. It's too much and would be so unfair to you."

Harper took her hand and kissed the crooked fingers, pressed them to her cheek. "It breaks my heart, too, Gramma."

Hearing Gram sigh, Harper squeezed her eyes shut before she lost it. Frankie's comforting hand on her back nearly sent her over the edge.

"Oh, my dear girl." Gram touched Harper's chin and urged her to look up. "I suppose change comes in many forms, doesn't it? Knowing what's best, which way to go…It doesn't always come easily." Her eyes shimmered and a sad little smile appeared. "It's all about crossroads, honey. Isn't it?"

# Chapter Twelve

Harper sat on her couch, viciously toed off one sandal, then hurled the other against the wall.

She'd hoped Frankie would stick around after Gram went to bed, that they would talk more, let the tension ease after the Great Discussion. And maybe it was selfish of her, but just having Frankie nearby for a while would have felt…But no. After only a few rambling comments, she'd split.

Harper struggled to process. But, shit, being the rational one was exhausting. Okay, yes, changes impacted Frankie, too, and it wasn't totally surprising that she'd chosen to process privately, but damn it all.

*And now I have this nightmare?*

"Tell me you are not serious. Please tell me." She returned to pacing with the phone, glad no one was downstairs to hear her stomping back and forth. *Thank God, for the time difference. Too bad it doesn't mean anything to my damn agent.*

"God, Sasha. I really don't need this right now. I'm in pretty deep at the moment. I can't possibly go—"

"The studio is being a bitch about this, Harper. If they weren't, you know I wouldn't be hassling you. The *Tonight Show* wants Storm the day after tomorrow and you front Storm. End of story."

Harper huffed. "Aren't we supposed to get some notice about gigs like this?"

"Irrelevant. Whoever was booked canceled suddenly, I guess, and Storm came up on the list, maybe because I've been beating the agency over the head about you guys for a year now. I don't know, but that's all beside the point."

"Well, we can cancel, too."

"The hell you can! Absolutely not."

Harper got the message. She wondered if Sasha got hers all the way out in California. Sasha had been her agent for four years, so shouldn't she?

"God damn." Harper slumped into the chair and pinched the bridge of her nose. "Running out on what I have going right now is…It's not doable."

"Sorry, hon, but neither is turning this down. How hard have you worked for something like this? A long freaking time. It's the career bump you've all been shooting for."

*True. But talk about bad timing.*

Sasha was right, dammit. Such a huge promotional opportunity couldn't be missed. Storm had been busting its ass for years for a break like this and deserved this chance. She had to grab it with both hands.

And abandon Gram's needs for her own? Right now? Knowing Gram, she probably would insist Harper prioritize herself, but that wasn't something a devoted granddaughter should do. She was still making amends for the years of devotion and support she'd let pass. Gram needed them now, especially now.

"Harper? You still there?"

"Yeah, yeah." She started pacing again. "Look, I haven't played or sung a note since we closed in LA. That was weeks ago. I'm supposed to be taking the summer to baby the voice, remember? This wouldn't be smart, and the studio should appreciate that."

"One song won't kill you."

Harper stopped at the window and the breeze flowed over her. Exciting opportunity pulled hard against profound responsibility. She exhaled toward the starry night, which was far more tranquil than she felt.

"If you knew what tonight was like…I can't justify leaving tomorrow. This is crazy and the timing sucks."

"Come on. It's not like you're going back on the road. It's only a few days. Is the world going to blow up without you?"

She knew Sasha really didn't expect an answer.

"Harper. The studio is pushing. They want this. Lawyers will start waving your contract in my face if I don't confirm tomorrow morning. Explain that to your people. They'll be excited for you."

Her heart pounding, she rested her forehead against the window. "You realize there's a lot involved."

"Of course. As soon as we're off the phone, I'll start making arrangements, get in touch with all the others, and email everything to you."

Harper ended the call and stared into the blackness outside. Her participation affected so many people and came with tons of complicated arrangements—a world that had begun to feel comfortably far away lately. She'd temporarily set it all aside for this world, but now it was back, in typical hair-on-fire fashion, and the contrast was eye-opening.

"All dried off and gotta jump back in the pool," she mumbled toward the parking lot. She wondered if she'd done too good of a job, acclimating to life here. Surprisingly, the prospect of returning to Storm's world actually unsettled her. "Going to New York means disrupting *real* life."

Frankie stood at her back screen door, sipping coffee as the morning's soft rain abated. The unexpected showers forced her to square off against her one enemy in life: recordkeeping. That was no uplifting matter, but at least it was black-and-white, unlike last night's family crisis.

She decided to find time today to talk with Stella, see how she was holding up after all that heavy stuff crashed down on her. Frankie couldn't imagine how someone in Stella's position, someone with a lifetime in one place, could cope with leaving it all behind.

She believed that Harper was right to start thinking ahead, considering Stella's age and limitations, but the simple facts didn't make it a simple decision. Harper had to know that. At least her struggle for composure had been written all over those glamorous features last night. Frankie had felt the tension in Harper's back, just by laying a hand on her.

The reality was hard for all of them to face. She certainly didn't look forward to losing Stella to some foreign place or Crossroads to some new incarnation. Stella and Crossroads were a package deal. Each thrived on the other, virtually inseparable, as Stella had declared to Harper. The hole their departure would create in Frankie's life would be enormous, but Stella's well-being *did* come first.

Frankie nevertheless struggled with the relocation and selling ideas, and figured Harper must have as well. But had she seriously considered the possibility of failure? What if Stella's golden years became sad, despondent years, longing for what used to be? If Stella wanted to stay with all her precious memories to the very end, shouldn't it be her choice?

Frankie leaned against the doorframe and sighed.

It wouldn't be easy if Stella stayed, that was obvious. Not long from now, she was bound to need some form of regular assistance, as well as someone to handle the store, and monitoring that and paying for it would require the family's diligence. Was family obligation the real issue here? If so, Harper apparently had been deemed the chosen one. Did she feel she'd drawn the short straw, pulled from her high-life down to this? At least her concern seemed genuine.

Frankie swore under her breath. "Overstepping or not, we have to talk."

*Damn. Sometimes, life just blows.*

She refilled her cup and tried to shift her thoughts back to her own world. Unfortunately, "paperwork" qualified because it only involved her, not three lives, two families, a generational business, and a bunch of broken hearts.

But forcing herself into work mode didn't promise to lift her spirits. She already knew what she would not see in her many calculations. Once again, she knew she wouldn't find a positive that she'd missed. None of the harvest projections or estimates or timetables she brought up provided an abundance of confidence or the financial optimism she needed.

If harvest went as planned and she netted every possible dollar from this first crop, the numbers still just showed *decent* profit. A monumental achievement for a rookie, but no safety net for the next twelve months.

Her bank account sounded pretty hollow these days and she worried that her best effort wouldn't fill it anytime soon. As things were now, she couldn't afford to replace any major broken equipment, or to let weeds, deer, or the sun claim her berries. Levees mustn't breach and drown sections, ditches mustn't sit stagnant… There was no room for anything but perfection, success on her first try.

She turned from her monitor and stared out at the back deck, wishing it had a roof so she could sit out there, rain or shine. Improvements to her cabin hadn't been possible for so long, either. She clicked on the folder of household expenses and compared her "priority list" to her "wish list." Everything would have to wait for harvest results and then, if she was anointed by some magic wand, she might be able to afford something on one of those lists.

Thankfully, she'd spent wisely when she moved in, addressing the cabin and the barn, and installing modern necessities. But everything else had landed on these lists, where they still sat after three years, and probably would continue to sit for a good while.

As the drizzle faded, she wandered to the barn and set out on the tractor to patrol the property, always a welcome chore, and today, highly therapeutic. This poor machine could use a break, she pondered, maybe retirement to simple mower status. If only she had known how much she would need a real heavy-duty multipurpose machine when she'd had the cash. The irony of putting something so tried-and-true out to pasture almost made her laugh.

Frankie motored along at a snail's pace with a keen eye to the state of her little empire. Still wet, berries and vines sparkled with promise beneath the sketchy, early-morning sun, while water in the ditches trickled steadily, riding nature's gentle current, no faster than the tractor.

Along the rear border, Frankie carefully inspected the levee that kept the swamp at bay. This area was her greatest concern, with the black water lying in wait, hardly a foot from the top where she rode and eager to get at her young crop on the other side.

Harvest couldn't come soon enough, and it was going to be an exciting trip-and-a-half, for sure. Already, she could see herself and friends maneuvering across planks that spanned the ditches, steering picking machines around the sections and amassing stacks of full boxes. Inconceivable, how those long-ago farmers scooped through acres of knotted vines by hand, but at least she wouldn't have those worries.

She occupied herself with the temperamental fourth picking machine for the rest of the day. Calling around to fellow growers, looking for spare parts or tips on the best resources was always a frustrating exercise, but it forced her mind off Stella's future and Harper's agonizing position.

Until a text message brought her work to a halt.

*Hi. Sorry to impose, but I have to ask a big favor. Got a minute?*

Frankie leaned against the picker, punched in a response, and waited eagerly for Harper's name to appear on her phone.

"Hey. Everything okay?"

"Hi. Yes." The tension in Harper's voice was palpable. "Everything's fine here. The issue is me."

"Are you alright? What's wrong?"

"Oh, I'm okay. Thank you, but see, I have to take off for New York. Like, tomorrow morning, first thing, Frankie. A big promo has come up for Storm and, honestly, I never expected to be dragged away like this. I'm sorry to be calling—"

"Harper. Take a breath." Frankie thought her fluster was as sweet as it was unfortunate. "You have to go, I take it?"

"Yeah. I got the call last night and I can't refuse. It's only for a few days and I'm coming straight back."

"But a promo is cool, though, right? For Storm, I mean?"

"Oh, well, yeah, but that leaves Gram on her own and—"

"Harper. We'll be fine. Go, take care of business."

"I'm not totally up for it, really, but promotions are contractual things, so…"

"I'm glad you called."

Harper heaved a sigh. "God, Frankie. You're a lifesaver. Thank you. I'm so sorry to lay this on you."

"It's no big deal, Harper. Besides, if you hadn't, I would've been pissed."

"Well, Gram's beyond lucky to have you around. *I'm* lucky. You're the sweetest."

"Relax. Stella will be in good hands."

"The very best. I'm sorry but I do have to go now and pack. But I'll see you in a few days."

"Looking forward to it already." *Just throw it out there?*

Harper took an extra second to respond. "Me, too, Frankie."

Frankie slipped her phone into her pocket. "Hurry back, Harper."

## CHAPTER THIRTEEN

Rolling into the Crossroads parking lot, Frankie was impressed to see a painting crew hard at work on the store's big sign. "Avon calling!" she shouted, strolling into the kitchenette. She snared Stella in a one-armed hug. "Morning, Ms. Proprietor. Big doings today, I see."

"Oh, Frankie! It's so exciting, getting the sign back to its original glory."

Stella glowed and Frankie tamped down a rising sadness, trying not to picture Stella separated from the place she loved so much. *Is this how it's going to feel from now on?*

"I'm glad they set up away from the steps." She observed Stella closely. The work probably helped take her mind off things.

"Me, too," Stella said. "I made sure they left plenty of room for customers, like Harper wanted. She beat me into the store this morning, you know." She took two glasses from the cabinet and poured Frankie's favorite combination of cranberry and orange juice for each of them. "She's getting the hang of rising early. And she's really catching on to things here, even though she's learned a few things the hard way."

"Oh?"

Stella smiled as she shook her head. "The other day, she let the delivery men leave things out by the back steps instead of on the landing, like usual. She thought she was doing them a favor, but she found out how heavy dog food and bird seed can be."

"Ouch."

"And she put so many squash in the upper bin, it fell over. Lord, we had veggies everywhere."

Frankie had to laugh. "We learn the hard way."

"Yes, we do. But she's really doing well. She does watch me like a hawk, though, and sometimes it makes me nervous. I just don't want her misinterpreting a little self-conscious fumbling. That's different from disability, you know."

Frankie took the offered glass with a nod of thanks. "Don't hesitate to point that out, Stella. I'm sure the last thing she wants is to make you nervous. And I'm glad you're letting her pitch in. You better." She nudged Stella's shoulder. "Busy morning today?"

"Yup. So different from the nights. I know we enjoy the porch, especially when you bring your guitar, but I do wish it was busier."

"If afternoons were like mornings, Stella, it might kill us both." She offered a good-natured grin to lighten the subject.

"Hm. You've got a point. Actually, I was about to rest a bit."

"Then, let's." Frankie led her to a table by the windows. "I'm bummed not to see Harper today."

Smiling, Stella patted her cheek. "Oh, really? Well, she wasn't very happy about going."

"Storm's a big deal and she had no choice." At least Harper hadn't been thrilled to interrupt her time with Stella.

"No. No choice. She said it's a big promotion for their album. They have a new one coming out later this year."

Frankie stood by the table and drank. "Must have been hard to go with the painters here today."

"She seemed torn, bless her." Stella sipped her juice. "Her agent called last night, insisting, so I rushed her out of here."

*Being here has to be growing more inconvenient for her by the day.*

"Well, then." Frankie sat opposite her and tapped the table with a firm finger. "How are *you* doing in the light of day, all things considered?"

"Oh, Frankie. I think I'm a little numb, to be honest. Every time I look around, I try not to see what I'll miss. It's hard." Frankie just nodded, not wanting to interrupt. "I know Harper's heart is in the right place. I can't really argue with her, can I? I mean, I know this all is bound to catch up with me eventually. I'm not going to live forever, for heaven's sake, and I refuse to become someone's burden."

"I felt for you last night, and I'm sure Harper did, too. It's painful for anyone, having to look ahead like that."

"You're a love, Frankie. I feel so badly that Harper's in this position because of me. I wouldn't want to be in her shoes, but I'm very glad you were here last night for her sake. It meant a lot to me and more to Harper than she knows, I think."

"I agreed with her because I want what's best for you, just as she does, and we want you to be okay with decisions that are made. Make sure you speak up, though, voice any concerns you have, say what you'd like."

"Oh, I suppose I will."

"Why do I worry about that?" She watched Stella grin into her glass. "Have you ever thought about where you'd like to live, besides here?"

Stella sat back and stared out the window. "Oh, my, no. I've never given that any thought. I guess I'll have to, won't I?"

"Someplace warmer?"

"Warmer than here in July? Ha. Florida would be awful. And too many hurricanes. Besides, it rains every day. Who needs that?" She leaned across the table confidentially. "And I love my daughter dearly, but anywhere in that state might be too close."

Frankie laughed as she tried to drink. "Well…the Carolinas?"

"They have hurricanes, too."

"So do we."

"Not like they do."

"We have blizzards."

"Oh, pooh. You think this Yankee's afraid of snow?"

*She's not going without a fight.*

"How about Arizona?"

"Too many old people."

Frankie laughed again. "California?"

"California? My God, that's far. And they're a little different out there, aren't they?" Frankie threw up her hands, laughing. "Well, I might think about that, if Harper lived close by. She'll be moving to West Hollywood soon. Did she tell you?"

"Is that right?" All part of that transient rock 'n' roll world, she figured, but the twinge of disappointment was her own fault. *You know damn well she can't wait to get back at it.* "She's never said anything about house hunting."

"She found a little place online and I'm happy for her. I guess her agent took care of things out there, and sold her old condo, too. So, I suppose I could get used to living there, if she was around." Suddenly, she frowned. "Oh, but then she's always on the road somewhere, isn't she?"

"This is going to take some thought." *A lot more.*

"Enough. It's a lovely summer day, the sign is coming back to life, you're here now, and Harper will be back. What more could I ask for? Life is good. Tell me how things are going at Cosgrove Bogs."

Frankie had to give it up for now. She tried to focus on Stella's question.

"So far, so good. All is well." Stella knocked three times on the wooden window frame for good luck. "I found the part I needed to fix my picker, so I'm happy. Not many growers have refurbished old machines like mine, so it took an hour of driving, but I got it."

"There's a lot to be said for the old things. They don't make 'em like they used to."

"I'm counting on it." Frankie winked as she stood. *Message received.* "Let's go see how the sign's coming along."

She walked with Stella off the porch to the painters' work area and they stood to the side, watching as old paint was scraped off the sign. She hoped seeing it restored also restored Stella's happy memories. She'd be leaning on them sooner than anyone ever imagined.

"I wish Harper was here to see this." Frankie thought she had just spoken to herself.

Stella drew her arm closer. "Me, too. It tickles me, you know, hearing you say that. I love that you two get along so well. It's just what I'd hoped when I heard she was coming."

"What's not to like? She's so much like you."

"Oh, Lord, you can pile it on, can't you?" Stella grinned, not taking her eyes off the sign. "Yes, I wish she was here, too. Rushing off for this important thing in New York City…" She wrinkled her nose. "She was looking forward to a quiet time here. I'd promised her a relaxing vacation. Well, I'd expected that, anyway. Now, she's running every which way, poor thing."

Frankie considered Harper's sudden trek to New York and didn't envy that life one bit. She was curious, however, because there were moments when the Harper she was coming to know didn't fit that famous musician image. She hardly seemed interested in music at all, and now, with some big promotional thing going on, she wasn't particularly psyched to go? Maybe responsibilities here were weighing her down, but shouldn't she be thrilled about the big-time opportunity?

Something apparently had put a hitch into it for Harper, and Frankie couldn't tell what it meant.

Terri slouched in Frankie's Adirondack chair, barely illuminated by minimal kerosene light. Stetson tipped down over her eyes, she hardly moved when Frankie stepped onto the porch and unlocked her front door.

"You asleep under there?"

"No, but after a half hour, I oughta be." Terri sat up and pushed her hat back in place as Frankie went inside. "Delivering a pony out to Northampton took all damn day."

"Your truck and trailer gave you away." Parked haphazardly across the front of the barn, Terri's rig said she'd been on the road too long. Frankie knew she probably wanted to talk to somebody, anybody, after hours behind the wheel.

"I needed to stretch before getting home," Terri said, straightening her long legs, "and thought you'd be here. Another ten minutes, and I was leaving."

"I closed Crossroads again tonight," Frankie said from the kitchen.

"Wasn't Harper due back today?"

"Tomorrow night." Frankie emerged with two bottles of beer and a jug of tequila.

"Whoa." Terri took the beer, her eyes on the alcohol. "Did you have a heavy night?"

"Eh." Frankie shook her head as she slid into the adjacent chair. "It's felt a little heavy to me for a couple days now."

"Uh-oh. No business?"

"Slow, like normal. Just three tonight—and Joe. Stella was about to go to bed, but he talked her ear off for a solid hour. The man shouldn't live alone with only his daughter checking up on him. He needs a sweetie in his life again."

"Sounds like he and Stella have a lot in common."

Frankie thought about that. "Yeah. I guess you're right."

"So, have you recovered from the *Tonight Show* last night?"

Frankie laughed. She knew Terri would get to the purpose of this visit eventually. "Not quite. Hell of a surprise, wasn't it?"

"Your text at eleven thirty scared the crap out of us." Terri took a blast of tequila and squinted. "Thank God you happened to be watching. We would've missed it. I almost didn't recognize her."

"I had to get out of bed and get closer to the screen. Talk about a transformation." She took a turn at the tequila and capped the bottle. "She's… God, she was…stunning."

"She has a body to die for, my friend. That leather didn't cover much. And all that eye makeup made her look like she's going to eat you alive."

"As if that look needs help."

Now, Terri laughed. "I know. She always looks you right in the eye and holds on. It's hard to break away—and you don't want to."

"And of all songs, they play 'Send Me Down'?" Frankie stared at her beer. "It's night-and-day from my version."

"You got that right. It was wild."

"I thought her voice sounded froggy at times, but, man, she can sing. And that instrumental break she did with the lead player, was that tight or what?" She took a long drink.

"Harper's really good, Frankie. But, you know, I think your version of the song is better. Did she write it?"

"I've never checked."

Terri was already looking it up on her phone. Within a minute, she raised an eyebrow. "'Lyrics by Harper Ashley Cushing,'" she read aloud. "That settles that. I'd avoid playing it for her. She might flip out."

"I don't think there's anything to worry about. I doubt we'll be playing much together, least of all that song. Isn't it weird that I picked *that* one to rework a few weeks ago?"

"Yeah, kinda. But the way you played it at Crossroads the other night, turned it into a ballad and changed the mood…I'm telling you it's a whole lot better. Most songs can't handle that much change, but your version holds up great."

"Thanks. I like it, too." *Wonder if Harper would.*

"She didn't bring an electric guitar with her here, did she?" Frankie only grunted, still lost in thought, and Terri sighed. "Wonder how she sounds on an acoustic. She sure burned the hell out of that electric on TV."

"No wonder she wants nothing to do with our music."

Without question, Harper was masterful at the guitar. Frankie had found herself glued to the screen, watching those skilled, nimble fingers fly up and down the neck. They pushed and pulled at the strings and formed chords so exotic they'd made Frankie cringe.

She drank heavily. *All that and looks, too.*

"I say give her time." Terri elbowed Frankie. "She'll be here a while, so who knows how things might change."

"Shit. That's the damn statement of the year." She reopened the tequila and downed a mouthful, then passed it to Terri. "Harper's trying to convince Stella to move, to sell Crossroads." Her eyes widening as she drank, Terri almost choked. "Yeah," Frankie added, "for Stella's own sake, before things get too tough for her."

"But Stella manages." Terri straightened in the chair and set the bottle aside. "How can Harper not see that?"

"Well, Stella 'gets by' right now. We all see that. But down the road?" Frankie shook her head. "I guess it *is* for the best, but, boy, it's rough."

"Why not get Stella some help, then?"

"Who's going to pay for that?" she countered, but it wasn't the first time that Harper's wealth had come to mind.

"But…sell the damn store?"

"It must all boil down to the family not wanting the responsibility."

"Jesus. Maybe Stella should sell it to you."

Frankie flashed her a look. "Seriously? She knows my dream is here and I can't be two places at once. I could never afford it, anyway."

"But, if she did, what would *you* do?"

"Hell, I don't know. I'd have to hire someone to run the place, wouldn't I? And rent out her apartment and the one upstairs." She shook her head before sipping her beer. "Totally not feasible for me. Besides, I'm not into playing landlord."

"Crossroads doesn't make enough to pay for hired help, does it?"

"No. And Harper has to be well aware of that now."

Terri sat back. "Hm. So, she's really looking to sell."

"Once the family's satisfied that Stella is happily situated somewhere else."

"Damn. Poor Stella."

# Chapter Fourteen

I t's not my old Beamer but it's fun to drive. I just extended the rental agreement."

Harper didn't mind having company on her ride back from the airport, even though Denise had been on the phone for the past half hour. But now, Denise paused, probably realizing the significance of what Harper had just said.

Finally, she sighed into the phone. "A long-term rental? So, you're staying a while, then."

"The whole summer, probably."

"You don't sound eager to leave *ever*."

"Oh, please. Right now, I just can't say when, exactly."

Another pause. "Well, when you come to your senses, let me know."

Harper really didn't feel up to this discussion. She was tired and actually looking forward to the comfort of her own bed and the background noise of crickets. She smirked at herself as Denise rattled on.

"Harper. I refuse to believe that being out there in the sticks is turning your head."

"I wouldn't go that far, but the peace is nice."

"Nowheresville is clueless. Does anyone there even watch the *Tonight Show*?"

"Online, maybe. I doubt anybody around here stays up late enough to watch it on TV."

"Well, damn. *I'm* sure glad I saw it. You guys crushed it, and that audience lost its mind."

Harper had to smile. "It was a good audience, wasn't it? We were pleased all around, even though I was pretty rusty. I did love seeing everyone again."

"And you met Jimmy Freakin' Fallon."

"What a great guy. He played some with us during rehearsal. Do you believe it?"

"No way."

"It was stressful, but fun. And jamming backstage with the guys? Hitting a couple of clubs after? God. It felt like forever, since we'd done that stuff."

"Who went out?"

"A woman Primma knew was playing a few blocks from our hotel, so Rhea, Zee, and I went with her."

"Did you guys end up on stage?"

"Yeah, but I just played. Rhea sang. She's great, you know. We ripped the place up for a half an hour."

"So, now, seriously, tell me you don't miss all that."

"Listen. Even without Decker and Smitty, Storm has an awesome sound. And we *are* family, you know, so…well, of course I do." Harper heard the tentative lilt in her statement and figured Denise had, too, judging by her prolonged silence.

"Real convincing." Another pause. "You know you're blowing my mind with this shit."

"I've just been so locked onto things here, Denni, it's a little hard to be one hundred percent into that scene right now. I'm just distracted, that's all."

"Well, are you making progress with your grandmother?"

"Yes." Harper glanced at the Cosgrove mailbox as she flew past. "I'm almost there, by the way. So, yes, we had the 'big talk' the other night and I think it went as well as could be expected. Frankie supported me, thank God."

"How's she taking it?"

"I haven't really gone there with her, although I'm sure she's on Gram's side. That's why her support the other night meant so much."

"You need more of that. Talk with Frankie. Sounds like the more she's in your camp, the more Gram will be, too. Then things should be easier to wrap up, right?"

Harper's stomach rolled at that thought. "We'll see. This whole thing is a master class in diplomacy. I don't want them thinking I'm trying sell the place out from under Gram. I'm trusting that Gram knows better, but I can't be sure about Frankie."

"She wouldn't think that. She likes you."

"Well, I like her, too, and I don't want to spoil that, but Gram's facing some heavy decisions, and Crossroads needs reno work to go on the market when that time comes."

"And Frankie's as attached to the store as your grandmother."

"For sure. But no one's ever had to worry about marketing it before." *How did I get into this again?* "An old friend introduced me to a big-time

Realtor the other night and she offered some serious advice. A buyer's not going to stick her neck out for Crossroads if the place doesn't show a healthy profit, and Crossroads just gets by." She sighed at the need for changes. "At the very least, it has to show potential, so there's a lot to do."

"How's your grandmother going to take it?"

"Reluctantly, at best, I think."

"And Frankie?"

"God. Frankie. I can't afford to turn her against me. She's been great about all this so far."

"Still just the supportive neighbor? Or is there more between you yet?"

"Ah, well, I don't know, exactly."

"How can you not know? Is she hot for you or not?"

"I wouldn't say—"

"Or maybe you're hot for her?"

"Doesn't matter, Denni. I'm not repeating the past. I won't put either of us in that painful position again."

"You're only there for a few months and she knows that, too, so what's wrong with mixing in a little play time?"

"A lot can happen in a few months, you know."

"Exactly. And you're wasting time."

"I am not. I'm focused."

"Uh-huh. So, answer my question. Something's simmering, isn't it? I just *know* it is. Don't even think of denying it."

Harper exhaled hard. "I have to be realistic, Denni."

"You want her, don't you? I *knew* this would happen!"

"Denni."

"She wants you, doesn't she? You've seen it in her eyes, haven't you?"

"Are you writing some B movie?"

"And your eyes always give you away, so she's seen it in yours, hasn't she?"

"You need to get laid. I'm ending this call."

"Ha! Come down off your high horse, Cushing, and jump on hers. Seriously, why the fuck not?"

Frankie tightened the last screw on the carburetor she'd just rebuilt and stood back, preparing herself for the test. She pulled the rip cord a few times, then gave it a commanding yank, and black smoke chugged out of the little engine and into a cloud around her head. Coughing as she waved it away, she adjusted the choke, and the picking machine began to purr.

"YES!"

It wasn't imperative that she have the machine operational this far ahead of harvest, but if she couldn't, a repair shop and time might be needed. The prospect of having her four pickers running simultaneously almost made her giddy. Six or so certainly would make for quicker work, but that was an expensive dream for another day.

As usual, the little triumph took her mind off Harper—briefly. Maybe tonight they could talk about the *Tonight Show*. Stella hadn't mentioned it, probably hadn't seen it. Frankie figured Harper must have kept quiet about it for some reason, so Frankie hadn't brought it up either.

But she was dying to talk about it and hoped Harper would enjoy that topic, something other than condominiums. Frankie wanted to bring up West Hollywood, too, but wasn't sure she should.

"This is a far cry from LA, isn't it, Harper? Living here must feel so weird." Frankie slid the barn door closed and began a long cursory stroll around the bogs. "Do you really miss it all that much?"

*You won't come this way again, will you? Not once Stella and Crossroads are gone.*

The subject seemed to spring to mind with every other breath. She couldn't escape the image of Stella on some sunny balcony overlooking the ocean, or of Crossroads as…as what? That was harder to see, but she supposed it should be obvious. Harper would sell it and some housing development would take over the intersection. Did Harper have anything more than a nostalgic tie to the place? No way, Harper would trade her successful life for an old general store. That was simply laughable. Stella had to know, too, and, guaranteed, she wasn't laughing.

She shoved a hand back through her hair. *Are there alternatives? How much leeway do you have, Harper, or did you just buy into your family's plan?*

She mulled it over for the thousandth time that day, now sitting on the Crossroads railing in the lantern light. A car approached from across the intersection, and she groaned at the idea of one last customer tonight. She'd thought Harper might arrive when Vicky and Tom were here, but their taillights were vanishing down the road.

They had stopped by, wired and eager to talk about the singer who looked a lot like Harper on the *Tonight Show*. Speaking to her directly had been their priority. Not up for discussing Harper's other life, Frankie claimed to have missed the show, that she'd been asleep, but promised to watch online.

Recognizing the Audi crossing the parking lot now, she smiled, despite herself. She was glad Harper was home, and quickly corrected her thinking. This wasn't "home" for Harper. Far from it. Frankie struggled with the idea of Harper putting so much change into motion and zipping back to her

LA world. Too bad, that *this* woman, the one constantly on her mind also unsettled her life.

In spite of it all, Frankie looked forward to time out here with her, just the two of them. She'd miss it.

Would there ever be enough hours in the day for them to talk about everything? She wished the store would close soon so they could sit here and not risk being interrupted. *What did she say about store hours...eight to eight?*

Harper swung through the screen door and grabbed the cowbell to silence it after a single clang. She handed Frankie a Coors.

"Six-pack in the fridge." She plopped unceremoniously into a rocker with a bag of Doritos. "Hi."

Frankie grinned at her relaxed air, at the very sight of her. Harper draped one knee over the other and closed her eyes as she chewed. In a sleeveless white Oxford and tight black jeans, she was sleek and toned all the way down to her bare feet and pedicured toes.

"I guess you're not going to bed right away."

"Beyond tired and too wound up." She took a handful of chips for herself, and carefully tossed the bag to Frankie. "After three days, I should be talked out, right? But I'm not. Just the opposite."

"Aren't you supposed to avoid lengthy orations?"

"Screw that."

Frankie sipped her beer, undeniably taken by Harper's presentation. "You're in a rip-roarin' mood, Cushing."

"Yeah, that's me. Rip-roaring." She chomped on a chip.

"How was New York?"

"An emotional blast. Now, I'm venting."

"I'll take that as a warning."

"Smart. Anything's bound to come out of my mouth when I'm wired." Frankie laughed, watching her drink. "It's safe to talk?"

"Do you want to?" Harper lunged forward. "Shit. I'm sorry to just assume you'd care to hang around longer. I-I wasn't thinking. Thanks so much for filling in. If you want to go—"

"No. I mean I don't mind staying. Hell, I just like—" She caught herself. This let-it-rip moment almost got away from her.

Harper rested her head on the back of the rocker and stared out at the stars. "You just like what? Sitting out here?"

Frankie pulled her gaze from the slope of Harper's throat, the extra button opened at her cleavage. A beautiful woman in repose, she was a powerhouse bathed in soft light.

"I just like the scenery."

Harper's eyes closed. "It's pretty good from where I sit, too."

Warmed by the compliment, Frankie smiled into her beer. "You blew it away, the other night, but...honestly? Storm's lead singer has nothing on you."

"Not even with all that makeup?" Harper finally looked her way. Those dark eyes had a way of seizing Frankie's every breath. They always seemed to search desperately for something.

Frankie set the Doritos aside and leaned on her knees. "You never said you were doing the *Tonight Show*."

"Storm's no megastar act. Not yet, anyway. And we only did one number. I really didn't think it mattered."

"You're kidding, right? Storm's big enough to open all across the country. Big enough to make the *Tonight Show*, which means you're really going places now."

"So, they say." She chugged the rest of her beer and went to the door. "Ready for another?"

Frankie looked up at her, the eyes a bit less electric now. "Not yet, thanks."

Harper's dull reaction came as a surprise, so maybe the topic was closed. Frankie decided to let her lead.

But she didn't, until she was back in the rocker.

"I just have a lot going on," she continued on a sigh, "and this damn thing with my voice comes back more frequently now. It's hard to take stock of everything when your world won't friggin' sit still."

Life in the fast lane had to be insane, Frankie figured, but, really, Harper had it made. Besides helping Stella, what did she need to "take stock" of? She had achieved her dream, didn't worry about money, and loved her work. Impressive. Frankie respected the achievement and even envied the financial freedom.

"What has your doctor said about your voice?"

"To stop stressing it the way I do and basically shut up for a while."

"What's 'a while'? A few weeks? A month?"

"Last Thanksgiving, she told me a few weeks, but then we had to hit the road. This past spring, she got pissed, and now, she's ordered a couple of months. Luckily, here I am."

"Luckily. Or else what?"

"Or else surgery. And no guarantees." She sent Frankie a sardonic grin, then drank and winced. It was a while before she continued. "We've worked so fucking hard for so long, you know? Storm is on its way now and we deserve it."

"It's finally paying off."

"Exactly. To gel like we do? You saw us, I take it? Damn, we're so good, all modesty aside. I can't let my voice screw everything up. I have to play this right."

*She's scared.*

"And you are. Your people understand your caution, don't they?"

"My lawyer's worried and my agent's ignoring the issue." She snickered. "I'm just a panicked thirty-six-year-old."

"Well, that's crap. It's not panic, doing the smart thing for your career."

"I reminded them that I want to stay 'off-line' for the summer and now they're freaking out. Everyone knows this pace is a grind, that it's going to get worse, the higher Storm climbs, but reminding them didn't do me any favors. Apparently, the label's asked if I'm going to bail. Thank God the band knows not to worry."

"Hell, talk about overreacting. Singers come back from stuff like this all the time, right? And don't your people know you're dealing with this huge emotional issue here, on top of that regular life?" Frankie finished her beer and sat back, watching Harper gaze into the darkness. "Harper. That's a heavy burden for anyone. They shouldn't be bitching about your time away. Hell, they should be thankful. You don't have to prove anything to anybody."

Harper shook her head. "My 'regular life,' as you call it, is at the heart of it all. It's not always pretty."

"No one's life is always pretty."

"Regular life is one thing, but it's *real* life that's the issue, Frankie. In my *regular* world, there's no room for it. Why do you think so many wash out or go this route," she held up her beer, "leaning on crutches like booze and drugs?"

"I don't see you surrendering to any of that. You're doing what you think is right for you and your voice, and for Storm and Stella, too. It's a load, but you're in charge."

"If only." Harper flashed her a grin as she stood. "But you're so good for my ego." She took another sip before setting her bottle on the railing, and then leaned heavily against the post and gazed across the intersection. "You know, Gram said this place was named Crossroads for just the reason you'd think. Decision-making." She shook her head and stuffed her hands into her pockets. "Is there such a thing as too God damn much irony?"

Frankie didn't know who or what Harper saw at the crossroads, but that weary expression said the pressure was tearing her up inside. *How much stress can a woman handle at once?*

Frankie moved to the opposite post, and they stared out over the parking lot. She couldn't look at her. Harper shouldn't feel she was under a microscope any more than she already was.

"Funny thing about Crossroads," Frankie offered. "I think my *real* life took shape on this porch."

"A good portion of mine did, so I can relate. And I'm thankful."

"I am, too. Endlessly."

"Maybe I should have let it shape my *whole* life."

"But 'should haves' never do anyone any good."

"True," Harper said through a little smile. "I'm not full of regrets, not by any means, but God, how things would have been different."

"Hey, we all make the best choices we can and cross our fingers. Sometimes they pan out. Mine did and yours, too. Because we didn't let bullshit get in the way of dreams."

Harper nodded vacantly. "It's been a slog, but you're right. And now, I have to shove all my crap aside somehow and focus on something far more important." She glanced down and exhaled hard, as if to force her thoughts into words. "Gram needs to move on while she can still enjoy life, Frankie. That stubborn pride of hers, to keep this place up, will kill her. God knows, it's already getting to me."

"Because you know how much it all matters." Frankie couldn't help herself. She crossed the distance between them and tugged Harper into a hug. She thrilled at Harper's surrender, more than pleased when Harper looped arms around her neck and dropped her cheek to her shoulder.

"Harper," she whispered, stroking her back. "You're not the bad guy in this, you know."

"Great. Just when I thought you'd been paying attention."

"Are you eager to off-load this place? Dump it in someone else's lap?"

Harper just raised her head and stared at her as Frankie continued.

"Are you eager to just stick Stella away somewhere so your family won't have to babysit?"

Harper's brows lowered and her eyes heated. Frankie could feel the irritation building as she inched her palms farther across Harper's back. She drew her closer, enclosed her a little tighter.

"*That*," Frankie added gently, "would make you the bad guy." She feathered her fingers along Harper's jaw. "I may not know you well, but I don't believe that's you. It's all about where your heart is, so trust it."

Harper's stiffness softened, and when she cupped the back of Frankie's head and drew it closer, Frankie's heart raced. She dissolved into the tenderness of Harper's lips, the blinding magic of that first, tentative touch, and the full yearning in the next. Holding Harper to her chest, being held to Harper's, feeling possessive fingers trail into her hair, Frankie succumbed to a euphoria she hadn't felt in ages.

She squeezed Harper closer as their kiss lingered, and relished the luxurious contours of her back, her sides, and hips. Frankie's knees almost buckled when Harper cradled her face in both hands. They trembled against her cheeks before slowly fluttering away to her shoulders.

Moving only inches apart, they each took a breath and Harper smiled wryly. Frankie bit back a grin.

*No regrets.*

Frankie's thinking process scrambled. She could fantasize all she wanted, but common sense told her Harper's stressed state of mind deserved the credit for this loss of self-control. Acting on impulse when you're tired and frazzled only led to trouble.

Harper set a palm on Frankie's chest. "We just crossed the line."

"Blew right over it."

Looking down at her hand still on Frankie's chest, Harper nodded, and Frankie wondered if she could feel the heart hammering beneath it. Crossing the line didn't matter at the moment, and she certainly hadn't spared it a thought during those kisses. She would bet a million bucks Harper hadn't either.

She tipped Harper's chin up. "Something that spectacular, I'm going to savor for a very long time."

"What you said about trusting my heart...struck a chord." She shook her head slightly and put a finger to Frankie's lips. "It's still ringing."

Frankie smiled beneath her finger. Impulse urged her to take it between her lips and suggest a whole lot more. But she fought it, unsure exactly why. Her hesitation felt too much like an old insecurity and she fought that, too. She didn't want to be second-guessing the wisdom of this attraction to Harper, at least not at the moment.

She drew her into a snug embrace, pressed a lingering kiss to her neck, and stepped back. Holding Harper at arm's length, Frankie's entire body hummed at the promising look on her face.

"I, um...I'm just going to say good night and go. It's the...the chivalrous thing to do."

She stepped quickly to the screen door, remembering to hold the cowbell silent as she went inside. She was through the kitchenette, out the back door, and driving away, and her heartbeat still hadn't returned to normal.

## CHAPTER FIFTEEN

Harper emerged from the steaming shower thankful to be rid of the showbiz hangover and the morning stiffness her old mattress had created. She wasn't happy to be so awake before sunrise, however. That had to change, and today was the day.

As if she didn't have enough on her mind already at this ungodly hour, a new issue had joined the others in her head. Its unsettling combination of arousal and worry had contributed to a restless night's sleep. *Did you toss and turn last night, too, Frankie?*

She didn't regret surrendering within that full-body embrace or initiating that first kiss or holding on for more. She couldn't remember the last time an impulsive act had knocked her so gloriously legless. But now what? Dare she even consider something more? A summer fling to pass the time like Denni had suggested? But there hadn't been anything casual about those long, consuming kisses. *What was I thinking?*

She sighed at her reflection as she brushed her hair. "Obviously, you *weren't* thinking, were you?"

She needed coffee. How else could she figure out what to do?

Thankfully, she smelled it brewing before she reached the bottom of the stairs, and then found Gram's apartment door open. Peeking in, she watched her study the sea of papers on the table.

"Well, good morning. What's got you so preoccupied at this hour?"

"Welcome back, honey. Good morning." Gram glowed with excitement. "Come see what I've been working on." Harper strolled in, daring to think Gram had begun inquiring about prospective places to move. She set an arm around her shoulders as she looked down at the pages of notations.

Gram slid one closer for Harper to read. "My shopping list to celebrate the Fourth. If it's going to be my last one here, I'm going out with a bang." She crinkled her nose, giddy.

Harper picked up a page and labored to read the ragged penmanship. "A list of party supplies?" She reached for another. "Look at all this food. Are you feeding the whole town?"

"And I want a sign out front and one by the counter, so people know." She showed her the sample she'd written. "I want to advertise that we're celebrating the day. Remember when you were little, how we celebrated?"

"You know I do. You and Grampa made a huge deal out of it, and it was a blast."

"Wasn't it?" Gram offered her more pages of scribble. "See, we can have some games for the little ones and horseshoes and that game where you throw beanbags. And maybe badminton, too. And we can have hot dogs and burgers, corn on the cob…Do it potluck-style so folks can bring their favorite dishes. We can have a bonfire in the parking lot and the musicians can play later. And Joey said Tom will pick up some fireworks in New Hampshire."

"Holy—Is that all?" Grinning, Harper poured herself some coffee. She would have paid megabucks for an espresso at that moment. "Remember," she pulled out a chair for herself, "it's a lot more expensive to do all this today than it was years ago."

"There's money in the bank, Harper. What good is it, sitting there, especially now?"

"Well…" Harper cut herself short. Gram's future needs were important, but she wasn't about to kill Gram's high with that painful subject. She scanned the papers again. "I'm exhausted just looking at all this."

Gram took Harper's hand and squeezed. "It'll be such fun."

"Okay, you win." Gram wiggled in her chair. "But," Harper added, "we should fine-tune these lists, don't you think? We'll work on it today."

Gram pulled Harper close and kissed her cheek. "Now, we need to hurry and make muffins. Let's go." Coffee in hand, Harper followed her out to the kitchenette, trying to imagine her this happy somewhere else.

Crossroads smelled like blueberry muffins in record time, and Gram bubbled with glee as she extended Fourth of July invitations to the early commuters. Party details needed to be finalized fast because Gram wasn't waiting to spread the word.

Harper set about cleaning up Gram's baking mess, considerably greater these days than in the past. Gram wasn't as steady or as careful, perhaps not as cognizant as she used to be.

"Oh, goodness!" Gram flashed her a panicked look. "I have to call Frankie and tell her about our big plan." She hurried away but turned back with a thought. "You two were up late last night, weren't you?" The twinkle in her eyes asked for more. "Was it after eleven when I heard her drive off?"

"Oh…We were just, you know, talking. I was too wired to sleep after that drive from the airport."

"Harper! I'm so sorry! I didn't even ask about New York!"

"Not to worry, Gram. It was fun being with the band again. We did a song on the *Tonight Show*. That television world is pure madness."

"You what? The *Tonight Show*? I wish you'd told me you—"

"It was a quickie, Gram, not worth staying up late for."

"I certainly would have! I'm very disappointed now."

"I'll bring it up for you on YouTube later on, if you want." That seemed to appease her, but Harper cringed at the idea of Gram witnessing what she'd interpret as a bawdy performance.

"I'd like that, thank you, after we open and work on our celebration. Today's going to be a busy day. Let me find my phone and tell Frankie about the Fourth, then we can talk about the *Tonight Show*—and about you and Frankie last night." She shuffled down the hall.

*Tell you what about Frankie? That her kiss melted me into the floor? That I wanted to climb into her shirt?*

"I wish you'd keep your phone with you all the time, Gram," Harper yelled after her, then spun around when the cowbell clanged.

"I told her that, back when she first got it." Joe sauntered up to the counter, eyeing the ceramic mugs sitting by the coffeepot. "I'll have one of those, please, Miss Harper."

"Coming right up. Black, right?"

"The only way." He scrutinized Harper's every move until he steadied the mug in both hands. He sipped cautiously. "Hits the spot every time."

"I'm trying to get Gram into the habit of carrying her phone around."

"Took me a while. After my Angie passed, Karen started harping until I got into the habit."

"Your daughter's right. It's important." He nodded. "Good. Maybe a little harping from you will convince Gram. I'd feel better about it."

"I can do that."

"Thanks, Joe. Hey, Gram doesn't have it all worked out yet, but she's throwing a party here on the Fourth. You and Karen have to join us."

"A party like the old days?"

"That's what she has in mind."

"So, *that's* why she asked about fireworks yesterday. Of course we'll be here." He waved a finger at her. "But she's going to get herself all fired up, so you keep an eye on her."

*Yes, Joe. Gram's full of spirit and drive and determination to keep Crossroads just like it's always been.*

"I'll do my best, but she's a hard one to control."

"When that woman puts her mind to it…She's always been too stubborn for her own good, you know."

"That's my gramma."

"She's got a damn good heart." He pulled out his wallet. "I'll take a couple of those muffins, before I forget." He pushed three dollars toward her. "Put the change toward the party."

Harper thanked him as he left, and put the bills in the cash drawer, knowing that a dollar-fifty for two muffins and a coffee was far too cheap. It would be another necessary change, like the price of bottled water or the store hours, to inch Crossroads toward some semblance of profit.

Gram's voice grew louder as she returned to the kitchenette, talking on her phone and gesturing as if whoever was on the other end could see her. Harper figured it was Frankie, and that revived the butterflies in her chest.

"Well, that's good," Gram said into the phone, grinning at Harper, "because if you did have plans, you'd just have to cancel them. This is more important." Harper shook her head at her. "Yes, she and I are getting everything planned today. I know we have to hurry."

"Let me know what I can do, Stella."

Harper turned at the dulcet sound of Frankie's voice and found her standing just down the hall, still talking to Gram on the phone. She winked at Harper. The sight of her, casual and cocky, leaning against the wall, sent a rousing buzz through Harper's system, and visceral memories of last night almost made her blush.

"I'm sure we'll need your help, Frankie," Gram continued innocently. "When don't we?"

"Well, I'll be over soon. It's time Harper and I hung the buntings off the porch."

"Oh, I can't wait. I love how that looks." Gram eyed Harper sideways. "Harper's waiting for you."

Harper straightened off the counter and slammed her hands to her hips. "Gram."

"Is that so?" Frankie asked.

"It is. Okay, I've said enough. See you soon, Frankie. Bye." Gram studied her phone, found the "End" button, and poked it. She raised a grin at Harper. "Well, you *are* waiting for her, aren't you?"

Harper felt her face heat. She tried not to look beyond Gram. Peripherally, she could tell Frankie stood with her arms crossed now. *And probably a very satisfied smirk on that delicious mouth.* "I have things to do, Gram. You and I have things to do. I'm not standing around, waiting for her."

"Okay, but I know you enjoy her company."

"Well, yes, and so do you."

"Uh-huh." Gram filled a mug for herself and picked up Harper's. "We'll take our coffee out front and talk. She'll be here soon." Turning to leave the kitchenette, she finally spotted Frankie. "Oh! You're here already?"

"Good morning, Mrs. Anderson."

"Were you driving while we were on the phone? You know that's against the law."

"I wove in and out of all the traffic and the cops couldn't catch me."

"Oh, you!" She returned to the coffeepot and filled another mug.

The exchange between them, like so many before it, warmed Harper's heart. A dash of manners and that debonair smile, and Frankie had Gram in the palm of her hand.

*Have you cast some spell over us Crossroads girls?*

Frankie tipped her head slightly. "Good morning, Ms. Cushing."

Harper's skin tingled. She could feel those arms around her, the silkiness of those lips at her mouth, and she remembered wanting more. *How could I not?* She'd spent another hour on the porch after Frankie left last night, just trying to figure out where her head was at, what the hell she should—or *shouldn't be*—doing. That had kept her awake for hours.

"Good morning to you, too."

Gram looked from Harper to Frankie. "So, we're putting up the buntings today?"

"I-I'll run up and get them," Harper said and slipped past Frankie.

"I'm taking your coffee outside, Harper!" Stella led Frankie to the porch and stopped to glare at the cowbell. "That thing's obnoxious. *Must* it be there?"

"Talk to your granddaughter."

Frankie leaned against the railing, preferring to leave Harper the rocker beside Stella.

The porch felt different today. *Crossing the line at Crossroads.* She smiled into her coffee, knowing they really hadn't *gone* very far, but their hot moment still smoldered, no matter how hard she tried to ignore it. Maybe she wasn't really trying.

"I'm so glad you two have become good friends," Stella said. "I know Harper's intentions for me and the store weigh upon you, too, and I'm sorry for that, Frankie."

"I think it's tough on everybody, but we'll all survive, you know. I'm sure of it."

"Don't play diplomat with me, missy. I know better." She sipped her coffee and rocked several times. "I do want you and Harper to come away from all this, knowing you did the right thing. It will be difficult for me at first, true, but I imagine I'll adjust. You two, however, you mustn't have regrets."

"As long as you're—"

"You know what I mean." She stopped when Harper arrived with the box of patriotic bunting from upstairs.

"What *do* you mean, Gram?" Harper set the box on the floor and sat beside her. "What's up your sleeve?"

"Not a thing. I was just telling Frankie that I don't want either of you to have any regrets about…all this."

"And," Frankie injected, "although she didn't let me finish, I tried to tell your grandmother that we wouldn't, as long as she was okay."

"That's right," Harper stated. "We'll be okay if you are."

Frankie opened the bunting box and shook out one of the decorative half-moon-shaped flags. Dwelling on what lay ahead would bum everyone out and, even though her common sense insisted on that private talk with Harper, she couldn't bring herself to ruin this sweet morning.

Stella muttered a little "hm" and Frankie wondered what she'd say next. Harper probably *worried* about what would come next, considering Stella had practically given up on filters.

"Once I'm…wherever," Stella began, "you two will keep in touch with each other, won't you?"

"Sure, we will, Gram." Harper stepped up to help Frankie tie the bunting to the railing, and they caught each other's eye.

"We'll keep in touch with you, too, of course," Frankie said quickly. Not wanting to think otherwise, she promptly pulled another bunting from the box, and they moved to another section of railing. "You better get in the habit of texting."

"But you'll come visit me?"

"Yes," they answered.

"No," Frankie added. "We'll never see you again."

"Now you're just being fresh." Stella pouted. "Will you come together?"

They stopped and looked at each other. Stella had meant something entirely different, of course, but the risqué double entendre hadn't escaped either of them. Immediately, they turned to Stella.

"Gram, who knows what each of us will have going on, but we'll try."

"She's right, Stella. Remember, I can't go anywhere around harvest."

"Exactly," Harper said, "and if Storm's on the road…I just can't promise."

Frankie hated envisioning Stella someplace other than here, hated the inevitability of it all, the feeling of helplessness. She forced herself to concentrate on hanging bunting all around the porch, and focused on how smoothly, wordlessly she and Harper worked together. She also recognized Stella's underlying mission, especially when she went to get her "lists" and left the two of them alone.

But Stella's maneuvering was all for naught. Wasn't everything about being "wise" these days? She couldn't allow her dusty libido to jump off the shelf and take charge, no matter how long it had been or how alluring the woman or how exciting the notion. She didn't live in Harper's fast lane. She wasn't built for that, and doubted her heart could handle the risk.

And Harper was too savvy to fall into some "thing" with a virtual stranger, wasn't she? Especially now, with so much bearing down on her? She certainly wouldn't, so far removed from her successful, glitzy world of rock 'n' roll. This was way out of her comfort zone.

*So, just let it go, dammit.*

Frankie went down to the parking lot and finished securing the bottom edges of the decorations to the porch. Above her, Harper began dead-heading Stella's hanging geraniums and Frankie's pulse quickened at her proximity.

"Gram's all worked up about the Fourth," Harper said. "Can I interest you in helping plan this big bash? She's looking forward to your input."

Scrambling for some impulse control, Frankie backed up to assess her work. She really couldn't afford to spend the rest of the day here; she had things to do, didn't she? She had to put some space between them because last night was just a moment of emotional weakness. Nothing more.

"This looks nice," she said, waving grandly at the storefront, "and the sign's so cheery." She walked back up the steps to where Harper waited, a hip against the railing.

*Asking what of me, exactly?*

"Well, I was on my way into town," Frankie answered at last, almost embarrassed by the excuse.

"Uh-huh."

"If there's anything you two need, I'll pick it up, no problem. Maybe things for the party?"

"We haven't decided much yet. Thanks anyway."

Harper's voice was as flat and emotionless as her expression and Frankie felt herself shrinking from both of them.

"Okay. Well, then, I...I probably should run." Her feet insisted she repeat last night's quick escape, but her heart hammered them to the floor. Her common sense turned away completely.

"Run?" Harper tilted her head as if to see around Frankie's fluster and read her mind.

*I said run, didn't I? So much for doing chivalrous things.*

"Well, I..."

"As in 'run away'? So, you're not in a talkative mood anymore."

Frankie finally gathered her pride and aimed it at Harper's challenge. "Should we talk about expectations?" she whispered, stepping closer.

"I'd like to. I think we should, don't you?"

"Do expectations include provocative kisses?"

Harper grinned faintly. "Are they mutually exclusive?"

*Damn, if this woman doesn't press all my buttons at once.*

"You tell me."

The last response Frankie expected was a kiss. Harper tugged her closer by the shoulders and Frankie's breath caught when those sweet lips nestled against hers so softly, too briefly. Her head spun as pleasure taunted her better judgment. When Harper stepped back, she appeared just as moved.

The yearning for more rose in Frankie right along with the warning bells. She refused to get hurt again, but, God, this...No. Harper was no fool. Yes, last night had been special, but *this*, well, this should be the period at the end of it all. Shouldn't it?

Harper offered a somber smile. "Frankie, last night—"

"Shh. Let's not spoil it."

## CHAPTER SIXTEEN

Things were actually running smoother than Harper expected, even though she was rapidly becoming counterproductive. Packages of hamburger buns and hot dog rolls lay scattered at her feet in the gravel and she swept them up with a muted curse, dodging three children running to the fire pit.

Buzzing around Gram's "July Fourth Fun Day" already had her overheated and bone-weary, so worrying about personal issues just ate away at her coordination and dwindling stamina. A tranquil moment with a cold beverage, preferably alcoholic, wouldn't arrive for hours and she had quite a few to go.

She bounded back up the porch steps and paused to check on Gram, who sat rocking blissfully with a friend. *The queen overseeing her realm.* But Gram's happiness was what this affair was all about, and, despite the madness, Harper was pleased so many families and friends had turned out.

"Harper, honey." Gram waved her over. "This is Mrs. Whitlock. Her son brought her today. He's the fellow with the twins." Harper smiled graciously at the millionth person she'd been introduced to today. Gram added, "Janice went to school with Grampa."

"Ah! I'm glad to meet you," Harper said, genuinely pleased. She plucked her tank top out from her stomach and fluffed air underneath. "Hot," she groused toward Gram. "So, was Grampa a rascal in school, too?"

Mrs. Whitlock laughed with Gram. "Suspended many times. He was always up to no good."

Harper gave her a thumbs-up. "Atta boy. I want to hear all the details," she added, stepping back, "but, right now, you'll have to excuse me. I'm on a mission. The cook is waiting for sausages and corn. Glad you could make it, Mrs. Whitlock."

Escaping inside, Harper appreciated that Frankie had removed the cowbell for the occasion.

*Haven't seen her in a while.*

They'd made such an efficient team yesterday and since early this morning, preparing for today, but something loomed behind Frankie's lighthearted commentary that felt like reservation. Maybe intimacy between them had left her as shaken as it had left Harper. Deep, prolonged kisses could do that, she mused. *Maybe I'm not the only one struggling to process.*

Turning into Gram's apartment, where the large refrigerator was packed with food, Harper crashed into Frankie coming out.

"Shit!"

Frankie's stacked tray clattered to the floor. "Whoa, Harper! Damn!"

They hurriedly restacked the tray.

"Sorry, Frankie. Looks like you've got the sausages I was coming for."

"Let me guess: Terri sent you for corn, too."

"Yeah. Did she send you for that?" Terri was never subtle. "I'll get it." She hurried to Gram's kitchen and grabbed the last basket of ears, sensing Frankie waiting in the doorway. "Maybe after the dinner hour, things will calm down."

"Keep dreaming," Frankie said. "How are you holding up?"

Harper slouched onto a hip and blew hair off her forehead. "Honestly? I'm running on fumes. How about you?" *God. She doesn't look half this frazzled.*

"I'm pretty spent, too. Listen, um, after I reload the cooler chest, I can help you. What's next?"

"God knows. Allie needs the old pallets out back brought around to the fire pit for later, so I thought I'd tackle that. Did you know that Tom recruited Joe to help with the fireworks?" Frankie's eyebrows shot up. "Yeah," Harper continued. "Not sure how wise that is, but Joe wanted to help."

A rousing cheer sounded from outside, and they started down the hall.

"The cornhole tournament," Frankie said. "I think a world champion has been crowned." At the kitchenette, she stopped and turned to Harper. "Let's throw all this at Terri and...Can we go hide somewhere, catch our breath for a few minutes?"

The invitation was refreshing for obvious reasons. It was time they stopped acting like neighbors passing on the sidewalk. Harper didn't know exactly *what* they were or what they should be doing instead, but that languorous kissing had to account for something. It surely reminded Harper of what she'd been missing.

Ignoring it all these past couple of days had kept them off Gram's radar, but those loaded, guarded moments in private had to go. Harper hated the hesitancy that grew whenever they were together, and wanted to believe Frankie did, too.

She nodded toward the front door. "Let's go. Meet me upstairs in ten minutes."

They arrived at the fire pit to Terri's boisterous thanks. She busied herself flipping burgers and snuck a grin at her wife, who made room on a side table for the sausages and corn.

"Guess it took two of us, huh?" Frankie said into Terri's knowing smirk. "Well, here you go."

Ginny looked up, feigning innocence. "We figured that carrying the basket *and* the tray would be hard."

Harper flashed her own smirk. "Don't *you* start."

"Frankie, do me a favor," Terri said, directing with the spatula. "Stack some of that wood here and toss a couple pieces on the fire? I've gotta get these burgers off."

Frankie hustled to comply, and Harper doubted they'd make their rendezvous in the five or so minutes remaining.

"I'm starting on the pallets out back," she said, stepping away, more than a bit disappointed.

Terri looked between them. Gesturing at Frankie, she told Harper, "This one will be there in a minute to help you." Ginny just grinned as she unwrapped the packages of sausage.

Harper pointed severely at Terri, who splayed her hands and offered too much wide-eyed innocence. The poorly disguised intentions had Harper shaking her head as she maneuvered toward the porch steps, aiming to take a shortcut to the back lot. *They're as bad as Gram. Does everybody want to watch us play with fire?*

"Harper!"

It took a second for Harper to spot Vicky at her car, parked with many others along the edge of the meadow. A large bowl tucked into her arm, Vicky shut the trunk and hurried toward her.

Harper glanced into the bowl as Vicky came to a stop. "Macaroni Salad Part Two?"

"Yeah. The first one went with lunch. This goes with supper."

"Good, because I didn't have any earlier. Thanks for bringing it. We really appreciate everyone doing the potluck thing. It's a huge help."

"Oh, no problem. Look, I know you're running around here like a chicken with your head cut off, so I won't keep you, but…Maybe we could talk sometime? I've been meaning to. Tom and I both have." She set her free hand on Harper's arm. "Just tell me. That *was* you we saw on Jimmy Fallon the other night, wasn't it?"

Harper's light-hearted mood clanged like the cowbell. No one had raised the subject, not yet anyway, and she had been glad to have only a dozen other things to think about—none of which centered on her professional life. She had labored to keep that off of her mind today.

She straightened and shoved both hands into her back pockets. "It was, yes."

Her jaw dropping, Vicky almost lost the macaroni salad. "Oh. My. God. Tom thought it was you and I told him he was crazy. I-I'm embarrassed to admit that I'm not too familiar with the music, I'm sorry, but…God, you were *something!*"

"Thank you, but I'm really just trying to escape it all for a while."

"Ah. I get it. Undercover." She eyed Harper sideways. "But *so* seductive."

Harper laughed lightly. "It's a schtick that grew over time, I guess. We struggled to get noticed."

"Oh, you're not struggling now. You've been noticed." Vicky chuckled. "It's hard to miss a sexy vision strutting front and center." She leaned closer. "You have no idea how exciting this is for a homebody like me. God, the highlight of my month thus far was painting the bathroom. So, *this? You?* Wow."

"Honestly, I really hope it's not brought up. I haven't said much about it to Gram because she'd broadcast it everywhere. She'd mean well, of course, but I just don't want to bring all that here, into her world."

"Not even when it's spreading the word about you guys?"

"Maybe in time."

"Well, before you go back to Storm again, would you autograph something for me?"

"Geez, Vicky. Yeah, sure. Thank you. I'm flattered."

"Later on, when the instruments come out, will you join in?"

Harper playfully punched Vicky's bicep. "If you think there'll be strutting around the fire here later, please think again. But you're sweet to ask. I've been advised to rest the voice for the summer. The *Tonight Show* was just a one-off and I had no choice."

"Well, that's a real shame about tonight. Maybe some other time when you visit Stella."

Harper thought about that as she squeezed through the mingling crowd at the porch steps. Frankie would have to deal with moving the pallets by herself for a few minutes, because now Harper needed to regroup in the sanctity of her apartment.

She wouldn't be making many more visits here, that was true. She might need to come to facilitate the sale of the place, but once she helped Gram move, that would be the end of it. She tried to imagine Gram celebrating

Christmas somewhere else, Crossroads dark and hollow through the holidays. Out of the blue, she pictured Frankie sitting on the deserted porch railing.

When the apartment door opened, Harper's stressed expression instantly morphed into glorious relief. Air conditioning clearly impacted her as much as Frankie rising from the couch.

"I thought you'd appreciate it," Frankie said, having cranked the unit up minutes earlier.

"You have no idea. Thank you." Harper bent over the sink and splashed her face with cold water. "I'm so glad I bought that last week, even though Gram probably will never turn hers on."

"When you didn't show up out back, I figured I'd find you here. The door was unlocked and when I stuck my head in, I almost suffocated. I'm sorry to intrude."

"Don't worry about it. I'm grateful." Harper saturated a hand towel, rung it out, and draped it across the back of her neck. "Vicky caught me out front."

"She's been dying to talk about the *Tonight Show*."

"That's the last thing I want to think about right now."

Frankie watched her drop into the upholstered chair. "We need cold drinks. I'll raid Stella's fridge, if you want."

"No need." Harper nodded toward her refrigerator and closed her eyes. "I hate to ask, but would you mind? I'll trade you my house in WeHo for a vodka and cranberry with ice."

Frankie's nerves twitched at the subject of Harper's new home. "What's it like?" She went to the kitchen and began making the cocktail.

Harper laid the towel over her face and spoke from beneath it. "It's just a three-bedroom cottagey place, rare, so I was lucky to find it. But I bought it sight-unseen, based on pictures and friends' recommendations. It looks cute."

"A new home's pretty exciting. Congratulations."

"Thanks, but, all things considered, it just feels like another project right now. I know that's weird." She sighed. "Speaking of projects, what time did you start yours this morning?"

The subject change struck Frankie as odd. Harper never seemed eager to talk about her real life. Apparently, all that reflection the other night on the porch was a rarity.

"I had to run the sprinklers for a few hours. You don't want to know when that was." *I couldn't sleep, anyway.*

"Before dawn? How *do* you do it?" Harper laid the towel across her throat. "I always thought I was in good shape. 'The life,' you know, it keeps you moving hard, but being here?" She chortled at herself, and Frankie turned from the counter to see her, to see something that reflected attachment to *this* place. "Being here, keeping up with Gram, with Crossroads, with *you*…"

Frankie lowered the glass to Harper's hand and the dark eyes opened directly up at her. She fought the urge to dive in.

"Look, about the other night, Harper… There's heavy stuff going on now, with Stella and Crossroads, stuff I'd like to get into with you, but what happened between us…Let's agree to not add to the stress. Call it an indiscretion and put it behind us. I mean, we're not kids. We know the score."

Elbows on the armrests, Harper stared at the glass she now held in both hands. "Yeah."

Frankie took a seat on the couch, touched to hear that the difficulty was mutual, but curious as to how close they were to ignoring it. *Dismissing "us" is freaking impossible and I actually suggested it? Certifiable. That's me.* She dropped her face into her hands.

"Alright. I take that back," she said. "I can't just let it go."

"Honestly, Frankie?" Harper swirled the ice in her glass without looking up. "Is that what it felt like to you? An 'indiscretion'? I don't think so, either. But you're right. I'll be out of here soon." She shook her head and drank.

Looking away, Frankie tried to gauge the raging battle between her common sense and her overexcited heart. The twinge in her chest said her heart was losing because Harper's was somewhere in LA. Nevertheless, her head kept pointing toward pleasure, even for the short-term. Realistically, she had nothing to offer beyond that, anyway.

*Neither of us would have to overcome obstacles or risk taking any giant leaps.*

"Frankie, once Gram is…Once things are situated here…" She set her glass on the table with an emphatic clack and went to the window. "Shit. See? I know I just can't. I really can't."

*Hell. If I can, can't you?*

Frankie just stared and waited for more. Her heart shook as she stepped up behind her.

"I know you're trying to be fair, and I appreciate that."

Harper's heart rate spiked. The soft words fluttered down her spine and she closed her eyes. "Don't stand so close. I'm having a hard enough time functioning."

"Why not just take things as they come, one day at a time?"

Harper fought for composure. Her calendar flashed to mind, the disappearing days, the commitments, and the distance they would create. On top of them was the risk. Her heart had taken one of those before and lost brutally. She *had* to be practical.

She shook her head. "I don't know how smart that is. In fact, I probably should just apologize—"

Frankie turned her around by the hips. "We're thinking too God damn much."

Harper had to smile at that—and at the concerted, wily glint in Frankie's eyes that swept all reservations aside. And that made her sigh with resignation. "You know," she whispered, "I am *so* damn tired of thinking."

Frankie took a hesitant step closer. "Then, for Christ's sake, let's not."

"Just throw caution to the wind?"

"With all *that* going on out there?" Frankie tilted her head toward the window and the noisy crowd in the parking lot below. "I'm tired of thinking, too."

She took another step. Harper backed up against the window frame and grinned.

"Are you cornering me, Frankie Cosgrove?"

"If that's what it takes, because I'm going to kiss the famous Harper Cushing and she's going to let me."

"The 'famous' one be dammed," Harper said, sliding her palms up Frankie's arms. "The *real* one says, 'Bring it.'"

Harper tugged her in and didn't even try to stop the dreamy moan that escaped when Frankie kissed her. The full measure of Frankie's strength pressed her against the woodwork, and Harper clutched her closer, holding on to deliver her share of this penetrating, luscious kiss.

Her senses reeled when Frankie squeezed her waist. Hands roamed higher and Harper kissed her harder. Fingers flexed into her ribs, cupped her breasts, tripped across her nipples. The stimulation electrified Harper's every nerve, made it impossible to stand still.

Her arms locked around Frankie's neck, she leaned decisively into their kiss and turned her from the window to the wall, reversing their position. Frankie's hands immediately slid down her back to her ass, pulled her hips in tight, and Harper's breath caught as her pelvis instinctively ground against Frankie's.

She returned her kiss possessively and let her fingers wander down the front of Frankie's chest. She kneaded the small breasts heavily and Frankie's guttural moan made Harper smile as she licked her lips. Having Frankie succumb was a dizzying concept, a tidal wave of pleasure and satisfaction Harper hadn't enjoyed in so long.

She tucked her fingers inside the front of Frankie's shorts, gripped the waistband as she trailed kisses along her jaw. "God, you feel so fucking good."

With a hungry groan, Frankie pulled Harper's tank top out of her shorts and Harper squirmed at the feel of hands on her bare back. Her mind went blank except for Frankie's hands, broad, strong hands so reverent on her skin, and Harper craved them everywhere. She wanted Frankie's skin beneath *her* hands. She yanked the T-shirt free, pushed it up Frankie's ribs, and took a breath when Frankie flung it aside.

Instantly, Frankie returned to Harper's mouth, their tongues meeting, stroking, while Harper lost herself in the feel of Frankie's abs. Dazed, she felt her tank top slip over her head. Bras were abandoned next, and when Frankie dipped her head and lifted Harper's nipple to her lips, Harper thought she'd sag to the floor.

But Frankie held her within both arms now, Harper's breast firmly at her mouth, and a wanton surrender flooded Harper's system. She slid her fingers through the mussed auburn hair, holding that hot, eager mouth in place, and closed her eyes at the sensation.

Her entire body shimmered, vibrated, but oddly, it didn't jibe with that unusual buzz she heard coming from the wall.

Frankie laughed as she raised her head. "Shit."

Harper was puzzled, more than a little disoriented by the hard landing. Her nipple sat erect, wet, and cold, just part of why she shivered. She desperately missed that snug fit to Frankie's body.

As Frankie straightened and reached for her back pocket, Harper rolled her eyes and stepped back. "Oh, you've *got* to be kidding me."

Frankie held her phone out for both of them to read the text from Terri.

*"Hey. Wherever you are. Cops are here. Brenda needs your word about fireworks."*

Frankie punched in an "okay," and put her phone away. She cupped Harper's breast and pressed a gentle, lingering kiss to the nipple.

Harper trembled at the tenderness and steadied herself with a palm to each of Frankie's breasts. She squeezed playfully, urged her back to the wall until no space remained between them, and spoke against her lips. "I'm looking forward to fireworks."

## Chapter Seventeen

It took playing her guitar amidst some two dozen adults, many seemingly tone deaf, singing Garth Brooks's "Friends in Low Places" to keep Frankie's mind from straying. Too bad there hadn't been time for a cold shower before this finale of their celebration. Her body still hummed. She might have been strumming along, but she definitely wasn't humming to Garth Brooks.

Typically, Terri took full advantage. She made it her mission to look pointedly at Harper and tease Frankie with suggestive expressions whenever she could. Frankie showed her appreciation by scratching her nose with her middle finger.

Thankfully, the collective musical effort around her quickly became as hysterical as it was fun, proven by Stella's tears of laughter. Frankie relished everything about that, particularly having Harper among them, even if she wasn't singing. This was what Crossroads was all about and there was no way Harper couldn't feel it. She would take it with her when she left.

And that thought lowered Frankie's bubbling libido to a steady simmer. Remember, she advised herself, there are plenty of good times in store and every reason to enjoy them. Harper would leave in a couple months, but that was not going to kick the world off its axis. *Well, maybe a little.*

The roaring fire at twilight had everyone gathered around, munching on leftovers and telling stories, yelling out song suggestions. The handful of children worked diligently at their s'mores, energizing their batteries to play in the near darkness. Fireworks would close the evening soon, but until then, everyone amused themselves with silly or well-known tunes, even patriotic ones.

Frankie went to Joe's side, teaming her guitar with his banjo, and kicked off a light-hearted tune for the kids. She repeated the chorus enough times to include the name of every child nearby, and soon had kids hopping around her, excited to hear their names sung. Adults clapped along, which only made the kids happier, and the ending drew an enormous cheer.

As she returned to her seat, she could feel Harper's welcoming smile clear down to her toes. The music hadn't whipped the audience into a writhing mob the way Storm's did, but she knew Harper recognized all this happiness just the same. They had that in common, and there was no denying it.

"You need your own TV show, Cosgrove. You aced that." Harper passed her a beer and held onto it until Frankie noticed. "You have a great voice, you know."

Frankie shrugged a shoulder. "Thank you. I love the effect that song has on everybody. It's all about those smiles, especially by firelight."

"Sitting here, watching everyone, all ages getting into the music together…It's so different from what I'm used to, but I never realized how much I liked it."

Frankie watched her gaze at the faces around the fire. "Special, isn't it?"

"It is, so carefree, uninhibited. No one's worrying about perfection or portraying an 'image.' It's relaxing, and when you can play relaxed, you're at your best."

"There's an honesty about it."

Frankie hoped she hadn't insulted Storm's image-driven personality, but she was proud of the raw joy her friends' music conveyed. She let her comment sink in as Harper watched the quartet currently playing.

"That's it, exactly," Harper said, distantly. "It's all such a treat for me. And I'd forgotten how sweet it is to hear so many instruments unplugged."

"I know this stuff isn't your thing, so thank you for being open-minded about it all. I'm glad you're enjoying it."

Harper quickly turned and squeezed her arm. "Enjoying it? I'm loving it." She leaned closer. "When Joe did the *Beverly Hillbillies* theme song, I was impressed that so many still knew the words."

"The power of TV reruns, I guess, but the song's timeless."

"He did a great job on it. Earl Scruggs, the banjo master, would be proud."

Frankie lowered her head to Harper's ear. "And Joe's not proud of his voice, but he knows Stella will sing with him."

"I like that between them." Watching him chat with Stella, Harper tipped her head closer, confidentially, and accidentally bumped her cheek against Frankie's nose. "She, um…" Her words caught and she smiled at the unnerving effect of such a simple touch. Frankie grinned. "Gram," Harper finished, her eyes finding Frankie's. "She still calls him Joey and I think that's adorable."

"It's a special friends kind of thing."

"Uh-huh." She tipped her bottle toward two middle-aged men talking with Terri. "Those two. The one with the beard comes in at least once a week. John, maybe? Is that his husband, the one with the stand-up bass?"

Frankie nodded. "John and Iman. They married about a year ago. Stella shamed Iman into bringing his bass to our get-togethers. He's a beginner but we love having him. She brought him out of his shell."

"If anyone could do such a thing, it's Gram. Makes me proud."

Terri stepped into the firelight with her mandolin and summoned all the musicians to join her.

"I guess that's my cue," Frankie said and left Harper grinning.

"Got time for just a few more," Terri told the crowd, "so let's party in Margaritaville!"

All the voices rose again, and Harper took note of the young girl struggling with her own guitar. She sat between her parents, apparently, but they were too caught up in their singing to notice the girl's difficulty. Harper scooted around the fire and crouched before her.

"Hi, honey. I'm Harper. What's your name?"

"Wendi."

"Nice to meet you, Wendi. Is this your guitar?"

"It's my mom's but she's letting me use it."

The woman beside her leaned into the conversation. "Wendi's taking lessons, aren't you, sweetie?"

"On this?" Harper thought the full-sized D40 was way too big for her little arms and hands.

"I can play some chords, but…Well, not fast like everybody else."

"Hang on a sec."

Harper walked up behind Frankie and slid her hand around her hip and into a front pocket of her shorts. Frankie jumped but didn't miss a beat. Then Harper whispered in her ear.

"Keep right on playing. Don't mind me." All innocence, Harper reached in deeper, her fingers privately flirting at Frankie's groin. "Just borrowing this." She pulled the capo from Frankie's pocket and hurried back to Wendi.

"A capo might help," Harper told Wendi and her parents, "but I'd try a smaller guitar going forward." Whoever was teaching Wendi should know this. "We'll put the capo up here." She attached the device higher up the guitar's neck. "Try your chords now. See, you don't have to stretch your fingers as far and that might give you more strength."

Wendi managed three chord changes in decent time, fast enough for her to notice the difference, and she flashed an amazed smile at her mother, then at Harper. "This is way better! Thank you!"

"Have fun." Harper returned to her seat, absently singing along.

She searched the crowd of musicians until she caught Frankie's eye. Frankie tapped her lips and wagged a finger at her, and Harper remembered her doctor's orders. She stopped singing in mid-note, then shook her head at Frankie and continued singing anyway.

She couldn't help it. The mood around the fire lifted her into song. This was a hell of a long way from belting out lyrics to thousands, yet she found herself enjoying every second. And it had to be obvious. Frankie's knowing smile spoke volumes. They shared this in their bones, and after this afternoon, they shared something more.

Frankie launched into a lively old country favorite of Gram's that everyone seemed to know, and the pace picked up. Confident and encouraging, Frankie met all the smiles and voices around her as she sang, always welcoming, giving.

Harper knew she'd never met anyone like her, never felt so instinctively drawn to someone before. Regardless of where their lives led, she'd remember Frankie by firelight for a very long time.

Once Tom and Joe shot off all the fireworks, the meadow of cars slowly emptied, and the police cruiser finally pulled away from the intersection. Even the crickets found it safe to come out of hiding. A refreshing stillness settled over the parking lot as she and Frankie finished the last of the clean-up together.

For her part, Frankie was still wired from playing and didn't want the night to end. She returned from the dumpster out back and found Harper tying the last bag of trash, her yellow T-shirt glowing against her tan in the waning firelight. She forced herself not to stop and just stare.

"Stella all settled?"

"God, yes. She was exhausted. I think she was asleep before we reached her apartment."

"She'll smile about it for days." Frankie hefted a large cooler and doused the fire with melted ice. "I would love to have played some Jim Reeves tunes for her. She loves his soft songs, but it would've snuffed out the mood just like this fire."

"You really like that old, classic country, don't you?"

"Some, yeah. I like to mix it up, but tonight was for easy songs everybody could do, including the kids."

"Well, you have the voice for old mellow country. I just love it. You're really good, Frankie. Truly."

"Thank you, but I just mess around. I'm honored, though, coming from you."

"Seriously. I wish you had soloed more. You have a very smooth sound, almost a contralto."

Frankie laughed. "Not a rock voice, huh?"

"No, and yours will outlast mine by years."

"Well, I'd like to hear yours in person."

Harper touched her arm, stopped her from poking the embers. "Only if you sing for me."

A wave of melancholy rose in Frankie's chest, right alongside a surge of pleasure. If they had little else beyond this summer, at least she'd have their musical connection.

## Chapter Eighteen

Harper started a fourth pot of coffee at eight o'clock, wondering if she'd still be coherent by the afternoon or a zombie. The morning rush had been true to form, and thank God Gram had appeared, bright and chipper, and helped satisfy the loyal horde. Four hours of uneasy sleep hadn't done Harper any favors, and Gram—at eighty-three—had put her to shame and effectively shoved Harper's plan for retirement talk right back into her face.

Harper hadn't been looking forward to their discussion this afternoon, but fine-tuning a plan for the future had to start soon. Maybe just not in the afterglow of Gram's enormously successful "July Fourth Fun Day."

*We'll see how the day goes.*

When her phone chimed, Harper turned from the chattering bunch at the counter. She left Donna to help Gram recount every last detail of yesterday's bash to a customer, and winced when she saw her mother's name on the screen. She grabbed her coffee and retreated to the back landing for some sun.

"Hey, Mom." She settled onto the top step and tried not to groan from the effort. "Happy Post-Fourth."

"Hello. Is everything alright up there? I couldn't reach a soul yesterday."

Harper remembered ignoring a call as she blew up balloons for the kids. She wondered if Gram had missed any on her phone.

"Everything's great here. Sorry we missed your calls, but we celebrated the Fourth yesterday with a neighborhood party. Remember when Gram and Grampa used to throw those big—"

"*Someone* needs to be more responsible, wouldn't you say? I mean, what are we supposed to think when we get no answer and no one returns our calls? Really, Harper."

"Sorry, Mom. It was wild. We had food and games going all afternoon and into the evening, and then music and fireworks till almost midnight. It was great and Gram was thrilled, but we're wiped."

"Midnight? Teenagers disturb the peace at that hour. Adults are supposed to know better. And how is Gramma after all that? There's only so much she should be doing at her age, you know."

"Hey, she's doing better than I am." Harper had to chuckle. "Not sure how either of us is going to last the day, but it was worth it."

"So, have you accomplished anything with her yet? You've had a whole month already, haven't you? I expect she'll be here for good by Christmas, won't she?"

*Which question do you want me to answer first?*

"How much caffeine have you had this morning?"

"What?"

"Did you and Dad go out for breakfast?"

"Breakfast? Well, no. We had plenty of it right here."

"Brunch?"

"Harper. We had an early tee time, so, yes, afterward we did brunch with the Nielsons."

"Uh-huh." Harper put the phone on speaker, and laid it on the step beside her. She rubbed her eyes. For this, *she* could use a caffeine IV. She took two huge gulps of coffee as her mother ranted.

"Now, I have plenty of questions because *Miss Independence* still thinks she lives on some planet without phone service. Other people are affected by Gram's situation, you know, not just you."

"I realize that, Mom." *It's always been about you.*

"And there's obviously nothing wrong with your cell phone."

"Look, you asked me to do this, so let me. You know damn well how Gram feels about all this and no way am I going to force anything down her throat. Some things take time and I'm lucky to have it. Just give me a break, okay? Some understanding would be nice."

"Are you through?" Harper stared at her phone and wished she could be rude enough to dump the call. "So, I assume that means you've made no progress? When do you expect to? We'd like to know that Gram's settled here by Christmas, Harper. I'm going to email you the particulars about the facility near us, so you can make inquiries. I happen to know they have several units available right now. You can't be dragging your feet. Who knows what will be available by the time you get around to it."

"Send what you want, Mom." *Knock yourself out.*

"Fine. I'll do that. Time's precious, so, for Heaven's sake, get down to business. You know, you could call with updates, occasionally. Once a week would be considerate."

"For more of these endearing family chats?"

"Why must you be so obstinate?"

Harper sighed. She hadn't thought it possible, but she was even more exhausted than when she'd waited on the McKinney family at seven thirty, all six of them, hyped up and heading off on vacation. "I'll do my best, Mom."

"Excellent. Thank you. We'll talk soon, then."

Harper almost kissed the printer when the test sheet emerged. She'd configured her laptop to the new printer so Gram could read from paperwork and not a screen, which she abhorred. The afternoon had been arduous. At least they had gotten this far.

With both of them running on precious little sleep, Harper bravely guided Gram through the tenuous details of "her future." She knew it was a strange world for Gram, and hoped the endless possibilities would interest and not intimidate her.

But Gram appeared entertained, not amenable, as they reviewed the myriad of housing options and locations. The condos and assisted living sites had her perusing printouts with unexpected curiosity, but nothing genuinely appealed. Nothing loosened that entrenched stance.

Harper then resorted to one last idea, actually a concession she had only recently begun to explore, that of in-home services. Maybe it was far-fetched, but Harper secretly held high hopes for this one. Although complex, it could keep Gram here and in charge of Crossroads, keep it off the market for the foreseeable future. Gram *had* to see that. Regular visits by an aide might enable her to stay as long as she wanted, but getting her to agree was another matter entirely.

Gram listened intently as Harper explained the requirements: someone, maybe part-time, would have to help in the store, and Crossroads' business would need a boost to cover that expense. Without question, the store had to start paying for itself, but at least initially, Harper could infuse some of her own cash or Mom and Dad could. The entire concept wouldn't go over well with them, but Harper was willing to fight that battle.

She reorganized the mess of papers on the table and refilled their iced tea glasses as Gram just sat, lost in thought.

Harper sat, too, and covered Gram's hand with hers. "I know it's hard, but please try not to be overwhelmed by all this."

"Harper, you know I want to stay, so those condo places…" She shook her head. "And I don't want that aide thing either, someone coming here all the time to check on me." She made a face. "I don't need that."

"Not necessarily every day. Maybe a couple times a week. It's a flexible thing. And not exactly *checking* on you, but, well, yeah, kind of, but making sure you're okay, happy and safe, eating well. Think of it as a friend stopping by."

"Frankie does that."

Harper frowned at her. "And how often do you feel bad about that, taking her away from her own life? No, this is how it *should* work."

"Well, Joey comes by every day, remember."

"And that's great. Visits from him and Frankie would complement this system perfectly." Gram stared vacantly at the list of services a visiting aide could provide. "You know," Harper added, "I've heard some great stories about how aides become good friends, and I bet that would happen here. I think you'd be surprised by how much you would enjoy the company, a new friend."

Gram touched the list, as if trying to relate to a stranger through the page. "Well, a new friend's not a bad thing."

Harper patted her hand. "Just think about it for now, okay?"

"I don't know if I can even do that without you, Harper. It's a lot. And you won't be here much longer."

"Not to worry. We'll figure things out." Gram nodded but didn't seem convinced. Harper inched her chair closer and wrapped an arm around Gram's shoulders. "I haven't brought this up before because I don't want you worrying about it. You're already thinking too hard, but—"

Gram turned to face her. "What is it? Is this going to be painful, too?"

"Like you, *I'm* laboring with a 'thing' these days, too. My voice might be trying to send a message. I'm not sure if it's going to quit on me, once and for all, and it's in the back of my mind constantly."

Gram leaned back in Harper's arm. "Really? I thought things were going well and you were happy."

"Oh, they are, and I am. Storm has never been so popular, but if I'm not smart, I may not be able to stick with it much longer. So, I think a lot about the what-ifs, you know? And about letting the guys down."

"Have you thought about changing careers?"

"No. Our music is taking off now and that's thrilling." Doubt brought her up short. "Well, to be honest, I might be a little afraid to think that through."

"You're still going to live in California, aren't you?"

"Oh, yeah. It's the center of the music universe. So, once the voice thing heals, I should be good to go. You and I have a lot on our plates, and I just wanted you to know that I understand the pressure."

"Honey, I wish things were easier for you."

"Likewise, Gram. But I'm going to do everything possible to help you because we're a team." She squeezed her shoulders. "*You* are my priority, though. Please remember that."

"But, Harper, if you're concerned about your career, you shouldn't have to be worrying about me. I'll just go anywhere. It doesn't matter. I don't want you—"

"Oh, no, no. That's not how this is going to go. End of debate." She kissed Gram's forehead. "So." She offered a hopeful grin. "Now, let's see what we can do about Crossroads' business. We have to beef it up."

Gram settled back into her chair, leery as she eyed Harper's list. She obviously knew what was coming.

"I know this isn't a popular subject, Gram, but we have to start making a real profit."

"*Not* to make Crossroads appealing to buyers, though, right?"

"Correct. For this plan, we'd shoot for self-sustaining, not saleable. It's critical. You know, we're incredibly lucky you're so good at bookkeeping." She nudged her shoulder. "I don't think I could've deciphered half your penmanship if you hadn't shown me, but...You're amazing. *You* told *me* that the bottom line is sketchy, and your numbers prove it. We both know something has to be done."

Gram sighed heavily and said nothing.

Harper pushed on. "Let's make Crossroads pay for itself, stand on its own two feet. It doesn't have to make millions, just enough to stay comfortable—and pay for a part-time employee. Maybe there's someone you know and trust who could help out here, say nine-to-three or whatever."

"We've never needed to hire anyone, all the way back to when my grandfather ran this store."

"And I appreciate that, Gram, but, first off, bread doesn't cost a nickel anymore. Secondly, there's only you here. We can't compare anything to the old days, unfortunately, but we still have Crossroads and its spirit." She took a breath. All this was wearing on her, and she couldn't imagine how Gram was coping.

"Honest, Gram. Everyone wants you and Crossroads here for years to come. No argument. What I'm saying is that I think there's a way, if we play our cards right and make the most of what's available to us. But turning a profit is absolutely an integral part of the plan."

Gram looked down at her hands in her lap. "What do we need to do?"

That stopped Harper in mid-sip. "Are you in?"

Gram picked up her glass and sent her a helpless smile. "I guess I am."

"Yes!" Harper clinked their glasses together. "We'll send out for pizzas tonight to kick off this campaign." She kissed Gram's cheek. "I love you."

"And I love you, honey. And I love your gumption. No wonder you're such a success at what you do."

"I don't know about that, Gram. All I know is I'm Stella Anderson's granddaughter." She winked and they clinked again. "We have to start by saving in any way we can...like closing on holidays and changing the store hours to eight to eight."

"What?" Gram recoiled as if she'd been slapped.

*Oh, now that was tactful. Shit.*

"Well, some changes—"

"Change the...Harper, our hours are a tradition. Our morning hours, in particular, are some of our busiest. And we *have* to offer coffee and muffins."

"Then, how about just shortening closing hours to eight? How often do we get more than a couple customers after that?"

"Not often, that's true."

"There are some other things we can do, too, such as accepting credit cards. How many sales do you turn away every day because you don't take them?"

"A few."

"The number's a little higher than that, isn't it?" She patted Gram's arm. "We don't have to go crazy with credit, because it's not all that profitable unto itself, but at least customers wouldn't leave empty-handed. It's an easy fix. You'll see."

"Do I have to get rid of the cash register?"

"No way! That's priceless." She was glad to see she'd pleased her with something. "And, as much as we enjoy the coziness of those lanterns on the porch, a brighter, more welcoming entry would help. Something livelier, more inviting—and safer."

"Electric lights?"

"Yes, Gram."

"But not get rid of the railroad lanterns. They've been on that porch since before you were born."

Harper shook her head vigorously. "They belong here, just not as the main lighting source."

"Then that sounds okay." She nodded at the list. "I suppose it is long overdue."

"We should add a little more lighting inside, too—to supplement what's here. And maybe replace the countertops, spruce up the woodwork. Would you like to have the cabinets refinished?"

Gram looked a bit bewildered. She gazed around as if seeing the place for the first time, and Harper feared she, again, had blown her away. A few seconds passed before Gram spoke, and, to Harper's relief, she sounded thoughtful.

"Well, I enjoy the feel, the look of wood, so, yes, I think I'd like that."

"Then, you got it." The heaviness in Harper's heart lifted as Gram's enthusiasm grew. She just wished these improvements had been made years ago, when Gram could have gleaned more from them.

Harper pointed to the last item on her list.

"And we *have* to review the merchandise, Gram, take stock of the stock. Let's get serious about what sells and what just collects dust. Fresh produce is Crossroads' biggest seller, right? So, what if we enlarged the area, got rid of some other stuff to make room?"

"I could tell you right now what people shop for. It depends on the season, you know."

"Well, I didn't think of that. I'm glad you did. You know best. The rolling racks will be great for adjusting space according to the season."

"They were Frankie's idea."

"Smart move by you, Gram, making such a wonderful friend."

"Smarts had nothing to do with it. Frankie's just a love. And I know you see that, too."

"Without a doubt." Harper certainly couldn't afford to think about Frankie right now and avoided Gram's probing eyes. "How about we tackle our merchandise project over the next week or so?"

"Do you think we could afford to redo the floors?"

Harper couldn't hide her surprise. "And take away the antique look of the place? You'd want that?"

"I've been pondering it for a while now. Nothing too severe, mind you, but it would be so nice to see the sun shining off these floors again. Oh," she set a hand on Harper's arm, "is there any chance we could have the outside painted?"

Harper was jubilant. *This will work.*

## Chapter Nineteen

"Honestly, Harper, how are you surviving there?"

"Stop making it sound like prison." Harper sighed as she and Denise walked out of the parking garage and hurried through the rainy Boston nightscape. "Believe it or not, I'm into it. I even sat in on one of the impromptu 'picking sessions' they have on the porch. Didn't sing, of course, but…" she nodded at the memory, "it was good to make music again. I enjoyed it."

"Struggling to picture you on the ol' hay bale, strumming away."

"Stop. It wasn't *that* countrified. Acoustic jams can happen anywhere, and you know it."

"Well, did you break out a Storm tune?"

"No, and the thought never crossed my mind. Weird, huh? It was tough enough, remembering some of those songs they tossed around. God, was I rusty. They change musical eras and genres like you change shoes, but I needed that exercise, the challenge, as much as the escape. I've been a madwoman for over a month."

"Yeah, well, so much for time flying when you're having fun. Your grandmother freakin' kicked you out for the weekend, so she knows you need *something*. And you called your bestie to save your sanity."

"She knows I'm dealing with a lot and wanted me to unwind. Plus, I think she wanted time with Frankie to talk about all the changes."

"And that's another thing. I was looking forward to meeting your farmer. Are you hiding her from me?"

Harper smiled as she opened the restaurant door. She hadn't had much private time with Frankie since the Fourth, but serious kisses in the parking lot at the end of that wild day had her eager for more. And that half-naked moment in her apartment still made her nipples tingle.

"The timing just didn't work out for you two to meet." She followed Denise into the Saturday night revelry at the bar. "You were only there for the day and now we're here."

"Awkward times between you? Did you two flame out already?"

*Quite the opposite.*

Baiting Denise was always fun. "I wouldn't say that, but we know we should at least *try* keeping a lid on things. God knows, it's not easy."

"And that's what your face says right now. So, what's up? Your clock's ticking. You told her you want to get back to Storm and your regular life. Right?"

"Oh, she knows. We just faced facts." Harper shrugged as they settled on stools at the bar. "I knew Gram's situation would be hard, but I never expected this."

Denise squeezed her hand. "You paid the price once before, Harper."

"I know and I'm not going through that again. It was hell for everyone."

Denise eyed her sideways. "Uh-huh."

"God, Denni. It's a tenuous thing and it can't get out of control."

"So, there's a shaky truce? Or have you been *fucking* out of control?"

Harper released a short laugh. "Not *fucking* out of control." She flashed her a sly look. "Not yet."

"Huh?" She leaned back, suddenly aware. "You're going for it, aren't you?"

"I'm a little scared."

"I *knew* there was a 'but' coming!" Harper just grinned into the mirror behind the bar. "You're into her now, aren't you?" Denise leaned against her shoulder. "So, you haven't done it yet? Wait—she fucked you, but you haven't fuck—"

"No. Jesus, Denni. Down, girl."

The bartender arrived and Denise rapidly ordered a mojito and menus. Harper appreciated the interruption, a moment to slow her rising pulse. She asked the bartender for bourbon on the rocks.

A true friend to her core, Denise momentarily let Harper off the hook. "I really like this place," she said, looking around. "Our kind of people. You didn't hit many like this on your tour, at least not the ones you took me to."

Harper always enjoyed the boisterous, primarily female crowd here, a must-do nightspot when Storm played in Boston. But, from where she sat tonight, the dining room appealed like a sanctuary compared to this packed bar area, and she was stricken by the temptation to relax at a table. Just yesterday, it seemed, wouldn't her preferences have been different? Around her now, the chatter and bustle were pronounced and distracting, almost irritating.

An arm suddenly shot between her and Denise, and extended to the bar. A short, curvaceous woman squeezed into the space. "Harper Cushing! I'll be dammed!"

"Vita!" Harper met the welcoming smile of the restaurant manager and completed the hug. "How are you?"

"Freakin' terrific, seeing you! Is Storm in town? What brings you to Boston?" She eyed Harper's crimson silk shirt. "Whatever it is, it sure as hell looks great on you."

"Family business. You're looking pretty slick these days. Business is good, I hope?"

Vita rolled her eyes. "Hey, if only Saturday night could be every night." She waved at the bartender, who had just delivered drinks. "Put those on the house, Merri. Anything these ladies want."

"Thanks, Vita. This is Denise, my partner in crime."

Denise offered a handshake. "Her sister in sin."

Vita shook her hand eagerly. "So, you won't be keeping her out of trouble?"

Denise grinned at Harper. "I've been failing for years."

"Well, you two have a good time tonight." She leaned in and hugged Harper again. "I'm thrilled you stopped by. I expect big things from you, but don't you dare forget us little people." She cupped Harper's cheek and spun off into the crowd.

"She's a dynamo, isn't she?" Denise stirred her drink.

"I don't think she's sat down once since she bought this place eight years ago." Harper sipped her bourbon and smiled. "Rhea and I played here when we were in college and Vita's been a supporter ever since. In fact, she connected me to Sasha."

"Speaking of Sasha, what's the latest since the *Tonight Show*?"

"Actually, I've been avoiding her calls. Our studio is up her butt and she sent paperwork I need to sign a while ago, but I haven't felt like dealing with it. I know I need to get on it."

"Uh-oh. A contract?"

"An addendum."

"For what?"

Harper heaved a sigh. "They're rushing the live album release up to October and want us back on the road through New Year's. The studio's kicking everything off by dropping a song from the album in early September."

"But, shit. Again, through the holidays?"

"Yeah, we'll go into rehearsal after Labor Day."

"Well, at least your voice will be in good shape."

"Yeah. Hopefully, by then, the doctor will give me the green light." She took a long sip of her drink. So much tumbled together in her head, Gram,

Crossroads' renovations, her voice, the holidays, life on the road, leaving…
"Managing the situation with Gram is going to be tricky. There's a lot to get done in a short time."

"Have you two reached an agreement yet, like where she wants to go?"

"She's not going anywhere. She doesn't want to. Hell, nobody wants her to. And she shouldn't have to for quite a while. I'm not going to force her, that's for sure, no matter how much my mother bitches."

"Wow. That's big, Harper. Ballsy. Man, she must be so relieved."

"Yup. She's not too thrilled about having an aide checking on her regularly, but that's part of the deal. We're going to make Crossroads earn its keep. It'll take some upgrades, though, and I'm about to tackle that nightmare."

"How does Frankie feel about that?"

"Well, Gram and I just settled on everything the other day, so I haven't had a chance to talk it all out with her. I figured we would tomorrow. She'll be all-in, I'm sure."

"So, you two don't see each other every day? I thought she was at the store all the time."

"No, not since I arrived. She's backed off a lot, which I do appreciate, because I need to make up for all my lost one-on-one time with Gram. But she flashes in and out, just as busy as I am."

"Have you spent time at her place?"

"We haven't had matching chunks of spare time, but I expect we'll get there."

Denise toyed with her drink and Harper could feel the heavy statement forming in her friend's head. *Yes, I want to "get there." Yes, I know what the calendar says.*

"Harper. It sounds like you're going to get there just in time to leave."

"Remember what I said about tenuous? Yeah. But, damn, it's wild because we…Well, even for a short time."

"I *am* psyched for you, but thank God you're going on tour. It'll be your emergency brake, should you need one." She leaned against Harper's shoulder. "Don't forget: Thelma and Louise had to drive straight off a cliff."

"Yeah, I suppose the tour *will* yank me back, won't it?" Harper kissed her cheek. "I love you for caring."

"Honey, tour will save you from yourself, but what's going to save Frankie?"

Harper straightened on the stool, knowing they'd each wrestled internally before giving in, all too aware that the calendar showed an end date. The absolute last thing she wanted was to kick Frankie or herself in the heart. She didn't have an answer for Denise, though, other than her own decision to walk away. She'd made that decision for Chelsea, too, and it still hurt.

"Girl, losing once before did a number on you, on your music, the band. I mean, of course I want you to be happy, but, shit, Harper, hold onto the reins."

"We're both being careful." *But the feelings are consuming.*

"You're hard-headed, Harper, not hard-hearted. You've always defied the distractions and sometimes you need a kick in the ass to wake up, but when you do, you go deep. For you, giving one hundred percent for the short term is tempting fate—for both of you, really."

Harper signaled the bartender for another round. Sometimes Denise knew her better than she did.

"We're moving on, Denni. I'll be back after tour and more frequently, actually, because of Gram, but our lives are open to change at any time."

"Oh, as if either of you are into playing the field." She snorted. "Until this, that is."

Harper swirled her ice cubes and drank, knowing Denise was right, as usual. She nodded as she lowered her glass to the bar top. It was best to let her continue. She was going to, anyway, and always managed to say what Harper needed to hear.

"Just watch your step, Harper. If this thing with Frankie takes root, remember," she gestured around her, "there's still this. Crowds and parties and red-eye flights, the studio hours and promo gigs, not to mention the lovely concert dates that go on for-freaking-ever."

"Okay, so I know it's rough sometimes."

"Not 'sometimes.' That's your 'normal.' But it's also mind-blowing glorious. *For you guys.* For everybody else, though, for your lover, your partner…"

At least Denise knew to shut up before ruffling the Chelsea debris pile. Thankfully, a short-term romance wouldn't lead to a repeat of that nightmare. Or shouldn't. Besides, Frankie wouldn't be content in Storm's world, anyway, so…

Denise suddenly laughed. "Like I should be the voice of reason? You're slipping, girlfriend. You should've slapped me down a whole paragraph ago. I totally suck at playing therapist." She held up her new drink. "Okay, so let's toast to a successful tour and your pain-in-the-ass vocal cords."

"God, yes." Harper clinked their glasses and drank, relieved to drop that subject. "I sang a little over the Fourth, just a neighborhood party around the fire, but still. It didn't hurt."

"Well, that's great news for you and the tour."

"Definitely. The voice is going to hold up. It better or I'm screwed."

"Oh, big time. Hell. What will you do if it doesn't?"

"Whenever I start thinking about that, I get nauseous. Things *have* to work out, that's all. After a whole summer of healing, if it still gives out?" She shrugged. "I don't know. I mean, what does that say, if it continuously fails me? That I should give it all up?"

"Jesus. You insist on messing with my head." She took a long drink. "Down the road, there's gotta be a way."

"There's surgery but they say that's no guarantee. Or I could lighten up on my material, like if I went solo."

"Oh, now, I can't believe you're even saying this. Solo?"

"I have stuff I wrote a long time ago and I suppose I could go that route if I had to." She chuckled. "Actually, I'd like to write more of that, but my songwriting muse died somewhere."

"So, you'd seriously pack it in and go soft? No. I don't believe it." She flipped her curls away from her face. "Like that would go over big. Sure. I can see it all now…" Reaching out, she spread her hands and read from an invisible marquee. "'Concert tonight: P!nk featuring songs by Bing Crosby.' Yeah, right." She looked hard at Harper. "You okay?"

"No. My brain's going in a million directions."

"No shit."

"Well, not *that* version of 'soft.' A solo guitar is a powerful thing. Think Etheridge or Sheeran or Springsteen, and tell me those acts don't work. All of *that* churns around in my head every so often."

"How long have you had this condition?"

"It's nothing new, Denni, but that one-off on the *Tonight Show* left me a little sore."

"Well, of all songs to do, Harper. 'Send Me Down' is no fucking lullaby. No wonder it did damage."

"Yeah, but I wanted a good test. So, cross your fingers for this tour."

Denise suddenly stiffened. Harper followed her gaze and turned around to a woman in jeans and leather vest and nothing else. Green eyes glinted as the woman smiled and settled a hip against the bar.

"Excuse me, but I have to ask," she said. "You're Harper Cushing, aren't you? From Storm?"

Harper whispered confidentially. "The disguise isn't working, huh?"

"No way! It *is* you! I-I saw Storm when you guys played TD Garden and, God, you fucking blew everyone's doors off."

"Thank you. We love Boston audiences."

The woman scrambled for a cocktail napkin and scribbled in the air at the bartender for a pen. "Just an autograph, please? I don't mean to bother you."

"Let me guess," Harper said, taking the bartender's pen. "Your friends dared you to ask."

"We all went to the Garden that night. In fact, a few of us remember when you played a party at Northeastern. That was some years ago. You guys are even hotter now."

Harper smiled at the compliment as she began to sign. "Thank you. We appreciate that."

"Oh, could you make it out to Carolyn?"

"You bet." *This really doesn't get old.*

"I bought both your albums, you know," Carolyn went on. "When's the next one due?"

"October, they tell me. It's live."

"Excellent. We'll be waiting for it." Carolyn took the autograph in both hands. "Listen, if you're going to be here a while, I, uh, well, maybe you'd feel like dancing later?"

"Thank you, but I'm here with—"

"Oh, right. Sorry. So, maybe a drink then?"

Harper bit back a grin. "We're not staying too long, but thank you for the offer."

Her face coloring, Carolyn nodded and held up the autograph. "Well, thanks so much for this. It's great to meet you. Have a good night."

Denise watched her go. "Was it my job to protect you?"

"You would have failed miserably."

"Carolyn was *very* nice."

"And we're probably ten years older."

"Like that matters."

Harper laughed. "Hey, we have to get food or I'm going to eat this menu."

The bartender committed their orders to memory and winked before hustling away.

"It's nice having everything on the house," Denise said, watching her go.

Harper shook her head. Such gestures were commonplace and commonly accepted, especially after Storm started opening for mega-stars two years ago. Tonight, though, it felt different, far more humbling.

Meanwhile, Denise sighed for effect. "I'd almost forgotten how it feels to be seen with a star."

"God. Please."

Lately, she hadn't been feeling much like Storm's celebrated singer and she hadn't fretted about it one bit. Flattery and recognition had accompanied her for the past two years or so, buoyed her from concert to concert across the country, through countless solitary nights and empty days. How weird, that now, with Storm comfortably riding high, it all felt a little foreign.

She didn't want to drift off into self-analysis, not here at the bar with Denise, but some reminders refused to be ignored. She was, according to one reviewer, Storm's "in-your-face-thrust," but, realistically, for how long? At thirty-six, should she be bracing for a career that wouldn't render her mute? Maybe *Harper Cushing* music deserved more consideration after all, but it sure as hell would cost her.

"Storm's no superstar act, Denni. And, in the grand scheme of things, Harper Cushing's actually pretty obscure."

"Ha. Spare me that shit. You can have any woman you want here tonight, Harper. And you're not allowed to forget your wingman."

"You know I don't play the one-nighter game. The Storm image is complicated enough."

"Not even with a hot butch farmer within your grasp? Maybe you *should* think of it as a string of one-nighters. It might be easier—"

"For an entire summer?"

"A whole summer of one-nighters sure sounds like fun to me."

"Need I point out that a whole summer's worth of the same woman equals a short-term thing?"

"Oh, true. Well, hey," Denise elbowed her, "at least you've moved from fantasizing about her to reality."

Harper brought her drink to her lips. "Oh, it's real, alright."

"I wish you luck, girl, and lots of rolls in the hay…although I think the hay part's disgusting. So, when one of these fine women here tonight slips her number down your pants, you damn well better give it to me."

## CHAPTER TWENTY

Blinding rain forced Frankie to switch her windshield wipers to high and her focus to the dark road. Slowing to a crawl, she preferred to be focused on the great music they had made at Crossroads tonight. Until the skies opened, they had been on a roll and Crossroads regular Donna had even videoed a little of it, intriguing Stella with the notion of posting it on the web.

But Frankie just wished Harper had been among them to share the fun. She'd been gone since midafternoon, off to Boston clubs with her best friend from Chicago, according to Stella, and Frankie couldn't help missing her. She wondered what Harper would think of Tom's idea that they do open mics in the area. When Iman suggested they search out a paid gig, the brainstorming had been inspiring and hard to stop.

"Maybe if the money is good," she said to her empty truck. "Man, could I use that."

She'd been plagued by that issue for a couple of days now. The closer the calendar moved toward harvest, the more anxious she grew about the final yield. Anything less than a stellar return would have her scraping up pennies. "I might *have* to find a real job."

So, when Iman said he "knew a guy" who might hire their little group, the prospect of extra money rang in Frankie's mind like the Crossroads' cash register. Terri had missed tonight's session, stuck at home sick, but they would hash it out when she felt better.

She squinted through the windshield. The forecast hadn't called for this deluge, but she had faith in her regular maintenance efforts. They should weather this wicked storm.

She shut off the music in the truck and listened to the rain pound her roof, the wipers slapping out a rhythm similar to one they had found tonight. How did a band as big-time as Storm work out its set list? She chortled at the thought of Harper worrying about catering to certain audiences' tastes. For her own little group, catering would be critical.

*Gotta please the audience if you want to get invited back.*

Finally, she motored through the lakes that had formed on her dirt driveway and pulled up to the cabin. She dashed onto the porch and shook rain out of her hair as she watched water pour off the roof. Checking the downspouts, she added another chore to her running list: fill in the muddy troughs being made by this fire hose effect.

She straightened with a jolt. *What the hell! Have I been asleep?*

Erosion from the downspouts rammed home her deepest fear about her levees. Reality stung when it was thrown right into your eyes.

She flung open the door, grabbed her slicker off the hook, and raced back to the truck. Tires spun in the soupy gravel as she backed up and shot to the barn, and once inside, she frantically tried to anticipate what she might need.

"Shit! Where was my mind?" She swung a large spotlight's strap over her shoulder, snatched a spare slicker off the wall, and stuffed a bunch of gloves into the pockets. "And…in case I need…" She added a set of chest waders to the load. "God, I hope not."

Hood flying off as she ran to the truck, Frankie threw everything into the passenger area, then ran back. She seized two different shovels and a rake, and jammed as many burlap sandbags as she could into a ten-gallon bucket, then grabbed two dozen more from the stack. She gave up trying to keep her hood on outside and heaved the barn door closed. She dumped her load into the truck bed and jumped into the driver's seat.

"Okay," she said, breathing hard, "fingers crossed."

She swiped back her dripping hair and drove onto the narrow perimeter road, where the terrible visibility demanded her utmost attention. Land on either side dropped off sharply to the bogs, and ahead, where the swamp threatened from one side, she crept along with an eye to the banking's edge.

She stopped to plug in the basketball-size spotlight and set it atop the dash. The mammoth beacon could cut through anything, like acres of sprinklers or this monsoon.

Curving around the hearty sections of old bog, she worried about the patch far ahead that she had fought with not long ago. Was it holding? Had it washed out? If there was trouble, that's where it would be. She aimed the spotlight forward, to the acreage she had planted.

Some three hundred yards on, she gasped and hit the brakes. She thought her heart stopped, too. Already, a lake had formed over a third of her new growth and was expanding fast.

Tears threatened.

"Fuck me." She slapped both hands to her face.

*No. Focus. There's too much to do. Focus. Can I fix it? Don't think, just do.*

Frankie crept along, tensing by the inch as she watched for the spotlight to fall upon the levee break she knew was out there. Finally, it appeared, a ten-foot gap in the road, allowing the swamp free passage onto her fledgling crop.

"Jesus."

She had to stop it. Then drain all the water off, too. Three years of hard work would drown before her eyes—and take her income with it.

She inched closer, stopping a good thirty yards shy of the break, in case the swamp decided to chew up more of the road. Peering through the windshield, she saw it was doing exactly that. Gravel trickled away with the incoming water, widening the gap by the second. At some point, she would need to get a dump truck out here somehow and rebuild the road before she could drive around the bogs again.

*How the hell can I do this? It's beyond me already.*

Resigned to her only option, Frankie jumped out and flung off her slicker in the downpour. She stepped into the chest waders and set the shoulder straps in place before throwing her slicker back on. She didn't like the waders. They were a necessary evil, if you fell and they filled with water. She'd heard plenty of stories about cranberry growers drowning.

*Just get to it, God damn it.*

With spotlight and headlights illuminating the area, she started shoveling all along the road, both sides of the gap, taking what could be spared to fill sandbags. She cursed the width and depth of the old perimeter ditch each time she slid down into hip-deep water and her cloddy boots settled into the mud. Hauling each foot out only added to the strain of carrying bag after bag through the water and lifting them, stacking them against the persistent incoming flow.

Hoodless, splattered with sand and mud, and soaked with sweat inside and rain outside, she shoveled and lugged for more than an hour. Yet to fill half the gap, her back and arms were giving out and she knew she had to get help. With Terri barely recovered from the flu, Frankie reluctantly accepted that she had no choice but to make this call.

Leaning against the truck, her phone tucked beneath her hood, she listened to the ringing on Harper's end of the line. She closed her eyes and tried to relax her joints and muscles. Even breathing was a chore. The phone continued to ring.

*It's almost two in the frigging morning. Please forgive me, Harper.*

"Frankie?" Harper sounded remarkably alert and her voice sent shudders of relief through Frankie's bones. "Frankie? Are you alright? It's two o'clock."

"I'm sorry, Harper. Yes, I-I'm okay, but…Fuck. I've got an emergency here. My bogs…Shit. I can't stop the flood. I've been trying, but—"

"You need help? I'm on the road, about ten minutes out."

"God, thank you. I swear I'll make it up to you somehow. I swear I will. I'm so sorry to ask."

"Just tell me where to go."

"I'll meet you at the barn."

Harper squeezed another element of stress into her brain and this one demanded to be front and center. "Jesus, Frankie. What have you gotten yourself into?"

*What have I?*

She certainly hadn't expected to end a night of clubbing by rendezvousing with Frankie. Not that she wasn't aroused by the idea, but the tromping-through-the-rain aspect did put a damper on things. She'd deposited Denise at her hotel just an hour earlier, survived the tearful send-off, and had almost come to terms with her own challenges.

She slowed at Frankie's mailbox. "At least I can do something for you, for a change." Crawling through the huge puddles on Frankie's road, she wondered what awaited her, wished she wasn't wearing her favorite silk shirt and designer jeans.

Bare light bulbs hanging in the barn helped her spot Frankie's silhouette in the open doorway, and she pulled up close and raced inside.

"Harper."

"I may not be much, Frankie," she said, carefully wiping raindrops from her eyes, thankful for water-proof makeup, "but I'll do what I can."

Now in the bright light, exhaustion and desperation stood out on Frankie's face. Her hair was plastered to her head, her slicker and waders dotted with mud. The compulsion to make it all better tugged at Harper's heart.

"Hi." She wiped a smudge off Frankie's cheek with a fingertip. "If I'm going to look like you soon, I'm in trouble."

Frankie hurried to the hooks on the wall and brought back a slicker and a cotton shirt.

"I could look at you all night. God, if I wasn't…" She glanced down at her own weathered condition and sent Harper an apologetic look. "You take my breath away."

Harper felt her face heat. "A friend came in from Chicago, um, just for the hell of it, and we went out to catch up on old times. I'm afraid I'm not too prepared for…whatever."

Frankie held up the shirt. "As much as yours makes me drool, I'd rather you wear this."

Harper accepted the yellow and green checkered shirt, admittedly grateful. "And now you want me to take mine off."

Frankie rubbed a hand over her face. "Oh, I do, trust me." She glanced around, suddenly shy, and Harper had to grin. "There's a..." Frankie stumbled. "...a pair of boots here, and some gloves. I-I'll go find them." She took off and Harper exchanged expensive silk for well-worn cotton.

The softness was comforting in the damp air and the fresh scent was unexpected. She finished buttoning the front and hung her silk on the wall hook.

"It's clean, by the way," Frankie said, returning with boots she set at Harper's feet. "These might be a little big for you, but they're tall and should keep you dry." She handed her gloves and the slicker. "And you'll need these."

Harper pulled off her dress boots and slid her feet and legs into the high, roomy waders. "Well, I won't be dancing in these, that's for sure, but I'm good." She put the slicker on as Frankie watched and jammed the gloves into the pockets.

"You have no idea how much I appreciate this, Harper. It's going to be tough, messy. Jesus, I hate having you go through—"

"Frankie. If I've learned anything, being back, it's that helping each other is still a way of life here. And, yeah, honestly? This is way the fuck out of my comfort zone, but I'm a big girl and not easily intimidated." She squeezed Frankie's arm, hoping she sounded encouraging—and braver than she felt. "So, let's go."

In seconds, they were creeping through the rain in Frankie's truck. Headlights and the huge spotlight were a godsend. It was black as hell out here and the gravel road atop the levee was barely wide enough for the vehicle. There was no pull-off area available, no way to turn around. To leave, they'd have to back up the entire way.

Harper tamped down her trepidation. It was little comfort, knowing they were hemmed in by low-lying bogs, somewhere out there in the darkness. And farther along, when she spotted swamp water just a few feet from their tires, she had to steady her breathing.

"That's it up there, isn't it? The end of the road."

"It is now, yes."

The skinny road wasn't much to begin with, but it had been fairly secure ground, or at least she'd assumed as much. Up ahead, it was gone. A chasm interrupted the road and swamp water streamed through, creating a turbulent pool on the bogs. An assortment of tools littered the top of the banking where Frankie had left them, and Harper wondered how she'd managed—how *they* would—on hardly any level ground. Then, she realized that this level ground had nothing to do with the problem they needed to address.

"I've got two rows of sandbags across the bottom already," Frankie said, "although you can't see them from here, but I need another six or seven."

"Six or seven *rows*."

Frankie nodded solemnly. "Yeah. I know." She clasped Harper's hand over the console. "Ready?"

Harper flipped up her hood, knowing her hair already was a lost cause. "I'm ready." She gave Frankie's hand a supportive little shake. "Where do we start?"

Frankie lowered her head and kissed Harper's hand. "Come on. I'll show you."

Her head bowed beneath the torrential rain, Harper followed Frankie over the side of the road, and learned about her boots' traction the hard way. Two steps down the steep banking, she slipped and skidded feet-first into several inches of ditch muck. Water splashed up, over the tops of her boots, and soaked her thighs.

"Ohhh, shit, that's cold!"

Frankie immediately put a tall shovel in her hand. "Your walking stick. Can you pull your feet out?"

"They're out," Harper said, finally freeing her second foot from the muddy suction, "as long as my boots come with them." Balanced by the shovel, she plodded to Frankie's side.

"We have to pack the side walls." Frankie pointed to the gap's edges. "Otherwise, it'll keep widening, crumbling, especially when we start blocking up the water." She handed a bag to Harper. "If you hold this on the banking, just above the water, I'll fill it."

Harper set her feet and kept the burlap sack upright as Frankie shoveled in sand, clay, rocks, and anything within reach.

"I dumped extra material along here when I put the new sections in," Frankie said between shovelfuls, "hoping I'd never need it."

"Well, count your blessings, farmer." Harper fought with the bag's growing weight. "Getting heavy." She prayed her musician's muscles could meet this challenge.

"Enough for that one." Frankie speared her shovel upright into the ditch. Together, they carried the bag against the flow to the gap. "Two people make such a difference," Frankie said, smiling as rain pelted her face. "I can't begin to thank you." She nodded toward the target spot. "On three, okay? One, two, three." They swung the bag into place and Harper staggered.

"Damn, there's some force to this water. It's deceiving."

"Pay attention to your steps or it'll knock you down."

"It's all fun and games, right?"

"Yup. Until someone goes swimming in the ditch."

"Yuck." She readied another bag as Frankie retrieved her shovel. "Hey? Wouldn't it be faster if we each filled our own bags?"

Frankie emptied her shovel into Harper's bag. "Sure, but it's trickier."

"Well, I'm game." Harper waded to the second shovel nearby and claimed it. "So, I've got this bag. You get your own."

*A little levity can only help this disaster. As long as I can keep up.*

Harper filled hers first and Frankie helped with the transport. Getting through the turbulence required patient footwork. Each step left only one foot at a time anchored in the muck, hardly stable, and barely a match for what flowed against her legs.

"I gather this edge of the bog is full of berries?" Harper studied the black water around her knees. "I mean, there *is* an edge of a bog right here, somewhere, isn't there?"

Frankie nodded as they went back to shoveling. "The whole place is full of berries, but this general area is probably ruined. Definitely everything immediately around us. With the water pressure and the sheer volume, these berries won't make it."

Harper stopped and stared at her. Frankie just kept shoveling.

"There's no saving them?" She hurried to fill her bag.

"Not these here. Out there, maybe, if I can drain the water off fast enough. But first we have to stop it." She grunted as she stooped to pick up her full bag.

"Don't!" Harper plowed through the water to help. "You're supposed to wait for me." She hefted the other end of the bag, and they dumped it into place.

"It's a catch-22 now," Frankie said, a dozen bags later. She leaned into her shovel and Harper plunked down on the banking, both of them exhausted. Frankie bent backwards, stretching. "Shoring up the sides narrows the gap which increases the water pressure which does more bog damage."

"But the pressure is going to rise, regardless, whether we build up across the bottom or in from the sides." Harper patted herself on the back for the analysis.

"You're exactly right." Frankie grinned. "But at least now, with the walls staying put, we can go like hell *up*."

Harper laughed. "I'd like to see either of us 'go like hell' anywhere right now." She moaned as she rose tenuously on the incline. "But I'll give it a shot."

Harper had no concept of time anymore. She had arrived at two, but it felt like she'd been at this for twenty-four hours and every inch of her agreed. Exertion had soaked through the shirt and forced her to abandon her hood. At least the downpour had diminished to a steady rain, and it felt good, drenching her head and trickling beneath her shirt. Even wet socks didn't bother her, although reliable footing had become a concern.

She straightened her sandbag and took aim with another shovelful, but a misstep tipped her sideways. Her foot slid out from under her.

Yelping as she went down, she saw Frankie high-step toward her in a hurry, but she didn't reach her in time. Harper landed on her side, full length in the ditch. Water flowed over her head and most of her chest, filled an arm of her slicker, her gloves, and both boots. Raising her head and spitting, she saw Frankie slip and land with a hard splash beside her. Again, waves of ditch water sloshed over her face, and she shoved both hands into the muck to push herself upright.

Sitting in water to her breasts, she spit again. "Fuck!" She flung muck off her gloves and dragged them through the water to rinse them. Hair dripped onto her face. "This shit is beyond gross!"

Beside her, Frankie rolled over and fought to rise to her knees. Harper tried to follow suit.

"God damn it, Frankie. Can this suck any worse?"

Her waders bulging from chest to thighs, Frankie tossed away her slicker and peeled the waders down to her hips. Some of the water inside drained out. "I doubt it." She staggered to her feet and pulled Harper up.

Legs and feet still weighed down, they trudged out of the ditch, up the banking, and sat heavily.

Harper shook a boot upside down. "And I thought the rain felt good." She tossed her slicker and gloves onto the weeds next to her. "I might have crap in places I don't want to think about."

"Yeah, me too. At least we were pretty much soaked to begin with." She combed her hair back with both hands and gave her waders one more shake before putting them back on. Harper watched her stand and pull them up, slide her arms through the straps, and set them on her shoulders.

*If I had half your stamina, your determination.*

"Please take a break," Frankie said. "Catch your breath." She tromped back to her half-filled bag and resumed shoveling.

Until now, Harper hadn't given the automatic nature of her assistance a thought. She'd immediately said "sure" and plunged right into this foreign, dark, wet, exhausting project that was such a part of Frankie's life. But she was up to her eyeballs in it now, literally—and felt driven to help. What that said about her and how she felt about Frankie, she would definitely have to assess later. Not right now.

Drenched to the skin, she fumbled into her boots, retrieved her slicker and saturated leather gloves, and hurried back to work.

Renewed diligence helped pass the next hour, as they set bags into the gap, but with each one, Harper begged for strength to do another. In fact, she knew they both were slowing down.

Frankie hadn't said much since their "swim." She just soldiered on, probably numb beneath a thick cloud of anguish. Harper remembered the sobering words about losing a year's income, so this had to be a genuine nightmare.

She looked up when Frankie stopped. Leaning heavily on her shovel, she watched her step back, sink a bit in the muck, and assess the wall they had built. Hours of hard labor finally had grown the barricade of bags to the height of the levee. They had stemmed the tide. It was a wonder Frankie didn't just drop to her knees.

## CHAPTER TWENTY-ONE

Soaked to the skin, Harper laid her head back on the headrest and closed her eyes. She didn't care that a masterful driving exhibition was underway beside her. Somehow, she just knew that Frankie would back up all the way to the barn in virtual darkness without incident. Lucky for them, because straying a few feet off track would be a hell of a lot more *inconvenient* than she cared to consider at the moment.

She internalized her moans because Frankie didn't need to hear that she had reduced Harper to a useless heap. She tried to recall ever feeling this wiped out. Even one of Storm's blistering three-hour shows had never left her this debilitated. The after-burn exhilaration of those shows always overpowered the exhaustion, whereas *this* afterburn just *couldn't possibly suck any more.*

As Frankie drove in silent concentration, Harper's back and shoulders ached, and her hands throbbed. Her arms and thighs felt too long, stretched beyond their bones, rubbery and hard to control, and her hips had begun a torment that was bound to last for days.

She envisioned the glorious shower awaiting her in her apartment. Maybe she'd just go in clothes and all. She wouldn't have the strength to take them off anyway. She would probably have to sit and let the water do what her arms and hands couldn't. But first, she had to drive home.

"Come on in," Frankie said, parking beside Harper's Audi. "A shower will feel good, and I'll get you some sweats to throw on."

Considering she was a total mess, Harper was sorely tempted. "That's okay, Frankie. I'll just head home. It's only a few minutes down the road. Thank you, though. You need to—"

"I'll live. You're my hero and you're dead on your feet." She waved her out of the truck. "Come on."

Harper's reservations mounted as she followed Frankie into her cabin for the first time. The last thing she needed was doubt about her own wobbly self-control, and having Frankie find her naked and melted like Jell-O on the shower floor.

At the flick of a switch, the cabin's open floor plan greeted Harper with a cozy kitchen/living room combination that invited her to collapse anywhere. The pale rose-colored walls were highlighted by soft gray woodwork, and a leather couch and recliner beckoned near the fireplace.

Frankie set two shot glasses on the kitchen table and rummaged through a driftwood cupboard until she produced bottles of tequila, Grey Goose, and Johnnie Walker Black.

"Not sure of your preference," she said and shoved her disheveled hair back, "but you're welcome to choose your poison." She turned to the fridge and spun back with juice. "Cranberry, of course. As a chaser." She brought over two juice glasses, then poured tequila for herself and downed it. "I'll get you something to put on."

"Please, Frankie," she tried as Frankie rushed off. "Don't fuss."

*Where the hell are you finding this energy?*

"No fuss," Frankie yelled from down the side hall.

She *was* fussing and Harper was touched as she stood, looking around. She wasn't about to sit, even if her ass was dry, because she probably wouldn't be able to get up again, but a short blast of something on the table could help. She was wrangling some Johnny Walker Black down her throat when Frankie appeared with a bundle of clothes.

"Whatever fits best. A couple of T-shirts and pairs of sweats, some socks. I'll put them in the bathroom. It's…It's right here." She disappeared again and came back, empty-handed and looking relieved. "You. Go." She pointed to the hall. "Just sing out if you need anything. Oh, well, not *sing*, but…you know…"

Harper moved as directed but hesitated in front of her and placed a palm on her chest. The drenched T-shirt clung to her like a second skin, and Harper couldn't tell if she or Frankie smelled more like ditch water. What mattered most, though, was the trauma in Frankie's eyes.

"Thank you. I wish you'd sit and try to unwind."

Frankie rubbed her eyes. "If I sit, I'll think, and I'm not up for that."

"We did all we could, Frankie. Rest is important now. Maybe things will look better in the light of day." Frankie tilted her head slightly, as if she doubted that statement, and Harper desperately wanted to distract her, take her mind off the heavy subject. She patted her chest. "I'm getting in the shower. If I'm not back by tomorrow, please don't worry."

She was pleased to see Frankie's harried look fade slightly. The weak smile said she might relax soon.

"I think you'll find everything you need. I don't have company often, so I suppose I'm out of practice."

"Chill, please. Now, go, sit."

Harper closed the bathroom door behind her and gazed with surprise at the spa-like world. Frankie had created a luxurious retreat, a woodsy décor of deep greens and bronze, hanging plants, elaborate tile work, and ultra-modern fixtures. The spacious glass-walled shower offered a teak bench and five glistening showerheads at varying levels.

Somehow, Harper found herself standing naked in the barrage of hot water. Snippets of leaves, bits of twigs, and trails of black water flowed off her skin, and her muscles flexed with gratitude. The scent of Frankie's fruity shampoo made her grin inwardly, and the lavender body wash almost relaxed her too much. The thought of Frankie sparing her the effort of washing led her mind dangerously astray.

As she dressed, she wondered if she would be invited to stay. The sun *was* about to rise. She stopped, hand on the doorknob, unsure if she'd accept. Yes, she could feel Frankie's strength wrapped around her, kisses and hands where she needed them most. Going to bed with Frankie would be… She took a breath. Not tonight. But everything about tonight had been so surreal, a night like no other, so one night…

"Jesus, I'm driving myself crazy." She straightened her hair, collected her wet clothes, and went out to thank Frankie again.

She found her sound asleep, head on her folded arms on the table.

Harper set her pile of clothes by the door and quietly walked back to her.

"Frankie?" she whispered. She laid an arm across the wet shoulders and gave her a little squeeze. "You can't sleep like this." She stroked strings of Frankie's hair from her cheek. "Hey," she tried at Frankie's ear. "You need to shower and go to bed."

Frankie groaned but didn't move.

"Come on, farmer." She rocked her gently by the shoulders. "Frankie. Sweetie."

Finally, Frankie's head turned. She lifted it slowly, as if against her will, and blinked. "Huh?" She sat up abruptly. "Oh. God, I went right out. I'm sorry." She scrubbed at her eyes.

"Don't apologize. It's your turn in that amazing shower of yours, then you're going to bed."

Still blinking, Frankie hurried to her feet. "I didn't mean…After all I put you through—"

"Stop. I survived. Look, I'm all squeaky clean now."

"No." Frankie shook her head, insistently. "It was a lot. I was in your shoes once, a long time ago, so I know."

"Y'mean my soggy boots?" Harper wanted to lift her spirit somehow.

"Yeah. Soggy everything."

"But we did it, Frankie." She set a hand on her shoulder. "I'm sure you did, too, back then." She watched Frankie's eyes grow distant, her attention shift to the alcohol on the table. "Back then, did you do it alone?"

"Ancient history." She poured herself another shot of tequila. "What matters—"

"No way. You could *not* have done what we just did by yourself."

"Well, she figured I could handle it." Frankie downed the shot and coughed at the burn. "She was busy with other stuff. It was just a rough night because I was a rookie, that's all."

"So, she…your partner? She just what? Took off and left you to it?" Harper bristled at the scenario. Something told her it had been one of many rough nights.

"She had to fix the generator because we needed a pump. Oh, I tried to be her knight in shining armor, you know?" She grinned feebly. "Shit, I was clueless. It was just one of those times when you paid the price for not knowing what you didn't know."

Frankie's old nightmare was kicking her while she was down, and she was *still* hoping someone would understand.

"What *I* know is that you've been a 'giver' for a long time and 'givers' deserve to be happy."

Frankie snickered. "Eh. Lessons learned."

"Yeah, true, but that's not always a bad thing. Look at all you've done on your own, Frankie. I'm glad you called me, glad I could help."

Frankie gazed at her for an extra second, as if for the first time, as if to assure herself Harper was real. She reached out and tucked strands of Harper's wet hair behind her ear.

"You didn't just help, Harper. You showed up like an angel of mercy." She managed a pained little grin. "Nothing like a shit-show tour of my world, huh?"

"Sh." Harper cupped her cheek. "I want you to rest. I'm heading home. We'll talk tomorrow…or, actually, later today. Okay?" She wished she could erase the defeat in her eyes.

Frankie's skin was cold, gritty in her palm, and Harper was sorely tempted to lead her into the shower and restore warmth and vigor to that body she admired. But she wasn't about to disrespect Frankie's worries with intimate suggestions.

She drew Frankie's chin closer and kissed her softly. "Now, please. No more thinking until you've slept." She inched back and smiled. "First, though, get in the shower. You stink."

❖

Frankie saw Terri strolling toward her from the barn but needed to slide one last board down into the pond's sluiceway. She had to block this flow of water—before she died like some lithium battery.

"Hey, Frankie. How's it going?" Terri looked down at her from the pump house, healthy and rested, hands in her pockets, not a care in the world. Frankie wanted to throw something at her.

Straddling the sluiceway's cement sides, she backhanded sweat and hair off her forehead and squinted up at her. "Just your typical morning workout."

"Wow. The pond's wicked full. Did last night's rain do that? How'd you make out?"

Frankie used a hammer to pound the board down into its slot. The remaining water draining off the bogs now would be redirected into the creek, which emptied back into the lower end of the swamp. If she could muster one last ounce of energy, arranging that would be her next project. *These days, every damn thing is about choosing which way to go.*

She hauled herself up the banking and sat on the ground near Terri's feet, counting on the sun's heat to keep her muscles from seizing up.

"Last night was a fucking nightmare."

"Oh, no. No wonder you look like hell. How long have you been at this?"

"What time is it?"

"A little after ten."

"About four hours."

"Did you sleep, for God's sake?" Terri squatted beside her. "What happened?"

Frankie gestured over her shoulder toward the bogs. "The swamp got in. A break in the levee flooded nine sections."

"Aw, shit! The new ones?"

Frankie nodded. "If I ever see another sandbag, another shovel…I could hardly pour my coffee this morning."

"Damn. You shoveled and stacked all night?"

"Harper helped me. I had to call her."

"What? On the bogs? In the rain?"

"Be thankful you've been sick. I would've called you at two o'clock."

"Holy crap. How'd she do?"

"She was beyond amazing. Both of us fell in, too." Frankie shook her head, still hating that she'd put Harper through all that. "She toughed it out. Fucking amazing."

"Well, that's a sight I would've paid to see. How is she this morning?"

"I don't know. I hope she's still sleeping."

"Here?"

Frankie eyed her sideways. "She showered and went home."

"Damn."

Frankie threw a rock into the pond. "Hell, after last night? She'll probably book a flight back to LA when she wakes up."

"That would suck, Frankie."

"Yeah, well…" She stood with effort and stretched her back. She really didn't want to think about it at the moment. She was depressed enough. "I had to get back out here and get this water running off. I lost the bloom on seven sections. It's hard, watching cash float away."

Terri shuffled in place, obviously not knowing what to say. "This runoff should help, though, right? It's a good thing?"

Frankie nodded. "Getting the water off should save the rest. This is as much as the pond can hold, though, so I'm sending the rest back to the swamp."

"Anything I can do? How much sleep did you get? Or did you get any?"

"I don't know. After I showered, I was in the recliner for a while, maybe an hour." She stared at the pond until she realized she was sleeping with her eyes open. She picked up her hammer. "Thanks for the offer, but you're just getting over that bug, so you're not allowed to help."

She started toward the creek at the back end of her property and Terri followed.

"It hit me pretty hard, I have to admit," Terri said. "Ginny booted me out this morning, said it was time I saw daylight. How was the jam last night, before all this, that is?"

Frankie chuckled. All that fun had washed away long ago.

"Good, but we missed you. Iman said he knows somebody who might hire us for real money—if we dare."

"Hey, now that would be cool."

"I was going to call you this morning to talk about it." She stopped them at the property line, prepared to play traffic cop with the draining water. "Later today, okay? I have to tend to this before it backs up."

"So…the damage is bad, huh?"

"Yeah. The closest sections were really under. This is the water, still coming off but not fast enough. I know they'll just be mush." She'd been seeing negative return figures in her head since last night. "I might need to pursue that gig thing, just to make ends meet."

"It's early, Frankie. The damage might not be so bad after all. But, we'll talk more about gigging. Hey, Harper might get a kick out of you in a band. You'd have that in common."

"Oh, right. As if we'd compare to Storm."

"Well, you know what I'm saying." Terri kicked the dirt around. "I stopped at Crossroads earlier and traded my green beans and tomatoes for muffins. Didn't see Harper around so I filled a couple of bins for Stella. It's tough, seeing her fight that arthritis more each day."

"I know and it's not just her hands and shoulders. Her knees bother her, too. I don't know how she manages, but she does."

"Is Harper still going ahead with relocating her like you said? With the price hikes she's made, it looks like she wants to sell the place."

"As far as I know, that's the plan. It's hard to talk about it at length, so we haven't. Not yet, anyway. I'd like to know if Stella's on board with whatever Harper's planning."

"You should call Harper."

"I'll get to that eventually. Right now…"

"Stella said Harper should invite you to dinner, there's stuff you two need to talk about."

"Really."

"She wants Harper to call you. You got your phone?"

"Eh, in the house. I forgot it. Harper's not calling right this minute."

"Well, it's not smart to be out here alone with no way to get help—or to reach or *be reached by* the hottest woman you've ever had in your life."

"Jesus, will you stop? I'll call her, okay? I want to talk to her, too."

"About selling?"

"And about keeping Stella happy. I don't really think Harper would just do her own thing, but Stella still deserves to participate in it."

"Is she *not* participating?"

"That's why I want to talk with them."

"Careful, Frankie. Don't freak out if Harper tells you to mind your own damn business." She adjusted her Stetson and crossed her arms. "That dinner-with-Harper thing is starting to make sense. Have dinner before you talk, before she kicks you out."

"I doubt she'd do that. I *do* see her point, you know. I'm not blind. But inside, I can't bring myself to agree."

"She doesn't need you to agree with her. She already holds all those cards. My guess is she wants you on her side for Stella's sake—and hers, too, 'cause, well, she's into you. I just know it."

"Uh-huh. And I'm on both their sides. But, damn, these decisions… Stella moving, Crossroads being sold, Harper going back to LA…"

"But, things between you two are good, even after last night?"

Frankie stretched her back again and laughed lightly. "Yeah, they're very good. I just wish I didn't have this mess on my hands now. It's going to take time away from us."

"What was that? There's an 'us'? What have I missed?"

"We've let the guard down, you could say."

"Really? Hallelujah!" Terri clapped Frankie's back. "You really didn't let her get away last night, did you?"

"Timing is everything and last night sucked all around."

"So…you haven't, um…"

"I have to focus on this, Terri. We're doing the one-day-at-a-time thing."

"But she's not going to be here forever." Frankie flashed her a severe glance and Terri briefly turned away. "Sorry. But you *are* going to call her today."

"Yes, I'll call her. Jesus. You're impossible."

"Excellent. Your spirit will thank me." She waved as she walked away. "Okay. I'm out. My work here is done."

Frankie watched after her, too exhausted to yell a clever response.

## CHAPTER TWENTY-TWO

Gram adjusted her clip-on earrings in her bathroom mirror, bemoaning her difficulties handling "those frustrating little pierced-ear ones." Harper hovered in the doorway and continued their conversation via their reflections. She didn't want to nag, but she was far more concerned about this shopping trip Gram was taking with her old friend.

"Harper. I wish you wouldn't worry so much. I have my routine. I'll have the shopping cart to lean on. And we're only going for a couple of hours. Now, tell me why Frankie is coming tomorrow instead of this evening?"

"Because she's exhausted. She got almost no sleep last night and was back out there right after the sun came up. She apologized but said she'd feel up to it tomorrow."

"Oh. Hang on a minute." Gram hurried off to her bedroom and returned with Harper's red silk shirt and dress boots from last night. "*Someone* was thinking of you very early this morning. I found them on your steps."

Harper accepted them humbly, her mind instantly back in the barn, half naked at Frankie's command. The fact that Frankie had delivered her clothes, had thought of her in the midst of her own nightmare, said so much about her.

Gram took Harper's arms. "I'm so proud of you, you know, doing what you did for her, even if you did sleep half the day away."

"I can't say I'd look forward to doing it again, because it was beyond exhausting and *so* gross, but I don't regret doing it for a second. She's pretty devastated."

"Well, I'm glad it was you. I'm sure she is, too." She kissed Harper's cheek. "I love you."

Harper hugged her. "And I love you. Now, you won't be too long, will you? I know you, Mrs. Anderson. You'll...What do you call it? You'll 'lollygag' over every little thing."

Gram pushed her away playfully. "Oh, stop. I need ingredients for my cookies and that cheesecake I want to try. Oh, and a new springform pan."

Excited about her excursion, Gram hurried down the hall to wait on the front porch.

"Gram, be honest. Is Mrs. Gaffigan *really* a good driver?"

"She's only eighty, Harper." Gram pushed through the screen door and, as usual, scowled at the cowbell. "I'd still be driving if my reflexes hadn't gone dull on me."

"No doubt. Do you have your phone?"

"Yes, now stop worrying. Here she is."

Harper waved from the porch as they left. Now, she tried to decide which of her many life-altering issues to worry about—in addition to Gram out in the wild world with Mrs. Gaffigan.

Alone now, Harper allowed the quiet and warmth of the afternoon to soothe her mind and body. An unexpected temptation rose from within, a melody's call to grab her guitar, and she decided to play, once she had Crossroads in order. The urge really wasn't all that unusual, but thinking of gentle, lighthearted tunes definitely was. Knowing that Storm's music hardly fit that bill, she ran through a mental list of other artists while she dead-headed Gram's geraniums.

She grinned as images of tiny white cranberry blossoms came to mind. "Hey, Ms. Cosgrove. Maybe you should teach me some John Prine."

Her phone chirped with a text and snapped her consciousness back in line.

*STOP avoiding me*, Sasha wrote, and Harper dropped onto a stool. *Need signature PRONTO. Sending doc for e-sig. Acknowledge, PLS!*

Harper leaned back against the building and stared out at the parking lot. She'd received the initial paperwork shortly after arriving here and had read it with disengaged attention. Today, she felt more disengaged than ever.

But, as she'd told Denise, there was no avoiding it. Not that she *didn't* want to rejoin her Storm family, but even she could see that she wasn't jumping to make it happen. And she wasn't sure why.

In September, Storm would reunite for rehearsals at Rhea's house in New Jersey, roughly two months from now, which hopefully was enough time to accomplish all she needed for Gram and Crossroads. And maybe way too much time for this growing attachment to Frankie.

She needed to squeeze an awful lot into what remained of her hiatus from Storm. She had to get options for Gram about home aides, find out exactly what that person could do and how she or he would be paid. The store's renovation projects required quotes and scheduling, and decisions about materials. She couldn't spare any of that time on herself, on something as trivial as a summer "thing."

At least she and Gram had eliminated the relocation issue, and that was a massive relief for both of them. And, as long as Crossroads could turn a sufficient profit, there would be no need to worry about selling. Having those matters off her plate made tackling the other tasks less formidable and the breathing room was invaluable.

Pulling all this off in just over two months might take a miracle, but she owed Gram that much. She reminded herself that she'd offered Gram this solution, so she had damn well better be here to see it through. For Gram, and, admittedly, for a little more quality time with Frankie. And for herself. She couldn't dismiss that surprising desire. She *needed* to be here, *wanted* to be.

*That's where the hesitancy's coming from.*

Gazing around the porch, she acknowledged that this deep-rooted connection she'd foolishly abandoned many years ago had snuck up on her in grown-up proportion. It really wasn't a surprise. She'd seen the signs, felt them. Since her arrival in early June, nostalgic fondness had been blossoming into something far more vital, a comfortable, *livable* place to be herself, a place her heart was happy.

A lifeline she shouldn't release.

"God help me figure all this out."

She remembered the phone in her hand. She brought up Sasha's text, sighed at it, and sent back a teary-faced emoji, apologizing for her delay. Then, resigned, she scanned the contract addendum. *There's no choice, so just do it.* She signed the document electronically and hit "Send."

Back inside, she put an oldies record on Gram's little stereo and began sweeping. She willingly lost herself in the memory of Frankie's appearance that first day, and sang along to "Old Cape Cod," although her own voice didn't resonate the way Frankie's had. But it didn't sound like a pathetic impersonation of Janis Joplin either, so she was heartened to hear that some of her own vocal quality had returned.

A vehicle's door slammed out front and a young delivery man clanged his way inside, the vase he carried bursting with yellow roses. A single red rose sat centered among them, and a single name sprang to mind.

"Harper Cushing?"

"Hi." She accepted the vase reverently. "Wow, they're gorgeous."

He bobbed his head. "Have a nice day, ma'am." He pivoted and was out the door.

"Thank you so much!"

As captivated by the flowers as by the gesture itself, she set the vase on the counter and opened the attached card. The trembling in her fingers almost made her blush.

*"Harper. For saving my sanity, for helping keep my dream alive, for giving so much of yourself. Above all, for being so very special. Thank you. Frankie."*

Her heartbeat kicked up as she set the card among the leaves. She pressed her face to the blossoms and inhaled. "You're pretty special, too."

She pulled out her phone to call her, but the cowbell clanged again.

"Joe. Good to see you."

"Same here. Those are pretty."

"Thank you. Yes, they certainly are."

She watched him wander the aisles aimlessly and hoped he was just preoccupied. According to Gram, Joe managed well on his own since his wife passed. Daughter Karen checked in daily and, as Harper had learned, his banjo kept him sharp. A friend of her grandparents for as long as she could remember, Joe could walk around Crossroads blindfolded and know where everything was.

But now, he combed the aisles at length as Harper waited. When all he ultimately brought to the counter was a loaf of bread, she knew his mind had been elsewhere.

"We have two muffins left, Joe. Good with coffee later tonight. They have…Let me see." She lifted the glass dome and gave the muffins a closer look. "Yup. Your name's on one and Karen's is on the other."

"Sure, why not," he said, and took a newspaper from the rack nearby. "That daughter of mine wants me to stop buying the paper and use my phone." He made a sour face. "You believe that? Well, heh. That ain't happening. And those muffins will be good for watching the ballgame tonight."

She wrapped them in waxed paper and put them in a small bag as he looked around, distracted. Whatever he had on his mind was bound to come out eventually. She pressed the cash register's metal keys and rang up his purchases, and the noise brought him around.

He squared his shoulders and his orange VFW T-shirt tightened across his shallow chest. He was ready to speak.

"I have to say, nobody's too happy about your new prices. Bet Stella isn't either."

"I understand and we agree with you," she said, making change from the drawer, "but Crossroads really needs a boost, Joe. It was a painful decision, truly. Times are hard for everyone these days. I'm sure you feel it."

"Oh, we all do, but I hope there's no more coming." His eyes went from the money Harper put into his palm directly up to hers. "Is Crossroads going to be sold?"

Harper's throat jammed. She didn't know where to begin.

"Geez, Joe. Gram can't hang onto it forever, now, can she?" She hiked a shoulder. "So, yeah. Eventually."

He frowned hard. "What the hell's that mean, 'eventually'?"

"Without Gram, Crossroads will go on the market."

"Y'mean when she dies?" He slapped both palms to the counter. "Is she sick?"

"That isn't—"

"I didn't know she was sick. How come I didn't know? She never said anything." He shook his head. "Damn. Proud woman, she is."

"Joe—"

"She never complains, you know, keeps everything to herself. Old-fashioned girl, bless her. And stubborn, too. Can you tell me what's wrong? Is there anything I can do?"

Harper rounded the counter and took him by the shoulders.

"Slow down, Joe." She sent her most reassuring smile into his wide-eyed worry. "Gram is fine. She's not sick." She patted his shoulders with both hands and saw relief sweep through him. "Come on, now. I'll walk you out."

She led him onto the porch, and he moseyed along, as if in a daze.

"You had me scared for a minute there," he said.

"I'm sorry. You panicked on me." She poked his arm. "Do you think Gram would keep any such news from *you*?" She laughed. "Rest assured, if Crossroads was going on the market, you'd be among the first to know. Please have no doubt."

He nodded, apparently satisfied. "Okay. That's good to hear." He went to his old Ford wagon and opened the door.

"Hey, remember," Harper added, "one of those muffins is for Karen."

"Ha. She'll have to find it, first."

She waved a hand at him in feigned disgust, and he chuckled as he drove off.

Harper returned to the counter and leaned on it with both arms. Changes to the store obviously had started the regulars talking. She couldn't reveal how close it was to failing, that was private, but everyone cared so much. Her plan *had* to succeed. If she accomplished anything this summer, it would be what was right for Gram.

Her phone rang on the counter. A contractor she had been trying to reach was returning her call and she took it as a sign that things would move in the right direction. She leaped at the chance to start the process.

"I was on the phone all morning, too," Frankie said, moving from her kitchen to the recliner. She shifted her phone to her other hand and relaxed into Harper's much-needed voice. "Looks like I won't be getting the loan I need, not when all I can show is 'potential' yield." She snickered. "And the flood's probably killed some of that."

"The loan for that machine you talked about?"

"Yeah. It was just a small loader, secondhand from a grower who's upgrading, but when you're a first timer…"

"Listen, 'first timer,' what you've done is mind-blowing, so give yourself a break. How are you doing, really? Did you get the damage estimate yet?"

"Not yet. Someone from my co-op will come soon and assess my crop. I know it's not going to be good news."

"Maybe it won't be as big a loss as it seemed that night."

"Thanks to you, maybe not. I needed the time to calm down, get my shit together, and wait for the facts. I can't be crying over finances without the facts."

"Well, something very beautiful is brightening my days, I'd like you to know. There are some absolutely spectacular roses beaming at me right now. Thank you, Frankie. I just love them and the sunshine they bring to the room. But, honestly, you did *not* have to do this."

"You're welcome. And I did have to. And right away. Not very original, I know, but it was the one thing my frazzled brain could handle. I owe you so much more."

"No, you don't owe me a thing. God, I owe *you* for all you do here, for Gram."

"Can I at least buy you a new pair of jeans?"

Harper laughed. "No."

"I love hearing your smile as much as seeing it. I'm glad the roses are doing their job." She took a breath. "What have you been up to on this misty, ugly day?" She pictured Crossroads and both apartments washed and spit-polished by now. Harper probably had little else to do, except maybe play her guitar or finalize changes that Frankie wanted—and didn't want—to think about.

"Just getting things ready for dinner later. You'll be here, won't you?"

"Absolutely."

"Good. Gram already made a chocolate cheesecake. First time with this recipe and she's excited for us to try it."

"I swear she wants me to gain weight."

"No, she loves you just as you are, but she does love to feed you."

Frankie was touched, but the thought of all this "family stuff" coming to an end made her retreat deeper into the recliner. "She's something else, Harper."

"Believe me, I know. When her mind's set on something, she doesn't let it go. She never ceases to amaze me, although sometimes I think she overdoes it." Frankie had to smile, hearing that Harper had learned what she already knew so well. "Like our dinner, later," Harper continued. "She likes it when we cook together, but she wants to do so much herself."

"It's what she's used to."

"And I really don't think it's a matter of pride or anything. To her, it's fun. She's oblivious to the fact that she's running herself ragged."

"But it keeps her young, Harper."

"I think so, too. Right now, she's taking a nap."

"At least she knows when she needs one."

"Yes, I've noticed that, too. I haven't had to nag. Listen, why don't you come over now?"

"Now?"

"Yeah, if you're not busy. Hell, we're five minutes apart and we're on the phone? Besides, the store's pretty quiet this afternoon and if I do any more 'housekeeping,' I'll scream. And I'm not allowed to do that, so…"

The concept of quiet time with Harper brought Frankie to her feet. "Um…Sure."

"Because why are we on the phone when we could be face-to-face?"

*Face-to-face. Yes, please.*

"Let me get dressed and go out and lock everything up. Twenty min—"

"You aren't dressed?"

"Well—"

"Damn, you're killing me, Cosgrove."

"I like that."

"Give it up. What are you wearing?"

Frankie grinned into the phone. "Nothing that suits *that* tone of voice."

"Oh, really? And what tone is that?"

"Storm's lead singer is very seductive on the phone."

"Is she? She'll have to use it, next time she's on stage. She'll definitely have to call you more often."

"You better stop or I'll have to take care of some business before I leave."

"If you were here, I could…lend a hand with that."

"Bye."

She heard Harper laughing as she ended the call. That creamy voice flowed through Frankie's brain and coated her throat until she could taste Harper on her tongue. Even in the shower, the delicious sound played like a smooth, low-lying background for notes that begged to lead, like decisions, family stuff, and taking care of "business."

*And I'm supposed to switch this off when she leaves? When Stella and Crossroads and the summer are gone?*

Sliding the barn door shut, she eyed her picking machines inside, lined up and awaiting her call to action. "Harvest will save me, I hope." Who knew what October would bring, but she counted on every last berry, every day's decent weather to recoup every cent—and every stray dream that most likely would torment her heart. *Harvest's reality check will do me good.*

## CHAPTER TWENTY-THREE

The empty Crossroads parking lot bothered Frankie more than ever. It tempered the high she'd been clinging to since Harper's call. *So many decisions looming.* She wished she'd found a few customers at the store. Lately, she could use all the congeniality, the positivity she could get, but the empty porch looked beleaguered, too.

She parked around back and was headed for the door when she heard the guitar. Rapid chord changes on emphatic strumming stopped her on the steps. The beat was forceful, and the melody dramatic.

She looked up at the apartment window, as if she could see the source. Then, Harper's voice cut into a split-second pause, riding the beat hard, and sent conflicting emotions swirling through Frankie's head. There didn't seem to be anything impeding those vocal cords anymore, which was great, but it just made Harper's departure feel imminent.

She stepped inside, saw Gram's apartment door closed and went to the stairway. The door at the top was closed, too, but Harper's performance powered through it.

About to knock, Frankie caught herself when the music abruptly stopped.

"Shit," Harper said, and Frankie almost laughed. She could relate to an aggravating note or lyric jerking momentum to a halt.

She didn't want to knock now, and leaned against the stairway wall. Eavesdropping was rude, but eavesdropping on Harper in musician mode was a treat she couldn't resist.

Harper plucked out a quiet, ponderous melody in a higher key. Her precision drew a lighter, golden tone from her guitar, far sweeter than what she'd just driven out the window. Then, a familiar chord progression brought Frankie upright on the top step and she set her ear to the door.

Hearing her own reworked version of "Send Me Down" came as a shock. Only once had she ever played it for anyone, just that night on the porch. Harper must have overheard it and, obviously, remembered it—and liked it.

Frankie listened hard as Harper performed the song. Stopping occasionally to find a chord she preferred, Harper worked through the entire piece and finished on a single, glittering note.

Frankie blew out a breath. *Wow.* She had to collect herself. She backed halfway down the stairs and knocked on the wall.

"Anybody home?"

Harper swung the door open, and Frankie took a moment to appreciate the tight T-shirt and shorts, how the guitar standing at Harper's side paralleled those toned, perfect legs.

"Hey, you." Harper waved her in. "Come on up."

"Hi." Frankie climbed the steps again.

"Gram's still sleeping."

Harper set the guitar into its opened case on the couch and Frankie nearly drooled at the expensive custom instrument. She admired the roses on the coffee table, too, impressed by the florist's arrangement and ridiculously pleased that Harper had brought them into her personal space.

Harper gently gripped Frankie's bicep. "I'm happy you're here."

The warmth in Harper's voice, her hand, her expression buoyed Frankie's spirit like nothing ever had before. The weight of "looming decisions" dissipated and her breathing grew short.

She didn't know if she was about to be kissed or if she should kiss Harper or if she should just go for it and sweep her off her feet. Harper resolved that quandary perfectly by taking Frankie's face in her hands, a new, heavenly habit Frankie had started to crave.

"It feels good to be with you," she whispered, letting Harper draw her head down. She closed her eyes at the plush feel of Harper's lips, slid her arms around her fully, and surrendered to the swirling inside as Harper weakened against her body. "I love the feel of you in my arms, in my hands."

Harper leaned back, toying with Frankie's hair. "Getting carried away is so easy, it's scary."

"Very," Frankie said, a breath from Harper's mouth.

"I want to tell you some stuff, so…we can't."

"We can't?"

"Not just yet." Harper kissed her lightly. "I have important news I hope you'll like, so we have to talk. I need to share before you turn me inside out."

"But I want what's inside." She fitted Harper's hips to hers and set their foreheads together, pushed "news" out of her mind. "I like this."

Harper sent her a sly grin and stepped out of her arms. "Honey, trust me. I like it, too." She backed up an extra step, shaking her head. "Man, you're hard to resist. Please sit." She shoved a hand through her hair. "Over there, or I won't be able to think."

Frankie didn't see herself as irresistible in the slightest but had no problem reveling in Harper's opinion. But hearing that Harper had news, important enough to pull the plug on hard-charging romantic intent, well, that just twisted her insides into an excruciating knot. Suddenly finding herself standing weak-kneed as Harper moved to the couch, she obediently sat in the upholstered chair.

"We've made some decisions." Harper rubbed her palms on her thighs.

Frankie gripped the armrests, hoping her composure would hold up beneath roiling desire and whatever Harper was about to announce. "Decisions about everything here?"

Harper nodded, then her eyebrows rose expectantly, as if she was about to high dive into the unknown and didn't know if she should. "Gram's staying, Frankie. We're going to work it out."

"Really?" Frankie lurched forward and slapped her palms together. "Hooray for Stella! This is…This is excellent!"

"We're arranging for a home aide to visit several times a week, and we hope to hire Donna to work here part-time."

"Donna? What a great choice! She's a regular here, familiar with Crossroads. Plus, Stella loves her company."

"I think she'll be good for Gram, and Crossroads should benefit from her interest in business, her schooling. I haven't thought it through yet, but I'm considering offering her this apartment in lieu of some salary."

"Wow. I like it." Frankie stood and paced to the kitchen and back. "What a deal, even though Crossroads could use the full rent."

"I'm going to bankroll this for Gram to get things started."

"God, Harper, that's awes—"

"But Crossroads needs to step up, Frankie, *more* than cover expenses. So, there'll have to be some changes made, upgrades and such. The place *has* to start showing a decent profit. That's as much a part of the plan as Gram accepting a visiting aide."

"Yeah. You're right. She's really on board with all this?"

"She is. Believe it or not, she's excited."

"Holy…" Frankie stared down at Harper in amazement. "Who are you, Wonder Woman?"

Harper laughed. "Oh, yeah, as if my nerves aren't shot to hell. She didn't cry, didn't argue. We talked it out like teammates. She even said I deserved a gold star on my forehead."

Frankie urged her up and into a hug. "I'm as happy for you as I am for her. This is the best news I've heard in a long time."

"You have no idea how much of a relief it is, knowing she's genuinely all for it. And I'm glad you're happy, too."

"Happy?" She stroked Harper's back. "Beyond happy. And your heart deserves this victory. I'm so glad you trusted it."

"It was tough. A wrong decision would have broken Gram's forever."

Frankie held her out at arm's length. She needed to see happiness flicker in those eyes. "How did you win her over?"

"Crossroads," Harper said, fingering the sleeves of Frankie's shirt. "The damn store is her heartbeat, I swear. It *has* to keep going 'cause it keeps *her* going, and vice versa, of course."

"It does. I've been so worried about how she would get along. Without it, I really believe she'd start to fail."

"And I agree. Without this place, she'd be lost." Harper drifted out of Frankie's hold and picked up a framed photograph of her grandparents on an end table. "Taking it away would be her undoing, and I could kick myself for not really seeing how much it meant all along." She set the picture down and turned to Frankie. "We've always known how attached she was, but watching her, seeing how she compensates, how she makes do, there's no mistaking how much she loves giving to the place or how much it means to her." She sat down hard. "It was like, what was I thinking, you know?"

"So…Crossroads is not going on the market." Frankie returned to the edge of her seat for the answer.

"Not as long as it sustains itself, and Gram has a support system. I mean, why, right?"

"Exactly." Frankie flopped back into the chair. "Christ, this is wonderful. It's the perfect answer for Stella—and for Crossroads. The store has a heart, too, a long-standing one, just like Stella, and the community needs it just as much as she does."

Harper watched Frankie exhale and close her eyes in relief. She shared the feeling, appreciated Frankie's point. Gram and Crossroads were a family unit unto themselves and couldn't be separated, just as her great-grandfather's legacy was linked to this very spot.

This plan was a far cry from what she'd been sent here to accomplish, and her mother would lose her mind, but it was the only choice short of destroying Gram's life. Her mother had spent two-plus days here in May, nowhere near long enough to get it right, to see and feel what truly mattered.

*Thank God, I took the time. Look what I've learned? And I'm still learning.*

"Assuming Donna agrees to everything…She's stopping by tomorrow morning, by the way, and Gram swears she'll jump at this. And I've put the wheels in motion for some projects around here because the other half of this issue is profit. Crossroads has to be all about profit from now on." She cleared her throat to broach a touchy subject. "So, there's a bunch of reno projects I have to squeeze in…before I go."

Frankie's elation flattened. "When's that?"

"September sometime. I'm not exactly sure." Harper saw her jaw twitch. *That's almost your harvest time, I know.*

"So…it's a shame you'll miss all our fall color, being in LA."

*Uh-huh. Foliage?*

"I hadn't expected to be here even that long, Frankie. I thought I'd get called back before Labor Day, so having some of September is really a gift." Frankie only nodded. "The band's gathering in Jersey, not LA. Our lead player, Rhea, has a huge place for us to kick off the rust and rehearse. We're going back on the road in October."

"On tour again?"

"Yeah, for the album release. Promotion is built into our contracts, so… We're booked through New Year's Eve in LA."

"That's big."

"It is, yeah."

Frankie sat up straighter and appeared to collect herself. "Well." She studied the braided rug for a long moment before leaning forward again on her thighs. "Then, there are two months or so…" She looked up, but her promising smile didn't reach her eyes. "To get Crossroads into shape."

She'd forced their personal issue aside and presented a ready attitude. Harper swallowed hard and tried to do the same. *Yes, now the end has an actual date.*

"Yeah. But my problem now is that midsummer is a busy time for contractors, so I don't know how much luck I'll have booking any. If…if work isn't finished by the time…" She blew out a hard breath. "Dammit, Frankie. I—"

"I'll keep tabs on things, Harper."

"I *do* recognize what time of year that is for you. I know you'll be busy."

"I'll manage. So, whatever you need me to do…"

"I'll pay you for your time."

"No, you don't—"

"No, *you* don't. Don't argue."

"Like hell, I won't. I'll be stopping by here no matter what you arrange, so—"

"No, Frankie. It's not right."

"Okay. Pay me and I'll just give it to Stella."

"Jesus Christ. She'll refuse to take it."

"What projects are you looking at?"

"This isn't settled yet."

"Sure, it is."

"Are we going to argue?"

"If you want. So, what projects?"

"God, you're stubborn." Harper dropped back against the couch. "Refinishing the cabinets, the woodwork, the floors—"

"The floors? Stella's okay with that?"

"I was surprised, too. Turns out, she's wanted it for a long time. Anyway, there's lighting work and painting the whole outside, too." She paused, trying to read Frankie's mind before adding more. "On top of that, there's making sure 'new employee/tenant' Donna fits in smoothly—*plus* whoever becomes Gram's visiting aide. How *that's* going to fly is anybody's guess but it has to work out."

Frankie sat forward in the silence, obviously trying to digest it all.

Harper went to the kitchen and poured iced tea for each of them. *It's a lot, I know.*

"Well," Frankie began from the living room, "it's a safe bet that Stella and Donna will do just fine, but Stella letting an aide—a stranger—keep her in line? Hm. I don't know. At least…At least we have a little time to work on that."

Harper handed her the drink. This was tough for both of them, and she admired Frankie's valiant effort to skirt their underlying drama. Frankie's message, her tone had softened a bit of the sting, and Harper reeled it in while she could. Impulsively, she ran her fingers through Frankie's hair, not surprised when she didn't react.

"Yes, we should," Harper said quietly. The word "we" hung in the air between them.

Returning to the couch, she tried to ignore the feel of Frankie's eyes on her backside. She wanted nothing more than to drop into those arms and hide from the world.

"An aide making two or three short visits a week shouldn't be hard for Gram to take. I'm hoping she gains a special new friend. So, with this aide coming regularly, and Donna close by, and you and Joe popping in, don't you think it should work? Actually, you being around should be a comfort to Gram, make it easier for her to adjust to a new routine."

"It sounds good, Harper. You know I'll watch out for her."

Harper just gazed back at her, wondering how in her world of devoted fans, boundless artistic expression, and intoxicating celebrity, she had ever developed this attraction to a selfless farmer. And she definitely had. She'd thrown herself into this damn short-term "thing," and known from the start that she would run head-long into a wall—and that it would hurt like hell.

She almost sighed out loud.

"Hey, there." Frankie waved through Harper's line of sight. "Where'd you go?"

Harper smiled toward her feet. "Sorry," she said and sipped her tea. "There's just so much in my head these days."

"We need music. Play some more. You need it. *I* need it. I interrupted you earlier."

Frankie longed to escape into Harper's sound, especially right now. She needed Harper's every nuance, every breath to envelop her, one-on-one from such close range, and take her away from difficult thoughts.

"We probably should go back downstairs. It's been—"

"No. You have to do 'Send Me Down' again."

"You heard that? I guess it sounded familiar, huh?"

Frankie couldn't help but grin at the blush on Harper's cheeks. "Forgive me, but it never sounded so good."

"Sorry I stole your rendition. That night you did it downstairs, you totally threw me, like, spun me around and forced me to look at it differently. And it came so easily. *You* should do it more often."

"I think you need to record it. The softness of your voice…Man, it was perfect. *That's* what's hiding behind Storm's lead singer?" She sat back dreamily, still hearing it in her head. "What a waste." Then she threw herself forward. "Not that Storm's work is a waste. I just meant that you—"

Harper laughed lightly. "Thank you. I confess I was taken by your voice, too, you know. I could listen to you all night." She saluted with a tip of her glass. "And one can only take so much of Storm's lead singer."

"Not true. Not for a second. Shit, Harper. I'm flattered as hell that you like my version, and I'm grateful you didn't kill me for reworking it. I *do* think you should record it."

"Okay, then. Maybe I *will* give it some thought." Harper grinned as she stood again. "Unfortunately, it's getting late, and we *did* invite you to dinner, remember. Gram's going to have a fit that I didn't wake her up long ago." She stopped at Frankie's side. "She's been worried about you."

"Let her rest," Frankie said, taking her hand and entwining their fingers. *Am I begging? Shamelessly.* The only thing she really wanted was time together. Considering what she now knew of Harper's tour plans, every opportunity mattered. "Play. Please? Anything."

Harper cupped Frankie's cheek, bent down, and whispered against her mouth. "I can't say no to you." She leaned on both armrests and, with apparently no regard for Frankie's throbbing libido, kissed her back into the chair. She tugged at each lip with her teeth, teasing, and then withdrew before Frankie could capture her.

Frankie returned to Earth in time to catch Harper's devilish smile and watch her settle on the couch with her guitar.

Harper began a staccato intro and Frankie's foot started tapping automatically.

"When I was putting Storm together," Harper said, talking over the notes, "I made each musician join me on various songs." She glanced at her chording hand, an unnecessary, disembodied look. Her mind, voice, and hands were on different tracks yet subconsciously in sync, a practiced skill Frankie understood well.

As taken by Harper's musicianship as much as her presence, Frankie marveled at the proficiency, the effort. She could relate to it, but that vision before her was enthralling.

Harper's brow furrowed as she sang. Hair swung around her shoulders, and shadowy waves teased her face. At times, her eyes closed as she squeezed out the lyrics, and when she opened them, they were impossible to ignore. Frankie could see how easily stage makeup would transform the sensual Harper Cushing into Storm's foxy lead singer.

Harper eased up on the strings and faded the song to a close. She flung her hair back and leaned on the guitar. "Think I woke up Gram?"

"Nah." Frankie pressed toward her on her knees. "God, you're just fantastic. That was…perfect. Thank you."

Harper fussed with the tuning. "We *have* to start dinner, so maybe we *should* wake her up?" She winked and Frankie's heart skipped.

Harper's fingers danced over the strings. It was a deceiving intro to P!nk's unapologetic "That's All I Know So Far," and Harper launched into the song's defiant, tumultuous world with a vengeance. Her voice sounded steady and well-healed, higher pitched than Frankie's and just high enough for those breathtaking notes.

Glued to her seat, Frankie almost shivered when Harper's voice soared, and she wondered if Storm performed this in concert. She didn't think the band covered other artists' work, so it was a shame that Harper couldn't knock out an audience with this demonstration of her talent. Fleetingly, Frankie hoped Harper's upcoming tour wouldn't push her terrific voice too far and end up damaging it permanently.

When Harper finished, Frankie could only stare, awash in awe and admiration. Harper raised her eyebrows.

*Is she asking if I liked it?*

Out of control and swept away, Frankie swiftly closed the distance between them. She took Harper's face in both hands and kissed her long and hard, then stepped back. Harper's surprise melted into appreciation.

Frankie shoved her hands into her pockets before they did something else she couldn't stop. She felt her cheeks flush. "I…well, I-I had no words, so…"

Harper laid the guitar in its case and rose into Frankie's personal space. "Really? I thought you spoke very well."

"Let's *talk* some more." The invitation came from somewhere very deep inside, unexpected and unencumbered, and made her blood rush with excitement. Or maybe caution. *Since when is my heart smarter than my brain?* Nevertheless, she allowed her invitation to linger.

Harper slid two fingers into Frankie's palm. "We *have* to do dinner."

"After dinner. My place."

# Chapter Twenty-four

Enjoying time she hadn't had on her first visit to the cabin, Harper studied the array of antique tools hanging above Frankie's fireplace. The mammoth two-man ice saw and the scythe, with its four-foot curved blade, were almost intimidating enough to keep her mind off why she was here.

Frankie hardly seemed more relaxed than she had the other night, when she'd made it her last-gasp mission to care for all Harper's needs. From the living room, Harper could see her pouring rose-colored drinks for them in the kitchen—and hurriedly wiping up a little spill.

They had left for Frankie's once Gram started yawning, and even felt compelled to provide a proper excuse. Harper grinned at that, as she flipped through a case of Frankie's classic albums. Gram had been thrilled to see Harper leave with guitar in hand, knowing they finally would be playing music together. Her reaction would be *very* interesting, however, if Harper waltzed in tomorrow morning, but Harper refused to worry about it.

Just like she refused to worry about *this*, tonight.

Dinner itself had gone well, except Gram spent all of Harper's prep time cautioning about vocal cord damage, and all the social time afterward coaching Frankie's "entrepreneurial spirit." Gram had run out of gas by eight thirty, and, for the first time, was willing to close Crossroads early.

Returning to Frankie's cabin, Harper didn't expect to feel such an undercurrent of freedom and relief. Being aware of it meant it was palpable, along with an unexpected, pathetic dose of teenage jitters. But having a little place like this for private time with Frankie was undeniably welcome, no matter what her conscience said.

She took a glass jar off the bookcase shelf and inspected the marbles inside. "Are these antique? Some look very old."

"Yup. Some are clay. I find them around here, every now and then." Frankie approached with their drinks. "A good friend once told me to keep them in a jar. That way, no one could ever claim I'd lost my marbles. Not even me."

"Ah. Wise friend." She met Frankie's raised glass with her own. "I'll drink to her."

"And to cranberry infusion."

"That's what this is? Pretty color." They drank together. "Ooo. Very nice, too."

"Berries, sugar, and patience. Good vodka helps." She took Harper's hand. "Let's go see if the mosquitoes will let us sit out back."

Harper grinned as Frankie led her through the kitchen. No doubt they each had the same thing in mind, but Frankie's old-fashioned propriety was adorable.

*We aren't kids anymore.*

Outside on the deck, Harper paused to listen to the ongoing debate between the frogs and crickets. She took in the surrounding blackness, the incredible canopy of stars, and, as her eyes adjusted, a trace of the sandy perimeter road emerged like a familiar ghost. The bogs were out there somewhere, but she felt more respectful of them now than spooked, which was a curious surprise.

"It's like another world," she said, finding Frankie watching her from the glider. "I can feel how special all of this is."

Frankie lit a large, squatty candle and set it on what appeared to be a homemade table, an old wooden crate inverted over a fat slab of tree trunk. She dragged it closer, sat back, and put her heels up on the corner.

"You're here, so it's even more special. And you're welcome anytime."

She draped an arm across the back of the glider and Harper didn't hesitate to settle into a snug fit against her side. She put her feet up, too, and rested a hand on Frankie's thigh, and when Frankie set her arm around her shoulders, the intimate sensation forced Harper's eyes to close.

"We are *so* playing with fire." Frankie's deep whisper made her skin tingle.

"Tell me about it." Harper slammed the door on her common sense and relaxed within Frankie's hold. "But this feels…" She nestled her head onto Frankie's shoulder. "God, it feels so good to just slow down this way."

"I'm glad we escaped. This is a beautiful night."

"Your bullfrogs have a lot to say."

"They're a talkative bunch, aren't they? When I croak back at them, they shut up. I think I confuse them."

"You're so easily entertained."

"They listen when I play out here, too."

Harper laughed lightly. "Bullfrogs like music? Who knew?" She splayed her fingers across Frankie's bared thigh, along the edge of her shorts. "Have you always lived in places like this?"

"God, no. The Boston suburbs and then the city itself. And then," she paused and sighed, "then love struck."

"Ah. Enter cranberries. So, you didn't always want to be a farmer."

"No. Does wanting to be a cowboy count?"

Harper laughed. "The wide-open spaces? Yeah, sort of."

"Hm. Maybe it does. Well, working the bogs *and* a relationship opened my eyes, I know that much." She squeezed Harper's shoulders. "How about you? A rock star at five years old, strutting around the living room, singing into a hairbrush?"

"Six years old with my best friend playing badminton racquet guitars. But summers here meant reckless bike rides with neighborhood kids." She shook her head. "Poor Gram. We were renegades on *motorcycles*, of course. I think I was around thirteen when I started dreaming of singing for real."

"I bet college got in the way. It did for me. It was a necessary evil, so I wouldn't starve while writing the great American novel. Little did I know, a relationship would stomp that dream into a whimper."

"Dreams matter, Frankie. They come from who we really are. Sometimes they're impossible and don't work out, but we have to take our shot."

"It took me fifteen years to find the courage, until I finally saw we were more in love with the land than each other. But she refused to see it and probably never will. It got messy."

"When it's no longer a two-way street…Yeah. I get it. Fifteen years is a chunk of your life." She squeezed Frankie's leg. "I'm sorry you went through that."

"Thank you. But I learned a lot." She snickered. "You can't let years blow by, trying to be who someone else wants. I tried so hard for so long and that was a big mistake. You lose sight of who you really are and, the next minute, you can't find what makes you happy." She spoke softly into Harper's hair. "We all learn from our dark times."

Harper flashed back to lessons learned and felt the wound she'd inflicted upon Chelsea as tangibly as if it had happened yesterday. That lesson loomed large now, considering.

"Sometimes love can be so damn blind. In my last relationship, we both failed to see the writing on the wall and lasted three years."

"I hope yours wasn't as messy as mine."

Harper swallowed hard and sat up, out of Frankie's hold. She needed some distance between them to gather the strength for this. "Christ. We'd *better* learn, hadn't we?" She scanned the darkness beyond the deck. "I wouldn't call my breakup messy, really. More like crushing. We just weren't working out. Careers, you know? Two ambitious women. But I should have been kinder."

*And I won't make that mistake again.*

Frankie slid her palm up to Harper's shoulder and tugged her back within her arm.

"Fate's impossible, sometimes, Harper. Look where we are today."

Harper nodded, praying she wasn't destined to repeat that heartache. "I've learned to read that writing on the wall, Frankie."

"So have I."

"It's up there in big, bold print."

"Can't ignore it."

"Because it'll hurt."

Frankie rested her cheek in Harper's hair. "Are you scared, too?"

Harper twisted slightly to face her. She figured her look said it all, but *this* she needed to convey unequivocally at point-blank range, for both of them. Would admitting it out loud help control these feelings? They had a mind of their own.

"Yes, I'm scared, too."

Because this was more than fun. This was want—and not just for some masochistic summertime tease that neither of them deserved. They each had paid a price, after all, and Frankie cherished her solitude, and Storm ruled Harper's life, so, really, what the hell were they doing?

Harper's fingers trembled as she touched Frankie's neck and drew her to within a breath. However ill-advised, this kiss would set her adrift. She just knew it. Or would it anchor her to the support her heart didn't know it needed?

She lost herself in delivering every ounce of sincerity, and in receiving all the tenderness Frankie offered. She shifted to face her more directly, urgently wanting to feel Frankie against her, and both those arms around her, tight and possessive.

"Harper." Frankie gripped her by the waist and whispered between kisses. "I know a more comfortable place." She urged Harper off the seat and stood with her, strong hands flexing nervously on Harper's hips.

*No, Frankie. I'm not going to object. There's no way I'm spoiling this by thinking.*

She hoped Frankie saw the welcome, the enlightenment she felt at this moment, because the feelings were genuine and powerful enough to throw discretion aside.

She ran a fingertip across Frankie's lips. "A more comfortable place is where we need to be." She gladly let Frankie lead her inside.

## CHAPTER TWENTY-FIVE

Frankie switched on the small light atop the bedroom dresser just as Harper placed her palms on her back. Their heat, their message took Frankie's breath away. She turned into them and kissed her as Harper's hands slid over her breasts and around her shoulders. Her heart rate quickening, Frankie inched her back against the bed, kissing each lip delicately.

"Even if your time here were to end tomorrow," Frankie said, her mouth at Harper's throat, "we'll have this."

Harper drove her hands up through Frankie's hair, drew their lips together. "Right now, Frankie."

Frankie kissed her fully as she eased her down onto her side and pulled Harper's lower body against hers. "You'll have to explain all the wrinkles in your shirt tomorrow," she whispered, nipping at Harper's ear, "so you should take it off now."

Harper pushed her onto her back and settled onto her hips. "My, my. This is the second time you've wanted my shirt off." The cocked eyebrow was deliciously arousing, even in the poor light, and Frankie's sex clenched. When Harper peeled off her shirt, grinding against her, Frankie's entire body pulsed.

The vision above her simmered with intoxicating intent, and Frankie wanted to give everything she could right now, mindfulness be dammed. And just as eagerly, she yearned to take.

"It's just the second time you know about," she said, squeezing Harper's ass. "Next time, I'll take it off you myself." She sat up quickly, captured Harper's mouth with a penetrating kiss, and urgently released her bra.

Frankie turned her onto her back, straddled her hips, and kissed her onto the pillow as she pinned both Harper's hands to the bed. She trailed kisses along Harper's throat to her breasts, lingered at each nipple and tasted, grated them gently with her teeth.

"God, Frankie…" Harper writhed beneath her, and Frankie desperately wanted them both naked.

"Mmm." She released Harper's hands to massage each breast and kissed her way upward until their mouths met.

Harper moaned into it, wrapped her legs around Frankie's hips, and pulled her against her crotch. Every nerve electrified, Frankie rocked into her, and when Harper sucked her tongue deeper into her mouth, Frankie rocked harder.

She claimed Harper's throat and heard her gasp, felt the guttural moan vibrate against her mouth. She reveled in the moment, to feel Harper's body *sing* in this intimate way. She stroked Harper's hardened nipples, the satin of her stomach and abdomen.

Taken by the luxury of her skin, she skimmed her fingers along the inside of Harper's waistband and teased them both. Harper squirmed impatiently. She parted Frankie's lips with a delicate finger and dipped suggestively into her mouth.

Frankie captured it with her tongue. She slid her palm inside Harper's shorts, eager to feel all of her, and when Harper surged upward, Frankie kissed her hard, back onto the pillow, and sent her fingers deeper. Harper's hips rose in welcome and, aching to reach farther inside, Frankie cursed the clothing between them.

Harper's talented fingers dug into her back. Unable to wait any longer, Frankie abruptly withdrew her hand and leaned back on her heels.

"Jesus, Frankie!"

Frankie pulled Harper's clothes down her legs. She tossed them aside and slid her hands up her calves.

"Oh, no. Not yet," Harper snapped, grinning. She grabbed the front of Frankie's shirt and hauled herself up, nearly popping the buttons when she forced it over Frankie's head. "I need you naked." Frankie hurried to kiss her, but Harper pushed her back, a palm at each breast. "You're not done." She tugged hard at Frankie's shorts. "Take. These. Off."

Frankie flung her remaining clothes to the floor, and knelt between Harper's legs, ready to pounce as Harper lay back. But she caught herself, taken by the view.

"I could devour every inch of you in a heartbeat."

Harper grinned slyly. "If you don't do something with that killer body right now—" She inhaled sharply when Frankie caressed her stomach and hips. The creamy skin rose and fell with each excited breath as Frankie kissed a path from one hip to the other.

"God, you're beautiful." As she nuzzled the inside of Harper's thigh, a tremulous hand settled onto her head, and she dipped her tongue into the wet flesh, relishing the heat, yearning to crawl inside.

Harper's hips rose to meet Frankie's broad, languid strokes, and she inhaled deeply when Frankie slid fingers inside, repeatedly. Shudders began against Frankie's cheeks and Harper's mounting groan grew into a prolonged, rapturous moan.

She flailed for the comforter as Frankie nursed at her sex, her body stiff and arched off the bed. Frankie rose with her, greedily, growling into her flesh.

Harper's hips clenched at the tip of Frankie's tongue, and she trembled long and hard. Raw hunger, a desire Frankie hadn't experienced in years, held Harper at that peak for a blissful eternity, until she had devoured the last surge of Harper's energy. Spent and listless, Harper finally took a breath, and shivered when Frankie tenderly withdrew.

Frankie's system raced madly, and she worked to steady her own breathing. There was so much to treasure, so much she wanted to give all at once, so much to be thankful for. She inched back just enough and gently slipped her fingers inside again. And again.

"Frankie…God, that was—"

"I can't get enough of you."

"You're amazing."

"Shh."

She reeled at Harper's reflexive response, how her eyes closed at the penetration, how she clung to Frankie's bared shoulders, offering herself to each stroke. Harper's inviting whispers would stay with her forever.

❖

Harper could smell the coffee before she opened her eyes. Sensing she wouldn't find Frankie beside her, she blindly reached out anyway, and her heart sank a little. But Harper was *here*, at Frankie's cabin, and that said plenty. She peered at the window and saw that dawn had also risen before her this morning. *And Gram, too, no doubt.*

She had to smile at that, imagining what Gram pictured the two of them doing.

She took a deep, cleansing breath and exhaled slowly. The bedclothes around her were a disaster, a reminder of a night she would never forget. She'd had her share of sexual forays in the past, but never one she relished through an entire night.

*Did I fall asleep first?*

She stretched her arms over her head and accidentally hit the headboard. She gripped it automatically, as if she did it all the time. Just like last night. And she remembered leaning on it for balance, straddling Frankie's head, looking down into those eyes as Frankie took her a third…fourth time?

Harper moaned as she curled onto her side. Her stiff legs protested, and her sex tingled.

"Ohhh, I'm *so* out of practice."

But all that exquisite surrender had come with just as much divine triumph, and Harper rolled back and smiled at the ceiling. *That strength of yours melted, didn't it, Ms. Cranberry Farmer?*

"Yes, it certainly did," she said aloud, pleased to have pleased. Nothing compared to having the rugged, indefatigable Frankie Cosgrove dissolve into her mouth.

"So, where might you be?"

Harper flung the sheet aside and managed to stand. After a quick glance into the closet, she slipped into that sleeveless denim shirt she liked on Frankie and snapped it closed. It hung just low enough on her to tease, and she ventured out to the kitchen.

Frankie was nowhere to be found but couldn't be far. She helped herself to coffee and had taken her first sip when she heard motion on the back deck. Within seconds, Frankie stepped inside, completely naked.

"Wow!" Harper almost choked. "Hell-o!"

"Shit," Frankie muttered, turning scarlet.

"Oh, yes. By all means, please come in." She grinned as she set her cup on the counter and stepped closer.

"Well, see, I got…" Frankie gestured frantically toward the deck. "My clothes are soaked, so I…I didn't want, you know, I-I didn't want to drip on—"

Harper gripped Frankie's hips. "Drip on me." She grazed her palms upward and massaged Frankie's breasts as she spoke. "Wet is very nice. You wet *and naked* is heaven." She plucked at the nipples and watched Frankie's eyes flutter. "This makes you dizzy, doesn't it?" She wrapped an arm around her waist and dipped her head. "And you love this." She drew a nipple into her mouth and sucked luxuriously. Frankie staggered in her grip and moaned her name with the same surrender that had stoked Harper's fire so many times last night.

Despite the warm morning, Frankie's skin was cool and damp from whatever water she'd gotten into, and Harper enjoyed the feel of it on her face. She urged her back against the door, still nursing contently, and rubbed her free hand down Frankie's torso, working her fingers into the firm muscles.

Frankie reached between them with both hands and ripped open the snaps of Harper's shirt. Her arms heavy atop Harper's shoulders, Frankie pulled her against her chest and Harper relinquished the luscious nipple as she surrendered. She met Frankie's mouth half-way down to hers.

Consumed by Frankie's kiss, she clasped her back with a splayed hand and sent the other into the slick fire between Frankie's legs, toying with her sex until Frankie began to wobble.

"Jesus." Frankie's head lolled back against the door. "Your fingers are magical."

Harper licked her way up Frankie's throat. "I could play your music all day."

Frankie's breath hitched when Harper circled her clit, and she squirmed when Harper squeezed it. Her words came out tight, strained. "Please...don't stop."

"Oh, I won't."

Wiggling her fingers, Harper dragged her mouth down Frankie's chest, bit at a nipple in passing, just to feel Frankie's sex clench. She crouched as she kissed a path down the chilled, hard body, and knelt to knead Frankie's ass as she licked her thighs.

She nuzzled into the tuft of hair and parted Frankie's legs, then opened her with both hands and drove her tongue inside. Frankie hissed at the sensation, her hips lurching against Harper's face, and Harper welcomed them with immense satisfaction. She pressed inward, sucked harder, and hummed with delight when Frankie slapped at the door for support.

Harper paused. "Please don't fall through the screen."

"God, Harper!"

Eager to take, to pick up where they'd left off last night, Harper sucked purposefully, felt Frankie shake, then slid two fingers up inside just to be as close as physically possible. To hell with the outside world and all its demands, right now *this* was what she wanted.

Frankie surged against the door and Harper repeated the motion, established an insistent rhythm. She didn't know how much longer Frankie would be able to stand, didn't know how she was standing *now*, but drove Frankie over the top. Last night's many orgasms would not be the only ones.

Frankie's thighs shook against Harper's shoulders. Her breathing came short and fast, and she sank her fingers desperately into Harper's hair, holding on, holding her head in place.

Harper happily obliged and reached deeper with a firm tongue. She surrounded the bottom of Frankie's clit with her lips and sucked the full shaft hard, forcing Frankie's sex to tighten around her fingers. Instinctively, Harper increased the commanding drive of her thrust.

Groaning, Frankie grabbed both sides of the doorframe. She almost twisted away, and Harper looped an arm around her thigh. Tremors threatened to break her hold. When Frankie's body went rigid, Harper stilled her motions, her fingers curled inside, and drew hard on Frankie's clit.

Frankie rocked through the vibrations and Harper marveled at her strength, her power, both so freely surrendered, both of which she'd turned on Harper last night with mind-numbing tenderness.

Frankie's arms dropped lifelessly to her sides, and Harper withdrew from her, lingered over a farewell kiss into her sex before standing. Withering against the doorframe, Frankie was visibly shaken, and Harper smiled at her blush.

"Holy..." Frankie dragged a hand over her face. "Those fingers..." She touched Harper's lips in wonder. "This mouth...You're lethal."

"As if you didn't slay me last night." She squeezed Frankie's hips into hers.

"Last night *was* fantastic, wasn't it?"

Frankie could beseech her without even trying. The warmth and sincerity in her eyes, the unguarded set of her jaw, the dimple that softened her entire face, Harper could gaze upon her for...for a long time. They reached inside and cradled her spirit like nothing else, ever. Not to mention the caress of her hands, the soothing draw of her lips, or the exquisite deliverance in each stroke of her tongue.

Uncontrollable emotions crept into Harper's confidence. Usually, she escaped into her music whenever she felt overwhelmed, but at this moment, she was on her own.

She cupped Frankie's cheek. "Last night was incredible."

Frankie turned her head and kissed Harper's palm. "We make some pretty impressive music together."

"Do you feel up to trying the literal version of that?" The idea shot forward from the back of her mind. Why, she wasn't sure, but it felt right.

"You mean, play some? Now?"

Harper laughed at the incredulous expression. "Well, not right this *second*, but isn't that what Gram expected?"

"Ah, yes." Frankie drew her in, and Harper wriggled at the sensation of their bodies pressed together so tightly. She tingled all over when Frankie combed fingers through her hair and whispered at her ear. "I'd love to, but we really don't have time."

The idea of leaving brought Harper's dreaminess and their "moment" to an end. She wondered if Frankie felt as disappointed. With Gram running Crossroads solo since six o'clock, there really was no choice. As it was, Harper had worried about not having been there earlier.

Frankie lifted Harper's chin on a finger. "Stella assumes we played last night, so we could just continue at the store. And nothing says we can't have another 'play date' here soon."

That prospect buzzed through Harper's system and lifted her heart. She didn't want to think about their summer evaporating in a flash. *Because they really are just "play dates," and I want more.* She couldn't let those concerns weasel in and ruin last night's high.

"I think it's a great idea," she said. "I'll call Gram and let her know we'll be there in a few."

"First, let's grab a quick shower." She nestled her mouth beneath Harper's collar and Harper closed her eyes as arousal coursed upward between her thighs. Frankie sucked at the base of her neck. "Oh, but we'll have to put clothes on, won't we? Damn." She grazed her palm down the front of Harper's body.

*Go ahead. Take it.*

## CHAPTER TWENTY-SIX

Frankie's mind and body reeled at this scene. Considering she had no idea how they'd even managed to get dressed, being here on the porch with Stella felt like a dream. But coping with a mind-blowing night *and this* seemed damn near impossible. She hadn't picked up her guitar in days, and now she was playing with Storm's lead singer? After devouring every inch of her last night?

Playing a duet with Harper for the first time was like stepping into someone else's YouTube video. Frankie battled her nerves as they worked through a song, as she watched someone—*it can't be me*—match Harper's playing, chord for chord, and her singing, word for word.

Thankfully, the guitar kept her hands occupied, but her senses refused to lose touch with last night, and Frankie had no idea how she was pulling this off. If she thought about it too much, the autopilot guiding her musical effort would disengage and she'd crash and burn.

She had often imagined what playing with Harper would be like, just the two of them, if they'd do it well, if she could keep up with her. But with a sex hangover? Apparently, it *was* possible.

Ridiculously warm and fuzzy, she wondered if Harper felt this high. *Is she wrestling with all this, too? Exhilaration comes in so many forms.*

"I've always liked that song," Stella said. Her concerted look said she'd been attuned to the song at hand, as usual, and Frankie was relieved. Stella had been focused on the music, not the two glowing women who'd just spent the night satisfying each other beyond all common decency.

Harper grinned and Frankie saw the same appreciation in her eyes.

Showing up together here at eight thirty hadn't knocked Stella off her stride at all. With a knowing grin and a bright "Good morning," she had welcomed Harper's assistance at the counter, set Frankie to work cleaning the griddle, and then had them playing music by ten.

Stella resumed rocking and looked from Frankie to Harper and back. "You two do a good job with that song. It's serious but in a crafty way." Harper leaned on her guitar. "You know, you're right, Gram. 'Pink Houses' drove home a point that too few noticed back then. Mellencamp's very underappreciated as a songwriter."

Stella's affinity for all types of music always made Frankie proud and she suspected Harper shared that feeling, but having Stella appreciate *this soft side* of Harper's work, up close and personal, was extra special.

Stella might forget the day of the week, but she could remember hits from the sixties, seventies, and eighties—and their messages—like it was yesterday. Sometimes her fondness for even older crooners made it easy to forget she had lived through that legendary rock 'n' roll period. But Stella seldom missed a beat.

"Well, you two must have practiced that a lot because it sounded great." Stella sipped her coffee. "What else did you work on last night?"

*Nowhere near as innocent as she seems.*

Frankie quickly turned away to adjust her tuning, biting back a grin so hard it almost hurt. She couldn't look at Harper but figured she had jumped away from that question just as fast. To her credit, Harper suggested another song in a carefree voice, and Frankie *had* to look into that innocent, loaded expression.

It was impossible not to smile, even though she hadn't played the song in years. Now, she prayed she could produce something that sounded like they'd done it last night. "Eh...E minor?" she asked, miraculously remembering the right key. Thankfully, Harper nodded while attaching a capo to her guitar neck and didn't look at her.

"Do I know this one?" Stella asked.

"I think it will be familiar, yeah," Frankie said. *If I don't butcher it.*

Ultimately, neither of them did, and Stella was delighted. She didn't notice Frankie's missteps. Harper, having played the song more often, breezed through it and only flashed Frankie a knowing smirk at two of her fumbles.

The hour's entertainment they provided Stella—without having practiced a single note together last night—staggered Frankie. Like Harper, she simply had offered songs she was familiar with, gambled that Harper would be familiar with them, too, enough to catch on quickly. A risky thing for two disparate musicians, especially with someone sitting a few feet away expecting to hear polished work. Hell, Frankie surprised *herself*, having kept up with the far more polished pro.

The excitement struck her so deeply, it felt indelible. Harper was bound to have felt it, as well. Rarely did synchronicity just materialize out of nowhere, but theirs had. Effortlessly. And it resonated to her bones.

Stella next raved about their spot-on harmonies in an old folk tune. Harper's higher reach wove into Frankie's lower lead like a hand in glove, remarkably good by anyone's standards. That they could pull off songs without ever having played together was dramatic enough, but *harmonies*? That just pushed "sweet" to "unreal."

*What just happened here?*

Frankie felt rather stunned beneath Stella's praise. Harper had leaped up with a high-five, glowing at the finish, and still shook her head in wonder.

Stella rose dutifully when a car drove into the lot and Frankie took the moment to regain some composure.

"You two keep playing," Stella said. "This beats my record player any day." She smiled at the college-age couple on the steps. "Good morning. Every day should start with music, don't you think?"

The customers agreed and the young woman removed her sunglasses and set them on her ballcap. "Your own personal concert," she answered, smiling at Harper. "Don't stop on our account, please." She followed her boyfriend inside and Stella trailed after them.

Harper leaned across the little table that separated them and whispered. "What the fuck did we just do?"

"Something magical happened."

"No kidding." She tugged the scrunchie out of her hair and put it back, neater. "We should've been too exhausted to pull that off."

"Hell of a way to follow up a busy night."

"I have no idea how we're doing this, Frankie. Where *did* all that come from? How?"

"Don't ask me. I'm still in awe. Sweet, wasn't it?"

Harper set her hand on Frankie's guitar as if to confirm all this was real. The simple, intimate gesture radiated through the instrument and into Frankie's chest.

"Way better than sweet, Frankie." Harper's astounded smile lingered. "I want more of it. Let's press our luck a little further." She realigned her capo and Frankie followed suit, hoping her luck continued.

Much to her relief, she recognized her own intro to "Send Me Down" immediately and deferred to Harper's voice. She was grateful to know the chord changes by heart. That allowed her to override her excitement, concentrate more on Harper's presentation, and enjoy the sensuous delivery.

At the second verse, Harper tossed the lyrics back to her, and Frankie carried on without a hitch. Harper filled the instrumental break with some impressive riffs, riding Frankie's rhythm until the final verses and chorus arrived, and they sang them together. Their harmony had clicked on earlier songs, but on *this* song, it sent goose bumps down Frankie's legs.

As their last notes lingered, Frankie sat motionless, hardly breathing. *If I move, will I wake up?* She shifted her gaze to Harper, saw her head rise cautiously, and when their eyes met, a spectacular connection flared throughout Frankie's body. They'd proven to be musically in sync, but Frankie knew this went far deeper. Some transcendent spell had woven them together. She couldn't speak.

Awareness showed in Harper's eyes, a revelation that slowly lifted the corners of her beautiful, sumptuous mouth. Frankie knew she couldn't speak, either.

Unfortunately, the customers burst onto the porch, and the cowbell clanged rudely.

"Wow!" the young woman exclaimed, and her boyfriend agreed.

"Yeah, wow!"

To Frankie's supreme delight, the rapturous spell defied this interruption. Neither she nor Harper looked away from each other.

"My goodness!" Stella exclaimed, just inside the screen door. "That was so pretty! Whose song is that, Harper?"

The young man said, "Yeah, I know that song. It's um…"

Harper gathered herself and her eyes finally fell away to look at Gram. "The band Storm."

"That's it!" The young woman caught her sunglasses as they fell off her cap. "I *knew* I knew it."

"Yeah. We watched a bunch of their videos the other night," her boyfriend said. "Savage stuff. The song's huge right now, but not this version. What a switch." He chuckled and looked at the women around him.

Frankie eyed Harper, wondering if she would explain.

"Well," the girlfriend said, "whoever created *this* version did it justice."

Frankie lent her a slight nod. "Thank you."

Not catching on, the boyfriend shrugged. "But the original kicks down walls. For sure, whoever wrote the original didn't expect it to sound this way. He'd probably be pissed."

Harper winked at Frankie. "Not at all."

"Wait." The girlfriend stepped closer and looked from Harper to Frankie and back. "You know him, the writer?"

"Her."

"No way."

"You know Storm?" the boyfriend asked, moving to his girlfriend's side.

Frankie watched Harper cast a grin to the floor. They both knew where this was headed.

"You know?" The girlfriend retreated a step to scrutinize Harper. She sent her boyfriend a brief, curious look, and squinted back at Harper. "Now that I think about it, you look an awful lot like Storm's lead singer."

"Yeah, she's right," her boyfriend added.

Stella giggled from the door.

Harper turned to Frankie with an apprehensive look, as if asking permission. Frankie simply folded her hands atop her guitar and smiled. *Go ahead. You've earned it.*

Guitar in hand, Harper stood. "Yeah. Storm's my band." She offered the couple a handshake. "Nice meeting you." The woman's jaw dropped as she shook Harper's hand.

Her boyfriend laughed. "No shit?"

Harper smiled as she shook his hand. "Thanks for thinking of the songwriter. I'm pleased you like the song."

"Well, damn." The boyfriend shrugged. "So, you're really down with this...this heartthrob stuff?"

Frankie chuckled. "That's what it is? 'Heartthrob stuff'? I never realized."

"It's tender and moving, different for me," Harper said, correcting him, and acknowledged Frankie with a smile. "My vocal cords are very grateful. Banging out Storm tunes takes a lot out of them."

Frankie was tempted to add her gratitude. Harper would be back to "banging out Storm tunes" soon enough.

"Well, so, you on vacation?" the boyfriend continued. "Is Storm playing around here?"

Harper sent Stella a smile. "I'm enjoying a long-overdue visit with my grandmother."

"Oh, cool. And what's next for Storm?"

"We're going back on the road this fall. Our live album drops in October, so maybe you'll check it out."

"Count on it," he said sharply.

"Do you have dates scheduled for around here?" his girlfriend asked, "you know, Boston or Providence?"

"I think Foxwoods casino in Connecticut is on the list."

Frankie wanted a peek at that schedule. She made a mental note to check Storm's website. Maybe she could swing a trip to Connecticut for that show. *If harvest is done.*

Harper looked up from prodding the fire to watch Frankie cross the dimly lit parking lot, her arms loaded with broken pallet pieces. Her strength never seemed to waver, and despite the late hour, neither did her energy. Harper appreciated having the view all to herself.

"Is that the end of it?"

Frankie deposited her load beside the firepit. "It is. All cleaned up. Until next week's delivery." She brushed her hands against her shorts and pointed at the flames. "Good job with the fire."

"I'm learning." Harper prodded the burning pieces into a taller pile. She almost smiled at herself, having developed this fondness for tending a fire, being mesmerized by dancing flames, just like Frankie appeared to be now. "Hey," she grazed a palm across Frankie's back, "today was a landmark day. I finally finished inputting Gram's year-to-date."

"You're kidding. You've been at that for weeks." Frankie turned in the firelight. "Getting that done is huge. You are amazing."

"No, I'm not. It's just a big relief." She dragged two lawn chairs to within poking distance of the fire, and sat, tugging Frankie down beside her. She linked their arms atop the adjacent armrests.

"So, now, Gram likes seeing her accounting so readily, so legibly. She may hate typing, but she's great at poking the keys with her pencil."

Frankie laughed. "I noticed she doesn't curse the technology as much."

"What a coup, huh? Actually, it *is* a big thing, especially now that Donna has started here. I think Gram likes having that business mind around to guide her."

Harper stopped short of acknowledging how the modernized bookkeeping would help once she was gone. Time was fleeting. She wanted to enjoy the three weeks that remained, not just cope with losing it.

Reflecting on that nostalgic, dutiful hiatus she'd anticipated, Harper worked hard not to be overwhelmed by the decidedly personal turn it had taken, these past weeks. Since this "thing" started with Frankie, keeping her own "big picture" in mind grew harder by the day. And those flashing caution lights seemed brighter lately. Would their brakes work when applied? *Depends on how fast we're going.*

Evenings like this had become almost routine now, whether here or at the bogs, and the intimacy filled a void dangerously close to her heart. She dared to think Frankie cherished these moments as much as she did.

"Stella can't wait to introduce me to her new aide, Marybeth."

"Her new *friend*, Frankie. Gram won't use the word 'aide.'"

"I just missed meeting her the other day, but it sounds like Stella scored some points, making her famous BLTs for their lunch." She leaned against Harper's shoulder. "Thank God they get along."

"I'm thankful for lots of things." She squeezed Frankie's arm. "Gram's excited about all the renovations, despite having carpenters underfoot everywhere. The work's really moving along." *And hopefully won't fall on you to see it through.*

Frankie covered Harper's hand with her own. "Stop stressing. I can feel it."

"I just want it all finished." Harper combed some of Frankie's rebellious hair back off her forehead. Touching was reflexive now, and for someone who had guardedly avoided attachment, it was new and thrilling and freeing. Risky, too, considering arousal usually followed. "I don't want to dump things on you. It's no way to treat that huge heart of yours, a hell of a way to repay all you've done for Gram these past few years—years *I* should have been paying attention."

"What did I say about 'should haves'?"

Harper sighed as her own issue leapt to mind, demanding to be spoken. "Plus, there's tour to think about." The excitement of playing again felt a bit muted these days. To revive it, she needed to throw herself back into action soon.

Frankie took Harper's hand onto her thigh. "We have to just take each day as it comes, Harper. It's all we can do."

Harper scanned the starry sky, grateful Gram had retired to her favorite TV show and bed. She needed to think out loud, to talk with Frankie, but knew she had to do the heavy lifting. When tour ended in LA, would she really come back here? What if her voice didn't last for the whole tour? What would she do then? Go home? *Should* Frankie figure into any of it? Maybe those were things she should just tackle internally.

As if she could sense Harper's plight, Frankie lowered her voice when she spoke. "Some days I feel a little awed by my own situation, you know? The land, the work...It took a while before I realized I shouldn't turn my back on them. And thank God. So, you never know."

Harper entwined their fingers on Frankie's leg and nodded. "I get it. Some days I'm in awe of what I've done, too, how far I've come, but I don't want it owning me." She shrugged. "Sometimes it feels like a smothering relationship."

"But you enjoy the band, the music."

"Oh, I do. It's been a part of me forever. There's this...*need* for it." She searched Frankie's eyes for recognition. "It's just hard to know if it's dictating too much, if I'm letting it."

"But you're on the right track, Harper. You're not running blindly through life." She laughed lightly. "*I* did and I'm here to tell you don't. It sucks."

"You went too long with your eyes closed."

"Yeah, probably. But you're not. You love what you're doing. Your heart's in it. Mine wasn't. Well, not at the end, anyway. I wanted and deserved something better but couldn't get there. I had too much self-doubt and was too worn down by then to take a stand."

It was hard to imagine Frankie lost and insecure, her spirit broken by someone she had loved, and Harper's temper flared for her. But the experience had created *this* Frankie she'd grown to treasure, released that strong, generous character and let it flourish.

*The things we endure for love.*

Harper could feel the message burrowing into her conscience. Her own difficult relationships had been dramatic with quick, pull-the-Band-Aid-off endings. Par for the course in her fast-paced life. But did her relationship with Storm fit the mold? Even though Frankie's past sounded far heavier than hers, it still rang unsettlingly familiar.

"I hear you," she said, staring into the flames. "Storm's is a crazy world, for sure, but we've all put our hearts and souls into it and we're proud of what we've accomplished. We love what we do. It's just…trying, sometimes. That's all." *It's a hell of a lot more than that.*

Frankie nodded. "Harper Cushing needs to get back into her groove."

"Yeah, I guess I do."

That wasn't what Frankie's big heart wanted to hear, but Harper had been honest. Storm mattered, especially these days with its success rising, and she was expected to lead the way. They couldn't squander everything. Band members had given too much to this *relationship*, the years of hardship and pitiful pay, of fighting for sorely deserved recognition and this opportunity of a lifetime.

She had to trust that Frankie understood.

"Fire's almost out," Frankie said. She emptied a nearby water jug onto the embers, and created a gasp of steam filled with a finality Harper didn't want to hear, see, smell, or even acknowledge. Frankie took her hand and drew her to her feet. "Come home with me tonight."

# CHAPTER TWENTY-SEVEN

It's shaped like a fucking triangle," Terri groused. "How the hell is it *not* supposed to tip over?"

Frankie knelt on the plywood and drove in another screw to join the double layers of wood. "Because," she said, straightening, "you pay attention. You don't step on the front corners or weigh them down off balance."

Terri screwed her corner tight and stepped back, eyeing the little flatbed vehicle. "Yeah, but a rectangular bed on a triangular chassis? I mean, the bed part's strong now, but…I don't know." She took off her Stetson to wipe her brow. "I suppose it ain't bad for being days away from the scrap heap."

"Hey. One man's junk, you know? That flood messed up my finances, so finding this thing answered my prayers—and I *had* to have one for harvest. This little buggy is going to cart a lot of berries off the bogs, especially now that we got the motor working."

Frankie beamed at her newest acquisition. Not much bigger than a golf cart, the three-wheeled little flatbed was worth its weight in gold. Now, she could get loads of full boxes to that beefy truck she planned to rent in October. Someday, she'd own one of those, too, but that was a long, long way off.

Terri pulled the rip cord and the motor at the front of the buggy sputtered, then settled into a steady hum. Gripping the long handle that extended forward from the motor, she stood in front like holding a dog's leash. "So, I push the handle down?"

"Yeah. Down feeds the gas. Let up on it, and it'll stop."

"No brakes?"

"No brakes."

Gearing up for the challenge, Terri tugged her Stetson down harder and squared off with the vehicle. "Well, okay." She pressed down on the handle and the wheel below the motor just spun in the gravel.

"Get on," Frankie said, taking the handle. "It needs some weight." Terri crawled aboard carefully, avoiding the front corners, and grunted into a cross-legged position. Frankie flipped the handle back over the motor, toward her. "Here you go. You're in the driver's seat now, sort of."

"Right. *Driver's seat.*" Terri huffed. "My ass on rock-hard plywood, is all." She took the handle, but the heaviness of her hands weighed it down. The buggy took off. "Yo! Shit!" Slammed onto her back, Terri fell away from the handle, and it bounced into a level position and slowed the buggy to a stop.

Laughing, Frankie ran after the runaway Stetson.

"Real fucking funny!" With a roll of her hips, Terri sat up and planted her feet on the ground. "Cripes, this thing's got some muscle." She settled her hat back onto her head.

"Good," Frankie said, sitting beside her on the edge of the bed. "It's going to need them to get a twelve-hundred-pound load up the planks and onto the road."

"Twelve hundred?"

"Yeah. I figure three boxes across, double-stacked, so that's six, and then five rows like that should fit. Thirty boxes at about forty pounds each, that's twelve hundred."

"Hell of a load for this thing, Frankie."

"I know. And keeping these three wheels aligned on planks up those steep angles is going to be tricky. We might have to push to help the motor."

"Gee. I can't wait."

Frankie turned where she sat to watch Terri circle the buggy. *The matador taunts the bull.*

"So, this thing may need our help?" Terri asked, sounding cocky now. "It's not as tough as it thinks, huh?"

"We'll find out in a couple of months."

Terri flipped the handle back to the forward position and squared off with the buggy again. Carrying Frankie's weight, the vehicle was equally ready.

*Don't do it, Terri. At least step aside or...*

"Listen, um, I wouldn't—"

With a quick, taunting jerk, Terri pumped the handle down. The buggy jumped at her like a jousting knight and the handle jabbed her in the chest. She landed hard on her ass as Frankie flew off the side.

They sat up in the gravel, Terri cursing the buggy, Frankie cursing Terri.

"You just *had* to play with it. Are you okay?"

"Eh. I think it's got enough power." They stood and brushed themselves off, and Terri rubbed her solar plexus with the heel of her hand. "Might be a little sore tomorrow."

Distant applause spun both of them toward the cabin.

"Encore!" Harper yelled, laughing as she approached. "That was hysterical."

Frankie pointed at Terri. "Wasn't my fault." She made no attempt to hide her appraisal of Harper in yellow shorts and white T-shirt, and heard Terri whisper pointedly behind her.

"You're drooling."

"Shut up," she whispered back.

"You have a new toy?" Harper asked, now agonizingly within reach. Hands on her hips, she shook her head. "Who needs to read directions, right?" She poked Frankie's stomach, then quickly rubbed the spot. "Hi."

*High is exactly what this feels like.*

"Hi, yourself, rock star. Come on. We were just going for a test drive." She showed Harper where to sit—in the center with Terri.

"Go easy on us," Terri said. She bumped a shoulder to Harper's. "Freakin' little kid at Christmas."

"Have you driven this thing yet?" Harper asked as Frankie stepped aboard.

"Nope." Standing front and center, where the vehicle's only wall rose some four feet and separated them from the motor, Frankie lifted the handle back toward herself and pressed down cautiously. "I'll take it slow." The buggy crept forward and picked up speed the more she depressed the handle. "Cool, right?"

"Your own cranberry chariot," Harper said, leaning back on her hands. "You'll be bringing this onto the bogs?"

Frankie nodded. "Once the picking machines go around a few times and clear the way. Then, this can collect the full boxes and truck them off." They cruised away from the barn and around the bog perimeter. "You think Stella would like a ride? I've always wanted to bring her all the way out here."

"I think she'd love it." Harper quickly swept loose hair from her face and put her hand back down before she fell over against Terri. "She'd need a cushion or something, though."

"Yeah," Terri added. "My ass is killing me already."

Frankie let up on the handle and the vehicle slowed to a stop. "Then, here. You drive." She traded places with Terri and put her lips to Harper's ear. "Hope I didn't just sign our death warrants." Harper laughed.

Looking steadfastly in command, Terri inched them forward until she got the hang of it. Then, she sped up as if she was late for lunch.

"Whoa!" Frankie yelled. "No helmets back here!"

"Or seat belts!" Harper added.

"Slow the hell down!"

Terri laughed but obliged, angling toward the barn doors just a bit too fast. All three of them yelled when the buggy's front corner pitched down into the turn, and impaled itself into the gravel. The sudden stop flung them all to the ground.

"Shit!" Frankie shouted, rushing to Harper's side. "Are you okay?"

Thankfully, Harper was laughing as she swept dirt off her legs. Frankie fired a glare at Terri, and brushed grit off Harper's shirt. Her dirty hands made it worse.

"Jesus, Harper," Terri said. "I'm so sorry. I forgot—just for a second—that this was a tricycle. I'm really—"

"It's okay. I'm good." She looked up at both of them and laughed again. "Honestly, you two are a menace."

Terri slunk back to the buggy. Frankie figured Terri's embarrassment probably lent her the brute strength to haul it upright by herself.

She turned to Harper. "I'm sorry, too. And about your shirt. I think I made a mess."

"Stop. It's just a shirt, Frankie," she said, looking down at it, "although Gram might be amused by the well-placed handprints."

"I may have missed a few spots."

Harper claimed her hand as it moved to her chest. "Another time, another place."

Frankie grinned at the invitation. "Aren't you happy you came by today?"

"Actually, I wanted to ask you both if you'd seen the Crossroads webpage."

"What webpage?"

"Since when does Crossroads have a webpage?" Terri asked, sitting on the buggy. She shook gravel out of her work boot.

Harper started searching her phone. "Almost a week now, apparently."

"A week?" Frankie looked at Terri and back to Harper. "How come we didn't know? Who—"

"Donna." Harper showed her the image on the screen. Minus one boot, Terri hopped closer to look over Frankie's shoulder. "Gram said Donna 'mentioned something about the internet' a while ago. I guess Donna sold her on the idea, but Gram forgot to tell anyone."

Frankie took the phone and studied the page, which showed the storefront on July Fourth, buntings and all, along with a few pictures of the inside. "Will you look at that?" She lifted her gaze to Harper's, momentarily distracted by the grin on her lips. "What does Stella think?"

"Well," Terri offered with a laugh, "*I'd* say that if Donna did this by herself, she did a great job. Don't you think?"

Harper smiled broadly. "Oh, I do. Gram's a little blown away by it, though, seeing the actual thing. The concept is still tough for her to grasp, and I think she's kind of afraid to be excited. The internet has such a *lovely* reputation."

"But this could be a shot in the arm for Crossroads," Frankie said, absently passing the phone to Terri. "I probably should have—"

"No 'should haves,' Frankie." Harper tapped her nose. "I don't know why *I* didn't jump on the idea when I got here in June. I'm sure it will help Crossroads."

"And check this out." Terri read from the screen. "'Several times a month, friends gather on the porch and extend the Crossroads neighborhood feel into evenings of homespun music and familiar sing-alongs.'"

"And *that's* what brought all this to light," Harper explained. "Just an hour or so ago, a customer asked me when there would be music on the porch." She tipped her head at Frankie. "She'd seen the page and asked if you participated and when I said yes, she said she and her wife would love to come and listen."

"Me?"

Harper tugged on Frankie's shirt. "Musically or otherwise, looks like a handsome cranberry farmer has made a *very* nice impression."

Frankie ran a hand back through her hair, floored by all of it.

"I'm glad you don't have to check in with the doctor for another six months." Harper parked behind Crossroads and hurried to help Gram exit the car. "It's good news, if these meds are all you need."

"I know. I'm happy you were with me for this appointment. The doctor's nice, isn't she?"

"Very. She knows her stuff *and you*. You're lucky to have her."

"So, are you off to Frankie's now? Weren't you going to help her do some weeding?"

"I thought I'd surprise her, yeah, but I have to jump on a Zoom call and that could take a while. Maybe I'll bring her something for dinner later."

"Your band friends have been calling a lot lately. You must miss each other."

"They've had too much time off," Harper offered with a laugh. "They're restless and toying with new material." She waved to Donna at the front of the store and followed Gram into her apartment. "Unlike them, I've had a wonderful vacation."

"Oh, sure you have. A 'wonderful vacation,' hanging out with a grandmother and her old store, working your tail off, and going to doctor appointments."

"Stop. I love being here, doing stuff with you. Look what we've done around here together—and that includes celebrating the doctor's visit with yummy ice cream sundaes. Have I been brooding about missing the band? No, ma'am."

*If anything, I've been brooding about going back to it.*

Harper did miss their creativity and family feel, but the past month or so had tempered her passion for Storm's signature fury. Maybe she needed this upcoming Zoom meeting more than she thought.

Upstairs in her apartment, she poured herself an iced tea and settled on the couch with her laptop, waiting for the connection to kick in. When the image of Rhea's home studio materialized, she leaned forward, searching for her lead guitarist.

"Whoa! There you are! Tell me that's not a mullet I see."

Rhea's ear-to-ear smile flashed against her olive complexion. Harper couldn't see her eyes behind those ruby lenses, but knew they were dancing.

"Yeah, so, the hair's grown some since the end of May, but it's coming off this week. Looks like you've been beaching it. I'm digging the tan."

"No beach, just outside a lot more than usual."

"Honey, being outside *period* is more than usual." She draped a guitar around her neck. "So, listen. It's just you and me today, but Primma and Zee sent me this tune they've been working on. I told them I'd mess around with it, then run it by you. See what you think."

Harper sat back as Rhea flipped a switch on her amp and picked through several crisp bars at a blistering pace. The sound pierced the tranquility in Harper's living room and brought her upright on the couch to lower the laptop's volume. But she couldn't. The "feel" of the song mattered, even if it assaulted her senses. The progression intrigued her, and she wanted to hear where Rhea took it.

The powerful notes stopped abruptly, replaced by chords barely restrained enough for Rhea's singing to be heard. Harper listened keenly to the pace Rhea applied to every line, the poetry in the clever lyrics, how well suited it was to the melody. The combination was solid, and the demanding tone made for a gripping sound.

Ending the second verse, Rhea suddenly asked, "For the break, I thought we'd flip back to this." Her fingers leaped into overdrive, and she cranked the power to match those wild, opening bars. Harper just sat with her chin in her palm, accepting the musical blows but mesmerized by riffs she could never do herself.

Rhea downshifted whenever words were called for, and jumped back into high gear whenever they weren't. Not a subtle ride for singer or listener, but it definitely grabbed you. And when Rhea closed by ratcheting up the emotion, Harper dropped back against the couch, exhausted.

"Wow. Intense," she said, watching Rhea chug a glass of water. "That's definitely a Storm tune."

Rhea relaxed onto a stool and smiled. "Yeah. I thought so, too. I think this is our next 'Wicked Angel.' I can hear you already."

Harper didn't think her voice could handle another "Wicked Angel." One of Storm's most requested songs, it demanded everything from her, left her physically drained each time she sang it, which was why it sat as the encore finale on their set list. But Storm could use another massive tune that kept the audience screaming for more.

"I'm not sure I should try singing it yet, but I vote yes. Get it out to everybody. Did you video this, I hope?"

Rhea was nodding. "Yeah. I thought you'd say that. I'll send the clip to the guys, and we'll go over it."

"Sounds good, although getting together like this doesn't really cut it."

"Hey, maybe I'll take a little road trip."

Harper laughed. "Right. As if you miss living on the bus."

"More important: How's that snarling vixen voice? It's coming along, right?"

"Definitely. I saw a Boston doctor a week or so ago, on the recommendation of my guy, and he said things are healing just fine. He was impressed, actually, so I'm testing it more often now." *Although not on tunes like this.* "I don't expect any more trouble."

"Shit, yeah! I like it. Less than two months, girl. I'm itching to get back out there and kick some ass."

*This is where I'm supposed to agree.*

"So, hey," Rhea went on. "What do *you* have to share? You working on anything at Granny's or just soaking up the sun?"

"No tunes to offer, I'm afraid. Well, not yet, anyway. I finally got Gram's situation ironed out. That was tops on my list. We're about halfway through all the renovations and breaking in a couple of new people. It's taken some doing, but she's happy, so I'm happy."

"Mission accomplished?"

"Getting there."

"But it can't be all work and no play. Come on."

"I do play now and then, but I'm being careful, doing mostly softer stuff. Besides, I can't drive Gram out of the house."

"Sounds like progress, at least, but not the kind of 'play' I was talking about. You better be getting some on the side, girl. That's what summer vacation's for."

"Uh-huh. And how many fine Jersey ladies are on your list?"

"Oh…a couple. It's been a great summer, so far. Charging up the batteries to hit the road, you know?" She set her guitar aside and pointed at the screen. "Okay. Look, I'll send you this clip and you can try it out, but start playing more. It really doesn't matter what, just start getting your smokin' self ready."

## CHAPTER TWENTY-EIGHT

F rankie accepted the three dollars from the heavyset man on the porch and sympathized with his weary look. Worn and sweaty, he gulped down the Gatorade, exhaled a thank you, and resumed his jog to God-knows-where. She maneuvered around the stepladders and workers finishing the recessed lighting, and then around Harper, Stella, and Joe, who were rearranging the porch furniture.

Inside Crossroads, the ongoing dance between business and renovation looked more like wartime chaos. Of all times for business to pick up, Frankie mused, did it have to be right now? Did the new webpage have anything to do with this?

Just beyond the door, a worker stood guard at a stepladder while another affixed a paddle fan and light to the ceiling. Frankie sidestepped them, listening to carpenters sand the woodwork at the dining corner. Amidst it all, Donna rang up purchases for a customer at the counter while another waited for the grilled cheese sandwich Stella had obviously forgotten.

"Be right with you," Frankie told the young girls pondering the candy case and hurried to the griddle. "Apologies for this," she said to the man waiting. "We're perfectly in sync around here right now, as you can see." She wrapped his sandwich and Donna took care of the money.

Back at the candy case, Frankie folded both arms on top and grinned at the three girls. "Any decisions yet?" All three spoke at once, but Frankie managed to bag their choices, tallying things in her head as she went. They paid her happily and she was relieved she didn't have to crowd Donna, who already had a man and a restless toddler at the register.

She took a breath, glad to see customers under control. *Thank God, we'll close for a few days to do the floors.* But looking around now, Frankie had to smile at the three weeks of progress, at what would be in a couple more, and she credited Harper's devotion to the cause. First off, though, she sorely wanted the kitchenette's cabinet doors reattached.

"When will all these doors be refinished?" she asked Donna, who was cleaning the Formica countertop.

"They're going back up tomorrow, I think, and Harper said the butcherblock countertop will be here, too. Hopefully, the sanding around here will be done soon, too, before this dust kills us all."

"Don't you worry about dust." Stella led Joe and Harper in from the porch. "I'm taking care of that." Behind her, Harper rolled her eyes.

"Got a little crazy just then, didn't it?" Joe chuckled and brushed off a stool at the counter before sitting. "It's a good sign, I say."

"Joey's right," Stella said. "Folks don't mind all this going on. They understand. But what would I do without you?" She patted Frankie's cheek as she shuffled into the kitchenette.

Harper patted Frankie's cheek, too, imitating Stella with a tease, and began dusting off the other stools.

Frankie just shook her head and stepped up behind Stella. "*Someone* left a sandwich on the griddle."

"Oh my God!" Stella whirled to the griddle in disbelief. "I *did*, didn't I? Dammit. That's not good."

Frankie steered her back to the counter and transferred her to Harper, who urged her onto a stool. Frankie poured her a glass of iced tea and Stella took it with both hands.

"Could've happened to any of us, Gram, but we all have to be on our toes. It's a little hectic around here, right now."

"Well, it won't happen again." Stella sipped her tea, deep in thought, until Joe tapped his palm on the counter repeatedly to get Donna's attention.

"Did you put that video of us on the internet last night?" he asked her.

"What video?" Frankie interrupted him, thinking somebody better start checking the damn webpage.

She exchanged a curious look with Harper. It had been a while since their last picking session, but she remembered Harper joining in and the boost that had given to the whole evening. No one had noticed it being recorded.

Donna nodded, her smile bright and proud. "Yup. Just a tiny one, like thirty seconds."

Harper looked more than concerned. Her dark eyes deepening, she inched onto the stool beside Stella. "At the risk of sounding ungrateful, I'd like a peek at things before they go up."

"Sure, of course." Donna grinned at Stella. "We thought it was great, that Roy Orbison song."

Stella nodded vigorously. "It certainly was, although you didn't need to film me singing along, too, Donna."

"I have to see this." Harper pulled out her phone and, in seconds, they all heard the chorus of voices on the recording. "I remember this," she said, looking at Frankie. "You nailed it, you know."

"Everybody did."

"So," Joe said, leaning forward to question Frankie, "we're on for tomorrow night, then? That's what we agreed to last time."

"And that's what I posted," Donna added, looking a little guilty.

"Yeah, I guess." Frankie kicked herself for forgetting, but the idea that Harper might join them again sent a buzz down her spine. "Maybe you'll try some singing this time?"

"I'll give it a shot, sure."

Stella cornered Frankie in the storage room as the full-throated group on the porch launched into another song. "What if I haven't made enough? There's an extra dozen people out there now, like Memorial Day."

Although a little part of her agreed with Stella's concern, Frankie enjoyed tonight's turnout. A half-dozen cars were lined up along the porch, windows down, as passengers listened to the music. Several people sat on their hoods, singing, and a couple even brought their own guitars to play along, all while little ones bounced around in the twilight.

She put down the carton of potato chip bags and took Stella's hands. "Will you relax? You've made enough cookies for a small country. And not everybody's going to hang around forever anyway."

"I could make a few dozen more. Oh. No. I don't have enough chocolate chi—"

"Stop. People are buying other stuff, too, you know. Look. Harper just reloaded the cooler chest and I'm already refilling the chip shelf. Stop worrying." She pulled her in for a quick hug. "Between you, me, Harper, and Donna, we'll handle it. Now, get out on that porch and sing, relax."

"You'll be right out?"

"Yes, in a minute."

Stella didn't look too reassured, but she went, and the applause her appearance drew from the crowd outside made Frankie chuckle. As she bent to pick up her chip box, a stiff-arm forced her against a stack of cartons.

"You've been in here too long." Harper stepped into her chest and drove both hands up into her hair. Frankie's head spun as arousal rocketed through her. Harper whispered against her mouth. "We're missing your voice out there and you're missing all the fun."

Harper kissed her slowly, languidly, back to the boxes, and had Frankie wet in an instant. At Harper's sweet hum of satisfaction, Frankie's self-control slipped away, and she squeezed her closer, returning every long, deep, delicious stroke of her tongue. Harper destroyed Frankie's hair, clutching her head tighter, and squirmed as Frankie's hands roamed down her back.

Frankie sucked Harper's tongue hard, dug her fingers into Harper's ass and crushed their hips together. She broke away to breathe and nipped along Harper's neck.

"Much more fun right here." She spun Harper against the wall and with a muffled growl, recaptured her mouth, oblivious to time, place, everything except want. One hand over a breast, the other at the zipper of her shorts, she groaned against Harper's lips. "Right here. Right now." She yanked the zipper down and shoved her hand inside.

Harper arched into her, took her mouth with a moan as Frankie stroked her hard and fast, relishing the feel of her. Harper's breathing fell short and when her head rolled back against the wall, Frankie devoured that luscious throat. She pinched the stiff nipple through Harper's shirt and bra and thrust inside her again and again.

"Frank—Oh...Fuck!" Harper's ragged voice crackled at Frankie's ear.

"Exactly."

"So...good!"

"Not good," Frankie breathed at her cheek. "So *fine*." She plunged deeper with each thrust, could feel Harper tensing, tightening around her fingers.

"Jesus. Oh, don't stop!"

"Let it come, Harper."

"Fuck, yes! I'm..."

"Yes, you are. Come for me now."

"God...Yes, Frankie!" Her words melted away and she shook against Frankie's chest, in her hand, rigid and fisting Frankie's shirt. Frankie licked the clenched eyelids, the moist cheeks, the tender lips. She swirled her fingers and made Harper twitch one final time. She hated to withdraw. She wanted more, could so easily drop to her knees.

Harper's chest heaved as she went limp against the wall, and she offered a dazed smile, straightening Frankie's mussed hair. And, because she could, Frankie reached between her legs again and cupped her possessively. Because Harper would let her. Because Harper wanted that hand exactly where it was, just as much as she did. The wet heat around her fingers took her breath away.

When she squeezed, Harper ground into her hand and Frankie squeezed again, unable to stop but somehow knowing she had to. *Remember where we are, for Christ's sake.*

Harper exhaled against her cheek. "If you keep it up, I'll—"

"You'll what?" Frankie leaned hard into her chest and outlined Harper's lips with her tongue. "You'll come again, won't you?"

"Oh, you're wicked."

Frankie's hammering heart left her shaky and she fumbled, zipping Harper's shorts, but she kissed her as delicately as she could. "You're magnificent, Harper Cushing." She inched back to share a serious look. "What you do to me, how you make me feel, I—"

"How I make *you* feel? God, Frankie." Harper pulled her in and spoke against her mouth. "To think I'd just come in here, hoping to steal a kiss."

Frankie kissed each lip carefully. "It's going to be a very long night."

# CHAPTER TWENTY-NINE

Playing from a stool beside Gram, Harper eyed Frankie on the opposite side of the porch and added her voice to the many. After an hour of singing and playing, she had settled into a comfortable groove among the folk, blues, and country tunes, and was grateful to discover her voice and guitar work could meet the challenge. The early going hadn't been easy, however, considering Frankie had turned her focus into a hot throbbing mess.

But the rumble of Iman's bass notes in the floorboards lent her the same familiar stability as Zee's thunderous bass guitar, and she couldn't help but compare the acoustic and electric instruments. *Just as stirring, yet so different.* The very presence of Iman's portly upright bass seemed to empower everyone in a welcoming, communal way Harper hadn't appreciated before, and she wondered if Iman realized the humanizing effect of his instrument.

Soloing on guitar and mandolin, Allie and Terri led the group through a pop song and drew a vigorous round of applause.

"I love it when they play that one," Gram said, watching Allie and Terri wave thanks to the people in the parking lot. "It's made for them."

Harper nodded as she clapped. "It's made for *all* of them. They have that one down to a science."

"Uh-oh. What's Frankie up to now?"

"We're going to try a little something," Frankie announced, glancing at the others and stepping to Joe against the railing. "We've toyed with this for a while now, so bear with us." Harper leaned on her guitar and watched as Frankie set a hand on his shoulder and nodded encouragement. Her connection to him was endearing, and Harper flashed a smile at Gram.

His full attention cast down at his picking hand, Joe cautiously plucked several solitary notes from his banjo, repeated them to establish an intro, and Frankie inched back, her own hands idle at the guitar. She began singing the humble, prayerful words of "Stand By Me" in a voice that flowed down into Harper's core like some rich, warm potion.

Frankie sang gently to Joe's notes, then played single, pointed chords in soft strokes when the chorus came around. The twinkling sound of Terri's mandolin fell in atop the melody and filled in the quiet background.

Harper sat fascinated by such a different take on the classic song. *A banjo, no less.* When Allie's guitar stepped in for the instrumental break between verses, Harper was tempted to add her own harmonic compliment, but she held back. This was their creation, and it was enchanting.

Around her, everyone appeared to agree. They sat transfixed as the overall sound grew. The closing chorus brought Iman's bass and Frankie's and Tom's guitars into the mix, and a few extra voices dared to join in. By the third and final repetition of the chorus, everyone was singing—including Harper. There was no escaping the spirit of the moment.

At the end, Harper jumped to her feet, cheering as the place went nuts. The musicians high-fived each other, clearly elated by their final product. And rightly so. Not only did their arrangement respect the popular tune, but their musicianship totally blew away any amateur imitation. For a casual little band, they were remarkably tight, far better than Harper expected, and she chided herself for being surprised. *Come down off that high horse, Cushing.*

"I hope Donna can put that song on the internet!" Gram shouted over the noise.

Harper nodded as she put thumb and forefinger to her lips and whistled. *She better. It was freaking fantastic.*

Had it been Frankie's doing? Lord knows, she'd done a masterful job reworking "Send Me Down." Harper pointed directly into Frankie's smile and winked.

Without their motors running, Frankie's picking machines stubbornly resisted being tucked deeper into the barn, no matter how much she and Terri swore at them.

"Thank God, there are only four," Terri said, flexing her shoulders.

"What's a few hundred pounds here and there?" Frankie started sweeping what now was a very roomy space. "They'll be easier when they're running on the bogs. You'll see when the time comes."

"Month and a half?"

"Maybe two. Harvest may not come till mid-October."

"God. Where does the time go?"

Frankie tried not to think about time flying. Harper would be gone in a month.

"Thanks for the help. I know you didn't stop by to be put to work."

"Eh. No problem. I came by 'cause I'm nosy." She went to the open doors and scanned the driveway. "So, they're late?"

"Should be here any time now." She set the broom aside. "We might need to help them with their stuff, too."

"Yeah, well, that's okay. I always wanted to be a roadie. Hey. Guess who's here first."

Harper parked at Frankie's cabin and strolled toward them, smiling behind oversized sunglasses. Knowing Harper would be her roommate for the next few days did absolutely nothing for the "friends with benefits" self-control Frankie was supposed to have. These days, just the look of her made Frankie take an extra breath, and right this second, she could strip her naked in this summer sun and lose her damn mind.

*Oh, the fantasies we keep.*

In a pink short-sleeved shirt and cut-off shorts, Harper looked more like a savvy, vivacious athlete than a rock star. Sometimes, Frankie set reality too far back in her mind for her own good. Like she had just now.

"Morning." Harper took off the sunglasses and beamed at each of them. "Terri, nice look." She gestured to the sleeveless T-shirt, snug across her broad shoulders. "Have you been working out?"

"Me? Um." She looked down at herself. "No but, you know, horses 'n' all." She fidgeted with her Stetson and Frankie almost laughed at her fluster.

"Well, I bet Ginny likes it," Harper added with a wink and turned to Frankie. "Rhea just texted. They're a few minutes away." She surveyed Frankie from the bottom up, from dusty boots and jeans to faded old T-shirt, and toyed with the rip at her ribs. "You've been hard at it again."

Frankie squirmed a little at the tickling sensation, which brought a very satisfied smirk to Harper's lips.

"We're just getting ready." Unable to resist some contact, she twirled a loose strand of Harper's hair behind her ear. "Is this space okay?"

Harper looked past her into the barn. "God, yes. That's plenty. Thank you for going to so much trouble."

"No trouble. I had help."

"Well, thank you both." She leaned upward and kissed Frankie lightly. "And thank you for offering your place, helping make this happen."

Frankie snared Harper by the front of her shorts and tugged her in. "I'm all for it, believe me. They get your apartment for four days and I get you." She returned the light kiss. "Perfect."

"Two white Suburbans," Terri proclaimed, and Frankie released Harper to wave the SUVs to the barn.

Harper grabbed her hand and headed for the closest vehicle. She hugged the driver the minute she stepped out, a tall, slim woman with a blazing smile and red goggle-shaped sunglasses.

One by one, Storm assembled in her yard and Frankie found herself a little starstruck. A sandy-haired man in a muscle shirt stretched loudly, while a man in ragged jeans and a petite woman rounded their SUV, headed for Harper. Three months had passed since Harper left them in LA and, judging by all the hugs and kisses, it had been too long.

Terri whispered at Frankie's shoulder. "Harper's like the little lost dog who finally found her family again."

Frankie couldn't disagree, despite the twinge of envy. Harper glowed among her bandmates, fondly touching and squeezing, answering and asking questions she didn't need to rush but obviously couldn't help. But then, to Frankie's surprise, Harper quickly turned and slipped an arm around her waist.

"Frankie Cosgrove, this is Storm." Frankie started shaking hands. "Rhea, our lead player; Decker, our drummer; Zee's on bass and Primma on rhythm guitar. And, you guys, this," she snuggled Frankie against her hip, "this handsome devil owns this cranberry farm—and her singing voice will croon the freaking pants off you."

"No way." Rhea slid her goggles up to her forehead and glanced at the others.

Decker clapped. "Sounds good to me. I like it when pants come off."

Rhea arched an eyebrow at Harper. "We'll talk later about how you know this." She extended a repeat handshake to Frankie and winked. "Oh, I *really* need to do this again."

Frankie knew what Rhea heard and saw, what they all did, and she cursed the heat in her cheeks, but kept her arm around Harper's shoulders proudly as she shook Rhea's hand. *Yeah, we're…close. For the summer.* "Thanks, but Harper's exaggerating. My music's nothing serious compared to yours."

"Bull," Harper said with a squeeze.

Zee plucked his T-shirt out from his chest. "Before I forget, Smitty sends apologies for skipping out."

"What's his excuse?" Harper asked and whispered to Frankie. "He's our keyboard player."

"His girlfriend's due date is today." Primma smirked at Frankie. "Baby number two."

"Well, I'm glad you guys could make it, at least. I'm happy to meet you all." Frankie looked back for Terri, and she stepped closer. "My friend Terri, who helped me get the barn ready. We'll give you a hand unloading, if you want."

"Hell, yes, we want." Decker said, sweat already shining on his thick arms. He shook Terri's hand eagerly. "Nice to meetcha. Let's get it on, huh? I'm ready to play sun god and crash."

Storm's organization was impressive for a bunch that seemed so laid-back. One SUV contained personal items and guitars while the other held gear and drums, and Zee quickly backed that one up to the doors to unload. A half hour later, Frankie's barn could have been a *Rolling Stone* photograph, the rustic studio filled with just enough high-end equipment.

It was enough to make the amateur musician in Frankie salivate. She was thankful to have no neighbors nearby because the sound that would emanate from here this week would surely shake the ground.

At dinner that evening, milling around Stella's dining room, the musicians clearly tried to win her favor with exemplary manners, and Frankie couldn't help being impressed. Actually, she was relieved by their appreciation of Stella's meal prep and hospitality because this motley group would be Stella's upstairs "tenants" for the next few days.

Zee settled in beside Stella with plates full of salad and spaghetti and tipped toward her, confidentially. "Thanks for all this, Mrs. A. A home-cooked meal?" He laughed. "Like, this is *so* good."

"And thanks for the barn space, Frankie." Rhea stabbed at her salad as she leaned against the wall. "We didn't bring the mighty stuff, just enough gear to shake off our dust. The last thing you need around here, I'd imagine, is megawatt sound."

Grinning, Decker refilled Stella's iced tea glass and then his own. "Yeah. Sorry, Frankie, but vibration alone would probably take down that poor little barn."

Stella gazed around her and, to Frankie, seemed a little lost in it all. But her eyes lit up when she caught Harper's attention, a safe harbor in the crowd.

"I was wondering how I was supposed to listen to you all if I was wearing earplugs."

Everyone chuckled and Frankie waited for Harper's response. Stella sitting in on Storm's raucous music couldn't be high on Harper's list, and Frankie figured everybody was thinking the same thing. To say Storm's music wasn't Stella's style was an understatement, but if she wanted to see her granddaughter in action, how could Harper say no?

*At least in the barn Harper won't be wearing basically-nothing leathers or getting off on a mic stand. Or would she?*

"We have some tunes that are…quieter," Harper managed, looking at her bandmates. They just nodded half-heartedly. That wasn't why they had driven all the way from Jersey.

*So, good luck with that.* "Quieter" was for the Crossroads porch, not a barn on fourteen isolated acres. "Quieter" simply wasn't Storm.

She hoped that, after reviving her Storm world for four days, Harper would still appreciate the relaxed atmosphere here, and the less frenetic music. It would say a lot about what really touched her heart.

# CHAPTER THIRTY

A llie motioned for Frankie to sit beside her, so she dropped into the Crossroads rocker with a long, worn-out groan. The long day of weed-whacking around the bogs had been as grueling as ever, but also odd. She had never been serenaded as she worked, and Storm's rowdy rehearsal blaring over the landscape had been…unusual, to say the least.

She really wasn't up for all the questions Allie looked eager to ask. But Stella and her visiting aide Marybeth were into a lively game of Yahtzee at the other end of the porch, so Allie no doubt felt this was an opportune time.

"Why didn't she invite you to go into Boston with them?"

"She did. I'm just wiped. Besides, this is their time to party. The band's leaving, day after tomorrow, and they won't get together again for a month, until September sometime."

"Well, listen. I just stopped by to ask if you two are free Friday night. Come out with Sunny and me?"

"Thank you, but by then, Harper and I will be back to keeping some space between us."

Allie sat back and squinted at her. "You mean as if four nights together never happened? On what planet does that work?"

"We're just bending our own rules for a few days. That's all, but I hear you. It's been beyond great. And so easy." The "roommates" arrangement with Harper made for spectacular nights together but ending it, when Storm left and Harper returned to her apartment, would be good practice. "We can't really 'date.' I mean, to what end, right?"

"Damn, I wish you could. *Everyone* wishes you two could." She sent her a sideways look. "Shit, Frankie. Messing around for a whole summer is…I don't know how you're doing it, to be honest. Has Stella said anything about the…*wisdom* of it all?"

"She's dealing with a lot, so where we're concerned, she's just happy and pretty proud of herself. She 'brought us together,' of course."

"Of course."

*For better or worse.*

"She'll be sad, too." Once Harper left, just looking around Crossroads would make Stella sad. Changes—and Harper's smiles—were everywhere, not to mention the effects Stella would detect on Frankie. She knew she'd have to buck up somehow when the time came, at least for Stella's sake.

"Well, then, Harper will leave with memories of great times, great music," Allie said. "I love that she gets into our stuff—and I never thought she would—but the way she steps up *and* steps back, not looking to dominate? And, man, the way you two click? That's special, Frankie. She'll take that with her."

"Thanks. I like hearing that." *Just tell me how to get through it.*

"Yahtzee!" Stella clapped for herself as Marybeth tossed her score sheet into the air, disgusted. They laughed as they stood, Marybeth gathering her purse to leave and Stella buffing her knuckles against her breastbone. "Champ strikes again!"

At the porch steps, Marybeth groused at Frankie. "I just need to know where she gets the marked dice." She called back to Stella as she headed for her car. "Until next time, *Champ!*"

Allie tapped Frankie's hand. "I have to shove off, too. Think about Friday night, okay?" Frankie nodded. "And Storm's little concert thing is still happening tomorrow night?"

"Eight o'clock, yeah. Harper says they're going to take it easy at first, or try to, then take a break, and then kill it for an hour."

Stella waved good-bye to Allie, packed up her Yahtzee game, and sat beside Frankie with a relaxed sigh. "Poor Marybeth. I whoop her butt every single time."

"You're merciless. Have pity on her."

"Next time, I think I'll make her some brownies to take home. A peace offering."

"You two are getting along famously—and that's scary."

"Isn't she wonderful? She's very professional, so knowledgeable and helpful—and funny. A lovely person." She grinned and elbowed Frankie. "And never nags. Hey, did you know her father grew up not far from here? He remembers Crossroads."

"Who wouldn't? She should bring him to visit sometime."

"Oh, that's a great idea! I bet he'd love that, wouldn't he? I'm going to suggest it."

Frankie rested her head back and tried to envision Crossroads' future. It was hard to picture Stella here too much longer, but this summer hopefully had given her at least a few more years of smiles, brownies, and porch time. Harper had done that. Frankie closed her eyes and smiled.

Stella curled her crooked fingers around Frankie's hand. "I know where your smile's coming from."

"Oh, you do, do you?"

"Harper had that same look on her face when we had our coffee out here this morning."

Frankie enjoyed hearing that. *Watching her put clothes on that fantastic body would've hurt if she'd been going anywhere else.* "She loves sitting out here with you."

"I'm happy the two of you are enjoying time together, you know. I'm not a prude."

"You weren't born yesterday?"

"Oh, you're a hoot."

"She has an amazing career ahead of her, Stella, and that's wonderful. And I'm glad for this summer. She's made it special for all of us."

"Well. That says a lot without saying much. I know there are feelings between you, Frankie. You're two very…heartfelt people." She squeezed Frankie's hand. "You know, no matter where she goes from here or what she goes through, she'll carry a piece of you with her."

Frankie looked down at their hands. "That works both ways, you know." She slipped her fingers between Stella's. "But when you're finally on the right track, Stella, what happens if you see there's more but you can't get there?" She shook her head. "I'm not sure how to handle that or even if I dare *think* about it."

"That's a tough one, Frankie, but I don't think you're alone."

Harper had so much on her mind, she struggled to remember lyrics and chords, and it showed. Initially, her bandmates laughed at her miscues, but the cute quips morphed into curious, rather irritated looks as her difficulties continued. The more she tried to keep her mates reassured, the more she stumbled.

Meanwhile, the Crossroads faithful sat attentively in their lawn chairs just outside Frankie's barn door, listening to the music. Harper knew the majority of them would leave once Storm launched into its "hard stuff." Already, she had lowered the overall volume and swapped out several songs to keep people happy, and the band had begrudgingly agreed, but it had been ages since she stressed about appeasing audience *and* band.

Beyond the mental gymnastics, Harper wrestled with an unfamiliar, gut feeling of exposure. Frankie seemed tangibly closer than the doorway where she leaned, and Harper would have relaxed beneath those discerning eyes if they weren't seeing Storm's lead singer in action for the first time, up close and personal. Support, respect, and even admiration showed in Frankie's expression, but longing and desire were there, too. Harper couldn't perform if she looked Frankie's way for too long.

As applause for their last subdued song faded, Joe stood to help Gram from her seat.

"Thank you all so much," Gram said. "What a treat this has been!"

He draped her sweater over her shoulders. "We're heading back now, but you guys are terrific. No doubt about that."

"Hang on," Harper said. "One more?" She turned in a circle, glancing at everyone, including her bandmates. "Frankie? Play one with us?" She grinned when Frankie's face went blank.

"But." Frankie straightened against the doorframe. "I don't know your songs."

Harper offered her acoustic guitar and took a spare for herself from the rack nearby. "There's one you know exceptionally well." Adjusting the tuning, she looked at her mystified bandmates. "Check it out."

Harper moved to within a few feet of Frankie and led her into the alternative version of "Send Me Down." Tension in her chest and limbs subsided as she sang the first verse, and then welcomed Frankie's voice.

Frankie eyed her cautiously and occasionally glanced at their chording hands, but held Harper's gaze as they effortlessly shared words and notes.

Distantly, Harper heard Zee's bass join in, and then Primma's wisps of slide guitar. At the instrumental break, Rhea added harmonic notes to Harper's lead, and Frankie's look of concentration softened into a grateful smile. Harper had all she could do to focus.

To her, this rendition had begun to feel like an old favorite, and in Frankie she saw the same rising exhilaration. They sang the final notes in harmony, their entwined voices sparkling to the last beat. Everybody clapped, including the band, as Frankie sent her a glazed smile.

Harper cupped her cheek and leaned closer until their guitars almost bumped. "Perfect." She kissed her lightly.

"Well, ain't that the truth!" Terri yelled from the doorway.

"Hell, yeah," Allie added, as applause finally faded.

Zee slumped onto a hip. "So, *that's* what you've been working on all summer?"

"Real nice take on it, Harper," Rhea said. "I don't know if the thousands who've already bought the original would like it, but it *is* sweet."

Decker, who'd sat silently at his drums through the song, leaned back on his stool and crossed his arms. "Have you changed any others?"

"No." *Was that a hint of resentment?*

"Don't blame Harper," Frankie said as she set Harper's guitar in the rack. "It's my doing. I liked the original, but of course I couldn't play it like

Storm does, so…" She shrugged. "Thanks for playing along, though. The way you guys filled it out was amazing. I'm flattered that you liked it."

"Well, it's *different*," Primma said and sent a skeptical eye to Decker.

"Huh." He arched an eyebrow at her. "Y'think?"

"*I* think it's lovely," Gram said, standing now between Joe and Donna. She raised her chin a bit and told the band, "You never know what your fans will say, but a little versatility only makes you shine that much brighter." She winked at Harper. "Thank you all for a fun time tonight. You're all so talented. It was a wonderful evening."

Harper walked them to Joe's station wagon, eager to thank Gram for withstanding an hour of music she wasn't likely to play on her stereo.

"You're a good sport, Mrs. Anderson." She kissed her cheek as Gram settled into the front seat.

"Good songs and good voices, honey. The music wasn't quite my style, but I *did* enjoy it. Especially you. And most of all, you and Frankie." She tugged Harper closer. "I think your musician friends might be a little jealous."

*I suppose that's possible, but I was thinking something else.*

Harper reached in and hugged her. "I love you, Gram."

"I love you, too, honey. See you in the morning."

Harper thanked Joe and Donna for seeing Gram back to Crossroads and returned to the scattering of loyalists at the barn. John, Iman, Allie, and her new girlfriend had left, but Vicky and Tom remained, along with Terri and her wife and daughter.

Frankie sat with them, and Harper wished for an extra minute alone with her, just to share more of that lingering high from their performance. But bandmates were gearing up for an hour of their powerful, signature music, and their eagerness was obvious. It was nearly impossible to talk over the loud burps from the PA system, blasts of random electric notes, and test raps off the drums. The hollow barn was simply a huge speaker cabinet for their sound and magnified it beyond anyone's chosen settings.

From behind her chair, Harper massaged Frankie's shoulders. "You guys ready for round two?"

"Hey, Harper!" Rhea held up Harper's electric guitar, a call for her to join them.

"Gotta go." She gave Frankie a squeeze and dashed into the barn.

Harper laid out various pedals next to her mic stand and began customizing the settings as minor chaos bubbled around her. This was far from a studio environment, where equipment never moved, and no roadies had spared them this setup, so issues like connecting specific cables, replacing guitar strings, or remembering equalizer levels forced everyone to actually *work*. She shook her head at how complicated band life had become and how much they took for granted.

Finally, with her guitar draped over her shoulder, she gave her strings a final tweak and cranked the volume. Her test notes fired out of the barn like gunshots. *Wildlife beware.* Getting nods from her bandmates, Harper grinned at Frankie, and with a windmill slash across her strings, Storm erupted.

# CHAPTER THIRTY-ONE

F rankie arranged hamburger patties and buns on the little barbecue grill in Crossroads' back lot, feeling as hot in the late afternoon sun as the grate itself. As hot as Harper looked in a loose-fitting white tailored shirt and blue shorts. She buzzed in and out, bringing things Frankie needed, and singing along to anything and everything Stella had playing in the kitchenette.

"Domestic bliss," Frankie quipped as Harper breezed by. *I could get used to this, damn it.*

Harper stopped. "It's fun, isn't it?" Frankie couldn't verbalize how much. She simply nodded. Harper leaned against her back to whisper in her ear. "I miss us waking up together."

Frankie half-turned, taken by the unexpected admission. "I do, too."

Harper slowly rubbed both palms up Frankie's back and across her shoulders, then trotted up the steps.

*Don't count the days, just your blessings. She's still pumped up because of Storm.*

Harper reappeared with a platter of shucked corn. "Any room for these? I talked Gram into Mexican street corn."

"I'll make room." She started shuffling things around on the grate and searched desperately for something casual to say. "Can't believe this grill doesn't get used more often. Stella loves her cheeseburgers, and this is better than the griddle inside."

"I don't remember the last time I had burgers on a grill. Not even back on July Fourth."

*She's avoiding the obvious, too.*

Frankie began laying out the ears of corn. "Then, it's about time." She bit back the rest of that thought. Harper didn't have much time left here, but there was no sense in pointing that out.

"The band would've loved them, if they only could have stayed longer."

"But they had a good time?"

"God, yes. I think Decker's going to adopt Gram, whether she's into the music or not."

"She's going to talk forever about having them here. Actually, she might even miss having that crew upstairs, cooking for everyone."

Harper laughed. "Yeah, she might." She hooked a finger into a back pocket of Frankie's shorts. "It gets nuts, sometimes, but I do miss them."

Storm had been gone two days and a part of Frankie wanted Harper to miss their own "roommate" arrangement just as much as her band. A big part of her. But neither of them was that oblivious to their situation to go there.

"You're already getting your groove back, Harper." She forced a smile as she flipped items on the grate. "Just a few more weeks."

"I'm looking forward to playing, to be honest. Their stay here brought so much back, that cohesion, the drive."

"And your voice was outstanding. Is it still okay?"

"So far. A dry throat, now and then, but no problems. Those new songs we tried are going to be amazing, so it's pretty exciting."

"I don't think they were too excited about our version of 'Send Me Down,' though."

"Well, no. They weren't, but that's because we worked so hard on the original and it raced up the charts. I'm kind of disappointed, but the softer version—*your* version—won't make our set list."

"I get that." She leaned against Harper's shoulder. "But it was *really* good, especially with the band added."

"No question, Frankie. I love it. I really do. It's just not a Storm tune."

"I wish you sang other stuff, too. Fans are missing out on that aspect of your voice."

"Thank you, but I'll leave that to you. Storm's material is what drives me. The soft stuff is just exercise."

"'Exercise'?"

"Yeah. You know, scales, pitch, tone, basic stuff and easy on the throat."

"Not stuff you take too seriously."

"Right. It's just part of crafting the real thing, and it's fun, like playtime."

Frankie didn't know what to do with that. *Did you hear what you just said?* She pondered the statements as she poked at the food on the barbecue.

If her own musical efforts had just been insulted, then it was a little hard to swallow and more than a little disheartening. Granted, it had taken a while, but everyone witnessed Harper's about-face to their music, and enjoyed how she'd taken it to heart. Or thought she had.

"We take our stuff seriously," she said, trying not to get defensive. "We can't do it professionally, but we're serious about it sounding good and doing it better every time."

"Of course. Everyone has her own musical taste and values. Storm just requires the best we can give."

*Yeah, well, so do we.*

"Right." Frankie shoved the spatula under the burgers and caught herself before she flung them onto the platter. She forced herself to ease up, and carefully took the food off the grate. "Time to eat." She headed for the steps.

"Hey. What's…Are you upset?"

Frankie stopped at the screen door. "Let's just say surprised."

Harper grabbed her arm just outside Stella's apartment door. "By what?"

"It's nothing, Harper. I'm probably overreacting, that's all." She stepped in and Harper followed.

"Overreacting to what?" She waited as Frankie put the food on the dining room table and Stella expressed her delight.

"We can talk later, okay? Right now, we—"

"No. I want us to enjoy dinner and I won't if I'm worrying about something I said."

Frankie sighed.

Stella stopped and stared. "Are you two arguing? What did I miss?"

"That's what I'd like to know," Harper stated, and planted her hands on her hips.

"It's just a difference of opinion, apparently." Frankie raised her palms haplessly at Harper. "A difference that surprised me. I'm sorry I got a little defensive."

"Well, if I put you on the defensive, then *I'm* sorry. But what—"

"Good," Stella said quickly. "Everybody's sorry. That's settled. Now both of you sit."

Harper put her hand on Frankie's arm. "Tell me what I said."

"I guess I just freaked a little about our music preferences, Harper, and I'm sorry." She sat, feeling her disappointment grow by the second.

Harper remained standing, her brow creased. "We have different preferences, that's true, but so what? Since when does that put either of us on the defensive?"

"Well, it was a little surprising to hear that mine amounts to some fun play-time exercise, compared to the grown-up thing Storm does."

"That wasn't intended to be demeaning in any way. But you guys *don't* perform for a living, and we do."

"True. But it doesn't mean we care or try any less. That's how it sounded."

Harper pulled out a chair and sat sideways to face her. "Of course, you all care, but it's our full-time job, Frankie. It's not that for any of you." She looked at Stella as if for support. "Am I way off base here?"

"No," Frankie said, pushing her burger aside. "I'd simply thought our music had come to mean something special to you, like it means to us. But, instead, I hear that it's just some amateur 'exercise' to you, and that kind of sucked." She dropped her hands to her lap. "That's all."

"Is this because Storm won't be doing your version of 'Send Me Down'?"

"God, no. It's beyond that, Harper. It's how you see our music here, *my* music."

"You think I don't like it?"

"Our 'simple, practice material'? How do you think that makes me feel?"

Harper threw up her hands. "I didn't mean it that way. You're definitely overreacting. Please stop."

"Yeah, maybe, but it does make me see things in a different light."

"And what's *that* mean? You see *me* in a different light?"

"Well, if that's how you value what I do—"

"Oh. Don't go there." Harper stood so fast, her chair almost fell over, and she spun to Stella. "Sorry, Gram, but I don't have much of an appetite right now."

Frankie didn't turn to see her leave. Numbed by a soul-deep chill, she saw their special musical connection in shreds.

The door to the upstairs apartment shut with force and Stella sighed heavily as she sat back in her chair.

"Well, I never thought I'd see either of you be so childish."

Taking a whole day to stew over Frankie's ridiculous tantrum did nothing for Harper's peace of mind. A foolish waste of a day, although she hadn't had a spare moment to do anything about it. Crossroads' renovations were wrapping up, Gram was being cranky and demanding about her decorating "wish list," and there never seemed to be quiet time at the store anymore.

At the moment, Harper reviewed a delivery receipt for Donna while a flooring contractor explained details about the last project on Crossroads' list. The phone jammed between her cheek and shoulder didn't help.

"Hear me out," Rhea pleaded, almost breathless with excitement.

"What did you say about next week?" She had said something about leaving, that much had registered. Harper begged the contractor to wait fifteen minutes and signaled Gram that she'd be right back. "Hang on," she told Rhea. "Let me go upstairs."

If only Frankie was here to help Gram deal with that contractor, she mused, running up to her apartment. "Why didn't we talk this out yesterday? Damn it, Frankie. *One* of us should have called, at least. This is just stupid." She shut the door and dropped onto the couch, winded. "Okay. Sorry. So, what did—"

"It's the perfect prep gig for us," Rhea charged on, "and Harry's off the frigging wall about it. We can fit it in, Harper. We just bump rehearsals back a week or so and we can do it."

"Wait. Slow down. A prep gig?"

"Two nights at the *fucking Fillmore*, for God's sake!" Harper's heart skipped at the thought of the historic venue. "I mean, I'm not as nostalgic as you, but still. San Fran's not one of our tour stops, so this covers that base. It's exactly what we need for some last-minute polish, you know? We'll hit the road a week later."

Obviously, Rhea couldn't wait to get back into their routine. Zee, Primma, and Decker had talked that up, nonstop, while they were here, and said Smitty was just as hot about it. Harper had almost forgotten what the anticipation felt like.

"So…First, we'd do this at the *Fillmore*?"

"Yeah. This is *sick*, right? What a lucky break!"

"But since when does the Fillmore have an opening?"

"No clue, but Harry found out about it yesterday and called Decker. If Sasha hasn't called you yet, call her. Decker said we can crash at his place. Remember that night we all sat around, dreaming of the old venues? You wanted the Fillmore *so* bad."

"For sure. If only."

"Well, here it is, Harper. We *have* to do this."

Rhea had a point, and her excitement was contagious. Playing the Fillmore as a warm-up to tour was a brilliant idea, an amazing opportunity, and where *that* place was concerned, it didn't take much to ignite Harper's fantasy. The iconic 1960s Fillmore concert hall would check off a lifelong bucket list item with a flourish.

*No question, this is a wise business decision.*

"Alright. I'm in, but…" So much crowded her mind besides rehearsals, flight reservations, and packing. There was *leaving*. Leaving Crossroads to stand on its own, leaving those sweet nighttime breezes and the damn crickets, leaving Gram. And leaving Frankie.

"I have…*stuff*, you know?"

"No shit. You sure do. Time to cut that fucking cord, girl."

Harper winced. "When would you get to Decker's?"

"Next weekend. Is that doable for you?"

"Today's...Saturday." Harper's brain swirled and she frowned hard. "God. Yeah, I guess it's doable."

"Excellent. So, hey, call Sasha, and keep in touch."

Ending the call allowed the immediate present, Gram, the store, and the contractor to come roaring back to mind. They waited downstairs. *One thing at a time.*

Harper forced herself to realistically, systematically assess her situation. The Fillmore gig effectively cut off her last two weeks here, so there was a lot to cram into the one she had left. At least renovations would be completed by then. The last of them, refinishing the floors, required closing Crossroads for a while, which actually would be more of a respite than a hardship, and Gram was excited about the reopening. Harper had been, too, but would miss it now.

And with a mixture of affection and relief, Harper knew that Marybeth and Gram had settled into a comfortable routine. Thankfully, Donna also had become a welcome fixture here, and couldn't wait to move into this apartment.

Harper sat forward on the couch, staring at but not seeing the old wallpaper. Such an insane day and rebellious focus had made it a long one. And now she had very important news to share.

She folded her arms across her knees and lowered her head onto them. Changes had worked out for Gram, thank God, just as Harper had hoped when the summer began, and *almost* everything would be on cruise control when she left.

## Chapter Thirty-two

W hen she emerged from the trees along Frankie's driveway, Harper switched off her headlights and drove up to the porch by moonlight. Frankie was playing her guitar in the minimal light, and blasting her with headlights would have been rude, if not painful.

Harper tried to steady her breathing. At least she wouldn't have to knock. She still didn't know where to begin and that's why she hadn't called ahead. Besides, Crossroads had been crazy-busy. Hopefully, Frankie wasn't still brooding, but then, she hadn't called, either. They hadn't spoken for two days, but now they'd *have* to. This "disconnect" just couldn't go on. It ran too deep.

*And that's the real issue.*

Frankie set her guitar aside but didn't get up. "Hi."

Harper stopped at the bottom step. "I'm sorry to interrupt." Frankie just shrugged, as if interrupting her music shouldn't be a big deal. "We need to talk, Frankie."

"I was coming over tomorrow morning."

"Like yesterday morning? To bake muffins and disappear?" Harper climbed the steps. "Not good enough. There's too much to be said."

"Maybe the fact that we're from two different worlds says enough."

"Well, we are, but…after everything we've shared?" She drew a stool closer and sat. Summarizing everything in such elementary terms seemed so insufficient. It just shortchanged their harmonies, their private exchanges, and God knows, their intimacies.

"It was fantastic, Harper. All of it was."

"So, what are you saying? That's *it*? Uh-huh. No. This is a misunderstanding we need to fix."

"Do we?"

"You don't think so? You think a…a childish disagreement should come—"

"For me, our 'disagreement' hits a lot closer to home than that. You seeing it as 'childish' just says that the rock star can't see through her designer sunglasses—or really doesn't want to."

Harper's temper drove her to her feet. "That's just not true and you know it. How can you even *think* such a thing?" She paced to the steps and back. "When have I ever put down your music? Never. *That's* why this whole argument is absurd. And, yes, it's childish."

"Then, let's leave it at that, Harper. Leave us right there. We're not going to get anywhere."

"Apparently, that's just fine with you."

Frankie hiked a shoulder. "Look," she stood and faced her, "our summer's almost over, right? So, maybe this is how it happens. Maybe we would have reached this point eventually. Maybe it's for the best."

Harper just stared at her. Those eyes held no warmth or welcome, just gloomy resignation, and Harper felt the chill of defeat and loss.

"This is the *easy* way, isn't it?" She wasn't asking. Her heart pounding in protest, Harper half-turned away. "Well, then. Just as an FYI, you might be interested to know that this *rock star* is leaving next Saturday. Something's come up."

Frankie stiffened.

*Like you suddenly give a shit?*

"Next weekend?"

"Yeah." Harper headed back to her car, trying not to scream every swear she knew or kick the gravel with her sandals or just shatter. "My schedule's been cut short. So, maybe I'll see you around before then."

Frankie doubted Stella was paying attention to the Britbox show she had insisted they watch tonight. Supposedly, the crime drama was good, but Frankie's mind was far from it and Stella's probably was, too.

With Donna not scheduled to move in until tomorrow, the entire building echoed in Harper's absence.

Saying good-bye on the porch this morning had been painfully awkward, and Stella and Harper had cried as if they'd never see each other again. Through an emotional fog, Frankie had fought her own composure, managed *not* to stroke that satin cheek, and only squeeze those magical hands.

At least Harper had smiled. Weakening beneath that penetrating gaze, Frankie had wished her good luck and success as Stella looked on, sniffling. Now, as she sat facing the TV, Frankie could still hear Harper ordering her to stay safe. She could still feel that palm on her chest. The pressure on that spot was so real and heavy.

She figured she'd still feel it in November, when Harper returned around Thanksgiving. Some things would be different then, but some wouldn't. She'd still yearn for her as much as she did right now, even months from now when the whole tour ended, although the wisdom of all that failed her. Storm's musical fulfillment was bound to remind Harper of what she'd been missing. Music was her life, not just business, and an artistic calling was not to be ignored, so...

"Do you think she's reached San Fransisco by now?" Stella asked.

Peripherally, Frankie saw her looking for an answer, so she answered as reassuringly as possible. "Definitely. They are all probably having dinner at some restaurant."

"Oh, well that would be nice. She said she'd keep in touch. Did she say that to you?"

Frankie nodded, wondering if Harper had really meant it. They hadn't been on very cozy terms, these last few days. *And whose fault was that?*

"I hope she really can make it back for the holiday," Stella said. "We'll wait for her, Frankie, and celebrate Thanksgiving whenever she gets here."

Frankie forced herself to appear brighter. Stella was too perceptive to not see a moping lump on a log.

"That would be great. She'd appreciate that, I'm sure."

Stella shifted in her chair and Frankie knew she was being scrutinized. "I know this is difficult for you, sweetie. I'd hoped you two would become dear friends. Honestly, I didn't really expect...well, you know."

"We didn't, either, Stella." She forced a grin for Stella's sake. "But our eyes were open. We're big girls. Sometimes, two lives only intersect for a while." She glanced at her and shrugged. "They don't always have to work out together."

"Are you lecturing me or yourself?"

Frankie laughed lightly at the blush she felt rising in her cheeks. "Okay, I confess. It was magical. But Harper finds her own kind of magic with Storm. That's just how it is."

"I know the summer was short, Frankie, and no one can predict where your lives will lead or who'll pop into them someday, but you two connected like it was meant to be. Something *that* special doesn't simply fade away. There's no denying it. I know what I saw. You guys even *sound* wonderful together."

Frankie's heart nudged higher into her throat. It was hard to hear her own thoughts out loud.

Humbled, she turned to Stella and tried to look "normal," not like an uncertain, regretful, heartsick, generally pathetic mess. "That means a lot, Stella. Thanks. I kinda think so, too."

Stella relaxed in her chair, hands folded in her lap. "I said all that to Harper, too, you know."

"Did you?"

"I won't betray her confidences, but I can tell you she was very deeply moved."

Frankie took comfort in knowing their brief relationship had actually meant something to Harper. "I appreciate you telling me."

Stella was right. They'd always have the summer to look back on, the baking, the Fourth, the bogs, their music, their passion. Things to smile about, if only she could be content with just those few months. But there was still so much more to share.

She really had brought on this bitter ending. Honestly. Because of the music? And she was whining?

To hell with the differences in their music…or whatever had forced her over the top. Maybe jealousy, "losing" Harper to Storm, had shortened her normally long fuse, and she'd ducked behind the music issue. Regardless, she'd let it screw everything up.

Frankie stood and stretched. She had to take her sad, sulking self out of here, away from Stella's sweet nature and home where it could fester and hopefully break like some nauseating fever. "Busy day tomorrow. Donna's moving in, right?"

Stella's instantaneous grin felt almost too bright. "That's right. Wait until she sees how the floors came out."

"They're gorgeous, Stella. You can see yourself in them."

"I know. Everyone will love them. Once Donna gets her things upstairs, we're going to bake for the grand reopening Monday. It'll be a busy day, all right."

"If you guys need any help, be sure to call."

"Definitely. You're heading home now?"

"Yeah, it's been a long day." She hugged Stella where she sat. "I'll lock up. You get some rest and remember, do *not* hesitate to call if you need me."

She checked the Crossroads doors and turned the dimmer switch for the new inside lighting down to "nightlight" mode. Motion detecting flood lights also stood guard at four spots around the building now, and, as much as she disliked the change in ambiance, she was comforted to know the place and Stella had some security.

Before exiting the back, she jiggled Stella's doorknob and went upstairs to check Harper's, or what used to be Harper's. Her hand around the knob, she lingered in the memory of eavesdropping. She could hear the vibrance in the voice, the perfect pitch, the timely breaths. The recall was powerful.

## CHAPTER THIRTY-THREE

Her throat parched and tired, like the rest of her, Harper rolled onto her side in her bunk and listened for signs of life from her bandmates as the bus rumbled along. Somewhere up front, Primma tinkered with a song, and Harper lounged in its lazy vibe until Smitty added a rising, piercing whistle from his portable keyboard and Decker started drumming on the table. So much for a gentle morning.

The short curtain beside her blocked the view of whatever weather awaited them today but it didn't matter. Rain or shine, Storm would crank out shows tonight and tomorrow in the ninth different city. Readjusting to the old routine was taking longer than she'd expected, and that probably contributed to what felt like disorientation. Days dragged and nights flew and riding that roller coaster was exhausting. What day of the week was this?

As usual, sleep had been erratic, bouncing between planes and motor homes, moving ever eastward across the country, and she couldn't wait for the next hotel bed and shower. She would make the most of both, before and between the upcoming Indy shows, and recharge for the next three in Chicago. Hopefully, she could squeeze in a visit with Denise and hit the hair and nail salons. She called Gram whenever she could but was so grateful that Donna had managed to teach Gram the intricacies of texting.

Crossroads sounded like a busy place, these days, which was good to hear, and Marybeth was bringing her father to visit fairly regularly, all of which gave Gram way too much to talk about. The chill of October was upon them, she learned, and Frankie expected a bountiful harvest, once nighttime temps dropped a bit more. Her preparations had her working hard, Gram said.

Harper wanted to know so much more. What preparations? Was she manning her sprinklers in the frosty dark yet? Was Terri helping her? When would harvest come?

Earlier in the week, between shows in Kansas City, she had called while up to her chin in bubbles, and those twenty minutes of steam and moist heat had helped her throat and weary muscles, but didn't lead to much detail about Frankie. She actually wondered if she was intentionally being kept in the dark about her for her own good.

Maybe it was just as well. Maybe her thoughts did wander back to Frankie too often, and she shouldn't be traveling that dead-end road. But it *had* been a memorable summer, hectic at times, and a little stressful, but more enjoyable than any vacation she'd ever had. The comfort in being herself, the surreal romance with a woman who literally caressed her soul, those were experiences to be treasured, and she kept them close, day and night.

She peeked at the blue-sky morning and wondered if Crossroads had sold out of its muffins by now. She chuckled at herself. Yes, she missed the bucolic mornings. She missed the way the simplest things made people smile, the ease with which feelings flowed, the honesty in those jovial porch sessions. *Shame on me for frowning on them back then.* Not for the first time, she figured Frankie may have been right to call her on it, after all.

And the daydreams of "home" didn't help her professional focus, either. They disrupted her sleep, muted her struggling songwriting creativity, and distracted her during rehearsals, which often frustrated the band and led to more disagreements than any of them preferred.

Having a new house in LA meant new opportunities in the heart of this vibrant, electric industry, but before she started buying furniture, maybe she'd return to Gram for a post-holiday get-together. Maybe stay a little while. And what was a 'while'? She missed that twinkle in Gram's eyes and the heartfelt messages in Frankie's. Damn, she missed so much about Frankie.

Harper followed Rhea into the hotel room they shared and closed the drapes against the bright afternoon sunshine. Each of them flopped onto their beds.

"Your alarm or mine?" Harper asked, eyes closed.

"I'll set mine." Rhea yawned at her phone. "Five o'clock?"

"Sure. That'll give us time for showers before Harry comes pounding on the door."

Harper gulped down half a bottle of water, determined to keep her vocal cords content, and willed herself to fall asleep. Arrivals were always insane, and Harper had grumbled as much as the others as Harry rushed them through unpacking, eating at the hotel, and a two-hour rehearsal/sound check at every venue.

Much later that night, Harper gratefully threw herself into the rear seat of their waiting van, still wiping makeup from her eyes. Their performance had run long, but the crowd loved those extra thirty minutes, and band members still buzzed with adrenaline, soaked through their clothes.

Decker and Zee squeezed in beside her, wired and talking nonstop. "The encore in K.C. was better," Decker insisted as Zee shook his head. "No. Indy. They wouldn't let us go until we did 'Wicked Angel.' We should've ended with that tonight."

Smitty slumped down in the second row. "Ask Harper what she thinks about that."

Sitting up front with Harry, Rhea barked at him over her shoulder. "Stop whining. You just wanted your keyboard solo."

Primma elbowed him and passed out bottles of water.

"How about if we close with it in Chicago?" Zee asked.

"Close with it tomorrow night," Harry stated from behind the wheel. Everyone shut up and looked at him. "What? It's the best finale. My opinion counts too, you know." He found Harper in the rearview mirror, two rows back. "You have a problem with doing that song tomorrow night?"

She looked away and drank heavily as they entered the parking garage. Apparently, he hadn't heard her voice cut out twice during the second encore.

Knowing glances on stage told her everyone else had heard it, so, thankfully, they hadn't attempted "Wicked Angel" and its hard-driving lyrics. *Never would have made it through that.* It was why they had agreed to skip the song tonight in the first place. She feared that doing it the other night in K.C. had set her vocal recovery back considerably.

"I vote we save it for Chicago," she said, hoping those extra days would make a difference.

The Crossroads faithful had a serious crowd on its hands, despite the aggravating chill. Bundled up in her winter coat and wrapped in a blanket, Stella "supervised" the porch from her rocker, as usual, but the musicians struggled to keep their cold hands nimble. The audience, however, was another matter.

Thanks to Donna's webpage efforts, dozens of cars filled the parking lot tonight, and people streamed in and out of Crossroads for snacks and hot drinks. Donna alternated between videoing the music and tending the register, as songs filled the night air for two-plus hours.

Guitar around her neck, Frankie bent to Stella's ear. "I think we've all had enough cold for one night. Don't you?" She wasn't about to let Stella's stubbornness land her in the hospital. And Stella's raised eyebrow said she knew what Frankie meant.

"After you do a couple more," she said, grinning toward the sea of cars, "because they're yelling for *you.* And those beeping car horns mean the natives are getting restless—in case you hadn't noticed."

Frankie had noticed, although disbelief made her shake her head. The vigorous applause for her own effort was certainly humbling, but she felt her work lacked a certain sparkle. Knowing exactly what that was, *who* it was, she did her best to ignore it.

Terri helped with that effort. She whistled across the porch to get Frankie's attention and kicked off a lively bluegrass tune. Welcoming the heated, energetic pace, everyone jumped into the music, and they were off.

But Mother Nature ultimately won the battle and Frankie soon had to call it a night, even though she was reluctant to let go of this camaraderie. Life had become far more solitary these days, now that she wasn't constantly needed at Crossroads, and time with friends kept her spirits from dragging, her mind off Harper and her woeful finances. Cars driving away and everybody packing up their instruments already had her eager for their next gathering.

Iman zipped a cover over his bass fiddle and called to her. "Hey, Frankie. We're ready to pick cranberries."

"Right," John added, swinging an arm around his shoulders. "I'm not just some handsome back-up singer, you know. When do we start?"

Frankie laughed at their antics, grateful for the support. "Very soon, depending on how cold it gets at night."

"It's not cold enough now?" Joe leaned on his tall banjo case. "If it isn't, what the hell does it take?"

"A spell of dry weather and nights in the thirties should do it." Just the sound of those temperatures pinched Frankie's nerves. Playing cat-and-mouse with the frost was intimidating as hell.

An hour later, Frankie had worked herself into a fret about the dropping temperature. She drove past her barn and onto the perimeter road, hardly needing headlights. Moonlight illuminated everything, including the steadfast trickle of water in the ditches.

*Thankfully, not cold enough to freeze.*

She stopped at the narrow bisecting road and stepped out, zipping up her jacket. The bitter, dank air enveloped her, penetrated her jeans, and chilled her thighs. A sporadic breeze buffeted her face and, despite the cold that made her blink, she was happy to feel it. Moving air helped prevent a freeze from settling over the low land.

She inched sideways down the banking and used her phone's flashlight to read the thermometer stuck into the ground. Thirty-four-degrees. *And six hours from now? How low will it go by five o'clock?*

Anxious to check the most recent co-op reports, she drove to the cabin. Hot coffee sounded really good right now, but she put it off until she found the printouts pertaining to her crop.

She sat down with trepidation when she read that the "tolerance" of her berries was twenty-six degrees. Based on the berries' current maturity, their outer skin could withstand that temperature before their insides froze. To be safe, she was ready to take preemptive measures at, say, twenty-eight degrees.

*Not gambling with a few degrees.*

She went through the motions of making coffee. Emptiness and silence seemed extra heavy in the house tonight, but she couldn't spare them the attention they sought. Her biggest test as a grower had to come first. She'd heard the stories, knew the consequences if she lost a single battle with the frost. Growers went through this regularly, combating the freeze, sometimes waging a dozen battles at this time of year.

Coffee in hand, she returned to her little computer niche and focused. The forecast indicated the temperature *could* drop from its current thirty-four to twenty-eight overnight. Easily. Especially if that sketchy wind died.

She glanced at the tiny black box on her hallway table and took comfort in the green light. The wireless device received readings from the thermometer on the bogs, and not only recorded highs and lows, but served as the alarm. It was active and receiving as promised, but she had never needed to set it until now.

The readout displayed the bogs' thirty-four-degree temperature, reassuring to see it matched what she literally had just seen on site, and she programmed the alarm to twenty-eight and turned up the volume. The beeping would scare the crap out of all the wildlife for a hundred miles but would never go unheard.

Sipping her coffee at the back door, she surveyed her property and shivered. Outside looked so much colder. Moonlight tinted everything in silver, too much like ice. The pond rested as still as glass, and even the pump house looked lonely and cold.

Again, she shivered, this time at the prospect of answering the alarm and calling on her army of sprinklers. She left her cup in the sink and went to bed, waiting and listening to the silence, wide-awake and alone between the cold sheets. Remembering.

# CHAPTER THIRTY-FOUR

Sweet bird songs on a warm spring morning were—without question—the polar opposite of what yanked Frankie out of a sound sleep. She nearly fell out of bed when the alarm went off, and as her feet hit the floor, she forced herself to stop and take a breath.

"Jesus Christ!"

She pulled on a thermal undershirt as she hurried to silence the alarm before it woke Stella, three miles away. Yup, the bog read-out displayed twenty-eight degrees. Time for the rookie's first test. Back in her bedroom, she finished dressing: thermal leggings, jeans, long-sleeved T-shirt, hoodie, heavy socks, and work boots. At the back door, she added a winter jacket and ballcap, grabbed gloves and the mighty flashlight, and headed for the pumphouse.

*Bring it on.*

The stillness of the night was consuming. Nothing moved, not even the air, and she wasn't happy about it. The crunching of semi-frozen gravel beneath her boots accompanied her to the pump house, where the cold embraced her with evil intention, as if she wore a tank top and shorts. Her arms began to shake, which made aiming the light difficult.

She checked the five-gallon gas tank unnecessarily and screwed the cap back on, then primed the pump several times, eager to wake the grumpy engine. But she couldn't grip the pump's ignition key wearing gloves. Aggravated and impatient, she shoved the right one into her pocket and turned the key.

Like the genuine old-fashioned motor it was, the engine protested, and she tried again. And again.

"Come on! This isn't any fun for me either!"

She cranked the key again and the motor sputtered.

"That's it. You can do it."

One more turn. The motor grumbled to life reluctantly, guffawing several times before it settled into a steady drone.

"Thank you, God."

She pivoted and hustled outside. The sight brought a relief that made her stop short.

Pressured to pop out of hiding, crystalline sprays rose in defense of her crop. Everywhere she looked, giant arcs of water revolved, glittering in the moonlight. *The cavalry throwing fistfuls of glitter into the air. This makes it all worthwhile.*

She smiled as the P!nk song came to mind and returned to the pump house to check the gauges. Pleased by the proper water pressure readings, she then went for her truck keys in the cabin. The berries were safe, as long as each sprinkler head was doing its job, and she had to ride the perimeter to be sure.

Luckily, it was almost five o'clock and her defense system would only see a few hours of active duty. Once the sun rose and lifted the temperature, she could shut the pump off. Two-plus hours of water on the bogs wasn't so bad, considering the alternative. If, instead, she had fired up the sprinklers at two o'clock, those six hours of water would have taken a day to drain, and the bogs two days to dry.

Delaying harvest wasn't smart when the berries were waiting at their peak. And the more days passed, the longer and colder the nights became, which required longer sprinkling time, which required more days of drying. A fellow grower once told her that his harvest season had dragged on so long, he actually finished on Thanksgiving Day—and no way was she going to spend her holiday doing that. Plus, there was always rain to worry about.

*Come on, Mother Nature. Work with me here, please.*

She drove to the far corner of the bogs, plugged in her spotlight, and powered down her window. From this vantage point, rows of perfectly aligned sprinklers spread out before her, one beyond the other until she couldn't quite see the output of the farthest few. She aimed the light along the row, catching each head's water in the beam, making sure it revolved and sprayed as intended.

Satisfied, she moved on to the bisecting road to check the view from the innermost point outward in every direction. Her headlights hit the archway of sprays that rained from either side of the gravel strip, and suddenly she could hear Harper's fascination with such a sight.

"You were taken by them in the daytime," she said, prepared to drive the gauntlet of sprays as they rotated on and off the road. "What would you think of *this*?"

Water buffeted her roof, and instinctively, she ducked as she drove. Splatter reached inside her opened window and soaked her sleeve, stung her cheek. Flipping on her wipers, she sped up a little until she found the spot where the sprays barely reached her window. She aimed the spotlight along the rows from different angles, then opened the passenger window and repeated the lengthy inspection on the other side.

Finally, she sat back, relieved to have verified each head. She dreaded the thought of finding one clogged or damaged. With temps in the twenties, marching out onto the berries and jumping ditches to fix a problem—getting drenched in the process—held no appeal whatsoever.

Water hit her face, startling her, and she closed the windows and cranked up the heat. Wiping her eyes and cheeks, she realized a breeze must have carried the spray inside, but just the existence of that breeze said her solitary battle would end soon.

"Eleven thirty isn't too early for wine, is it?" Denise opened the bottle anyway.

"Not this morning, it isn't. Where's your peanut butter?" Harper searched the kitchen cabinets. "Never mind. I found it."

"How are you supposed to sing for me with peanut butter stuck in your mouth?" She made a face, staring at Harper's project. "On toast?"

"Yup. Hotels are clueless. This is a treat, my new breakfast habit."

"Peanut butter toast and wine? Ew. Come on, we'll chill out on the bed." She grabbed two glasses and moved on. "So's that an oldie-but-goodie recipe from your grandmother?"

"From Frankie." Harper followed with her little plate. Just saying the name felt good. Sliding her guitar aside, she joined Denise on the bed and waited for some quip about Frankie.

"Uh-huh." Denise poured for each of them. "I can't believe you're here, you know, even for a few hours. This is like skipping school."

Thankfully, Denise hadn't pushed because Harper didn't know how she'd handle a Frankie discussion. "And you're skipping work," she said, wiping her mouth with a napkin.

"Hey, a *storm* has hit Chicago and I'm not missing it."

"VIP passes for tonight are in my case."

Denise bounced where she sat. "I can't wait! So, what did you want me to hear? Is this a new song?"

Harper shrugged as she wiped her hands and brought the guitar onto her lap. "New to me. And that could be as far as it goes." She started the first verse and Denise's eyebrows rose with recognition.

"Wow. You're kidding, right? 'Glory Days'? What a great idea—and a fantastic tune for you. I love it already."

Harper stopped to drink. "Thanks, but that makes all *two* of us. Not so popular among the Storm gang."

"What's wrong with a freaking Springsteen classic? Everybody loves it. What's the matter with them?"

"It's not 'our' sound. Smitty turned it into 'Smash Mouth Days.' Zee's pushing his latest creation instead, but it's too crazed, in my opinion, and too hard on my voice."

"Be careful with that."

"I'm trying." She set the guitar aside, having lost interest in playing. "Already, Rhea's had to take over one of my tunes and we had to pull another completely, and nobody's happy about it. I feel bad, but what can I do?" She looked up quickly. At least Denise would understand. Somebody had to. "I have to have *something* left in the tank to get through 'Wicked Angel.'" She almost laughed at her situation. "I swear, we could repeat that song for an entire set and nobody would mind."

"Except your throat."

"God, yes. So, I'm looking for a few easier numbers, mainly to pace my voice, but it's hard to please everybody. Apparently, I 'went soft' over the summer."

"So, you never got off on the mic stand on Granny's front porch?"

"Shut up." She clinked their glasses together. "I've missed you."

"I've missed you. And how about Crossroads? You miss that, too?"

Harper chose that moment to drink.

Denise leaned back on one arm. "I see. So, just how 'soft' *did* you get over the summer?"

"I didn't turn against my day job, if that's what you're asking."

"It's not."

"I couldn't do Storm material this summer. I *had* to do something else."

Denise laughed. "Well, you certainly did that."

Harper sighed and reclined against the headboard. "So, I got a little spoiled."

"Drink. I've never seen you look this confused." She set a hand on Harper's knee. "Storm has to cut you some damn slack. It's in everyone's best interest. Besides, it's your voice on the line, not theirs."

"We either have to change some of our material or give Rhea more of my lead vocals."

"Whoa." Denise refilled their glasses. "She's terrific, Harper, but—"

"She has a powerful voice."

"But she's not the fox you are up front, not who fans come to watch. She takes your lead vocals and where does that leave you? How long have you been dwelling on this?"

Harper shrugged. Admitting it out loud was like carving a marker into a tree; once done, it lasted forever. "Well, my voice started acting up about a year ago, so it's been a while. We almost canceled two dates on this tour before deciding to let Rhea handle things."

"On a temporary basis."

"Right. But, one way or the other, I need to make some changes and that will be hard for all of us. It could screw up Storm's entire image."

"But what you need," Denise leaned closer, "what you *want*, they matter, Harper."

"Yeah, and my voice has started casting its own vote."

"You know what's best for you. And, for God's sake, dialing back on the hard-ass material shouldn't sound Storm's death knell."

"No, and I really wouldn't mind dialing things back, but there are a lot of other votes involved."

"Since when have you let others dictate what you do? It *is* your band, after all. I say do what feels right, even if it means 'adjusting' Storm's precious image. Hell, even if it means thinking twice about Storm itself."

Harper exhaled hard as she put her glass on the nightstand. "God, Denni." She folded her hands atop her head and rolled her eyes. "Storm's been my life. Walking away doesn't compute in my head, but when you lay it out like that..."

"Hey, who loves ya, baby? Just want you happy, doing what you love. And if it's wailing in front of Storm and your voice says it's okay, then fine. If it's on a stool under a spotlight, that's just as cool. But *not* doing what you like isn't an option. It'll eat you up till you just feel like crap."

Harper couldn't pinpoint when it had begun, but already she was no stranger to that feeling. Concern about her voice had grown during the past weeks and allowed other emotions to run unchecked. Frustration, disagreement, stress, worry, all chipped away at her under the pressure of touring, and now, that rare, unsettled day wasn't so rare anymore.

The sooner she addressed this discontent, the better, even though that could open a whole box of crazy. Toning down Storm's "style" wouldn't sit well with bandmates who lived to blow holes in the sky, nor with Sasha or Harry or the recording company reps who thrived on pitching Storm's successful image to the buying public. And maybe not with the buying public, either. She didn't like this selfish feeling, messing things up for everyone at the worst possible time, but how much longer could she ride this uneasiness?

Tears threatened and she pulled Denni into a hug. "I love you."

"Yeah, I know, and I love you, too." Denise rubbed her back. "Now, let's hear the rest of it."

## Chapter Thirty-five

Frankie poured her leftover ice cubes into the cooler chest on the Crossroads porch. When she flipped the top closed, Stella flattened her hand to the lid.

"Harvest will get back on track tomorrow, Frankie, I'm sure. Don't look so discouraged."

"We should be almost done by now. Raining all night set us back even further than last week's cold spell. I'd hoped—"

"I know what you hoped, but there's no sense sulking about Mother Nature. Now, the weatherman said it should be breezy tonight and isn't that good?" Frankie nodded. "So, tomorrow, I'll make sandwiches for everyone's lunch, like the other days, and Joey will pick me up. We'll be there around one o'clock?"

"Thank you. Yes, I think that's good, if we can get on the bogs around ten-ish. The wind should have dried the dew by then."

"Stop worrying. I'm sure you and your army will get a good start on the day." Stella patted her shoulder and headed for the screen door to wait on a customer. "Go, get your mind off this for a while. Maybe make a *phone call?*"

Battling defeat, and lost in thoughts of equipment, her invaluable volunteers, and tonight's wind, Frankie couldn't handle placing a certain phone call right now. Harvest had been going so well, only interrupted once by a particularly dewy morning. But the subsequent week of unseasonable cold and each night's prolonged sprinkling had shut down the following day's work. And yesterday, a heavy rain had extended the delay.

She drove home, wishing she could have started that push to the Big Finish. Today should have been the day because Saturday was ideal, the least imposition on helpers who had real weekday jobs. No need to beg for anyone's holiday or vacation time. Hopefully, tomorrow they would make serious headway because, once Monday arrived, she would lose half her "crew" to other obligations and harvest would slow to a crawl.

She slumped into a corner of the couch, staring at her guitar in its stand across the room. No, she didn't feel like playing, although Harper's singing was so vivid in her head, she could have harmonized with it.

She pulled out her phone and brought up Storm's website, wondering where Harper was at the moment. A video from one of the Chicago concerts caught her eye, hard to miss with Harper front-and-center, barely dressed in black leather and a glossy white Flying-V guitar hanging across her hips.

The song was "Wicked Angel," and Frankie sat transfixed as music hammered out to a gyrating crowd. Harper's gaze through all that theatrical makeup felt as penetrating as the notes she played, reaching out eerily, hungrily, and Frankie couldn't look away.

"Such a different you," she said vacantly. "How are you hitting those notes?" The gravel in Harper's voice was sexy but Frankie wondered if it literally grated against the lining of her throat. *Doesn't that hurt?* She couldn't tell if the grimacing revealed discomfort or pure exertion, considering Harper's entire body seemed to clench, delivering the wrenching lyrics. *When you love what you do…*

The video ended with the song, the entire stage going black, and Frankie closed the site. It was then she noticed the voice mail and sat bolt upright. "How did I miss this at…?" She checked the time and realized she'd been in the barn, fixing the buggy's motor. "God damn it."

"Hey, cranberry farmer. It's me." The recorded voice was light but weary, and Frankie wanted to crawl into the phone to get closer. "We haven't talked in too long and leaving this voice mail isn't what I'd hope for, but… well, here I am, so…I just thought I'd ask how harvest was going. Gram said you started but the cold nights have been a pain. I, uh, I hope things pick up for you—pun intended." Frankie shook her head. "Yeah, so, uh, we're back on the road this morning, same ol' thing, you know? We're selling out everywhere and shows have been great. Rhea and I have been writing more together lately, not that it's been easy for me, but she's incredibly patient. We thought Decker had COVID, but it's just a bad cold, so we chain him to his drums and pour Gatorade down his throat every hour."

The image was amusing, and Frankie was touched by Harper's lighthearted effort. The tightening bond with Rhea sounded promising for her, although Frankie couldn't help the twinge of jealousy. There had probably always been something between them anyway, she mused.

*I should have called you by now. Long ago. I didn't because I cannot want to this badly. Even harvest wouldn't get you out of my head if I did.*

"Okay, well…" Harper paused and Frankie almost panicked, thinking she had ended the call. "I've been meaning to call you. And Gram's been on my case about it."

*She's been on mine, too.*

"Look, Frankie, I-I know things were awkward when I left. I mean, I suppose I know why, but…I think we've gone too long without talking. I did want to say hello and see how you were. I'm sorry we missed connecting here. So…I guess I'll hang up now. Please take care, okay?"

Frankie saved the message.

A crisp knock on her door interrupted her thoughts and she had to mute the lingering sound of Harper's voice in her head, blink away the lasting image of her smile. The effort left her adrift as she opened the door to Terri.

"Hi. Come on in."

"You look like you've seen a ghost. Or did I wake you up?"

"Huh? No, I was just listening to my voice mail." She wandered back to the couch.

"Yeah, I can tell you're busy." She smirked. "So, do you think we'll be a 'go' for tomorrow? Everybody's chomping at the bit."

"You have no idea how much I appreciate that. Yeah, if the wind cooperates. Ten o'clock."

"Right. Hey, Ginny's making pizza tonight and we want you to join us for dinner. You're cooped up here too much these days."

"Thanks, but I'm good."

"Yeah, you look it." Terri removed her Stetson and planted herself in the recliner. "You got a voice mail from Harper, didn't you? Finally? Bet you still hadn't called her, huh?"

"What's the sense, Terri? She's done here. She's back to living her real life now, doing what she loves. And good for her. I can't be expecting anything different."

"Well, Jesus, even a plain old friend gives a call once in a while, shows she cares."

"She knows I care."

"Does she?" Terri shook her head. "See? I was right. Staying cooped up *has* messed with your head. It can't hurt to show her you care."

"Yes, it can."

"Oh, poor you. Stop being an idiot."

"I'm facing the facts. The sooner I get my head on straight, the better." She went to the fridge, came back with two beers, and handed one to Terri. "Besides, it was supposed to end this way. We knew that."

"What way? Fighting or falling for each other?" Frankie just sent her a blank look. Terri laughed, the bottle at her lips. "Oh, spare me the denial. Spare *yourself.*" She leaned on her knees. "Stella's worried about both of you, you know. Every time I see her, she nudges me to nudge you to do something and I tell her it's like talking to the damn wall. If you didn't have harvest on your mind, Stella would be up your butt about it instead of mine." She took a drink and pointed the bottle at Frankie's phone. "That voice mail says she at least got through to Harper."

"I'll call her tomorrow morning."

"Do it now." She stood and put her hat on.

"I can't call right now. They're probably in the middle of a sound check for tonight's show."

"What is it with you and calling that woman? I'm leaving so you—"

"I'll return her call in the morning."

"Frankie." Terri moved to the couch and sat beside her. "Whatever she thinks of our music or wherever her nonstop life brings her, does that really matter? And who the fuck cares what style of music she plays? You know better, God dammit. You two have a piece of each other and that kind of harmony is too precious to let fade away."

Frankie didn't have a response to that little lecture. Wise words faded quickly in her current reality.

Terri chugged the rest of her beer. She gave Frankie's shoulder a squeeze, put her bottle on the kitchen table, and stopped at the front door. "One hour. Get in your damn truck and come over for pizza."

Harper's leather bra and low-slung pants could hardly have been any thinner or more revealing, but she was still beyond roasting. She broke from playing the electrifying guitar duet with Rhea and grabbed the mic by its throat.

Tears of sweat stung her eyes into a quick clench, trailed alongside each nostril, and raced over her lips. Salty and insistent, they burst on poetic phrases heaved from her chest, and sprayed against the mic just a breath away. Exertion engulfed her in a high gloss, dripped from her face, chest, and arms.

The song powered upward. Storm's second encore, "Wicked Angel," pushed band and audience to the frenzied heights everyone had been anticipating, and Harper reached for all her body had left, all her voice could give.

Split-second pauses replenished her empty lungs in perfect time, and she drove words from subconscious to tongue with mindless recall. Blinking through the sting, she surged onto the mic, growling instead of singing, until her last, throaty whisper vibrated back against her mouth. On that final note, she let her head and arms drop and the stage went black.

The audience lost it.

Band members hooted to each other in the dark and Rhea whirled her around in a hug.

"Fuck, girl. How do you do it?"

Harper wiped sweat off her cheeks with both hands. "No freaking clue." Her squawking voice surprised them both. There was a new soreness, a metallic taste as she swallowed, and her worst thoughts surfaced. Now, she also had a fear of speaking.

Decker jumped down from his drums and herded everyone to the front of the stage to bow as the houselights came up. Fans tossed flowers, candy, plastic nips of alcohol, clothing, gummies, and all sorts of delights at them. One nip was glass, however, and it broke in two as it ricocheted off a monitor by their feet, then bounced across Harper's throat and rattled against Rhea's guitar strings.

Shocked, Harper jerked back and slapped a palm to the sting. Someone pulled her off stage, and Harry gripped her by the shoulders and forced her into a chair.

"Shit, Harper. Let me see." The venue manager handed him a handkerchief and Harry turned her chin aside and pressed the cloth against the gash to stop the bleeding. "Christ." Seeing his always-perfect composure so frazzled, Harper would have laughed if she wasn't afraid to. "It's not super bad," he reported, "but a shitty way to end your finest performance of the tour."

Harper nodded in his hand. The wound was disturbing, infuriating, but wasn't her real worry right now. Harry's pressure against her throat caused her to swallow against her will, and the soreness, the taste of blood made her wince.

"You'll be okay," he said in reference to the wound. "You probably won't even need stitches. Hey, maybe having alcohol in the bottle was a good thing."

She returned a look that told him to "think again."

They were halfway back to the hotel before anyone realized Harper hadn't said a word since being on stage. Harper, meanwhile, was glad of it. The pain and taste persisted, and she avoided swallowing as much as she could. Apparently, Harry had arranged for a doctor to come and tend to her wound, but she wanted the *inside* of her throat checked. Their second Cleveland show tomorrow night felt impossible right now, and the upcoming two at the Barclays Center in Brooklyn? And the rest of the tour back west? She knew what it all meant.

*How often did I think about this happening? It was inevitable. Everybody knew it, including me. So now what?*

A swallow made her cough, and she gasped at the pain. She took the handkerchief from her throat and wiped her mouth. Specks of blood made her heart sink.

"How you doing?" Zee asked, patting her knee in the second seat of their van.

"Been better."

He raised an eyebrow at her gritty voice. "Fuck. You blew it out, didn't you?"

Harper nodded. "We have a problem."

"Jesus, don't talk," Harry snapped as he drove, and Smitty chuckled.

"That's not going to bring her voice back by tomorrow night," he told him. "She's right. We have a problem."

Decker hauled a case of Smartwater onto his lap and handed bottles to Primma, who passed them around. Harper accepted hers with great apprehension. She was dying of thirst, seriously dehydrated, but afraid to drink.

The whole situation was dire. She needed a medical evaluation fast. How many shows would she miss now? This nightmare meant she was letting everyone down—*again*, and this time looked more serious than ever. It was the issue she hadn't been able to resolve for so long.

*Maybe it's resolved now.*

Harry sat by the windows in Harper and Rhea's shared room, mindlessly wrapping and unwrapping his tie around his hands. Rhea put the room service tray on Harper's bed, and they studied the ingredients the doctor had ordered for Harper's throat.

"Is the tea supposed to be *pumpkin spiced*?" Harper whispered.

Rhea stirred in a huge amount of honey. "Who knows? Drink slowly."

Harper obeyed as Harry began to pace.

Rhea sighed at him. "Harry. Sit. I told you I can handle it."

Harper watched her turn and look at the others. Hand on her hips, she appeared as in command here as she always did on stage, but there was desperation in her eyes, and knowing who had put it there hurt.

Decker nodded as he munched on a sandwich. "Maybe add an extra hour to tomorrow's sound check," he suggested, and glanced at Zee as he spoke. "That should get us comfortable enough with the changes."

"We'll just be ready to jump in if Rhea needs help." Primma leaned into Harper's shoulder as they sat against the headboard. "Anybody's bound to forget lyrics here and there. We'll get her through it."

Harper sipped her tea again and rubbed her eyes. Damn, she was tired, and all this was her fault. Not intentionally, of course, but it had been preventable.

"It's a long haul ahead." Harry looked pointedly at Rhea. "We're barely halfway through."

Now, Rhea crossed her arms. Just as attuned to their schedule as Harper, she didn't need the reminder. Everyone was worried, agitated, and already the atmosphere in the crowded room was too tense.

"I think more rehearsal than sound check," Rhea stated. "We have work to do." She turned to Harper with a resigned but sympathetic look. "Don't worry. We'll get through it."

"That makes for a very long day." Harry shook his head.

Decker leaned back on Rhea's bed. "At least we've been through the drill before."

Sitting in the corner with an ice bucket from his room, Smitty popped the cork on champagne that nobody had felt like opening. He grinned into the distracted faces. "*Somebody* ought to drink this." He snorted. "We *all* need it." He took a lengthy blast from the bottle and aimed his attention at Harper. "Tomorrow night's one thing. But when we show up without you in New York? Huh. People might notice."

"They'll want to know when you'll be back." Harry started pacing again, his head pigeon-bobbing as he thought. "Actually, social media won't wait for the Barclays Center. Chatter will start tomorrow night."

Rhea slumped against the wall. "You should notify the company, Harry, get to them before they read about this and come screaming."

"I'll let them know. At least you have disability provisions in your contracts, so there is that. They won't be happy, but no recording company would, especially with the new album doing so well."

"I'm so sorry, guys." Harper swallowed more tea with difficulty. "The doctor tonight, well, you all heard him. He said a few weeks at best, but I'm afraid to put much faith in that. Been there and done that, you know?" She tried to clear her throat but couldn't. "He said this laryngologist he knows in Boston is the expert, so…"

"Boston?" Primma asked.

"So, you're out of here tomorrow." Zee sat beside Decker and sent him a foreboding look.

"Yeah. This doctor's calling his friend and thinks he'll squeeze me in Monday morning."

"So, you'll be gone for who knows how long." Decker looked from Primma to Rhea and down at the bedspread. Smitty just shook his head and drank.

Harper watched them process it all.

"Resting for a summer was no miracle cure, obviously," she said softly, "and there's no guarantee with surgery, either. I have no idea what the hell's going to happen."

Harry looped his tie around his neck and hung his hands from it. With his distressed hair and his slouching posture, he radiated defeat. "Regardless of what the Boston doctor says, you get a second opinion, pronto."

"I will." Her voice cracked. "I may have just pressed my luck too far." She frowned hard at what had to be said out loud. "I'm afraid they'll tell me to stop, period."

The quiet in the room clawed her insides to pieces. She thought she might even vomit. *God, please, no.* Setting her head back against the headboard, she tried not to see Storm struggling, her career coming to an end. *Bottom line's a bitch. I'm not the only one wondering.*

# CHAPTER THIRTY-SIX

I didn't expect this morning's shower. It only lasted an hour, but it killed the day before it even started." Frankie stood in the barn doorway, watching the last of her volunteers leave with a free Sunday to do as they pleased. Dictating this voice mail message had her feeling even more alone, and anxiety about netting the most lucrative harvest possible underscored that mood, but she wanted to keep all that out of her voice.

"Just a few more days are all I need. Tomorrow's *the* day, now, and it'll be slow without as much help, but I'll take it." *Does that sound upbeat?* "Hey, it's good to hear you're getting back into songwriting. Sounds like Rhea's a good partner. And I'm glad the tour is going well. You guys must be psyched about playing the Barclays Center. Tonight's the first of two, isn't it?" *Yes, I've looked at your schedule.* "Will it be Storm's first time there? Jesus, you'll just crush it."

Storm's music had never been her thing, too blaring and at times too wild, but she had plenty of respect for the band's skill and creativity—and its lead singer. They were going to kick the roof off the Barclays, and, honestly, Frankie couldn't have been prouder of Harper.

"I wish I hadn't missed your call. Really. And this phone tag blows, so I-I guess we'll try connecting some other time. Harper, I..." She bit back a sigh. "Yeah, well, we'll try again another time. Enjoy New York."

With a free afternoon on her hands, Frankie focused on the Crossroads decorations Stella wanted and headed off for Terri's farm. But poking around the hay bales and corn stalks inevitably had her thinking about her own crop—the mushy sections of bogs, the dent they would make in her profit, and her looming financial struggle. Hauling a second armload of pumpkins to her truck, she toyed with that idea of gigging for extra income. *No great windfall, but if there must be a second job...Seriously, why not that? It just might make ends meet.*

By dinnertime, Crossroads glowed with the crisp orange and gold accents of the season, and Frankie silently thanked the phantom crew that must have done this terrific job when she wasn't looking. She'd prevailed over her mental traffic jam, but hardly remembered the past couple of hours of work. At least Stella thought the storefront's transformation was magical. Maybe it was.

Watching Donna post pictures on the store's website, Frankie suggested a little music around the fire pit and texted the Crossroads faithful. "Even if only a few of them are free tonight, it would be nice," she told Stella. She needed a serious dose of friends.

*This* lifted her spirits and filled that emptiness in her chest. It required her to look away from images she longed to see and ignore the difficult emotions. Lately, she had so overloaded the back of her mind, that her most prominent thoughts flitted in and out like transients and often left her hanging.

But the usual suspects played with abandon now, and she marveled at how passersby had filled the parking lot. A few held up phones, videoing the impromptu session. Some contributed armloads of firewood from home. *Special times I wouldn't trade for anything.*

Between songs, a large woman in a sweatshirt and Red Sox cap stepped into the firelight and handed Frankie a bottle of cinnamon schnapps.

"I was on my way home with it," she said, grinning, "but after *that* song? My all-time favorite. I've never heard a woman do 'Pretty Woman' before and, damn, if you didn't slay it."

Frankie gestured to the musicians around her. "Thank you. Glad you liked it." She held up the bottle. "But this? I can't—"

"Oh, it's just a thank-you. Take it."

"Well, it's very sweet of you."

"Do you guys play out anywhere?"

*An ironic question, considering.*

Frankie heard Terri and Allie laugh behind her. "No. We just get together for fun."

The woman's painted eyebrows lifted. "Seriously? Well, would you consider playing at my place sometime? I own the Turnbuckle Tavern in New Bedford." She extended her hand. "My name's Lannie Millbrook."

Frankie glanced back at her friends' surprised faces. "Well...um..." She shook her hand quickly. "I'm Frankie Cosgrove and—"

"I know who you are, and I think you're outstanding. I've been here before, you know. My son lives a half hour away and he's mentioned this, here at Crossroads. So, what do you say?"

Frankie couldn't help a nervous laugh. She looked back at the others again, saw the eagerness. "Sure. Yeah, okay. Thanks so much. It'll be fun."

"I'll pay you, of course."

"Well, thank you. This is quite a surprise."

"Shouldn't be," Lannie said, reaching for her wallet. "Look at the crowd you draw." She passed her a business card. "Call me tomorrow and we'll set something up."

"I'll do that."

"Excellent." She clapped Frankie on the shoulder. "Nice meeting you."

"Same here." Frankie watched her maneuver through the cars until she reached her own and drove off. She turned to the others, and everyone cheered. She bent to Stella, seated nearby. "Do you believe this?"

Stella grabbed her hands. "Of course, I do, sweetie, and I'm thrilled!"

"It's just a gig, I know, but…"

Terri elbowed her arm. "Extra cash."

Serendipity had her in a daze.

"Hey, Frankie." Allie folded her arms atop her guitar and cocked her head. "Does that mean we need to name ourselves?"

Suggestions flew from everywhere and Frankie laughed at the enthusiasm among friends and spectators alike.

"Play some more," Stella said, tugging on her jacket. "That's what we need right now."

Frankie didn't know where to begin. Thankfully, Joe picked out a bluegrass intro on his banjo and reflex took over. Tomorrow was going to be a busy day.

Harper parked amidst the many cars at Frankie's cabin, grateful for the tranquil setting's soothing effect on her frayed nerves. Not a soul around, she checked her composure in the mirror and credited the golden afternoon light for improving her haggard face. Finally, she took a deep breath, stepped out of the car, and followed the sound of machinery around the barn to the bogs. *How is it that these wide-open spaces seem to help with the blues?*

Several acres away, workers swarmed over the maroon-colored landscape, and she spotted Gram sitting by herself, under a sun umbrella by Frankie's truck. The walk took a while, and she wondered if anyone could recognize her from this far away, how long she could maintain this surprise.

Thankfully, the trip to Boston, of all places, had allowed for her return here because she desperately sought relief in this familiar rural world. She still reeled at the morning's nerve-racking medical examination and surreal doctor-speak.

She inhaled deeply, a singer's expansive breath, hoping this sweet, fresh air would steady the maelstrom in her gut and keep the new chaos in her life from showing too much.

The Boston laryngologist had delivered crippling news, a gut punch, and although Harper had known it could come to this, reality struck hard. She had cried on the phone with Harry and then Rhea, and again while driving here, listening to "Wicked Angel" in the car.

Three quiet months, minimum, for her speaking voice to return to normal, the doctor had stated, and that was the limit of any stress and strain. Her physiology simply could no longer handle more. *"If you insist on singing like always, you'll be tempting fate, risking permanent damage. Take a year off, first."*

Determined to prove him wrong, Harper had left his office and spent the next hour in the parking garage, crying and frantically arranging for a second opinion—in LA. If she had to be sidelined for a while, she might as well face facts and go home, finally.

For now, at least swallowing didn't hurt too much, and her whisper even sounded a tad louder. *Humming is out of the question.* But after the upcoming holidays, if the band set aside a handful of softer tunes for her, she should be able to contribute. But, then again, just "contributing" to the band she'd created didn't sit well. She worried about the group's reaction on their Zoom call tomorrow. Another thing roiling in her stomach.

"Storm was *my* band," she grumbled, walking the perimeter road. "Storm *was* my band." She *so* wanted a clearer head to cope with this nightmare. *Storm's bigger than me now. It will go where it needs to—as it should, whether I'm "contributing" or behind the wheel or just a passenger… or not there at all.*

"How about cutting me some slack, you guys?" Whispering Denise's words against the sound of gravel crunching underfoot, she heard her own hint of snarkiness. "And if they don't?" *Already I feel like the "odd woman out."*

As a few voices yelled vague greetings from the bogs, she tip-toed up behind Gram, ducked under the umbrella, and wrapped her in a hug.

"Oh! Who's this?" Gram couldn't turn to see her, and Harper whispered in her ear.

"How's the world's best grandmother?"

Gram twisted in her grip and elation lit up her face. "Harper!" She scrambled to her feet and they hugged mightily. "Oh, my goodness! What are you doing here? Aren't you supposed to be in…Cleveland or wherever? I-I can't believe it!" She kissed Harper's cheek and hugged her again.

"It's so good to see you, Gram." The understatement nearly brought her to tears. Harper held her at arm's length. "You're lookin' great, Mrs. Anderson. Supervising this operation is the perfect job for you."

"Oh, Harper! Your voice." She dragged a lawn chair against her own. "Come and sit. You sound so rough, honey." She slipped an arm beneath Harper's and clutched it to her. "But I'm so happy to see you. Did Frankie know you were coming?"

"No. We'd played a little phone tag, but—"

"She'll be so excited."

"Eh, I don't know. Did I do the right thing, coming here? You know that Frankie and I..." She sighed. "We're not...I can't mislead her, Gram."

"But you're here. How can you *not* spend time with her?"

"Well, not *intimate* time." *Because I can't trust myself.* "That would be too dangerous."

"And why is that?"

Harper frowned. Gram knew why. "Because nothing can come of it."

"It can't?"

"No."

"Because that would hurt?"

"Yes, it would hurt. Both of us."

"Because you care for each other."

"Yes."

"A real lot."

"Well, yes, a lot."

"Amen."

"Gram."

"Oh, look." She jiggled Harper's arm. "Frankie's coming off the bog now. Wait till she spots you."

Watching Frankie high-step across the vines, examining the berries as she walked, Harper fought the urge to meet her halfway. The confident stride and tanned arms were tangibly familiar, and, despite her best effort to ignore them, she could feel those strong hands caressing her skin.

At the makeshift ramp up to the road, Frankie combed her hair back with her fingers, and came to a dead stop.

Harper's excited swallow made her cringe. "Hi, Frankie."

"Harper?" Squinting against the sun, Frankie took the ramp slowly, maybe cautiously. "Are you who I think you are?"

Harper gave Gram's arm a squeeze before standing. "It's good to see you."

Frankie came to within several feet and looked at Gram. "Is it really her?" Harper bit back a grin.

"I couldn't believe it either."

Frankie tipped her head and eyed Harper all the way down to her dress boots and back up to her eyes. Then, the scrutiny broke and that smile shimmered into Harper's chest. Frankie held out her hands, but Harper caved and stepped between them and hugged her.

"How are you?" The blissful sensation of Frankie's solid body against hers made her tremble, and she closed her eyes, fisted the sweat-dampened T-shirt across Frankie's shoulders, and held on.

*God, I need this.*

"Right now? I'm…I'm shocked." Frankie inched back, holding her by the waist. "What are you doing here?"

*If only this wasn't such a terrible idea.*

"I'm on the mend again."

The amber in Frankie's scrutiny darkened. "I've never heard you sound like this."

"You could say the doctor's put me on house arrest." She *had* to keep her chin up. She grinned at Stella. "Why not here?" As soon as she said it, she knew *why, not here*. But had she really wanted to go anywhere else?

Frankie just gazed at her, probably agreeing that anyplace else would have been easier on each of them. "For how long?"

Harper had to step away, break contact, and get a grip. "A few days. I've arranged for a second opinion in LA. I have to get my house up and running, anyway, so…"

"Oh, yeah. The house."

Gram sat forward. "But it's good that you're getting a second opinion."

"It's bad this time, isn't it?" Frankie asked.

"Yeah. Apparently, if I want to do better than this…this weird whispering, I need three months, minimum, like before, but no cheating. To do Storm's music, though, I'm supposed to wait at least a year, and even then it would be risky."

"Oh, Harper." Gram sat back, obviously distressed.

"Well, where does that leave you?" Frankie asked. "How's that supposed to work?"

"I don't know, exactly." She jammed her hands into her back pockets and tried to keep her turmoil in check. "Storm would have to make changes for me." She shrugged. "I'm not sure how receptive they'll be. I know *I* wouldn't want to change things that are working so well."

"Have you talked to them?"

"We're meeting on Zoom tomorrow. They're carrying on with the tour right now, and Rhea's singing my parts. She's really good at it, thank God. She's moving in with me, once tour wraps up, and we're supposed to start studio work on the new album in January. Somehow, everyone will have to deal with my mess."

"Rhea's moving in?"

"She is, yeah. We've been working on new material, although it'll all be for her now, not me. Everybody's riding along in limbo at the moment, and it kills me to put them through this."

Gram stroked Harper's arm. "Not to mention what it means for you, honey."

"Wait for the second opinion," Frankie said. "Who knows how things will turn out."

"True." Harper's throat tightened and she knew tears weren't far off. She *had* to get off this topic before she threw herself back into the sanctuary of Frankie's arms and embarrassed herself. "Hey. I'm still coming back for Thanksgiving."

Gram clapped her hands together. "Oh, yay! That's wonderful! How about Christmas?"

"Maybe for a week or so. I'll have to figure that out, though, because Mom's going to want me with them in Tampa." She snickered. "Although, after our two go-rounds about you and Crossroads staying put, Mom may not care to see my face for years. But you know where I'd rather be."

"Don't you worry about her. Just think about tonight. It will be so good having us together again for supper!"

Harper looked for agreement in Frankie, but she didn't appear overly enthused.

"Yeah, okay, sure." Frankie glanced over her shoulder nervously. "I... uh...You'll have to excuse me. I have to get back out there."

"Of course. I understand."

"I'm sad to hear your news, Harper. I bet the second opinion will come back better." She snatched a bottle of water from the cooler. "This was what I came for." She forced a smile at Harper. "If you were dressed for it, I'd put you to work."

Harper straightened and returned her own forced smile. "Tell me what time tomorrow and I'll report for duty."

"We can settle that later," Gram said. "Meanwhile, we'll have supper and then spend the evening together." She didn't wait for Frankie to come up with an excuse. "Harper, let's go back to Crossroads. You've had a busy morning, so you can rest while I plan supper."

Hoping Frankie's lukewarm greeting would improve, Harper touched her arm to stop her from leaving. She wanted to prolong this connection, however flimsy. Their talks had always been so thoughtful and companionable, and she needed some of that today, but right now, she could hardly think. "Well...How's it going out there?"

"Good. If the weather holds up, we should finish in two days." She held up two crossed fingers and walked away.

## CHAPTER THIRTY-SEVEN

Harper ran hot water into Gram's tub until steam filled the bathroom, and armed with a relaxing playlist on her phone and a massive cup of tea, she slid in up to her ear lobes. Gram's bubble bath was a bit much, but after tonight's stilted conversation with Frankie, the gardenia scent bothered her least of all.

Moisture helped the vocal cords. She had to concentrate on that, not the likelihood of a career disaster. *Singers often come back from this, right?* And not the prying it took to get Frankie to talk tonight. Granted, she'd had her own difficult moments, loosening up in the awkwardness between them, but Gram had helped, hadn't she?

"If it wasn't for you, Gram, I bet she wouldn't have mentioned the Turnbuckle gig, wouldn't even have stayed the whole hour." She dunked a washcloth and laid it across her throat. "It's difficult for me, too, Frankie, but can't we do better?"

But maybe if Gram hadn't been there, Frankie would have been more conversational, more revealing. Harper sighed, because there were things she had wanted to say, too, personal things, like "I miss us" and "I wish things were different." But battling Frankie's reticence and her own better judgment, she had kept them to herself.

They *did* lead separate lives, after all, but, damn, coping with this relationship "adjustment" was hard. *Are we supposed to pretend we've just met? Go back to that night you told me to trust my heart? To before we kissed? No one can turn the clock back that far.*

"Harper Cushing. You're driving yourself frigging crazy."

She stopped the music on her phone and switched to a YouTube video someone had posted of her last performance. She shook her head at her outfit. No question it was borderline erotic—and hot, literally.

"God, that was tough. I *really* need to go that route just to sing?"

She could still taste the sweat and blood. She had reached the dehydration danger level *before* doing "Wicked Angel," so singing the song had just crisped her vocal tissues into potato chips. When she punched out lyrics at the top of her range, the delicate little blood vessels had freaked.

*Guess it's pretty easy to explain what happened. The "why" is another matter.*

She cringed, watching herself. Muscles wrenched as she reached for notes, the strain in her throat and diaphragm evident throughout the entire song. Even her calves and thighs clenched as she drew strength from them.

"Shit. Watching this is exhausting, but, man, did it go over big."

Too bad, in a way, because now Storm fans wouldn't see the same show. *What they watch here won't be repeated live anytime soon. Maybe, ever.* Having Rhea take over as lead singer might cost the band some fans, but at least it wouldn't detract from the performance, and Harper found some solace in that.

Thin as a rail and sporting her new buzz cut, Rhea was aggressive on stage, guitar slung low across her abdomen, peeling off riffs like orgasmic strokes. She could handle the singing, too, although lacked Harper's range, but she always stood on solid ground. Any fans who missed Harper were bound to be won over very quickly, and new ones were sure to come along. Harper smiled as she lay inhaling the moist air, and let her conscience take a breath, too.

Her phone sounded in her hand, and she started so severely, she almost dropped it in the water.

"Hey, you."

Denise got to the point immediately. "I'm fucking bullshit at you, Harper Ashley Cushing!"

"Apparently."

"I have to *read* that you're quitting Storm? On fucking Instagram?"

"I'm not—"

"You actually pulled the plug and didn't give me a heads-up? Am I still your bestie or what? Jesus, how could you not tell me? Am I the last to know?"

"I'm not quitting." Harper sipped her tea carefully. "And I didn't post anything."

"Well, somebody did. Why are you whispering?"

"I'm just talking softly. Unlike you."

"It's the voice again?"

"The doctor says vocal strain."

"Aw, Jesus, Harper. Not cool. I'm sorry, hon. Why didn't you call me about this life-shattering decision?"

"It's not life-shattering."

"Life-*altering*, then."

"Because it just happened the other night and it's been crazy, going through everything with Storm and Harry and all the business bullshit, and getting a flight out, dealing with the doctor—"

"Stop. Where the hell are you?"

"Well, I had to go to Boston for—"

"Boston?"

"Yes. They have doctors."

"Like, they don't have any in Cleveland? Oh, gee, maybe there's one in Calie, Harper. Hey, maybe even here in Chicago, *near your BFF's fucking house!*"

"Denni. I'm at Gram's." Denise paused and Harper pictured that funny, perplexed look on her face. "My house in WeHo is still empty, remember? I had to come this way for the specialist, so I'm making the most of it. But it's only for a few days. I'm seriously out of commission now, enough to be getting a second opinion in LA."

"So, you *are* going back? And staying? Why the second opinion?"

"This doctor said to take at least a year, that doing Storm tunes again could cause permanent damage."

"Fuck."

"Yeah. But he *did* say that three months might bring my speaking voice back, so I'm thinking there's hope for doing gentler stuff with the band, if they haven't blown me off by then. Hopefully not, but this is asking a lot from them. We're supposed to start on the new album in January and Rhea's moving in until she can find a place."

Denise took a breath and exhaled. "That's a lot, but it's good to hear you're not really saying bye-bye to all the fame and all that hard work—and all that money."

"No, not if I have a choice." She heard the rest of that dubious truth come out automatically. "Who would want to part with all the lovely stress, the rat race, the insanity that threatens my health?" She coughed and winced at the pain, then sipped more tea.

"That shit's not going anywhere, you know. It'll all be there when you go back."

"Yeah. Hopefully, the guys will cut me some of that 'slack' you mentioned, and some version of me can get back in three months, in time to do decent stuff for the album. Otherwise…Well, I don't know."

"*If* you still really want it."

Harper just closed her eyes at that possibility.

"I assume you've seen Frankie? How did that go?"

"Okay, I guess, but it wasn't easy. I suppose she's being smarter than I am. I've already second-guessed myself about coming back. Not that my place was move-in ready, but, if it wasn't for Gram…"

"No more open-door policy from Frankie?"

"No. I should be so guarded."

"But, 'because of Gram'? Uh-huh."

"I really came back here for all of it, Denni, for Gram, for Crossroads, *and* for her because…" *Because why?* "I really needed some 'feel good' time."

"Yeah. Sounds like that's just what Frankie offered. Did I just hear you laugh?"

"Sorta. That 'feel good' time, staying here with Gram, includes sleeping on her couch, so it's lacking in that respect, too."

"Why didn't you grab that second bedroom you had upstairs?"

"It's Donna's place now and I'm not intruding. Besides, Gram wants us to be roommates while I'm here, and, before you bring it up, no way was I staying at Frankie's."

"Deep down, she's dreaming of you in her bed, girl."

"Oh, I'm not so sure."

"Maybe the sooner you get back to LA, the better *everyone* will sleep."

"Not so sure about that, either."

"Honey, she's the reason you're there. Admit it."

"I just need some time to—"

"To *honestly* see what you've been missing, if it's still real, if *Frankie* is. Come on, Harper. You're torturing yourself. Do you even *know* where you'd rather be?"

Harper finished her tea, mulling over the question and picturing *this* as her reality. She had entertained the notion many times since coming here last summer but had cast it off as ridiculously whimsical, staggeringly impractical at the very least. *If there was no Storm, would I choose this? What if I've just been too damn afraid to take a hard look?*

Right now, the image rose clearly, easily, and, to her amazement, overrode Storm's hectic life like a speedbump. But, the accompanying guilt was almost paralyzing. The idea of leaving Storm for a year loomed large, but the very real possibility of ruining her voice permanently threatened to force a decision she never dreamed she'd make.

Her bandmates depended on her, but, understandably, they grew impatient. Each time she delivered a medical update, their frustration and distress, maybe even resentment, seemed to have increased. Hell, she wasn't the only one scared shitless about blowing everything up.

Professional success hadn't come easily for any of them, she knew that, just like she knew her health *had* to come first. *Is it really "success" if it fails to measure up to genuine "feel-good" living?*

Denise had been silent for a while, probably just to let Harper think.

"Sorry, I got all heavy on you, Harper. Look, I watched clips of Storm playing without you. The YouTube stuff is really good. They did alright."

"I'm proud of them." No question, they'd worked their asses off.

"Hey, who knows? You could be back at that mic in no time, bringing the fucking roof down."

Yes, she'd miss the performance high, unless the band helped and she knocked herself out and her voice didn't disappear forever. "None of it comes cheap, remember. There's a price for all that."

"But, shit, Harper, your last song was beyond everything. What a memory you left that crowd. Did you already suspect it might be, like, your last hurrah for a while?"

Harper laughed and it hurt. "No. Blowing out my vocal cords made the decision for me."

"Well, lemme tell you…God, it was *the bomb*! Thank God the lights went out when they did, because, girl, you were almost like *there* there, you know? With the whole fuckin' world watching you come. *Seriously*?"

*Yeah, it was good, wasn't it?*

"Denni, take a breath."

"Jesus, Harper. I'll never see a mic stand the same way again."

Harper grinned into the phone. "Sweetie, nothing beats the real thing." Immediately, Frankie came to mind and Harper unconsciously ran a heavy palm over her nipples. "Gonna sign off now so I can soak and sulk, but I'll check in soon."

She ended the call and slid down until the bubbles tickled her chin and the tactile recall of Frankie's penetrating fingers blotted out her worries.

"Stella's getting all four boxes?" Terri set a crate of berries onto the bed of Frankie's truck and watched her add another from the little buggy.

"Yeah. And that one's for you guys."

"Whoa. Thank you! Ginny makes even better cranberry bread than you do."

Frankie smiled at that, appreciating Terri's attempt to lighten her mood. Concentrating on this project today had helped, but she really couldn't shake the shadow of financial loss that hung over her. And that certainly did nothing to strengthen her spirit in coping with Harper's presence.

She sighed as she brushed her hands on her thighs and stretched. Scooping all day had ruined her back, but she wasn't going to let the leftover crop go to waste. What her machines hadn't been able to reach, she—and Terri, to a minor degree—had picked the old-fashioned way, by hand.

"Yeah, I'm storing the rest in the half-cellar at Crossroads. I don't have a cellar, so the berries will do better, last longer at Stella's. I'm keeping one box because I'll probably go through it in a few weeks or so."

"How long will mine last?"

"Months, if you keep them cool and dry."

"Too bad we couldn't get them all, huh? Would've helped your harvest totals."

"Not much, actually." But she wished the same thing. "A thirty percent loss is too big to make up by hand-picking berries off the ditches."

She backed the buggy into the barn, reluctant to dwell on it. Then, again, maybe it would help to face the facts out loud.

"The co-op cut right to the chase. They said a ten or fifteen percent loss was common for rookies, but thirty percent? Shit. That's almost a disaster. I know I'll feel it through the coming year." She slid the door closed. "I can't let that happen again."

They sat on the tailgate in the fading sun, and Frankie tried not to think about her diminished income, the household improvements that would have to wait yet another year, bills she'd have to pay discriminately, if at all. She hadn't played that game since her college days, avoiding the landlord, cancelling her internet service… Until next season—when she made zero mistakes, she'd be living on a shoestring, at best, unless some windfall dropped into her lap.

She focused on harvest's triumphant moments now like a lifeline. She wouldn't forget the lessons learned or the friends who had seriously toiled for her. Even Harper had pitched in, those last two days. She'd nearly fallen into a ditch, but overall, she had lent valiant and invaluable effort.

Frankie laughed at the memory. "I can still see Iman grabbing Harper's ass."

"The poor guy was mortified." Terri laughed, too. "He grabbed her just in time, though. She was taking a dive."

"She did that last summer and wanted no part of a repeat."

Terri patted her leg. "I know she's leaving tomorrow, Frankie, but it's been nice having her back. Are you doing okay?"

"Yeah. I'm managing."

"Uh-huh. Too bad she won't be here for our gig next week."

"She can't pass up her appointment with that LA specialist. She said it was a miracle he had a cancellation and could fit her in right away."

"Well, look. Maybe things will work out for her, and Storm will come by this way eventually. Hell, you could always fly out and visit."

"Harper's got her work cut out for her now. Besides, she might have something going with Rhea. Who knows? I just let things between us go too far. Getting that close was my own fault."

"It's nobody's *fault*, Frankie. It's a bitch pulling back, but you'll get through it. Hang in there."

Frankie groaned as she hopped off the tailgate. "I should get these berries over to Stella's before the dew settles on them."

"You want some help?"

"Thanks, but I got it." They stopped at their respective drivers' doors. "And thank you for the help this afternoon. Take a few Tylenol before your back starts acting up."

"You should talk."

She offered Terri a grin as she slid behind the wheel. "Gotta run to the store and buy some."

"Yeah. Good luck with that."

Frankie shook off the grin as she drove to Crossroads. The combustible mix of emotions awaiting her was enough to make her turn around. She couldn't wait to see Harper, but hoped she wouldn't.

*I can be gone in ten minutes, if I can get these boxes into the cellar quietly enough. Too bad that bulkhead door squeals like a pig.*

She drove around to Crossroads' back lot and immediately abandoned any idea of a quick getaway. Returning from the dumpster, Harper scooted out of her path and waved. Then, she opened Frankie's door.

"You're staying for dinner." The coarse voice sent a tingle across Frankie's back, and the domineering tone was too arousing for her own good.

"I am?"

"Gram knew you were coming."

"How did she know? *I* didn't know."

Harper grinned, one hand on the truck roof, the other still holding the door. Frankie yearned to reach out and sweep her onto her lap. *We could sit here all day.*

"Somehow, Gram knew. She's been saying so since this morning. She knows you better than you think."

"Oh, now, that's frightening. Does she know I have berries to be stored in the cellar?"

Harper glanced into the truck bed. "Where did they come from?"

"Ditch berries, the ones along the bankings that the pickers couldn't get. I scooped them today with a little help from Terri."

"Scooped, as in by hand?"

*You asked me that on the day we met. You enchanted me then and it's worse now.*

"Uh…Yes, ma'am, and, if you let me out of this truck, I'll get them inside before the dew ruins them all."

Harper stepped back. "Can I help?"

"You could open that bulkhead, please." Frankie measured her shaky self-control as she lowered the tailgate and lifted the first of four crates. She grumbled at the weight, and how her muscles had relaxed prematurely, before she'd finished this chore.

Having opened the bulkhead, Harper passed her en route to her own box in the truck. "Careful," Frankie said. "They're heavier than you think."

Harper chuckled but needed two hands to drag a crate to the edge of the bed. "I lifted my share during harvest, remember." She grunted when she picked it up.

"You certainly did," Frankie said, maneuvering carefully down the dusty old steps, "but we were on a roll, all heated up and primed. Right out of the blue, however, forty-five pounds weigh a ton." She set the box on the cellar floor and turned to check Harper's footing on the stairs.

"Whew!" Harper blew loose hair off her forehead as she stacked her box on Frankie's. "You're right. It *is* heavier than the other day."

"Especially carrying it down a flight of stairs." Frankie trotted up and out for another crate. *Keep busy.* Harper followed, and Frankie handed her a crate. "Thanks for this help."

Harper rested her load on the tailgate and shook her head. "Does your strength ever give out?"

Drawing the last box into her arms, Frankie laughed at the irony of the question. "Oh, yeah." *The longer we're together, the less I have.* She led them back to the cellar.

Harper set the box atop hers again, then grazed those musical fingers across the berries, leveling them, maybe committing the image and feel to memory. This time tomorrow, she would be far from moments like this.

"Frankie." Harper turned to her, and Frankie's heart skipped. She was actually afraid to look up. "There's so much to say and I don't know where to start."

"Let's not go there, Harper." Frankie absently ran her fingers through the berries of another box. "I-I don't know either, but we probably should just leave it alone."

Harper clasped her hand amidst the berries and Frankie looked down at the sight, thinking she should take a picture. She could see it framed and hanging in her bedroom.

"Frankie, it was special. *You're* special. I want you to know how I feel. Nothing's going to change that."

Frankie didn't want *anything* to change, but she definitely doubted Harper's surety. Harper was moving on, just as she'd planned from the very start, no strings attached.

"You know I wish you success, all the luck in the world. Be happy with your life, Harper, your music. Like I said once before, your heart deserves it."

"So does yours." Setting both palms on Frankie's cheeks, Harper tugged her head down and kissed her.

The tenderness in her lips jolted Frankie's heart, rattled its wounded walls, and she had to tamp down very real tremors. She mustn't wrap her arms around Harper. She mustn't surrender as she had so cavalierly this summer. This kiss, this exhilaration had to end.

*She answers to a greater calling and we both know it.*

Frankie withdrew and watched Harper's eyes flutter open. They were teary.

Frankie summoned what remained of her resolve and steadied her breathing. "I'm not coming to say good-bye tomorrow. I'm leaving the send-off to Stella."

When Harper looked up from Frankie's shirt, the disappointment appeared genuine. "You are?"

"Jesus, Harper. This is too fucking hard."

"I-I know. God, I know, but...For Gram's sake, at least?"

"Donna will be here. I'll...I'll come by and check on Stella later."

"So..."

Frankie exhaled heavily. "So, let's go see what she's up to."

# CHAPTER THIRTY-EIGHT

Harper set the armload of grocery bags on her little counter and fished out the vodka, limes, and juice. Eager for a serious drink at two thirty in the afternoon, she found cracking open the cranberry juice unusually difficult. *Jesus. Can't something go right for once? And why the fuck didn't I buy grapefruit instead?*

She shucked her presentable clothes to resume painting her living room and chose a favorite old yellow T-shirt, but the pink stains shot her right back to harvest. Memories of saying good-bye to Gram—minus Frankie—were painful enough, and that was more than two weeks ago. Her eyes filled up.

She growled at the ceiling, unable to control herself. "Stop, already." She sat on the edge of her bed, wincing when she swallowed some of her drink, and wiped away another batch of tears. Today had been particularly tough, and it was going to get worse.

With music blaring throughout her new house, she managed to get a first coat on the spacious room before the dreaded Zoom call with Storm. She didn't have good medical news to report and feared everyone's reaction. The collective mood darkened with each call.

Making matters worse, no one had been very receptive to the songs she'd offered in recent days. Since her arrival in LA, she'd filled her time generating tunes she could handle on the new album, forcing her reluctant creative muse into action. She should have known better. "Forcing" rarely produced anything worthwhile. As with her second specialist appointment this morning, she knew—as the band would—that she still didn't have much good to offer. At least not yet.

"Hey, guys. How's Atlanta?" Happy to see them on the screen, she tamped down the distress rising in her throat. Ironically, her raspy voice helped disguise it.

"Fucking freezing," Primma said, lounging on one of the hotel room's queen beds. "Weird, with Thanksgiving coming up."

Rhea said hello as she moved the laptop to a better vantage point. Now, Harper could see everyone except Smitty, who probably was stretched out on the floor somewhere.

Joining Harry on the end of the bed, Rhea tried to look upbeat. "Hey, you. I see the painting's coming along. I like the color. What is it, peach?"

*The color of Frankie's place.*

"Rose," Harper said, leaning aside so they could see the walls. "It's pretty. I'm going with a light charcoal accent. I don't want it dark in here."

*Already, this small talk is too much.*

"So, um, are you sounding stronger," Harry asked, "or is it just my own wishful hearing?"

*It's too much for him, too.*

"Maybe a little."

"How did it go at the doctor's this morning?"

Harper took a breath. "Nothing new and more of the same, I'm afraid. She said at least twelve months, that I'd risk everything if I tried our stuff any sooner."

Everybody swore and Rhea flopped back onto the bed.

Harry ran a hand through his hair. "Aw, Harper." He shook his head. "Fuck."

Zee's arm shot up. "So, like, shit, it's too dangerous to try *anything*?"

"I pressed her, big time. She came back with science, hit me with things like regenerative tissue and healthy blood flow and so much stuff, I wanted to punch the frigging wall. I *still* do, as a matter of fact. And *then,* she gave me examples of other singers."

"And they've had to do what?" Decker asked, sounding skeptical. "Shut it all down?"

"Well, yeah. Some had to. The doctor said I'm basically next and for who-the-hell-knows how long. Apparently," she cleared her throat carefully, "apparently, I'm on the 'fringe of permanent damage.' Her words."

Rhea finally sat up and stared gloomily. "Shit. I'm so fucking sorry, hon. I know you had high hopes. We all did."

"But…" Decker paused, his face contorting, "but, damn. This album needs to get moving."

Rhea nodded toward the floor. "The couple tunes you and I worked out really have potential, and nothing says we can't keep fine-tuning them, but… Aw, Christ, Harper. I'm not sure how to put this." She blew out a breath. "Honestly, it's not worth you trying to come up with softer stuff anymore. I mean, you know that's really not who we are, anyway, and if you can't sing with us…"

Storm wasn't open to change, and she should stop trying. She couldn't blame them, really. It was her voice that had backed them to the wall, given them no choice but to plan, create, rehearse, record, and perform without her. But this surely sounded like she now actually was, quite literally, the odd woman out. The finality of it crept over her.

Decker lifted his head from his hands. "Harper, look. I'm sorry, man, but the fucking clock's already ticking on us."

"What about another specialist," Zee offered. "Maybe—"

Harper shook her head. "This one's at the top of the charts, Zee. Some of the biggest names have trusted her." His shoulders drooped.

"Contracts aside," Harry said, fidgeting with his tie, "you know this is Storm's opportunity to strike, right after Head Wind's success, right after the live album. Obviously, it's not your fault, but, well, this blows because the time for us to jump on it is now."

*Tell me something I don't know.*

"Oh, I hear you, Harry. Of course, I do. Storm…has to keep moving."

"You know we've been lucky to get through as much as we have," Primma said with a self-deprecating laugh, "and we've had our rocky moments, but now we're really up against it. Now, we have to *record* the stuff, make it…permanent."

The heaviness of "permanent" sank to the pit of Harper's stomach. After a year's absence, could she just pick up where she'd left off? *Should* she risk it? Would they even want her back? At that point, and with a stack of lighter creations collecting dust, would *she* want to return to this?

Smitty's voice sounded from somewhere off camera. "We finished our song list. It's done."

"The tone of the album is a given," Harry said. "It's signature Storm, all the way, the sound that the company demands and fans expect. Changing tone, type of song, would not only have thrown things off schedule, but raised holy hell with the company, not to mention the fans. You get that, I know."

*I get that you've built the album on your own, not that it'll be what fans expect.*

"Listen, I can't tell you how sorry I am for all this. I know what you guys are facing and, God, I hate it. I feel for all of you. You've gotta do what you've gotta do, I get that." She looked at each of them on the screen. "It's not easy for me, either, watching an entire album go by, but I suppose sticking to Storm's signature sound like you've been doing is for the best."

As much as she believed the band's sound needed her voice—and that fans really did expect it—she truly wanted to support her Storm family, and she felt obligated to respect whatever song choices they had made. But she still wished her tunes had been considered. They actually were decent. She'd looked forward to the band expounding on them, and audiences enjoying the occasional shift.

*The songs may not be Storm's thing, but I like them, dammit.*

"So, I guess I'm taking the year off," she said distantly, knowing no one would correct her. "I can't believe I'm saying this. What will the company say?"

"Disability is disability, Harper. What *can* they say?" Harry turned to Rhea. "You've got most of the leads down."

Rhea just nodded. She'd already assumed Harper's role. At least she didn't look happy about it.

"No one likes this, Harper. Please don't think we do." She slipped a finger beneath her glasses and wiped her eye. "I think we each could use a hug right now."

Primma suddenly sat up, looking all too peppy. "Hey, you could still play with us, you know." Harper almost laughed. "Yeah, we've been talking about it." Primma elbowed Zee.

"Sure, yeah. We could work in another full-time guitar."

Harper tried conceptualizing that sound. Another rhythm player besides Primma was totally unnecessary, although it would still allow her to play in complement to Rhea's lead. It wasn't much, but it was something. *My paltry "contribution."* Actually, she hated how *all* of this sounded.

Could she adjust to a year of that? Lighter songs might have expedited her real return, but already, business was outpacing her. And so was the band. Should she "settle"? Just play backup and keep her mouth shut? In her own band?

"Thanks, you guys, but…You know what I think? I really think I'm done talking for today." She swallowed hard against the direct punch to her gut. The storm in her head was sweeping her out to sea.

Joe brought fresh drinks for everyone to their table at the side of the little stage, beaming at Stella as he sat. Frankie had wanted him and his banjo to join her during her previous set, but he was so excited to be Stella's date tonight, she hadn't pushed. She was happy for them, too.

Besides, the Turnbuckle's full house seemed more than content with what she, Terri, Allie, Tom, and Iman had generated so far. In fact, just moments ago, after only their second set, Lannie had offered Frankie two months of Friday night gigs. Her financial woes could use the money, and by the looks of the overflowing tip jar, the Turnbuckle was *the* place to play.

Donna collected a wealth of videos of their performance for the Crossroads webpage, and already had shared a few with Lannie for

Turnbuckle's. She'd tried pitching Frankie a website for their little group, but Frankie was too keyed up and the room too loud to concentrate on that right now. Meanwhile, Marybeth advised Stella to brace herself for increased attendance at Crossroads' future porch sessions.

Frankie couldn't help being proud of their efforts. The lively Turnbuckle crowd had no qualms sending song requests to the stage or Stella's table. A flattering number of them even asked for Frankie, in particular, which she found humbling and a bit embarrassing. Especially when Terri insisted Frankie close the evening on her own. Frankie protested until they compromised; they would accompany her halfway, but she would finish the last set by herself.

*Now what? Should I just stick with the tunes we'd planned or pick out better solos? Damn, this break between sets is disappearing in a blink.* New song choices careened like bumper cars in her head.

"I think every Crossroads customer in the world is here tonight," Stella said, tipping confidentially against her shoulder. "It's wonderful. You're a natural up there. Everyone loves you. If only…"

Frankie sipped her drink and patted Stella's arm. Yes, in a way, she wished Harper was here, too, but figured it was just as well. How could she concentrate if Harper was sitting here, checking her out?

"You said she'll be here by tomorrow night, Stella. She's learning the hard way about getting a flight at Thanksgiving."

"I know, but she'd be thrilled to see you like this." Stella shifted in her seat. "Alright. I'm not going to dwell on it. I'm very happy we'll be having Thanksgiving together, even if it's in the evening. Now, get back up there and get this crowd going again."

"Could you convince Joe to play a few? I don't want to do bluegrass without his banjo. Tell him it's time to get this place stomping."

She left Stella giggling about her assignment and followed the others onto the stage, wondering where Harper was, what she would think of Crossroads musicians actually playing for money.

*Why does she always figure into every damn thought?*

Thankfully, sounds of Joe tuning his banjo drew her focus back in line.

They captured everyone's attention immediately, and the bright harmonies and quick picking kicked off a set of bluegrass and country songs, with several pop covers sprinkled in for good measure. Frankie followed Joe's sing-along version of "The Ballad of Jed Clampett" with a complex, punchy tune that featured solos by each of them, and the third set ended with another boisterous ovation from the crowd.

Back at Stella's table, Frankie could only shake her head at all the cocktails awaiting her.

"People keep sending them over here," Stella said, grinning. "Another one arrives every few minutes. I think people like you." She poked her arm.

Frankie leaned closer. "But, Jesus, Stella. Somebody better help me because I can't drink—"

"Look at this!" Lannie appeared beside her, wide-eyed at the five drinks. She laughed and patted Frankie on the back. "I think I'll send you some bread to help soak all this up."

"No way I'm drinking them all. Maybe two by the end of the night."

Lannie winked at Stella. "Turnbuckle has a new favorite, and I couldn't be happier." She bent to Frankie's ear. "I know we agreed to Fridays for the next two months, but how about something longer? Would you consider that?"

"Longer?" Frankie just looked at her in disbelief.

"Yeah, like through the summer?" She laughed again. "You look stunned and you shouldn't. You'd be ideal as a regular here, Frankie. Let's talk more later, but think about it, okay?"

"Well…Sure. Let's talk. Thank you." She watched Lannie hustle away, then turned to Stella. "What did she say?"

"You heard her. A 'regular here.' That's…" Stella literally wiggled. "I'm *so* excited!"

Too dumbfounded to be excited, Frankie looked around in a daze, hearing Lannie's words and trying to get them to register. She'd need quiet time to fathom what a "regular" gig actually involved. Could she juggle such a schedule? Should she learn more current tunes? Would she need more presentable clothes? And then there was the money.

She reached for the closest drink on the table, a margarita, she thought, and clinked it against Stella's glass. "Fate works in mysterious ways, doesn't it?"

# CHAPTER THIRTY-NINE

By the time Harper spotted Turnbuckle, she was past it. She slammed on the brakes, swung the car around on a quiet little side street, and cruised back, willing to park on the damn sidewalk, if she didn't find a spot soon.

Two blocks away, she hurried along the dark sidewalk, shivering as she adjusted her favorite white turtleneck beneath a painfully uninsulated red leather jacket. *LA weather, this is not.* She checked the time on her phone and quickened her pace.

"She's into her last set. Shit."

Harper flung open the thick door and stepped into the entryway's warmth and subdued lighting. From another room came the full sound of acoustic guitars, mandolin, and bass, supporting a voice that sent goose bumps along her arms.

She puffed out a breath to collect herself and peeked around the corner.

In a snug, emerald dress shirt and dark jeans, Frankie stood tall and slim at the mic, commanding as she sang, with Terri, Tom, and Allie grinning around her, and Iman at his big upright close behind them. Their confidence as a unit was evident and their delight was contagious.

Harper remembered to breathe. This was an image of Frankie she'd treasure for ages. *Thank God, I made it in time.*

She knew timing, musicianship, cohesiveness, and sweet sound when she heard it, and the bunch on stage had all of that and more. She had heard them play this lightning-quick song at Crossroads several times but, spotlighted like this, their musical skills and Frankie's voice shone like never before.

*Just as polished as any "professional" band in your world, Cushing.*

Harper settled against the doorway woodwork. She wouldn't dare make an entrance and throw them off-track. This was Frankie's moment, and she was glowing. Besides, with the way her heart was beating, Harper was too excited to move.

Arriving a night early, she couldn't wait to surprise them. But her mere presence wouldn't be the only surprise. She had a much bigger one in store, as long as she could voice it at just the right time.

For now, she cherished what felt like a very private viewing, even if she was sharing it with the audience. Heads bobbed, and fingers and toes tapped, and here and there, people shared comments as they watched. A few sang along. And when the tune finished, there was no mistaking the audience's appreciation.

Harper smiled so broadly, her cheeks hurt. She blinked away the onset of happy, proud tears and laughed lightly at herself.

*You deserve this, Frankie. People* should *hear you and the messages you sing. Appreciating the natural beauty of an unforgettable voice and raw, classic instruments is what it's really all about.*

Frankie thanked Terri, Allie, Tom, and Iman, making sure patrons knew their names, and renewed applause accompanied them off stage. Watching where they went, Harper spotted the tables of the Crossroads faithful, and Gram with Joe at her side, of course. The vacant chair at Gram's other side made Harper smile. But when to make her move?

Still between songs, Frankie drew a stool to the mic and Harper figured better to move now, than once Frankie had started another tune. With an eye on Frankie, she crossed her fingers and maneuvered to that empty chair.

"This next song," Frankie began, hitching a hip onto the stool, "is one I think you'll—" Adjusting the mic, she fell silent. "Harper?"

Harper stopped abruptly at the chair as every eye in the place turned to her. Gram looked up and gasped.

"Surprise!" Thankful she hadn't had to yell over the curious crowd, Harper raised both palms slightly. "I know I'm late but, really, I'm early." Her heart skipped when Frankie smiled.

"Either one is just fine, trust me."

Hardly intimidated in front of an audience, Harper planted her hands on her hips. "Listen," she said, playfully impatient. "I didn't fly all the way from LA to stand here talking. Play on, girlfriend!"

Frankie's head dipped when people clapped, and Harper knew she had made her blush. *Not sorry, hon.* She couldn't help smiling as she slipped out of her jacket. She hugged Gram, kissed her cheek, and relaxed into her seat.

Frankie stood and pushed the stool aside. "Talk about getting caught off-guard," she admitted to everyone, shaking her head. "Man. This is like having that extra person show up for dinner last-minute." People laughed.

She picked at a few random chords, watching her hand, as everyone watched her. Harper knew those actions were mindless, knew Frankie had abandoned whatever she'd planned, and now searched madly for just the right song. Her heart went out to Frankie in every way.

"So, I'm throwing down my own gauntlet," Frankie stated, and looked from Harper to Allie and then to Allie's guitar. Allie grinned back. "Ladies and gentlemen. I'm honored and *so* happy to have a very special friend here tonight. Please allow me to introduce the lead singer of one of the hottest bands in the country, Harper Cushing of Storm."

She extended a hand toward Harper and the audience applauded. They were words Harper hadn't heard in a long while, and the association sent a nostalgic shiver coursing through her. A few people shouted and whistled in recognition until she had to acknowledge them, and smirking at Frankie's tactic, she rose slightly and sent the crowd a humble little wave.

"Unfortunately for all of us," Frankie explained, "Harper's battling some voice trouble these days, but, if she's not too spent from her flight, maybe she'll join me on guitar."

Harper felt her jaw drop. Everyone cheered the idea, but Harper shook her head. Gram nudged her as the audience clapped louder.

Offering her guitar, Allie whispered at Harper's ear. "You both know you want to."

Harper's cheeks heated as she stood and accepted the instrument. It was her turn to blush, especially now that people were calling for her.

She draped the guitar over her neck as she approached Frankie, eyeing that sly smile for any clue, any advance notice of what they would play. She only hoped it was a song she knew or one they had done together. *How long ago?*

Instead, Frankie slipped an arm around her shoulders and squeezed. "I can't believe you're here. You've made my night."

"I couldn't miss this, Frankie." *Now will you tell me what you have in mind?*

But Frankie gave nothing away. She stepped to the side of the mic and went straight into fingerpicking the opening chord. Her first words sent a wave of affection through Harper's heart, and then relief to her nerves, because she knew the *love* song well. If only she could sing it with her. How often had she wished it fit into Storm's genre? And why had she never thought to ask if Frankie knew it, too?

She could hear the heartfelt promise in Frankie's voice and nearly lost herself in the lyrics. That was the point. Studying every nuance in Frankie's face, Harper fit supporting chords to Frankie's effort, and just as easily saw herself opening to Frankie's message. Fortitude, choices, and someone special. And she sang it *to her*.

As the chorus finished, Harper leaned closer until only the mic separated them, and adlibbed an instrumental break over the melody Frankie played. It fit seamlessly, a perfect substitute for their missing harmonies, and felt almost as surreal. Coming so off-the-cuff, the intensity of it made concentrating difficult. She struggled to stay sharp, not let it shake her. And she could see that Frankie felt every beat of it.

Frankie looked *into* her as she sang, and, on a breath as the song closed, Frankie shifted enough to face the audience and Harper followed suit. Inexplicably, they slowed the rhythm in perfect sync and let the final notes drift.

She met Frankie's eyes. *It happened again, didn't it?* "Damn, that was scary-good, you know."

People were on their feet instantly—and shouting for more.

She winked at Frankie and grinned to see her shake her head at another of their amazing miracles. When Frankie offered her hand, Harper gladly entwined their fingers.

"Ladies and gentlemen," Frankie said, raising their joined hands, "Harper Cushing!"

The crowd wouldn't quit, and Frankie queried Harper with a look, then drew her closer to be heard over the demands for more.

"Would you do one more, please?"

Harper tilted her head, moved by the unnecessary plea in Frankie's voice. "Anything you want."

"You choose."

"Oh, Jesus, Frankie. Um." Now, the shoe was on the other foot and Harper hurriedly racked her brain. *Something I know she knows.*

Frankie nodded at the audience and leaned to the mic. "She said yes!"

Delighted laughter added to the cheers.

Harper tugged Frankie to her by her sleeve. "Do you remember 'Everything Has Changed'? It's light pop, but it's upbeat, fun."

Frankie nodded. "Too bad we can't do the duet version."

"That's okay. I'd rather hear you sing it anyway."

"We've only played it together once, you know."

Harper held her gaze for an extra beat and admitted, "I've played it a few times, since."

"Yeah, so have I."

Frankie touched her hand where it rested on the guitar, then turned to the mic. "Okay, you guys. Here's Harper." She backed away, and Harper stepped forward to play the intro. Several people immediately applauded, recognizing the Taylor Swift song, but then quickly quieted to listen.

Frankie moved to the mic and Harper smiled with satisfaction to hear her first soft words. Turn-about was fair play, and now *she* had chosen lyrics that spoke of love and learning what really mattered. *I can't sing them, but you certainly know what I'm saying.*

When Frankie sang about opening doors and making up for lost time, Harper knew she'd nailed her song choice. *Yes, Frankie. It's all about truly saying "Hello" and coming home to each other.* Her composure almost failed.

The crowd's ecstatic reaction stunned them, and Harper was thrilled beyond words for Frankie. She gripped her hand firmly and gave it a little shake.

"My turn," she said and spoke into the mic. "Ladies and gentlemen, Frankie Cosgrove!" As the audience responded, Harper kissed her cheek and hustled back to her seat.

Frankie guzzled half of a glass of water as the audience—and her pounding heart—settled down. *How does something so spur-of-the-moment be that good? How the hell do I follow it? Too bad I can't go pass out somewhere.*

She returned to the mic, dragging the stool along with her. She didn't risk looking at Harper. She still needed her brain to function. As it was, she could feel her touch from this distance.

"Wow. I need to sit down after that." The audience laughed. "Gotta clear the brain fog," she said, tinkering with notes high up the guitar neck where her fingers rested.

She vacantly picked at chords as her hand descended the neck to a more relaxed position, slowly tripping down the scale. But those random changes actually weren't random at all, and the song finally surfaced from her subconscious.

*The other night this turned out pretty sweet, so here goes.*

"Before I close tonight, I want to thank Lannie for this opportunity and for trusting I wouldn't have you throwing glasses or furniture at me. And I want to thank you guys for sticking around, these past few hours. You've been amazing and that means a lot to someone who's never done this before, believe me."

The crowd clapped vigorously as she clamped the capo into position on the guitar neck.

"I'm not sure I'm brave enough for this, but…sometimes you just have to go for it, like, fling glitter in the air and watch what happens, prove to yourself you can land on your feet…or that someone really is there for you." She turned to Harper. "You can't let a moment like that pass you by. You hang on, you lasso it, and don't let go, because it could be very, very special. Just like tonight. So, thank you."

Frankie plucked at the strings, "walking" the notes down the scale repeatedly into the steady cadence of P!nk's "Glitter In The Air." She had learned this song with Harper in mind, believing they each should trust in their fearlessness, their inner strength to pursue love. And now she hoped the lyrics hit home. She leaned into them and sang directly to Harper, asking if she'd ever felt this way, promising they could have it all if they wanted.

Elbows on the table, her hands steepled at her lips, Harper gazed back at her through glistening eyes. As if alone in the room together, Frankie poured her soul into Harper's, knew she heard the lines about endless nights and owning the stars, and whether it could possibly get better than right now.

With the last notes lingering, Frankie watched her eyelids flutter, saw Stella pat her arm.

The blood rushing in Frankie's ears almost drowned out the audience's appreciation. Somehow, she'd made it through without a glitch and without choking up. *Sappy? Absolutely. And freaking perfect.*

Turning away from Harper was the last thing she wanted to do, but she had to acknowledge the ongoing applause. Her brain told her to face the crowd, and she was shocked to see a scattering of people standing and clapping. Forcing herself off the stool, she tipped toward the mic.

"You guys are the best. Thank you so much for a fantastic night. Have a happy Thanksgiving, everybody."

Friends swarmed her as she approached the table, and patrons on their way out stopped with compliments and thanks. Several hovered around Harper, waiting as she graciously signed autographs and spoke with a star-struck Lannie. The whole departure process took nearly an hour, while Frankie itched for a private moment with Harper.

Finally, they connected in the parking lot as the Crossroads faithful drove away.

Frankie set her guitar case down and hugged her. "I don't care that you're just here for Thanksgiving. I want to hold you right now."

"The best idea I've heard in ages." Harper returned the lengthy squeeze. "You were absolutely phenomenal tonight, Frankie, so, so good."

"Thanks, but it's amazing what inspiration can do, isn't it?" Frankie nuzzled her neck and kissed it lightly. Better judgment be dammed, she was giving in to desire. "And I thought *music* made me high. But *you*…God, I'm so glad you made it here."

"I had to, Frankie. I *needed* to." Harper slid her cheek along Frankie's as she leaned back. "When music calls us, we answer. What *type* of music we prefer has nothing to do with it. Truly. Just look what happens."

"I'm so sorry for acting like a kid about all that."

"No, Frankie. *I* was the thoughtless one—and I want to put that mess behind us."

Frankie dipped her head and kissed her with all the passion she could muster, and it was a lot. Harper weakened in her arms, moaned so sweetly, Frankie didn't care where they were.

But she couldn't forget the very temporary nature of all this. She knew better than to lose herself in it all over again but desperately wanted to. If only for a few days or even just tonight.

"I want to shut out everything but you, right now. I-I don't care."

Harper traced Frankie's lower lip with a finger. "We're in sync so often, it takes my breath away."

Frankie slid her palms down Harper's back and reached for her hands. She entwined their fingers and brought them to her chest. "Too bad we're in separate cars."

Harper grinned. "Lead on."

# CHAPTER FORTY

Propped up against Frankie's headboard, Harper sipped her honeyed tea, laid her head back, and closed her eyes. Muscles felt languidly fluid after that thunderous orgasm Frankie had summoned from her depths, and that was all she wanted to think about. Except for the delicious body draped over her and those precious lips at her breast.

*This* was what she'd come back for, *who* she'd turned her life upside-down for, after all those days and nights, tied up in knots, wondering where the hell her life was headed. She had no preconceptions, no misgivings about the future, whatever it might be. She knew she wanted Frankie in her life every day and, if Frankie shared that yearning, Harper knew what it would take.

Like being offered this cup of tea, the tenderness in Frankie's every gesture made her happier than she'd ever been. This time, for *this woman*, she was genuinely on the right track.

"I'm so lucky," she whispered as Frankie smoothed a palm across her stomach.

"*I'm* the lucky one. With you, everything feels right."

The words lingered as Harper filtered the cool softness of Frankie's hair through her fingers. Frankie just brightened her life. It would be empty without her, no matter how many crazed fans or euphoric songs passed through it. She'd felt the emptiness in just the weeks they had spent apart. Life would be...There was a reason she couldn't begin to picture it. And she really had known it for a while.

"*We* are right, Frankie," she said, stroking her back, the breadth of her shoulders, the solid slope to her ass, "and you make me feel more than anything's ever moved me, including music. You go so much further than that, just being you."

Frankie lifted her head from Harper's chest and rose up to kiss her. Harper had only a second to set her tea on the nightstand before Frankie began kissing her way down, between her breasts. She slipped along Harper's frame and settled between her legs.

"I need…" she kissed Harper's abdomen and moved lower, "I need the very essence of you like I need air to breathe." She slid her arms beneath Harper's thighs and scooped her hips to her mouth.

"Ohhh, Frankie." Harper's eyes slammed shut, and she arched within Frankie's arms. "Oh, God, yes."

A groan rose from somewhere deep in her chest, and she knew more were coming, that Frankie wouldn't rest until she'd made her explode again. Harper fully intended to let her do anything and everything she wanted.

Her legs quivered around Frankie's shoulders, and her body shook when Frankie bore down, ravenous at her center. Harper shuddered gloriously for what felt like days, her only reality being Frankie's merciless attention. When Frankie finally stopped, Harper exhaled for the first time in forever.

"My God, Frankie." She reached down and flittered shaky fingers across Frankie's mouth. "What such tender lips can do." She forced herself to sit up, grunting at the effort.

Her head resting on Harper's thigh, Frankie smiled. "I'm just going to lie here and love looking at you."

"You think so?" Harper forced her legs away and pushed Frankie back onto the mattress. She curled her body down and tugged on Frankie's nipples with her teeth. "I've got you now." She nipped across her stomach, heading downward to reach Frankie's abs, her hips, and slipped a hand between her legs. "You are *so* ready for me."

Restless, Frankie moaned as she flexed her fingers into Harper's ass and thighs. "When…when you come, I…"

Continuing her way down, Harper stretched out against her to lick her thighs, and felt Frankie seize her knees, draw them to her shoulders, and spread them at her head. Knowing Frankie would be inside her at any second, Harper had to take her at that moment.

Holding Frankie's thighs apart, she slipped her tongue inside as warm breath tingled her own center, just as Frankie's tongue filled her. Each of them writhed at the penetration.

Harper couldn't help but moan into her. She drove her fingers in and heard Frankie's sharp inhale, before her own hips were pulled feverishly onto a very hungry mouth.

Frankie's trembling soon matched her own, and Harper struggled to concentrate as Frankie's lips gripped her harder, forced her to stiffen. Harper circled Frankie's center with her tongue, played with her until they arched together and shuddered as one, neither able to stop devouring the other.

But Harper collapsed first, her legs sagging onto Frankie's shoulders, and Frankie's mouth dropped away. Harper lapped her center several times, teasing, making her twitch, before rolling off to her side.

"Harper." Frankie's voice was an octave lower, and thoroughly spent. "That was…Whoa. Is there a delicate word for a fuck like that?"

"Dammed if I know." Harper propped herself up on an elbow and smiled back, along their bodies, beyond Frankie's breasts to the wondrous smile on her face. "If there is, it won't come close."

Frankie propped herself up, too, and grinned. "If I could feel my legs, I'd say let's do it again."

"Ha!" Harper flopped onto her back. "Maybe next week when I'm able to walk." She popped back up, warmed just by the sight of Frankie lying there, gazing back at her. "Hey."

"Hey what?"

"You know…" Words were about to come from her heart. Maybe not fully formed or thought out, but the message building inside had been contained long enough.

"Do I know what?" Frankie asked, that edible dimple accenting her dashing grin. "I know you're beautiful and you're amazing…and…and, God damn, we're good."

*It's harmony, Frankie.*

"I love making love with you." Harper replayed the words in her head, watched them register in Frankie's eyes. She didn't know if Frankie wanted to hear them or even would believe them, but they were true.

"Harper." Frankie's voice dissolved into a whisper. "It's never felt like 'just sex' between us. Is that odd?" She glimmered with mischief. "Even though I can't get enough of you. Never could."

"Keep talking like that and I'll dive back in for seconds." She inhaled slowly when Frankie slipped two fingers deep inside her. "Jesus." She pressed a hand to Frankie's and held it in place. "Stay right there."

"I intend to." Frankie shifted onto her knees between Harper's legs and urged Harper's shoulders flat onto the bed. "And you stay just like that." She sat back on her heels, watching as she slipped her fingers in and out, gliding on slow, easy strokes. "Have I told you how exquisite this feels? How beautiful you are?"

"Frankie, you…God, that feels—"

"We've been making love from the start, Harper," she said gently, "and I love it, too." She withdrew her fingers, wrapped Harper's legs around her waist, and drew her upright against her.

Harper held on, her arms around Frankie's shoulders, and swallowed hard but not against pain in her throat. Her heart was rising to be heard, for the attention it deserved and had earned.

*This is where the afterglow emotions come out and the girl cries.*

"It's not about sex," she said. "We've always been about something bigger." She stroked Frankie's cheek. It was so good to be warmed by the amber glow of that look again. "Those weeks away...I know that's not a long time, but, God, I missed you. It was time enough to see that something *I* wanted and needed was missing, to finally see what really mattered to *me*."

Frankie looked down, sheepishly. "And I was afraid of losing again, losing what we had and hurting again. There probably was some jealousy thrown in, too." She lifted her eyes to Harper's and shrugged. "I tried not to be, but Storm had you and I didn't. Hell, even Rhea had you, and—"

"Rhea?" Harper cupped her chin. "Sweetie, there's nothing like that between Rhea and me."

"No?"

Frankie could only watch as Harper grinned sweetly and shook her head. The list of tonight's surprises just kept growing. But she couldn't get distracted by her own misguided assumption or the truth. She *had* to finish explaining.

"Harper. I had no right to be jealous, period. I know that, but...inside, things felt unfinished, like...like you and I were meant to do more." She brushed Harper's throat reverently with the back of her fingers. "Like more harmony."

The word rang with perfect pitch in Harper's heart, and she pulled her to within a kiss.

"I've rushed into relationships before, Frankie, even rushed right out of them. Shit, I've rushed through *life*, these past few years, and I've had it. I don't want to rush anymore." She kissed her lightly.

"Then, this is the perfect place to be, not California. I'm biased, I know, but..." Frankie drew her in tighter, whispering at her lips, "but there's no rushing here. No one sets your pace."

"I know. *You* make this the perfect place for me." Harper's heart pounded at the sight of tears. "You make a lot of things perfect."

"I can only dream of that, Harper. It's why I'm so thankful we at least have this. What's ahead for you—"

"Frankie." She stopped her with a fingertip to her lips. "I've left Storm."

Frankie straightened with shock, her hands frozen on Harper's back. "You what?"

"I did. It's been a rough few weeks, but, yeah. I finally read that writing on the wall. My voice had been trying to tell me all along, hadn't it? I was kidding myself, thinking I still fit into Storm's world."

"But you do. How could they let you go? *You* are Storm, Harper. They're nothing without you."

"Not true. They're cruising along just fine and more power to them. We'll always be each other's biggest fans, but there was a different route calling me, one of those crossroads decisions."

"So…I can't believe this. No more motor homes or concert tours? No shit?"

Harper grinned. "No more craziness and city-to-city living. I want to see sunny days, not sleep through them, Frankie, to create music that soothes the heart, not screams at it. I want to actually sing, for a change, and still have a voice when I'm old." She dabbed away a tear from Frankie's cheek. "My heart wants something more."

A smile blossomed across Frankie's face and made Harper's breath catch. *Yes, Frankie, it's what you think it is.*

"Well, wow." Frankie blinked to clear her eyes. "I-I don't know what to say. I mean, I *do*, but…There's so much I…" She laughed at herself. "Now, I feel like a damn teenager."

Harper cradled Frankie's face in her hands. "You're blushing."

"Well, it's just…it's been a long time since…"

"It's been a long time for me, too, Frankie, a long time since it's been real."

"This is *so* real, Harper. I'm crazy in love with you."

Harper wasted no time surrendering to *this* reality. "And I'm *so* in love with you."

Frankie met her kiss softly, almost tentatively, before seeking more. Her own lips trembling, Harper couldn't recall a gentler kiss moving her so deeply.

## EPILOGUE

It's so nice to hear you sing like that, Harper. It's been a long time coming." Stella beamed as they set their guitars aside. Frankie winked at Harper. An hour of playing on this unseasonably warm April afternoon showed just how far Harper's voice had returned and how far she could push it, as long as she kept things relatively peaceful.

"Six months have been plenty," Harper admitted. "Frustrating as hell, but I've been careful, and it's paid off."

"Did you play for your friends the other night on the Zoom call?"

"No. Frankie and I just had a few drinks with them and caught up on stuff. The whole band is staying at Rhea's in LA this month, and she's put them to work making changes. She took us on a walking tour, and I hardly recognized the place."

"It's good she bought your house, Harper. That worked out well for you *and* her."

"Everything's been working out. Storm's going back on the road again, and even Frankie and I have a little news."

Frankie handed Stella the list of gigs she and Harper had compiled.

"The farthest we're going is Connecticut, Gram, and that's only for two shows at the end of June."

"Oh, my. So, I see there's some work here. Nothing in New York City?"

Harper shook her head and Stella looked for confirmation from Frankie.

"No New York City," Frankie stated, pleased to reassure her. She drew her stool closer to their rockers on the porch. "I know it's only April, but those dates are all we're interested in through the summer, along with Turnbuckle, of course. And you *know*, we'll be here for the Fourth of July." She grinned at the relief on Stella's face. "Crossroads' annual Family Fun Day is a big deal."

"But it's not as big as performing in New York City. I thought that's what you two wanted."

"Not exactly. That city's too much stress," Harper said. "I'm done with that. Like Frankie said, we're not interested."

"We're keeping things closer to home." Frankie pointed to the printout on Stella's lap. "We like this arrangement with dates scattered here and there, Cape Cod, Boston, Providence. There's no 'road trip' string of them."

"Luckily," Harper said, "neither of us needs to make a killing at this." She clasped Frankie's hand and drew it onto her thigh. "I picked up a couple of small solo gigs, but there are three or four we'll perform together each month of the summer. Not a lot. And beyond that, who knows!" She flashed a smile at Frankie. "God, it's *so* liberating. What a comfortable feeling."

"And as for the Turnbuckle," Frankie entwined her fingers with Harper's, "some nights, just a duo might show up instead. Overall, it's a livable schedule for both of us. I can baby my berries," she turned to Harper, "and you can have all the time you need for songwriting and that solo album you've dreamed about."

"And *somebody* won't be worrying about her crop losses if I can help it."

The promise in Harper's eyes still felt surreal, still set Frankie's heart aglow every day. She still marveled at how much life had changed since Thanksgiving.

The summer had opened a door for each of them, but it had taken a few months to walk through it. A soul-deep bond had formed since, and the honesty of Harper's life-changing decision proved she believed just as firmly in what they shared. Frankie cherished everything about her.

"And don't forget, Gram. We're just five minutes away from you here." Stella sent them a sideways look. "So, when I make a pot roast dinner, there better not be any excuses." Spotting Joe's car arriving in the lot, she stood and straightened her sweater.

"Your date's here," Harper teased.

"Joey's not my *date*, silly. We're just going to lunch."

"Right."

"Like every Thursday," Frankie added.

Stella raised an eyebrow at her. "Don't change the subject. I hope your schedules won't interfere whenever I call you two for dinner."

Frankie raised her palm to promise. "No way."

"Uh-huh. And when are you going to expand your cabin?"

"Please. One thing at a time, Stella," Frankie said with a laugh. "We've talked about it, yes, and the barn, too, but—"

"God, Gram. Living through construction here last summer was wild enough. We're putting it off till next year."

"Well, I *do* like the sound of this, you know." Now, Stella's eyes twinkled with approval. "Yes, I like the 'comfortable' feel of it all."

"What feels comfortable?" Joe asked, climbing the steps.

Stella collected her purse from the side table and elbowed him confidentially. "These two."

Joe sent them one of his crinkly matter-of-fact frowns and draped Stella's arm over his. "Took long enough, if you ask me." He turned her toward the steps. "Come on, now. Aren't you hungry yet?"

"Actually, I am. I'm thinking about the pumpkin ravioli."

"What? Pumpkin ravioli?" He shook his head, grumbling as he walked her to the car. "No. Get the chicken parm." He shut Stella's door and ambled around to the driver's side, but she continued to talk.

"Joey, you always get the chicken parm. Get something different this time." She waved as he pulled away from the porch.

Watching from the railing, Frankie grinned at the typical back-and-forth between them, and slipped an arm around Harper's waist. They waved back. "They are a pair, for sure. And your grandmother's a clever one. She had us in mind all along, didn't she?"

Harper chuckled. "Yeah, probably. And I bet she never had any intention of leaving this place." She leaned into Frankie's hold. "Thank God, I didn't let Mom take charge."

"I'll second that. You came to the rescue just in time. Rescued me, too."

"Who rescued who?" Harper looked up and kissed her. "This is all just as hard to believe now as it was when I arrived. Who would've thought?"

"We've come a long way in a short time, Harper." The agreeable smile on Harper's face sent heat surging through Frankie's chest.

"So many changes. I love seeing Gram this happy now. Hell, even my mother's happy, or at least satisfied." She threaded her arms around Frankie's waist and sighed with contentment. "And I'm so far removed from where I was a year ago, this feels like a dream."

Frankie pressed her closer. "I'm happy, too, Harper. We're good together." She lowered her head and kissed Harper softly.

"We are, aren't we?" Harper kissed her back. "I never thought it could feel like this. I'd stopped thinking it could be this perfect."

Frankie wrapped her up tightly and nibbled her ear. "Just so you know, I'm holding you like this forever."

"Oh, please do." Harper sighed again as she returned the squeeze. "I love you, Frankie."

"Harper Cushing," she whispered, lifting her head. "I love you, too."

"I can hear the harmony when we say it together."

Frankie nodded. "Because love *is* harmony."

THE END

# About the Author

A life-long Massachusetts resident with backgrounds in journalism and telecom, CF Frizzell writes in various genres with a reporter's penchant for detail and depth. She is a Golden Crown Literary Society multiple-award winner for novels in both contemporary and historical romance. Her *Measure of Devotion*, set in the American Civil War, has been honored as a 2023 finalist by the American Fiction Awards in three categories: Historical Fiction, LGBTQ+ Fiction, and Historical Romance.

CF "Friz" Frizzell credits Bold Strokes Books powerhouse authors Lee Lynch, Radclyffe, and the generous BSB family for inspiration. Her introduction to BSB began as a rabid reader, advanced to volunteer BSB proofreader, and then to hopeful, aspiring writer, winning the 2015 GCLS Debut Author Award for her historical romance, *Stick McLaughlin: The Prohibition Years*. She is into history, sports, and Guild guitars—and her truly amazing wife, Kathy, and their chocolate Lab, Chessa.

# Books Available from Bold Strokes Books

**All For Her: Forbidden Romance Novellas** by Gun Brooke, J.J. Hale, Aurora Rey. Explore the angst and excitement of forbidden love few would dare in this heart-stopping novella collection. (978-1-63679-713-7)

**Finding Harmony** by CF Frizzell. Rock star Harper Cushing has to rearrange her grandmother's future and sell the family store out from under her, but she reassesses everything because Gram's helper, Frankie, could be offering the harmony her heart has been missing. (978-1-63679-741-0)

**Gaze** by Kris Bryant. Love at first sight is for dreamers, but the more time Lucky and Brianna spend together, the more they realize the chemistry of a gaze can make anything possible. (978-1-63679-711-3)

**Laying of Hands** by Patricia Evans. The mysterious new writing instructor at camp makes Grace Waters brave enough to wonder what would happen if she dared to write her own story. (978-1-63679-782-3)

**Seducing the Widow** by Jane Walsh. Former rival debutantes have a second chance at love after fifteen years apart when a spinster persuades her ex-lover to help save her family business. (978-1-63679-747-2)

**The Naked Truth** by Sandy Lowe. How far are Rowan and Genevieve willing to go and how much will they risk to make their most captivating and forbidden fantasies a reality? (978-1-63679-426-6)

**The Roommate** by Claire Forsythe. Jess Black's boyfriend is handsome and successful. That's why it comes as a shock when she meets a woman on the train who makes her pulse race. (978-1-63679-757-1)

**Close to Home** by Allisa Bahney. Eli Thomas has to decide if avoiding her hometown forever is worth losing the people who used to mean the most to her, especially Aracely Hernandez, the girl who got away. (978-1-63679-661-1)

**Golden Girl** by Julie Tizard. In 1993, "Don't ask, don't tell" forces everyone to lie, but Air Force nurse Lt. Sofia Sanchez and injured instructor pilot Lt. Gillian Guthman have to risk telling each other the truth in order to fly and survive. (978-1-63679-751-9)

**Innis Harbor** by Patricia Evans. When Amir Farzaneh meets and falls in love with Loch, a dark secret lurking in her past reappears, threatening the happiness she'd just started to believe could be hers. (978-1-63679-781-6)

**The Blessed** by Anne Shade. Layla and Suri are brought together by fate to defeat the darkness threatening to tear their world apart. What they don't expect to discover is a love that might set them free. (978-1-63679-715-1)

**The Guardians** by Sheri Lewis Wohl. Dogs, devotion, and determination are all that stand between darkness and light. (978-1-63679-681-9)

**The Mogul Meets Her Match** by Julia Underwood. When CEO Claire Beauchamp goes undercover as a customer of Abby Pita's café to help seal a deal that will solidify her career, she doesn't expect to be so drawn to her. When the truth is revealed, will she break Abby's heart? (978-1-63679-784-7)

**Trial Run** by Carsen Taite. When Reggie Knoll and Brooke Dawson wind up serving on a jury together, their one task—reaching a unanimous verdict—is derailed by the fiery clash of their personalities, the intensity of their attraction, and a secret that could threaten Brooke's life. (978-1-63555-865-4)

**Waterlogged** by Nance Sparks. When conservation warden Jordan Pearce discovers a body floating in the flowage, the serenity of the Northwoods is rocked. (978-1-63679-699-4)

**Accidentally in Love** by Kimberly Cooper Griffin. Nic and Lee have good reasons for keeping their distance. So why does their growing attraction seem more like a love-hate relationship? (978-1-63679-759-5)

**Fatal Foul Play** by David S. Pederson. After eight friends are stranded in an old lodge by a blinding snowstorm, a brutal murder leaves Mark Maddox to solve the crime as he discovers deadly secrets about people he thought he knew. (978-1-63679-794-6)

**Frosted by the Girl Next Door** by Aurora Rey and Jaime Clevenger. When heartbroken Casey Stevens opens a sex shop next door to uptight cupcake baker Tara McCoy, things get a little frosty. (978-1-63679-723-6)

**Ghost of the Heart** by Catherine Friend. Being possessed by a ghost was not on Gwen's bucket list, but she must admit that ghosts might be real, and one is obviously trying to send her a message. (978-1-63555-112-9)

**Hot Honey Love** by Nan Campbell. When chef Stef Lombardozzi puts her cooking career into the hands of filmmaker Mallory Radowski—the pickiest eater alive—she doesn't anticipate how hard she falls for her. (978-1-63679-743-4)

**London** by Patricia Evans. Jaq's and Bronwyn's lives become entwined as dangerous secrets emerge and Bronwyn's seemingly perfect life starts to unravel. (978-1-63679-778-6)

**This Christmas** by Georgia Beers. When Sam's grandmother rigs the Christmas parade to make Sam and Keegan queen and queen, sparks fly, but they can't forget the Big Embarrassing Thing that makes romance a total nope. (978-1-63679-729-8)

**Unwrapped** by D. Jackson Leigh. Asia du Muir is not going to let some party girl actress ruin her best chance to get noticed by a Broadway critic. Everyone knows you should never mix business and pleasure. (978-1-63679-667-3)

**Language Lessons** by Sage Donnell. Grace and Lenka never expected to fall in love. Is home really where the heart is if it means giving up your dreams? (978-1-63679-725-0)

**New Horizons** by Shia Woods. When Quinn Collins meets Alex Anders, Horizon Theater's enigmatic managing director, a passionate connection ignites, but amidst the complex backdrop of theater politics, their budding romance faces a formidable challenge. (978-1-63679-683-3)

**Scrambled: A Tuesday Night Book Club Mystery** by Jaime Maddox. Avery Hutchins makes a discovery about her father's death that will force her to face an impossible choice between doing what is right and finally finding a way to regain a part of herself she had lost. (978-1-63679-703-8)

**Stolen Hearts** by Michele Castleman. Finding the thief who stole a precious heirloom will become Ella's first move in a dangerous game of wits that exposes family secrets and could lead to her family's financial ruin. (978-1-63679-733-5)

**Synchronicity** by J.J. Hale. Dance, destiny, and undeniable passion collide at a summer camp as Haley and Cal navigate a love story that intertwines past scars with present desires. (978-1-63679-677-2)

**The First Kiss** by Patricia Evans. As the intrigue surrounding her latest case spins dangerously out of control, military police detective Parker Haven must choose between her career and the woman she's falling in love with. (978-1-63679-775-5)

**Wild Fire** by Radclyffe & Julie Cannon. When Olivia returns to the Red Sky Ranch, Riley's carefully crafted safe world goes up in flames. Can they take a risk and cross the fire line to find love? (978-1-63679-727-4)

**Writ of Love** by Cassidy Crane. Kelly and Jillian struggle to navigate the ruthless battleground of Big Law, grappling with desire, ambition, and the thin line between success and surrender. (978-1-63679-738-0)